The WHITE GRYPHON

Also available from Millennium

The Black Gryphon
Storm Warning

The WHITE GRYPHON

Mercedes Lackey & Larry Dixon

Book Two of *The Mage Wars*

Interior Illustrations by Larry Dixon

MILLENNIUM

An Orion Book

LONDON

This edition first published
in Great Britain in 1995 by
Millennium
An imprint of Orion Books Ltd
Orion House, 5 Upper St Martin's Lane
London WC2H 9EA

Second impression 1995

A CIP catalogue record for this book is available
from the British Library
ISBN: (Csd) 1 85798 430 7
ISBN: (Ppr) 1 85798 431 5

Printed and bound in Great Britain by
Clays Ltd, St Ives plc

Lovingly dedicated to our parents,

Edward and Joyce Ritche

&

Jim and Shirley Dixon

OFFICIAL TIMELINE FOR THE

by Mercedes Lackey

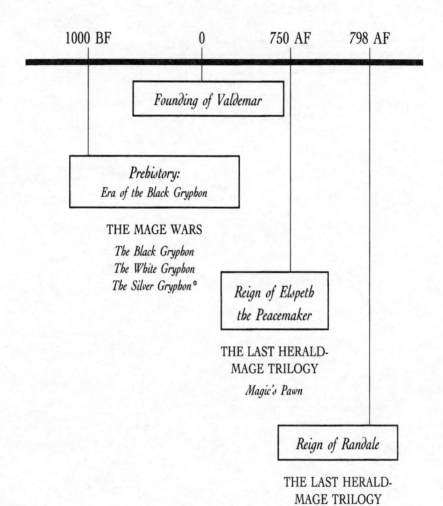

1000 BF   0   750 AF   798 AF

Founding of Valdemar

Prehistory:
Era of the Black Gryphon

THE MAGE WARS

The Black Gryphon
The White Gryphon
*The Silver Gryphon**

Reign of Elspeth
the Peacemaker

THE LAST HERALD-
MAGE TRILOGY

Magic's Pawn

Reign of Randale

THE LAST HERALD-
MAGE TRILOGY

Magic's Promise
Magic's Price

BF   *Before the Founding*
AF   *After the Founding*

HERALDS OF VALDEMAR SERIES

Sequence of events by Valdemar reckoning

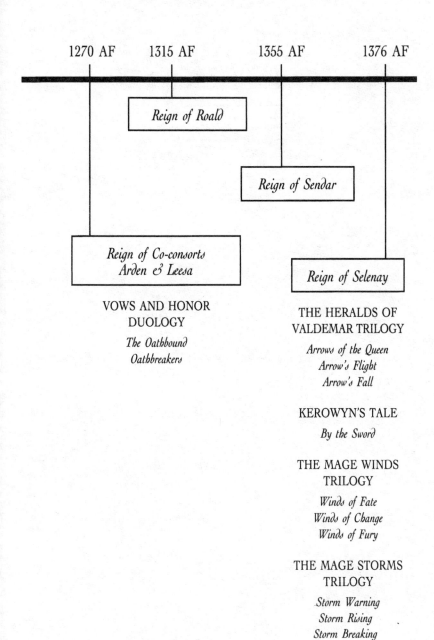

1270 AF   1315 AF   1355 AF   1376 AF

Reign of Roald

Reign of Sendar

Reign of Co-consorts
Arden & Leesa

Reign of Selenay

VOWS AND HONOR
DUOLOGY

The Oathbound
Oathbreakers

THE HERALDS OF
VALDEMAR TRILOGY

Arrows of the Queen
Arrow's Flight
Arrow's Fall

KEROWYN'S TALE

By the Sword

THE MAGE WINDS
TRILOGY

Winds of Fate
Winds of Change
Winds of Fury

THE MAGE STORMS
TRILOGY

Storm Warning
Storm Rising
Storm Breaking

Amberdrake

Skandranon

One

Light.

From crown to talons, tailtip to wingtip, it will be a sculpture of light.

Skandranon Rashkae rested his beaked head atop his crossed foreclaws and contemplated the city across the bay. Although his city was considered dazzling at night by the most jaded of observers, even by day, White Gryphon was a city of light. It gleamed against the dense green foliage of the cliff face it had been carved from, shining in the sun with all the stark white beauty of a snow sculpture. Not that this coast had ever *seen* snow; they were too far west and south of their old home for that.

Of course, given the way that mage-storms have mucked up everything else, that could change at a moment's notice, too.

Well, even if such a bizarre change in climate should occur, the Kaled'a'in of White Gryphon were prepared for it. *We build our city to endure, as Urtho built his Tower. Let the most terrible winter storms rage, we are ready for them.*

It would take another Cataclysm, and the kind of power that destroyed the twin strongholds of two of the most powerful mages who ever lived, to flatten White Gryphon. And even *then* the ruins of its buildings would endure, for a while at least, until the vegetation that covered these seaside cliffs finally reclaimed the terraces and the remains of the buildings there. . . .

Skan shook his head at his own musings. *Now why are you thinking such gloomy thoughts of destruction, silly gryphon?* he chided himself. *Haven't you got enough to worry about, that you have to manufacture a second Ma'ar out of your imagination? You came over here to rest, remember?*

Oh, yes. *Rest.* He hadn't been doing a lot of that; it seemed as if every moment of every day was taken up with solving someone else's problems—or at least look as if he was *trying* to solve their problems.

There was no one near him to hear his sigh of exasperation, audible over the steady thunder of the surf so far below him.

He dropped his eyes to the half-moon bay below his current perch, and to the waves that rolled serenely and inexorably in to pound the base of the rocky cliffs beneath him. On the opposite side of the bay, where the cliff base lay in shelter thanks to a beak of rock that hooked into the half-moon, echoing exactly the hook of a raptor's beak, the Kaled'a'in had built docks for the tiny fishing fleet now working the coastline. *One year of terrible travail to cross the country to get here, and nine of building. We have managed a great deal, more than I would have thought, given that we cannot rely on magic the way we used to.*

Now his sigh was not one of exasperation, but of relative content.

From here the half-finished state of most of the city was not visible to the unaided eye. Things were certainly better than they had been, even a few years ago, when many of the Kaled'a'in were still living at the top of the cliff, in tents and shelters contrived from the floating barges.

The original plan had called for a city built atop the cliff, not perched like a puffin on the cliff face itself. General Judeth was the one who had insisted on creating a new city built on terraces carved out of the cliff face. Like so many of the Kaled'a'in and adopted Kaled'a'in, she was determined to have a home that could never be taken by siege. Unlike many of them, she had a plan for such a place the moment she saw the cliffs of the western coastline.

Skan still marveled at her audacity, the stubborn will that saw her plan through, and the persuasion that had convinced them all she was right and her plan would work. Small wonder she had been a commander of one of Urtho's Companies.

The rock here was soft enough to carve, yet hard enough to support a series of terraces, even in the face of floods, winds, and waves. That was what Judeth, the daughter of a stonemason, had been the first to see. The cliffs themselves had dictated the form the city took, but once folk began to notice that there was a certain resemblance to a stylized gryphon with outstretched wings—well, some took it as an omen, and some as coincidence, but there was never any argument as to what the new city would be called.

White Gryphon—in honor of Skandranon Rashkae, who no longer dyed his feathers black, and thanks to the interval he had spent caught between two Gates, was now as pale as a white gyrfalcon. The only black left to him was a series of back markings among the white feathers, exactly like the black bars sometimes seen on the gyrfalcons of the north.

The White Gryphon regarded the city named for him with decidedly mixed feelings. Skandranon was still more than a little embarrassed about it. After all those years of playing at being the hero, it was somewhat disconcerting to have everyone, from child to ancient, revere him as one! And it was even more disconcerting to find himself the tacit leader of *all* of the nonhumans of the Kaled'a'in, and deferred to by many of the humans as well!

I thought I wanted to be a leader. Silly me.

Truth to be told, what he'd wanted to be was *not* a peacetime leader; he'd wanted to be the kind of leader who made split-second decisions and clever, daring plans, not the kind of leader who oversaw disputes between *hertasi* and *kyree,* or who approved the placement of the purifying tanks for the city sewage system. . . .

Council meetings bored him to yawning, and *why* anyone

would think that heroism conferred instant expertise in *everything* baffled him.

He wasn't very good at administration, but no one seemed to have figured that out yet.

Fortunately, I have good advisors who permit me to pirate their words and advice shamelessly. And I know when to keep my beak shut and look wise.

Somehow both the refugees and the city a-building had survived his leadership and his decisions. Most people had real homes now, homes built from the limestone that partly accounted for the city's pale gleam under the full light of the sun. All of the terraces were cut and walled in with more of that limestone, and all of the streets paved with crushed oyster shells, which further caught and reflected the light. There was room for expansion for the next five or six generations—

And by the time there is no more space left on the terraces, it will be someone else's problem, anyway.

Sculpting the terraces and putting in water and other services had been the work of a single six-month period during which magic *did* work the way it was supposed to. It had been just as easy at that point to cut all of the terraces that the cliff could hold, and to build the water and sewage system to allow for that maximum population. Water came from a spring in the cliff, and streams that had once cascaded into the sea in silver-ribbon waterfalls, carried down through holes cut into the living rock to emerge in several places in the city. It would not be impossible to cut off the water supply—Skan was not willing to say that anything was impossible anymore, given what he himself had survived—but it would be very, very difficult and would require reliably-working magic. It would also not be impossible to invade the city—but every path, either leading down from the verdant lands above, or up from the bay, had been edged, walled, or built so that a single creature with a bow could hold off an army. The lessons learned from Ma'ar's conquests might have been bitter, but they were valuable now.

Skan raised his head and tested the air coming up from below. *Saltwater, kelp, and fish. New fish, not old fish. The fleet must be coming in.* It had taken him time to learn to recognize those scents; time for his senses to get accustomed to the ever-present tang of saltwater in the air. No gryphon had ever seen the Western Sea before; his scouts hadn't even known what it was when they first encountered it.

Huh. "My" scouts. He shook his head. *I had no idea what I was getting myself in for—but I should have seen it coming. Amberdrake certainly tried to warn me, and so did Gesten and Winterhart. But did I listen? Oh, no. And now, here I am, with a city named after me and a thousand stupid little decisions to make, all my time eaten up by "solving" problems I don't care about for people who could certainly solve those problems themselves if they tried.* Now he knew what Amberdrake meant, when the kestra'chern said that "my time is not my own."

And I don't like it, damn it all. I should be practicing flying, or practicing making more gryphlets with Zhaneel. . . .

Instead, he was going to have to return for another blasted Council session. *They could do this without me. They don't need me. There is nothing I can contribute except my presence.*

But his presence seemed to make everyone else feel better. Was that all that being a leader was about?

:Papa Skan,: said a sweet, childlike voice in his head, right on cue. *:Mama says it is time for the meeting, and will you please come?:* Even without a mage-made teleson set to amplify her thoughts, Kechara's mind-voice was as clear as if she had spoken the words to him directly. It was another of the endless ironies of the current situation that the little "misborn" gryfalcon had become one of the most valuable members of the White Gryphon community. With magic—and thus, magical devices—gone unreliable, Kechara could and did communicate over huge distances with all the clarity and strength of teleson-enhanced Mindspeech. She was the communication coordinator for all of the leaders—and, more importantly, for all the Silver Gryphons. The Silvers were a resourceful policing organization formed of the remnants of the fighters and soldiers who had made it through the two

Kaled'a'in Gates, rather than through the Gates they'd been assigned.

Kechara's ability, combined with her eternal child-mind, would have caused her nothing but trouble in the old days, which was why Urtho had hidden her away in his Tower. But now—now she was the answer to a profound need. No one ever questioned the care lavished on her, or the way her special needs were always answered, no matter what else had to be sacrificed. She, in turn, had blossomed under the affection; her sweet temper never broke, and if she didn't understand more than a tenth of what she was asked to relay, it never seemed to bother her. Everyone loved her, and she loved everyone—and with Zhaneel watching over her zealously, making sure she had playtime and naptime, her new life was hundreds of times more enjoyable than her isolation in Urtho's Tower.

:*I'm coming, kitten,*: he told her with resignation. :*Tell Mama I'm on my way.*:

He stood up and stretched his wings; the wind rushing up the cliff face tugged at his primaries like an impatient gryphlet. He took a last, deep breath of the air of freedom, cupped his wings close to his body, and leaped out onto the updraft.

The cliff face rushed past him, and he snapped his wings open with a flourish—and clacked his beak on a gasp of pain as his wing muscles spasmed.

Stupid gryphon—stupid, fat, out-of-condition gryphon! What are you trying to prove? That you're the equal of young Stirka?

He joined the gulls gliding along the cliff face, watching the ones ahead of him to see how the air currents were acting, while his joints joined his muscles in complaining. Like the gulls, he scarcely moved his wings in dynamic gliding except to adjust the wingtips. Their flight only looked effortless; all the tiny adjustments needed to use the wind instead of wing-beats took less energy, but far, far, more control.

And a body in better condition than mine. I should spend less time inspecting stoneworks and more time flying!

He *could* have taken the easier way; he could have gone up instead of down, and flapped along like the old buzzard he was.

But no, I let the updraft seduce me, and now I'm stuck. I'm going to regret this in the morning.

As if that wasn't bad enough, by the time he got halfway across the bay, he'd collected an audience.

His sharp eyes spared his bruised ego none of the details. Not only were there humans and *hertasi* watching him, but someone had brought a dozen bouncing, eager young gryphlets.

A flying class, no doubt. Here to see the Great Skandranon demonstrate the fine details of dynamic gliding. I wonder how they'll like seeing the Great Skandranon demonstrate the details of falling beak-over-tail on landing?

But with the pressure of all those eyes on him, he redoubled his efforts and increased the complaints of his muscles. He couldn't help himself. He had always played to audiences.

And when he landed, it was with a clever loft up over their heads that allowed him to drop gracefully (if painfully) down onto the road rather than scrambling to get a talonhold on the wall edging the terrace. He made an elegant landing on one hind claw, holding the pose for a moment, then dropping down to all fours again.

The audience applauded; the gryphlets squealed gleefully. Skan bowed with a jaunty nonchalance that in no way betrayed the fact that his left hip felt afire with pain. Temporary pain, thank goodness—he'd been injured often enough to know the difference between the flame of a passing strain and the ache of something torn or sprained. He clamped his beak down hard, tried to look clever and casual, and waited for the pain to go away, because he wasn't going to be able to move without limping until it did.

Stupid, stupid gryphon. Never learn, do you?

The burning ache in his hip finally ebbed; he continued to gryph-grin at the youngsters, then pranced off toward the half-finished Council Hall before any of the gryphlets could ask him to demonstrate that pretty landing again.

Amberdrake took his accustomed chair at the table, looked up at the canvas that served as a roof, and wondered how many more sessions they would meet here before the *real* roof was on. Right now the Council Hall was in a curious state of half-construction because its ambitious architecture absolutely required the participation of mages for anything but the simplest of tasks to be done. The mages hadn't been able to manage more than the most rudimentary of spells for the past six months, not since the last mage-storm.

That left the Council Hall little more than the walls and stone floor, boasting neither roof nor any of the amenities it was supposed to offer eventually.

But the completion of the Council Hall was at the bottom of a long list of priorities, and Amberdrake would be the last person to challenge the order of those priorities. Just—it would be very nice to look up and see a real roof—and not wonder if the next windstorm was going to come up in the middle of a Council session and leave all of them staring up at a sky full of stormclouds.

The Kaled'a'in mage Snowstar, who had once been the mage that their Lord and Master Urtho had trusted as much as himself, took his own seat beside Amberdrake. He caught the Chief Kestra'chern's eye and glanced up at the canvas himself.

"We think the next mage-storm will return things to normal enough for us to get some stonework done," Snowstar said quietly. "This time the interval should be about nine months. That's more than enough time to finish everything that *has* to be done magically."

Including the Council Hall. Amberdrake smiled his thanks. Snowstar had been put in place by Urtho, the Mage of Silence, as the speaker to his armies for all of the human mages in his employ, and no one had seen any reason why he shouldn't continue in that capacity. General Judeth, former Commander of the Fifth, was the highest-ranking officer to have come through the two Kaled'a'in Gates before the Cataclysm—purely by accident or the will of the gods, for she was one of the Commanders who appreciated the varied talents of the nonhumans under her command and knew how to use them without abusing them. On Skandranon's suggestion, she had organized the gryphons, the other nonhumans who had served in the ranks, and the human fighters into a different kind of paramilitary organization. Judeth's Silver Gryphons had acted as protectors and scouts on the march here, and served in the additional capacities of police, watchmen, and guards now that they all had a real home.

Amberdrake liked and admired Judeth. *I would have willingly named her Clan Sister even if no one else had thought of the idea.* Members of the Kaled'a'in Clan k'Leshya comprised the bulk of the humans who had wound up together—and with no qualms on anyone's part, they had adopted the mixed bag of service-fighters, mercenaries, kestra'chern and Healers who had come through with them. The adoption ceremony had ended the "us and them" divisions before they began, forging humans and nonhumans, Kaled'a'in and out-Clan into a whole, at least in spirit. And the journey here had completed that tempering and forging. . . .

Well, that's the idealistic outlook, anyway. Amberdrake did not sigh, but his stomach churned a little. *Most* of the people of White Gryphon were folk of good will—

But some were not. The most obvious of those had marched off on their own over the course of the arduous search for a place to build a home, and good riddance to them, but some had been more clever. That was why Judeth's people still had a task, and why they would continue to serve as the police of White Gryphon.

Because, unfortunately, the Silvers are needed.

In an ideal world, everyone here would have had meaningful work, status according to ability, and would have been so busy helping to create their new society that they had no thought for anything else.

But this was not an ideal world. There were shirkers, layabouts, troublemakers, thieves, drunks—any personality problem that had existed "back home" still existed somewhere among k'Leshya. There were even those who thought Skandranon was the villain of the Cataclysm, rather than the hero. After all, if he had never taken Urtho's "suicide device" to Ma'ar, there would never have *been* a Cataclysm. And in a way, there might have been some truth in that idea. There would only have been the single explosion of Urtho's stronghold going up—not the double impact of all of Urtho's power *and* Ma'ar's discharged in a single moment. Perhaps they would not now be suffering through the effects of mage-storms.

And perhaps we would. Even Snowstar is not certain. But there is no persuading someone whose mind is already made up, especially when that person is looking for a nonhuman scapegoat. Not even Judeth herself could reason with some of these idiots.

As if the thought had summoned her, Judeth arrived at that moment. Her carefully pressed, black and silver uniform was immaculate as always. The silver-wire gryphon badge of her new command gleamed where her medals had once held pride of place on the breast of her tunic. She wore no medals now; she saw no reason to. "If people don't know my accomplishments by now," she often said, "no amount of medals is likely to teach them, or persuade them to trust my judgment."

She smiled at Amberdrake who smiled back. "Well, this is three—Silvers, Mages, Services—and I know that Cinnabar can't be spared right now for Healers, so where is our fourth?"

"On the way," Snowstar said promptly. "Zhaneel had Kechara call him."

"Ah." Judeth's smile softened; every one of the Silvers liked Kechara, but Amberdrake knew she had a special place in her heart for the little misborn gryfalcon. Perhaps she alone had any notion how hard Kechara worked to coordinate the Silvers, and she never once took that hard work for granted. "In that case—Amberdrake, is there anything you want to tell us before Skan gets here?"

"Only that I am acting mainly as Chief Kestra'chern in this, rather than as Chief of Services." With no one else to coordinate such common concerns as sanitation, recreation, medical needs, and general city administration, much of the burden of those tasks had fallen on Amberdrake's shoulders. After all, the kestra'chern, whose unique talents made them as much Healers as pleasure-companions, and as much administrators as entertainers, tended to be generalists rather than specialists. Amberdrake had already been the tacit Chief of Urtho's kestra'chern, and he was already Skandranon's closest friend. It seemed obvious to everyone that *he* should be in charge of those tasks which were not clearly in the purview of Judeth, Snowstar, or Lady Cinnabar.

Judeth raised an eyebrow at that. "Is this an actionable problem?" she asked carefully.

"I think so." He hesitated.

"I think you should wait long enough for me to sit down, Drake," Skandranon said from the doorway. "Either that, or hold this meeting without me. I could always find something pointless to do."

The gryphon grinned as he said that, though, taking any sting out of his words. He strolled across the expanse of unfinished stone floor to the incongruously formal Council table, the work of a solid year by one of the most talented—and unfortunately, disabled—woodworkers in White Gryphon. Since an injury that left him unable to walk or lift, he had been doing what so many other survivors at White Gryphon had done—used what they had left. He'd built the table in small sections, each one used as an example to teach others his woodworking skills, and then had his students assemble the pieces in place here. Like so much else in the settlement, it was complex and ingeniously designed, beneath an outer appearance of deceptive simplicity.

"So, what is it that was so urgent you had to call a Council meeting about it?" Skan said, arranging himself on the special couch that the same woodworker's students had created to fit the shape of a gryphon. "I know you better than to think it's something trivial—unless, of course, you're growing senile."

Amberdrake grimaced. "Hardly senile, though with an active two-year-old underfoot, I often wonder if I'm in danger of going mad."

Skan nodded knowingly, but Amberdrake was not about to be distracted into discussions of parenthood and the trials thereof. "I'm afraid that as Chief Kestra'chern, I am going to have to bring charges against someone to the Council. That's why I needed three of you here—I'm going to have to sit out on the decision since I'm the one bringing the charges. That means I need a quorum of three."

Snowstar folded his hands together on the table; Judeth narrowed her eyes. "What are the charges?" Snowstar asked quietly.

"First, and most minor—impersonation of a trained kestra'-chern." Amberdrake shrugged. "I do not personally *remember* this man being in Urtho's service, as a kestra'chern or otherwise. I can't find anyone who will vouch for his training, either. I *do* know that his credentials are forged because one of the names on them is mine."

"That's fairly minor, and hardly a Council matter," Snowstar said cautiously.

"I know that, and if it were all, I wouldn't have called you here. I'd simply have examined the man and determined his fitness to practice, then put him through formal training if he was anything other than a crude *perchi* with ambitions." Amberdrake bit his lip. "No, the reason I bring him up to you three, and in secret session, is because of what he has done. He has violated his trust—and if he had been less clever he would already be in Judeth's custody on assault charges."

Judeth's expression never varied. "That bad?" she said.

He nodded. "That bad. We kestra'chern are often presented with—some odd requests. He has used the opportunities he was presented with to inflict pain and damage, both emotional and physical, purely for his own entertainment."

"Why haven't we heard of this before?" Skan demanded, his eyes dangerously alight.

"Because he is," Amberdrake groped for words, "he is *diabolical*, Skan, that is all I can say. He's clever, he's crafty, but above all, he is supremely adept at charming or—manipulating people. He has succeeded in manipulating the people who came to him as clients so thoroughly that it has been over a year from the time he began before one was courageous enough to report him to me. Even the other kestra'chern were fooled by him. They couldn't tell what he was doing behind his doors. But I know—I have felt what his client felt."

Skan's beak dropped open a little. "What *is* this man?" the gryphon asked, astonished. "Some sort of—of—evil Empath?"

"He might be, Skan, I don't know," Amberdrake replied honestly. "All I know is that the person who came to me needed considerable help in recovering from the damage that had been done, and that there are more people who are more damaged yet who have not complained." Amberdrake had been very careful not even to specify the client's sex; while the victim had not asked for anonymity, Amberdrake felt it was only fair and decent to grant it. He spent several long and uncomfortable moments detailing exactly what had been done to that victim, while the others listened in silence. When he had finished—as he had expected—all three of them were unanimous in their condemnation of the ersatz kestra'chern.

"Who is he?" Judeth asked, her voice a low growl as she reached for pen and paper to make out the arrest warrant.

Amberdrake sighed and closed his eyes. He had hoped in a way that once the charges had been laid and the Council decision arrived at, he would feel better. But he didn't; he only felt as if he had uncovered the top of something noisome and unpleasant, and that there was going to be more to face before the mess was cleaned up.

"Hadanelith," he said softly, as Judeth waited, hand poised over the paper.

She wrote down the name.

"Hadanelith," she repeated as she sealed the order with her signet ring. "Can I deal with him now, or is there something else you want to do with him first?"

"Now," Amberdrake said quickly, with a shudder. "Arrest him *now*. He's done enough damage. I don't want him to have a chance to do any more."

"Right." Judeth stood up. "Skan, would you have Kechara call Aubri, Tylar, Retham, and Vetch, and have them double-time it over here to meet Amberdrake and me?" She handed the arrest warrant to Amberdrake, who took it, trying not to show his reluctance. "I'll be going with you to take this Hadanelith down. This could look bad—I am considered to be the military leader here. A military leader arresting a putative

kestra'chern under any circumstances will cause some discontent. Still, I don't want to be seen as being above getting
my hands dirty or unfit for service with the other Silvers. And
I definitely do *not* want someone like that loose to deal with
later. Hate to saddle you with this, Drake, but—"

"But I'm the one bringing the charges, so I had better be
there. It's my job, Judeth," he replied as he wrung the warrant
loosely in his hands. "Though it's times like these when I
wish I was just a simple kestra'chern."

Judeth snorted and gave him a sideways look. "Drake," she
said only, "you were never a *simple* kestra'chern."

"I suppose I wasn't," he murmured as she, Snowstar, and
Skan left the table and the Council Hall.

Hadanelith whittled another few strokes at the wooden bit
before setting it down. After some more cutting and rounding—not too much rounding, though, it needed to remain a
challenge for the client, right?—he'd add the pilot holes for the
wooden pegs and straps later. Carving wood was so much like
what he did for a living with his clients, it was natural that he
would be excellent at it. He could grasp the roughness, grip it
firmly, and then cut away at every part that didn't look like
the shape he had in mind.

Telica, here, was one of his works. A slice here, a chunk
taken off there, and before long she'd be another near perfect
item. Her mind was his latest work. She was nude, kneeling
on the floor, held in place by several lengths of thread binding her neck to her wrists, her wrists to her ankles. The
thread was completely normal in composition, which was
what made it so amusing to him.

Virtually any effort at all would have snapped them, without leaving so much as a welt; no, the real bindings here were
those of his will over hers. The regular training that made her
one more of his items held her as firmly in place as any set of
iron shackles or knotted scarves. She was one of his carvings,
inside, though she didn't presently show so much as a scratch
on her alabaster-smooth skin.

Every time Telica came to him for one of her appointments

she knew she would be trained and tested in a dozen ways. All of his girls knew this. They could be trapped or tricked, hurt or caressed, abused or set up for humiliation, and after a while, they came to love him for it—or at least obey him. Obedience was close enough for him; he'd take that over love any day.

So it was with no worry at all that he took three steps to stand before her steadily breathing, still form, and put a hand to her jaw. "Open," he said in his rich voice, and her lips parted in instant compliance to receive the wooden bit he'd been trimming. As he pressed it deeper into her mouth, he noted that it scraped the gums, and probably pressed the palate about *there.* Good, good. It would serve as another test of her training in itself, then, and the soreness that lingered after Telica's visit would simply be another reminder of his attentions, and who she served now.

Who *she* served? That was another delicious irony. Hadanelith was, as far as anyone else knew, serving *her*, but behind these doors, she was *his* as surely as any other of his whittled treasures. His treasures were six now; Dianelle, Suriya, Gaerazena, Bethtia, and Yonisse, and Telica here, each one a good but still slightly flawed carving.

There was always something wrong with them by the time he'd made them his artworks. Why was that? Why was the wood always unseasoned, or knotty, or split down the middle, when he'd finally carved away enough of the bark to make something beautiful? It was as if the wood that looked so promising on the outside failed to live up to the promise; that by the time he'd gotten enough of the useless wood shaved away to refine the details, the flaws in the material showed themselves.

Telica here, for instance, was too quiet. It was nearly impossible to get as much as a whimper out of her. He was no more lusty than any other man, he felt, and there were times, just as when one craved a certain dish or fruit, when he simply had to hear a muffled cry of anguish or a sob. Telica was mute as a stick unless he lacerated her with a blade or pierced her flesh with a needle. She was just as flawed in her silence as

Gaerazena was in her garrulous, hysterical chattering and Yonisse was in her shuddering anxieties.

It couldn't be his skill; it had to be the material itself. If only he could get his hands on a woman of real substance, breeding, true quality. A woman like Winterhart. . . .

That one he had yet to touch, although he had watched her hungrily for ten years. Now there was a creature fit for an artist! Not wood at all, she was the finest marble, a real challenge to carve and mold. But he could do it. He was more than a match for her, just as he was more than a match for any of them. What sculptor was ever afraid of his stone? What genius was ever afraid of his toys? The challenge would be to unmake and then remake her, but to do it so cleverly that she *asked* for every change he made to her.

What a dream. . . .

But a dream was all it ever would be. She would never come to him, not while she was mated to the oh-so-perfect Amberdrake. And not when the whole city knew how disgustingly contented she was with her mate. It was all too honey-sweet for words, just as sickeningly, cloyingly sweet as that sugar-white gryphon, Skandranon, and *his* mate.

It was just a good thing for him that not everyone in this little utopia was as contented with life as those four were.

He would certainly enjoy giving all of them a bitter taste of reality when the time was right. Especially Winterhart. Get under that cool surface and see what seethed beneath it. Find out what she feared.

Not the ordinary fears of his six creations, he was certain of that. No, Winterhart must surely fear something fascinating, something he would have to work hard to discover. What could he cut free from inside her? Now there was an interesting image; a hollow woman, emptied out slice by slice, with only a walking shell left for everyone else to see. How could it be done? And how thin could he carve those walls before the sculpture collapsed in on itself? Well. If the wood was good enough, he could scoop out quite enough to satisfy his needs.

These thoughts were on his mind as he lowered his knife

down between Telica's thighs. That, and his craving for her to make some noise for him.

The blade touched the birch-white skin of one thigh.

At that moment, a shadow moved across Telica's still skin. The lighting in the room shifted as someone—no, several someones—came into the room uninvited. Now *this* was an outrage! Hadanelith whirled, knife in hand, to confront these presumptuous invaders. Before he could utter more than a snarl, a boot to his face made things quite different than a minute before, when *he* was the one in control.

Amberdrake's trepidation had hardened into a dull, tight pain in his gut. It certainly wasn't because he hadn't seen horror in his life, or felt himself grow ill from feeling others' suffering. It wasn't precisely because he feared a violent confrontation, or the cleaning up that was always needed after such a thing happened. The sensation he had, as the group arrived at Hadanelith's home—or perhaps it should be called a lair—was dread for its own sake. Amberdrake had the feeling that nothing good was going to come of this arrest. Morally it was the right thing to do, by Law it was the right thing to do, yet still there was that gnawing in his gut that told him they were doing more harm than good.

Aubri, the Eternally Battered, apparently felt it also, although it might have just been a bad breakfast that caused his disgruntled expression. He was a gryphon who never had any good luck, if you believed what he said.

"It's too quiet in there, Drake," he wheezed, as they held themselves poised just outside Hadanelith's door. "We know he's got someone in there, so why isn't there any sound?"

"I don't know," Amberdrake replied, in an anxious whisper. "I don't like it, either. Judeth?"

"I've got a bad feeling about this," she said shortly. "Let's get in there—now."

With a wave of her hand, she led her group of ex-fighters through the door in a rush. Amberdrake trailed behind, warrant still held in his clenched hand, dreading what they would find.

So he didn't actually *see* Judeth kick Hadanelith in the jaw and send him sprawling to the floor, but once he saw what had prompted that action, he also saw no need to protest what might be considered an act of brutality.

The young woman was bound only by thread, in one of the most excruciatingly uncomfortable positions Amberdrake had ever seen. Her skin was sheened with sweat, and her muscles trembled with the effort of holding herself in place. There were faint scars in many places on her pale skin. With Hadanelith's carving knife lying on the floor where Judeth had just kicked it, there wasn't much doubt in Amberdrake's mind where those scars had come from.

But most horrible of all—she acted as if she were completely unaware of their presence.

No. She's not acting. She is unaware of our presence. She will not acknowledge that we are here because he has not told her to.

That was what held him frozen, and what made Judeth's eyes blaze with black rage; that one presumably human person had done *this* to another.

The scars are only the least of what he has done to her. This will take months to undo. This is a case for the Healers; my people can't possibly make this right.

With trembling hands, Amberdrake unrolled the arrest warrant and read it out loud. Hadanelith did not move from the place where he lay sprawled across his own floor, not even to finger the growing bruise on his jaw. He only glared up at Amberdrake in impotent fury as the kestra'chern read out the charges and the sentence.

"You've heard the charges. We've seen the evidence before our eyes. You've been caught, Hadanelith," Judeth said fiercely, biting off each word as if she bitterly regretted having to say anything to him at all. "Have you got anything to say in your defense?"

In answer, Hadanelith spat at her. Since he was lying on the ground and she was standing over him, it didn't get very far. The glob of spittle hit the top of her boot and ran down the side. One of the human Silvers snarled and pulled back a fist; Judeth caught his arm.

"No point in soiling your hands, Tylar," she said coldly. She looked around, picked up a piece of expensive silk that Hadanelith was using for a couch drape, and deliberately wiped her boot with it, dropping it at her feet in a crumpled heap. Only then did she turn to look at her prisoner.

"There are a lot of things I would *like* to do to you, scum," she said, her voice flat and devoid of all emotion. "However, we've got one Law to deal with people like you. Hadanelith, by reason of being caught in the acts described, you will be taken as you are to the plateau above White Gryphon in chains. You will be taken to the edge of the lands we have claimed and cultivated. There you will be freed of your chains, and you will be given from now until darkness falls to take yourself outside our border marker. If, by tomorrow at dawn, you are still inside them, whoever finds you is permitted to take any steps he deems necessary to get rid of you."

Hadanelith's rage showed clearly in his eyes, but his voice was as cold as Judeth's. "As I am? What, no weapons, no food, no—"

"You are a mad dog, scum. We don't supply a mad dog with food and weapons." Her lips thinned, and her eyes glinted as she looked down at him. "You think that you're so clever—I suggest you start using that cleverness to figure out how to survive in the forest with only what you're wearing." She jerked her head at the rest of the Silvers. "Chain him up, and get him out of here before he makes me sicker than I already am."

The Silvers didn't need any urging; within moments they had their prisoner on his feet, collared and manacled.

Amberdrake had expected Hadanelith to fight, to heap verbal abuse on them—to do or say *something*, at any rate. This continued silence was as unnerving as his continued certainty that no good was going to come of this.

He is a mad dog. The forest is going to kill him, but painfully, and perhaps slowly. Shouldn't we have at least had the compassionate responsibility to do it ourselves?

But his crimes had not warranted execution, only banishment. He could not be cured, that much was obvious, so the rulers of White Gryphon had an obligation to remove him from among those he was preying upon. That meant imprisonment or banishment, and White Gryphon did not yet have a prison.

Hadanelith glared at Amberdrake all the time he was being bound, and continued to glare at him all the time he was being hauled out of the room, as if he held Amberdrake personally responsible for what was happening to him. That just added another level of unease to all of the rest.

If they had found Hadanelith alone, Amberdrake might have turned and bolted at that moment—but they hadn't, and through all of this, the young woman had not moved so much as an eyelash. Amberdrake's personal unease gave way to a flood of nausea as he knelt down beside her.

He eased down his own shields, just a trifle, and touched her arm with a feather-brush of a finger to assess the situation.

He slammed his shields back up in the next instant, and knew he had gone as white as Skan's feathers by the chill of his skin.

He looked up at Judeth, who hovered uncertainly beside him.

"It's not good, Judeth, but I can take it from here." He took a deep, steadying breath and reminded himself that this was no worse than many, many of the traumas he had helped to heal in his career as the Chief Kestra'chern of Urtho's armies. He looked up again and manufactured a smile for her. "You go on along. I can manage. She'll have to go to Lady Cinnabar, of course, but I can snap her out of this enough to get her there."

One of Judeth's chief virtues was that she never questioned a person's own assessment of his competence; if Amberdrake said he could do something, she took it for granted that he could.

"Right," she replied. "In that case—I'll go along with the others. I want to make personally sure that chunk of *sketi* gets past the border markers by sundown."

She turned on her heel and stalked out the door, leaving

Amberdrake alone with the girl, a young woman whose name he didn't even know.

And that's the next thing; go through Hadanelith's records and find his client list. Where there is one like this, there will be more.

You knew it could be this bad, Drake. Just think how much worse it would be for her if you weren't here.

Hadanelith would not run, no matter how grim and threatening his captors looked. He walked away from them at a leisurely pace, as if he was out for an afternoon stroll, keeping his posture jaunty and his muscles relaxed.

It wasn't easy. The back of his neck crawled, and despite that officious bitch Judeth's assertions that they were not going to physically harm him—*themselves*—he half expected an arrow in the back at any moment.

But no arrows came, and he completed his stroll down the furrow of planted ground without incident, carefully stepping on each tiny seedling before him as he walked, and grinding it into powder beneath his feet. A petty bit of revenge, but it was all that he was likely to get for some time.

At the end of the furrow was the land that had not been claimed from the forest—forest that held so many dangers that sending him out here might just as well have been a death sentence. Even the field workers came out under guards of beaters to drive the beasts away, and Kaled'a'in whose specialty was in handling the minds of wild beasts in case the beaters couldn't frighten predators off.

And archers in case both fail. Thank you so much for your compassion, you hypocrites.

He did not pause as he reached the trees and the tangle of growth beneath them. He pushed right on in and continued to shove his way grimly through the bushes and entwined vines, ignoring scratches and biting insects until he finally struck a game path.

Then he stopped, a little out of breath, to take inventory of his hurts. He wanted to know every scratch, every bruise, for he would eventually extract payment for all of them.

There was the kick to his jaw, the other to his hand; the one had practically broken the jawbone, the other had left his hand numb. His guards hadn't been any too gentle on the trip up here, either; they'd just about dislocated his arms, wrenching him around, and they'd gotten in a few surreptitious kicks and punches that left more bruises and aching spots under his clothing.

Nevertheless, Hadanelith smiled. They'd been so smug, so certain of themselves—they'd said he was to be sent into this exile *as he was*, and then were bound by that word from searching him!

Fools. They assumed that a kestra'chern at work would be completely unarmed—but Hadanelith was not exactly a kestra'chern.

And Hadanelith was never unarmed.

He began to divest himself of all his hidden secrets, starting with the stiletto blades in the seams of his boots.

Shortly, he would resume his journey to the boundary markers, and he would be very careful to remain outside them for the few days it took to convince these idiots that some beast or other had disposed of him.

Then he would return.

And then the repayments would begin.

Amberdrake

Two

Skan cupped his wings and settled onto the ledge of the lair he and Zhaneel had chosen when White Gryphon was first laid out, this time only stubbing two talons upon landing. That wasn't unusual; he was often less careful when he thought no one was watching him, and the pain was negligible. This was his home. He could blunt his talons on the stone if he felt like it.

Together with a small army of hertasi, they had carved it from the rock of the cliff, used the resulting loose stone for mortared walls and furniture, then filled it with such gryphonic luxuries as they had brought with them. It had a glorious view of the surf on the rocks below, but was sheltered from even the worst winter storms by an outcropping of hard, black stone covered with moss and tiny ferns. It was easily the best lair in the city; mage-fires kept it cozy in the winter, breezes off the sea kept it cool in the summer, and there were plenty of soft cushions and carved benches to recline upon. Occasionally rank *did* have its privileges.

One of those privileges was absenting himself from the likely unpleasant confrontation with this Hadanelith character. He felt rather sorry for poor Amberdrake but, on the whole, rather relieved for himself. Perhaps he could soothe his guilt later by visiting Amberdrake with a special snack or treat.

At least that Hadanelith mess was one decision I didn't have to make. All I had to do was agree with Drake. What's happened to me, when not deciding someone else's fate is an event?

His wing muscles still ached, distantly, from his landing, and he felt a lot more tired than he should have been after two relatively short flights. *I'm going to have to increase the time I spend skydancing,* he decided. *No matter how I have to juggle my schedule. I shouldn't be tiring this quickly. After ten years you'd think I'd get most of my endurance back!*

He folded his wings, and glanced back down at the surf before pushing open the door to the lair. Cinnabar kept warning him, even after all these years, that the time he spent between Gates followed too quickly by the perils of their cross-country trek had burned away every bit of his reserves. He was stripped to the bone by the strain, so many years ago—but he should have gotten all of it back by *now!* Amberdrake, Gesten, and Lady Cinnabar had done their best for him, too. *This is all the fault of a sedentary life! I spend more time strolling around the streets than I do in exercises, and no one says anything because I'm Skandranon—but if I were any other gryphon, there'd be jokes about my sagging belly!*

He closed the door neatly behind him and stepped over the wall across the entrance—a necessary precaution to keep unfledged, crawling, leaping gryphlets from becoming hurtling projectiles off the balcony. The gryphons had never had to face that particular problem when their lairs had been on the ground, but a small inconvenience seemed a trivial price for the added safety of their youngsters.

Small mage-lights illuminated the interior of the lair—unusual in the city at the moment, as were the mage-fires that heated the lair by winter. Mage-lights and mage-fires were far down on the list of things the mages needed to create during the brief times that magic worked properly. Skan had made most of these, and Vikteren had done the rest.

There we are again. Another reason why I am such a feathered lump. Lying in place for days on end to make mage-lights. Staring at a stone to enchant it to glow like a lovesick firefly while hertasi and humans bring me enough food to sink a horse. What would Urtho think of me now?

The humans and hertasi had to make do with candles and lanterns; while mage-lights and mage-fires were in limited supply, they went first to the Healers, then the gryphons and *tervardi*, then the *kyree*. Only after all the nonhumans had sufficient lights and heating sources would humans receive them for their homes. This had been a decision on Skan's part that although it seemed slightly selfish, had a sound reason behind it. The Healers obviously needed mage-lights and heat sources more than anyone else—and as for the gryphons, tervardi, and kyree, well, the former had feathers, which were dangerous around open flames, and the wolflike latter didn't have hands to light flames with.

Freshly crisped gryphon and roasted tervardi, mm-mm! Served fresh in their own homes, in front of their children— Ma'ar's secret recipe! That was the very phrase he'd used to persuade the rest of the Council to agree to the edict, and as he'd figured, the invocation of Ma'ar's name did the trick, more than logic had.

He hadn't enjoyed manipulating them, though. Tricks like that left a rather bad taste in his mouth. He really didn't like manipulating anyone, if it came right down to it. Neither had Urtho.

There were many things Urtho didn't like, gods bless his memory. I always secretly pitied him for the position he was put in by others' need for him. He never liked being the leader of all those who craved freedom from Ma'ar, but it was something he had to do. I remember him looking at me once, with a look of quiet desperation, when I asked him why he did it.

Skandranon paused, eyes unfocused, as his memory brought the moment back in sharp detail. He said, simply, *"If not me, then who?"*

Now I know how he felt then. It wears a soul down, even though the sense of fulfilling a duty is supposed to make a soul enriched. A noble heart, the stories say, is supposed to live and find joy in the responsibility. But I am satisfied less and less, doing a great deal I don't like—including getting fat!

"Zhaneel?" he called softly, when a glance around the "public" room showed no signs of life, not even a gryphon dozing in the pile of pillows in the corner. "I'm—"

He'd called softly, hoping that if the little ones were sleeping, he wouldn't wake them. Stupid gryphon. Vain hope.

A pair of high-pitched squeals from the nursery chamber greeted the first sound of his voice, and a moment later twin balls of feathers and energy came hurtling out of the chamber door. They each targeted a foreleg; Tadrith the right and Keenath the left.

They weren't big enough to even shake him as they hit and clung, but they made it very difficult to move then they locked on and gnawed. And Amberdrake and Winterhart thought *they* had problems with their two-legged toddler! Young gryphons went straight from the crawling stage into the full-tilt running stage, much like kittens, and like kittens they had three modes of operation—"play," "starving," and "sleep." They moved from one mode to another without warning, and devoted every bit of concentration to the mode they were in at the time. No point in trying to get them interested in a nap if they were in "play" mode—and no point in trying to distract them with a toy if they were squalling for food.

Zhaneel followed her two offspring at a more sedate pace. She was more beautiful than ever, more falconlike. Her dark malar-markings were more prominent; now that she wasn't trying to look like the gryphons whose bodies were based on hawks, and now that she had learned to be self-confident, she carried herself like the gryfalcon queen she was. "Don't worry, I wasn't trying to settle them for a nap," she said calmly over their wordless squeals of glee, as Skan tried vainly to detach them. "We were just playing chase-mama's-tail."

"And now we're playing burr-on-papa's-leg, I see," he replied. Zhaneel took one bemused look at what her children were doing and began chortling. At the moment, still in their juvenile plumage, the gryphlets looked like nothing but balls of puffy, tan-and-brown feathers, particularly absurd when attached to Skan's legs. "The Council session broke up early,"

Skandranon continued, "and I decided that I'd had enough and escaped before anyone could find some other idiot's crisis for me to solve."

It came out a lot more acidic than he'd intended, and Zhaneel cocked her head to one side. "Headache?" she inquired delicately.

He succeeded in removing Tadrith from his right leg, but Keenath, being the older of the two tiercels, was more stubborn. "No," he replied, again with more weariness than he had intended. "I am just very, very tired today of being the Great White Gryphon, the Wise Old Gryphon of the Hills, the Solver of Problems, and Soother of Quarrels. No one remembers when I was the Avenger in the Skies or Despoiler of Virgins or Hobby Of Healers. Now they want someone to do the work for them, and I am the fool that fell into it. I am tired of being responsible."

He slowly peeled Keenath from his foreleg, as the young gryphlet cackled with high-pitched glee and his brother pounced on Skan's twitching tail.

"You want to be irresponsible?" Zhaneel asked, with a half-smile he didn't understand, and a rouse of her feathers.

"Well," he replied, after a moment of thought, "Yes! The more people pile responsibilities on me, the less time I have for anything else! All of my time is taken up with solving other peoples' problems, until I don't have any time for my own! And *look* at me!" He shook himself indignantly. "I'm *fat*, Zhaneel! I'm overweight and out of condition! I can't think of the last time I sat around chatting with Amberdrake and Gesten just because I enjoy their company, when I spirited you off for a wild storm ride, or just flew off somewhere to lie senseless in the sun for a while! Or for that matter, to lie on *you* a while. And the longer this goes on, it seems, the less time I get to even think!"

Zhaneel reached out a foreclaw and corralled her younger son before he reattached himself to his father's leg, nodding thoughtfully. "But the city is almost finished, except for the things that people must do for their own homes, which you cannot be responsible for," she pointed out. "So—surely they must not need you as much?"

He sighed and shook his head. "Except that the more things get done, the more they find for me to do. As the months go by, the things are always less vital, but they're frozen without my word of approval or decree. It's as if they've all decided that I am the only creature capable of making decisions—never mind that I'm only one member of a five-person Council!"

As she fixed her eyes on his, he struggled to articulate feelings that were not at all well defined. "I don't know if this is some twisted joke that fate has played on me, Zhaneel, but I'm beginning to feel as if I'm not me anymore. It's as if the old Skandranon is being squeezed out and this—this faded, stodgy, dull old White Gryphon is taking his place! And it is happening in my body, and I can only watch it happen."

As Tadrith raced around to attack Skan's other side, Zhaneel cornered him as well, tumbling both gryphlets together into a heap of cushions, where they attacked each other with exuberant energy, their father utterly forgotten. She sat down beside him and nibbled his ear-tuft, with an affectionate caress along his milky-white cheek. "The wars are over, my love," she pointed out with inarguable logic. "There are no more secret missions to fly, no more need to dye your feathers black so that you do not show against the night sky—no more real need for the *Black* Gryphon. We all have changed, not just you."

"I know that," he sighed and leaned into her caress. "But— that was more than a part of me, it was who I was and I miss it. Sometimes I feel as if the Black Gryphon died—with—with Urtho—and now all I have left is a shell. I don't know who or what I am anymore. I only know that I don't like what's happened to me."

Zhaneel clicked her beak in irritation. "Perhaps you do not care for what you are, but there are many of us who were very pleased to see a Skandranon who had learned a bit of responsibility!" she said crisply. "And we would be very annoyed to see that particular lesson forgotten!"

She glared at him just as she would have glared at a foolish young brancher for acting like one of the fledglings.

He shook his head, trying to bite back a hasty retort and instead make her see what he was talking about. "No, it isn't that," he replied, groping for words. "I—it's just that it seems as if I've gone to the opposite extreme, as if there just isn't any time for me to be myself anymore. I'm tired all the time, I never have a moment to think. I feel—I don't know—thinned out, as if I've stretched myself to cover so much that now I have no substance. My duty has consumed me!"

The slightly frantic tone of his voice was enough to make both the youngsters look up in alarm, and Zhaneel patted his shoulder hastily. "You'll be all right," she told him, clearly trying to placate him. "Don't worry so much. You gave a lot of yourself in the journey here. You lost almost all of your strength when you were trapped in the Gates. You just need more rest."

That's always the answer, any time I complain that I don't feel like myself.

"And that's just what I'm not getting," he grumbled but gave up trying to explain himself to her. She didn't understand; how could he expect her to, when he didn't really understand what was wrong himself?

The gryphlets came galloping over to him again, and he settled down on the floor and let them climb all over him. What *was* wrong with him, anyway? He had everything he had ever wanted—a lovely mate, a secure home, peace—and he was the leader he had always dreamed of being. Shouldn't he be content, happy?

Well—except that he *wasn't* the leader he had dreamed of being, back when he fought against the sky, *makaar,* and all the death-bolts an army could hurl at him. The stories he was raised on, of heroes and hopes, said nothing about the consumption of the leader by his duties. He had dreamed of dramatically-lit skies against which his glorious form would glide across the land he protected, and below him the people would cheer to behold him and flock to his presence.

Maybe the problem was simply that he was, at best, a reluctant leader when it came to peacetime solutions, and his discontent with that situation spilled over onto everything else.

Zhaneel nibbled his ear-tuft again, then disappeared into the depths of the lair, presumably with some chore or other to take care of now that he was keeping the youngsters out of her feathers for a while. Skandranon might be caught in chasms of distress, but he would always have affection for his little ones. He loved them day to day as much as he had enjoyed conceiving them. He fisted his claws and bowled the little ones over with careful swats, sending them back into the pile of cushions. They squealed and chirped, rolling around and batting at him in boundless exuberance—for the moment—and he wished that he could be as carefree and happy as they were.

Was everyone as unhappy as he was? He didn't think so. In fact, he wasn't quite certain when his current discontent had begun. It was simply that today, he was devoting concentration to realizing it was *there*, and just how deep it festered.

As arduous as the journey here had been and as fraught with danger and uncertainty, *his* job had actually been easier then than it was now. He'd only needed to offer encouragement, to keep peoples' spirits up. He could step up and make a rousing speech, inspire hope, and tell well-timed stories. He was the cloud-white cock of the walk at critical times. Judeth had been in charge of protecting the army of refugees, Gesten and Amberdrake in charge of keeping everyone fed and sheltered. Lady Cinnabar had taken over anything remotely concerned with the health of the group. All *he* had been asked to do was to provide a figurehead, a reminder of the old days, and what the best of those days had meant.

Skandranon snorted to himself. *In other words, vain gryphon, your job was to be their living legend.*

Now he had to make decisions—usually difficult, uncomfortable decisions. Worst of all, he was the only "authority" anyone could agree on to arbitrate in disputes between nonhumans and humans—and even though the disputants might agree on him as arbitrator, they were seldom entirely satisfied with him. Humans, he suspected, always were sure he was favoring nonhumans, and the nonhumans were always convinced he would favor humans because of his special relationship with Amberdrake. Annoying, but there it was. And that just led to another source of discontent for him; if people were going to insist he solve their conflicts, the least they could do would be to pretend that they liked the solution! But no matter what he did or did not do, *someone* would grumble about it!

It almost seemed as if the easier life became, the more *trouble* people caused! In the beginning, when White Gryphon was nothing more than a collection of tents perched on the terraces, people just never seemed to have the energy or time to quarrel with one another.

Maybe that's it. Maybe the problems are coming because people have too much spare time?

Surely that was too easy an answer. . . .

And it wasn't true for everyone, either.

Maybe it was just the curse of civilization. *I know that Urtho's army had all the troubles that plague any big gathering of people. It stands to reason that once people aren't completely absorbed in the business of trying to get the basic necessities, they'll go back to their old ways. Look at that Hadanelith creature, for instance! I'll bet ten years ago he was playing those same games down among the* perchi; *I'll bet the only reason he didn't get caught then was because his clients just didn't come back to him for more, rather than complaining about him. Or else—his clients just didn't come back from the battlefield.*

Or maybe Hadanelith hadn't been old enough, ten years ago, to ply any kind of trade; Amberdrake hadn't mentioned his age. That could be why he had been able to fake being trained—if he had lied about his training he could just as easily have lied about his age and experience. Most of the kestra'chern attached to Urtho's armies had *not* wound up with the Kaled'a'in Clan k'Leshya; instead they had gone through the Gate that had taken the noncombatants from the purely human forces. That only made sense, of course; why should they have gone where the skills they had trained for would not be needed? The Kaled'a'in Clan k'Leshya had chosen to go with the gryphons and the other nonhumans because of their own special relationship with Urtho's magically-created creatures—but the other Kaled'a'in Clans had not gone to the same refuge for purely pragmatic reasons. It was best not to put all the refugees in one place. If the Kaled'a'in were to survive as a people or even as a vestige of a people, it was best that the Clans split up, to distribute them over too large an area to wipe out. That Amberdrake was here was partly the result of his own friendship with Skan, and partly the fact that he had joined k'Leshya himself; besides him, there were only the k'Leshya kestra'chern and perhaps a handful of others.

So when there was leisure again, and people began to look for some of the amenities of the old days, there were some things—like trained kestra'chern, for instance—that were in short supply.

Which means that the more subtle unethical people will have the opportunity to revert to type, an opportunity that hasn't been there until now. That makes sense. Probably too much sense, actually. Urtho might have been the most principled creature in the known lands, but there were not too many like him, in his army or out of it. I suppose, given how many people were pouring through whatever Gate was nearest there at the end, that we shouldn't have expected that everyone with us was of an angelic nature. We shouldn't have expected anything. We were just glad to be alive at the time. And later—everyone was too busy to get into trouble, even the potential workers of trouble.

That only depressed him more. Perhaps he was overly idealistic, but he had really hoped that they had left things and people like Hadanelith behind them. *I suppose there is going to be crime now, theft and assault, fraud and chicanery, who knows what else.* He sighed. *More work for the Silvers; I'd thought Judeth was just creating makework for them, but maybe she had more vision than me.*

Or maybe she had just had less blind optimism.

Or maybe she is just smarter than the White Fool.

Well, whatever the reason, General Judeth had done her work well. The Silver Gryphons, with their silver badges and ornamented bracers to show their station to even the most drunken of viewers, were as well-trained as they were well-equipped. Fortunately for Skan's peace of mind, the stylized silver-wire badges they wore, created by a displaced silver-smith who was tired of never being able to make jewelry any-more, bore no resemblance to Skandranon, White *or* Black. After all, there was only so much adoration a sane mind could accept. The former soldiers had applied their military training to other matters under Judeth's supervision, and at the time Skan had only felt relief that she was giving them something to make them feel useful.

I thought that gradually we'd be able to phase all those old warhorses out, that once we knew we weren't going to need protection against whatever is out there in the wilderness, they'd become mostly decorative, rescuing children from trees and the like. Silly me. So now we have police; and it looks as if we are going to need them.

No wonder that Judeth had insisted that the Silvers always travel in pairs, with one of the pair being a Mindspeaker—and no wonder she had politely requisitioned Kechara's talents and service. Skan hadn't thought much about that, either, ex-cept to be glad that Judeth was giving poor little Kechara something to do to make *her* feel useful. He'd been too grate-ful to care, since that got her out from under Zhaneel's feet most of the day. The eternal child, she'd been fine until Zha-neel gave birth to the little ones—and the sheer work caused by the presence of three children in the lair, one of them half the size of an adult, was just a bit much for Zhaneel.

Even the addition to the household of another hertasi, a young lizard named Cafri, who was Kechara's best friend, playmate, and caretaker all rolled into one, had not helped un-til Judeth had come to Skan with her carefully-phrased re-quest. Now Kechara went up to a special room in the Silvers' headquarters in early morning and did not return until after dark—not that Judeth was abusing her or overworking her. The "special room" was very special; it had a huge open highsilled window, a fabulous balcony, was cooled by the breezes in summer and warmed carefully in winter. It was also crammed full of all the toys the grandmothers could make. There were playmates, too. The mated gryphons among the Silvers brought their own offspring to play there as well. It was just that Kechara of all the "children" would be asked from time to time to Mindspeak a message to someone. She would stop whatever she was doing, happily oblige, then get back to her latest game.

Mindspeech seemed to take no effort whatsoever on her part which, in itself, was rather remarkable. She often forget to say things with words, in fact, projecting her thought or feeling directly into the mind of whoever she was "talking" to, particularly when she was impatient. Acting as message-relay for the Silvers did not bother her in the least—in fact, she was rather proud of herself, insofar as Skan could tell, because *she* had a job, and none of her playmates did.

:Papa Skan!: said that cheerful little voice in his head, suddenly, and he wondered with startlement if she had somehow picked up his thoughts about her and assumed he was trying to talk to her. *:Papa Skan, Unca Aubri says you need to know something.:*

He sighed with mingled relief and resignation. Relief, because he didn't want to have to explain what he had been thinking to Kechara, and resignation because Aubri had been assigned to the unpleasant task of ejecting Hadanelith from White Gryphon. Something must have gone wrong. . . .

:What does Uncle Aubri want, sweetling?: he asked carefully, keeping his own feelings out of what he sent. She was quicker to pick up on emotion than thoughts.

Her reply was prompt and clear. *:Unca Aubri says to tell you he's up on the cliff and that there's a ship that isn't ours, and it's coming in to the docks and he wants you to come where he is right away please.:*

His head snapped up. A ship? A strange ship? Friend or foe? *:Tell him I'm coming, sweet,:* he replied quickly. *:Can you please tell Uncle Snowstar and Uncle Tamsin what you just told me? And ask Cafri to run and tell Judeth the same thing?:*

:Yes, Papa Skan,: she said with a giggle, largely because she really liked to Mindspeak with "Uncle" Tamsin. She told Skan it was because "he has a furry mind, and it tickles," whatever that meant. *:There, Cafri is gone, I'll talk to Unca Snowstar now.:*

Her "presence," as strong as if she had been in the same room with him, vanished from his mind. He leaped to his feet and called to Zhaneel, who came quickly out of the rear of the lair.

"Aubri's seen a strange ship coming in to the docks," he told her hastily, and her golden eyes widened as the hackles on the back of her neck stood up a little.

"Who?" she asked.

He shook his head. "We don't know. I've had the Council summoned; we'll have to go down and meet it, whoever it is. I don't know how long I'll be."

She nodded, and shooed the twin gryphlets into the nursery—which just happened to be the most defensible room in the lair. *She* knew; she was a child of the Mage Wars, after all. They dared not assume this was a friend, or even a neutral party. They *must* assume the worst.

"Stay safe," was all she said, over her shoulder, her eyes wide with worry that she would not voice. "I love you, Skandranon Rashkae."

"I love you, Brighteyes," was all he *could* say—then he was off, out the door of the lair and onto the landing porch, using the low wall to leap from. A wingbeat later, and the White Gryphon was clawing his way against the wind to the top of the cliff, where Aubri was waiting.

Amberdrake shaded his eyes and stared at the bobbing sail just beyond the mouth of the bay, even though he knew he would not be able to see anything. Even if he had not been half-blinded by the sunlight on the water, the ship was too far away to make out any kind of detail.

That, however, was not true of the gryphons, whose eyes were infinitely better than the humans'. Aubri roused all his brown feathers, then widened his eyes rather than narrowing them as a human would; his pupils flared open, then constricted to mere pinpoints, then flared again with surprise.

"They're black," Aubri announced, his voice startled and his beak gaping open, as he peered across the waves at the oncoming ship. "The humans in that ship, Skan, Drake, they're *black.*"

"They're what?" Skan craned his neck as far as it would go and widened his eyes as well. His pupils flared to fill his eyes. "By— Drake, Aubri's right. These humans have *black* skin! Not brown, not painted, not sunburned—they're really, really black!"

Black? But— Amberdrake blinked because he, and perhaps he alone of all of the Council, knew what that meant, and recognized who these people must be.

"They must be—but we aren't that far south—" He was babbling, he knew; speaking aloud what was running through his head, without thinking. He scolded himself. That would be a horrible habit for a kestra'chern to get into!

"They must be *what,* Amberdrake?" The Kaled'a'in Adept, Snowstar, stared at him out of silver-blue eyes in a gold-complected face, his expression one of impatience. He tossed his braided silver hair over his shoulder and stared hard at his fellow Kaled'a'in. "What are you babbling about?"

"They must be Haighlei," he replied vaguely, now concentrating on his effort to try to make out some details of the ship, at least, something that might confirm or negate his guess.

"They must be highly *what?*" Snowstar asked sharply, perplexed and still annoyed.

"Not *highly,*" Amberdrake repeated, rather stupidly, shading his eyes against the glare of the westering sun on the water. "*Haighlei.* From the Haighlei Emperors. You know, the Black Kings. They're called that because they *are* black. They're the only black-skinned people that I know of, but how on earth they came here, I haven't a clue."

Out of the corner of his eye, he saw Snowstar's mouth form into a silent "o," and the Adept also turned his attention to the boat that was tacking into the bay.

"Aren't we more than a bit north and west for them?" General Judeth asked, her voice troubled. She was right to be troubled; the Haighlei Empire was vast and powerful, even by the standards Ma'ar had set, and they were as mysterious as they were powerful. She shaded her sharp, dark-gray eyes with one hand, her strong chin firming as she clenched her jaw.

Amberdrake gave up trying to make out any details for the moment, and shrugged. "I don't know," he admitted. "I don't know of anyone from our lands who had even the vaguest idea how large their Six Nations are. For all *I* know, they could run from this Sea to the Salten Sea in the East!"

The only person he had ever met who knew anything about the Haighlei Emperors was his old teacher, the incomparable kestra'chern Silver Veil. At the start of the war with Ma'ar— had that really been twenty years ago?—she had been heading south, toward a promised position in the court of one of the Kings. She would be perhaps fifty now; no great age for a kestra'chern of her lineage and training—and she was one of those women who would never look anything other than agelessly elegant. Had she gotten that position? Was she prospering? He hadn't found out; the wars had eaten up all his time and energy, leaving none to spare for trying to trace his mentor's whereabouts.

He turned his attention back to the ship. The ship had entered the bay, now, and it was finally possible to make out the details of its fittings and crew. The White Gryphon "fishing fleet" was made up of fairly crude vessels fitted with oars and a single, basic sail—large enough for four men at the most. This was a real *ship*, clearly able to carry several dozen people, and Amberdrake didn't know enough about ships to know if it was of a type any of their few folk familiar with such things should recognize or not. It was quite elaborate, that much he knew on sight; it had three masts and several sails striped in red and white, and there were people swarming all over it. The hull was painted in blue and red, with a pair of eyes on the front; the sails were augmented by a network of lines and rope-ladders. There was a raised, houselike section in the middle of the boat that had a door and several windows in it. The men actually doing all the work were dressed simply, in white breeches, many with colored cloths wrapped around their heads and colored sashes around their waists, but there were three people in much more elaborate clothing standing in front of the door in that houselike section, peering at the people waiting on the dock. Rich hues of red, orange, and the gold of ripe grain, ornamented with winking glints of metal and the sharper gleams of gems marked the costumes of these three notables. The cut of their clothing was entirely unfamiliar to Amberdrake.

It did not comfort Amberdrake in the least to see, as the boat drew nearer, that every man in the crew had enormous knives stuck through their sashes, and that there were racks of spears visible behind the elaborately-garbed men watching them.

They're tall. They are very tall. The ship was finally close enough for Amberdrake to make some kind of guess as to the general appearance of these people. The thing that struck him first was their height. The shortest of them would probably top the tallest Kaled'a'in by at least a head. Their features were handsome enough, finely sculptured, although they were not as hawklike as the Kaled'a'in. Amberdrake was amazed by the garments the three—officials?—were wearing; although the material was very light by the way it fluttered, it was woven with incredibly detailed geometric patterns in bright yellows, reds, and oranges. The robes fastened high up on the side of the neck, with the openings running down the left of the front rather than the middle. The robes boasted high, stiff collars that matched the cylindrical hats each of them wore. Heavy, jeweled neckpieces lay on their breasts and shoulders, and heavy, matching brooches centered their odd hats.

Although their hair was as tightly-curled as a sheep's fleece, it was so black that it swallowed up all the light. The sailors wore theirs at every length, although perhaps "length" was the wrong term to use for hair that stood out rather than draping down the owner's back. Some of them had cropped their hair so close to the skull that there was nothing there but a short frizz; others had clearly not cut their hair for months, even years. It stood out away from their heads as if lightning had just struck them. But the three men waiting with folded hands wore their hair as short as they could and still be said to *have* hair. The hats fit too closely to allow for any amount of hair.

They were all, without a doubt, beautiful to behold. Unfortunately they did not look pleased, if Amberdrake was any judge of expressions.

They did not bring the boat to the dock; instead, they anchored out in the bay, with a sophisticated set of tensioned fore- and aft-anchors that held them steady against the waves.

And there they waited. The sailors formed up in loose ranks on the deck of the ship and remained there, unmoving.

No one spoke a word; the ship hung at anchor, with the only sound being the steady pounding of the surf on the rocks.

"It appears that they expect us to come to them," Judeth observed, in her usual dry manner.

Of course they do. We're the interlopers, the barbarians. Amberdrake would have called for a boat to take him and the rest of the Council to the strangers if there had been any—but there weren't. Every vessel they owned was out fishing or dropping nets.

"They aren't stupid," Skan rumbled. "They can see we don't have the means to come to them. Besides, if they came this far, they can go a few more feet."

And be damned annoyed when they do, Amberdrake thought silently, but he held his peace. There wasn't any way they *could* go out to the waiting vessel, except by flying, and he was not about to suggest that Skan go out there by himself. There was no point in wrapping a potential hostage up like a gift and presenting him to a possible enemy.

The tense moments passed, marked by the waves breaking against the rocks, as the Haighlei stared and the Kaled'a'in stared back, each of them waiting for the other to make the next move. But as it became clear that there were no other vessels available, not even a tiny coracle, the Haighlei leaders turned to the sailors, gesturing as they ordered their men to bring up the anchors and move in to the docks.

To make up for the loss of face, the Haighlei brought their

ship in with a smooth expertise that Amberdrake watched with envy. There were no wasted motions, and nothing tentative about the way the captain and pilot maneuvered the ship. Even though the dock was completely unfamiliar to them, they had their vessel moored and comfortably snugged in to the wooden piers in a fraction of the time it took their own people to do the same with a much smaller boat.

"They're good," Judeth muttered, with grudging admiration. "They're damned good. I'll have to remember to dredge some sandbars to hang them up on if they turn hostile and bring friends. It would cut back the effectiveness of the drag-fishing nets, but we could work around that. If there are hostilities, the gryphons and kyree wouldn't be free to pull nets in, anyway."

Amberdrake nodded, impressed all the more by the fact that Judeth's mind never seemed to stop examining resource management and strategy, even while watching the ship draw in.

Within a few moments, the Haighlei sailors had run a gang-plank down to the dock, and were unrolling a strip of heavy woven material patterned in bright reds and browns to cover it. Then they scrambled back aboard their ship, and formed a line of alert bodies along the railing—all this without another issued order.

Only then did the three envoys—if that was what they really were—deign to descend to the dock. And there, standing on the strip of material, they waited, hands tucked into the sleeves of their elaborate, fluttering robes.

Amberdrake started to step forward, hesitated, and caught both Judeth and Skandranon's eyes. Judeth nodded, slightly, and Skan made an abrupt motion with his beak. Amberdrake assumed the leadership position of the group, and the others followed.

He was the only one of the lot properly garbed to meet these people; Snowstar was wearing simple Kaled'a'in breeches and a wrapped coat, both old and worn. Judeth, though her pepper-and-salt hair might have given her the authority of age, wore one of her old black uniforms with the insignia removed and only the silver gryphon badge on the breast. Bearlike, red-haired Tamsin, who shared the Healers' Council seat with his love, Lady Cinnabar, was as shabbily dressed as Snowstar. Only Amberdrake kept up some pretense of elegance these days; somehow it didn't feel right for a Council member to show up in public dressed as if he had just been weeding his garden (as Snowstar had been) or scrubbing medical equipment (which was where Tamsin had been). As the best-dressed Council member, perhaps it was wisest for him to pretend to the position of leader.

He stopped, within easy conversational distance, but no closer. The stern, forbidding expressions on the faces of the envoys did not encourage hearty greetings.

"Welcome to White Gryphon," he said, slowly and carefully—and hoping frantically that these people *might* be able to speak his tongue! "We are the Ruling Council of the city. I am Amberdrake." He introduced the rest of his colleagues as the Haighlei stood there impassively, giving no indication of whether they understood him or not. "May we ask what brings you to our settlement?" he finished, a little desperately.

The man in the middle removed his hands from his sleeves, and cleared his throat. "You trespass upon the lands of King Shalaman, and violate the sanctity of Haighlei territory," he said, coldly, clearly, and in a precise but dated form of their own tongue. "You will leave, or you will be removed."

Amberdrake stood there, stunned. A hundred things ran through his mind. *Should I apologize? Should I beg for mercy? Should I explain how we came here? What should I say?*

Judeth stepped forward and folded her arms over her chest, matching the envoys stare for stare. "We will stay," she stated, baldly, her eyes meeting theirs without blinking. "There were no territory markers here when we arrived, and there are no signs of habitation for two days' *flight* in any direction. We can withstand any force your King may bring against us. We have been settled here almost ten years, and we are staying."

Amberdrake nearly bit his tongue off, suppressing a yelp of

dismay. What is she doing? Who does she think these people are? What—

"Drake," Skan said—as softly as a gryphon could—in Kaled'a'in, "Judeth's calling their bluff. They can't force us out, not now, not without bringing a lot of troops up here, way off from their own nearest city, and not without a big expense. They weren't using this land for anything. And Judeth knows we have to look as if we're operating from a position of strength or they won't take us seriously."

Judeth, who understood Kaled'a'in quite as well as any gryphon, nodded ever so slightly.

The impassive masks of the envoys cracked the tiniest fraction with shock, as if they had no idea that someone might actually *challenge* them. "You will leave," the middle envoy began again, as if by repetition he could make his point.

"I said, we will *not*," Judeth replied, this time with more force. She smiled, slightly, as the wind stirred her short curls. "We *are*, however, willing to make alliance with King Shalaman in return for the use of this land."

The envoys did not actually faint with indignation at Judeth's bold statement, but they were certainly shocked. They were shocked enough to turn away and confer together in buzzing whispers, all the while casting dubious glances over their shoulder at the Council members.

"I hope you know what you're doing, Judeth," Amberdrake muttered, watching the three envoys—though what he would do if they announced that they were leaving then and there, he had no idea.

"I had my hand in some of Urtho's diplomatic doings," Judeth said with equanimity. "Not a lot—but I know a bluff when I see one. Skandranon is right. These people can't possibly have any way of dislodging us without a lot of trouble. If we take a strong stand now, they're more likely to give us some respect. It'll suit them better and save face all around if they decide to make an alliance with us and pretend it was all their own idea."

Before Amberdrake could reply, the middle envoy turned

abruptly and centered his gaze on Judeth. "Flight, you said," he said to her, frowning. "Two days' flight."

Although it was not phrased as a question, it clearly was one. Skan read it that way, too, and stepped forward himself. The envoy had ignored his presence and that of Aubri up until this moment—a rather difficult proposition, considering that he was the size of a small horse.

"Indeed," Skandranon told the man in his deepest and most impressive voice, fanning his wings for emphasis. "We gryphons, who are also citizens of this settlement, made flights in all directions before we settled here." He tilted his head toward the man, whose mouth had actually dropped open in shock on hearing the "beast" speak. Skandranon looked up, with his head lowered at just the right angle to make his brows and eyes appear even more raptorial than usual. "You might be amazed at the things we do."

The envoy closed his mouth quickly, as if he had just swallowed a bug; the other two were looking a bit ill, with a grayish tone to their skin beneath the natural deep black color. The middle man looked at his two colleagues, who simply blinked at him uneasily. He turned back toward Amberdrake.

"We will confer," he said shortly, and without another word, he marched back up the gangplank, followed by his fellows.

Two sailors sprang down onto the docks and quickly rolled up the strip of carpet, taking it back aboard the ship. They did not retract the gangplank, however, which might be a sign that the envoys were not done with White Gryphon yet.

Amberdrake could only hope.

"Now what?" he asked Skan and Judeth. Judeth shrugged.

Skan actually chuckled. "I think that is obvious," he replied. "Now we wait. And of course—we eat. Is anyone besides me hungry? I think that if Aubri and I bite through a few leg-sized bones while we're in eyesight of these diplomats, they might just reconsider any conflicts and be friendly."

Judeth, at least, made one concession, a concession that really didn't do much to mitigate Amberdrake's anxiety; she suggested that the rest of the Council members drift off one at a time and return wearing clothing a little more appropriate to the situation. "Except Drake, of course," she added, with an enigmatic half-smile. "He is never underdressed."

Amberdrake wasn't certain whether to take that as a compliment or the opposite.

She also suggested that Tamsin send Lady Cinnabar in his stead, a suggestion that everyone else seconded.

Tamsin was hardly offended. "I was going to suggest that myself," he said, with obvious relief. "Cinnabar has a lot more experience at this sort of situation than I do!" He thought for a moment, then added, "I'll Mindspeak Kechara while I'm on my way up; I've got some ideas that may speed things up a bit."

He sprinted for the path to the top of the cliff; Amberdrake did not envy him the climb that was ahead of him. But when Lady Cinnabar appeared, long before even their most athletic youngster could have made it up the winding path, it was obvious that at least one of Tamsin's ideas had been to have Kechara send her down directly.

She was wearing one of her seldom-used court gowns, a lush creation of silver brocade and emerald silk that went well with her pale blonde hair, making her a fit match for Amberdrake's beaded and embroidered, bronze-and-brown finery. And with her were two *hertasi* laden with "proper" clothing for Judeth and Snowstar, at least by Amberdrake's standards of the clothing appropriate to diplomatic receptions. Judeth sighed when she saw the particular uniform that her *hertasi* had brought, but she made no other complaint. Both of them headed for one of the nearby boathouses to change, while the two gryphons, Amberdrake, and Lady Cinnabar waited, keeping their vigil.

It would not be too much longer before the fishing "fleet" came in, and what they were going to make of this imposing vessel, Amberdrake had no notion. He had confidence in the basic good sense of everyone out on the water, though; the sea was a harsh teacher, and those who were not possessed of good sense had not survived the first two years of experimenting with boats and fishing.

"I met Tamsin on the way down, and he told me everything you know so far," Cinnabar said, as she examined the Haighlei ship without appearing to pay any attention to it at all. "I don't entirely agree with Judeth's approach, Amberdrake. I'm not sure it was necessary to be quite so blunt with these people."

Amberdrake shrugged. "I feel the same way," he agreed. "But she'd already gotten the bit between her teeth and was galloping away before I could stop her. The little that I know about the Haighlei is that they are extremely formal, that their culture is very complicated. I'm afraid we shocked them, and I only hope we didn't utterly revolt them."

Cinnabar pursed her thin lips, but made no other change in her expression. "That could work to our advantage," she told him. "If we follow up on the shock in the right way, that is. Now that we have shocked them with our barbaric direct-ness—which could be a sign of power, and they can't know one way or another yet—we need to prove we can play the diplomatic game as well. We can't simply let them dismiss us as beneath them; we have to complicate the issue for them."

Amberdrake nodded, relieved to have someone on his side in this. "We also can't afford to have them out there, waiting, watching for us to make a fatal mistake," he agreed, "And if we shock and frighten them too much, that's exactly how they may decide to treat us." Then he smiled weakly. "Although on the surface of things, it does look as if it would be very dif-ficult for them to insert a spy among us without a boatload of makeup."

Judeth emerged from the boathouse at that moment, look-ing as if she had just come from a dress parade. Somehow, de-spite the fact that the stiff, severely tailored black-and-silver uniform she wore was over ten years old—this time *with* all her medals and rank-decorations on it—her *hertasi* had made it look as if it had just been fitted for her yesterday. With it she wore her favorite thigh-high, black leather boots, marking her former position as a cavalry commander.

"I'm glad to see you here so quickly, Cinnabar," Judeth said with a smile. "This is not my strong suit. Telling them they have no choice but to live with us—now that is my strong suit! But from now on—" she made a helpless little gesture with on hand. "—I'm in the woods. You and Amberdrake play this the way you see fit."

Amberdrake relaxed a trifle; it would have been very difficult to get anything done if half of the Council members were at odds with the other half. . . .

"I agree," Skan put in, "with one proviso. I do not believe that these people are familiar with gryphons or kyree— creatures that they *think* are mere animals—being intelligent. Look at the way they reacted when I spoke! If you wish, you may put me forward as the titular ruler here, and that will throw them further off balance, a state which we can use to our advantage."

"Now that is a good idea," Cinnabar said thoughtfully. "It might be the factor that turns us from mere barbarians into something so very exotic that we take ourselves out of the realm of anything they can calculate. We might be able to get away with a great deal more than we would as barbarians. They will certainly assume we are the most alien things they have ever seen, and make allowances. I like it."

"So do I," Amberdrake replied, as Snowstar emerged from the boathouse, garbed in one of his sweeping, midnight-blue silk robes, with dagged sleeves faced with white satin and a white leather belt. He had braided ornaments of white feathers and crystals into his hair as well, and now was more splendid than Amberdrake.

"Well, look who's putting us in the shade," Judeth chuckled, as Snowstar rejoined them. "Where were you keeping *that* rig all this time?"

"In a chest, where it belonged," Snowstar replied serenely. "It's not exactly the sort of thing one wears for building walls, weeding gardens, or trekking across the wilderness." He half-bowed to Lady Cinnabar, who smiled back at him. "One wonders what our visitors will make of our transformation."

They did not have to wait much longer to find out. As the

first of the fishing vessels came up to the dock and tied up—be it noted, carefully and cautiously—the three envoys emerged from the cabin of their ship, waited for the sailors to unroll the carpet again, and trooped down the gangplank to face the Kaled'a'in delegation.

The Haighlei did not miss the change in wardrobe; each of the envoys gave them a penetrating glance, although they said nothing. Skan did not pause to give them a chance to speak first.

"You surprised us with your coming," he said graciously, rumbling deeply despite the clear volume—offering an apology that was not an apology. "We of the White Gryphon Council are as much responsible for the work of our settlement as any of our citizens. We were dressed for labor when you arrived, as is our duty. Nevertheless, we deemed it important to be here at your arrival—and felt it was irresponsible to keep you waiting as clothes were changed. Healer Tamsin was required urgently above; in his place is the Honorable Lady Cinnabar, also a Healer and a member of our Council."

Cinnabar inclined her head toward them in an acknowledgment of equal status, and her formal, perfectly fitted gown left no doubt as to her rank. The meaning of the salute was not lost on them.

Amberdrake felt the appraising eyes of the two silent envoys assessing every detail of the new costumes, reckoning value, perhaps even assigning a tentative rank to each of them as the Haighlei judged such things. He thought he sensed a marginal relaxation, now that there were no longer forced to deal with what looked like a band of scruffy workmen.

The leader nodded graciously. "We see now that you are not the piratic interlopers we first took you for," he said, offering his own not-quite-apology for their first demand. "Our agents reported that they had seen something like a riever's base being constructed; we see that you have built a formidable settlement here, made for the ages rather than the moment, and worthy of the name of 'city.' "

I think he's saying that they've had a good look, and Judeth's right; they can't dislodge us without a nasty fight.

The envoy's next statement confirmed Amberdrake's guess. "We see that you would also make valuable allies, and we have been advised to offer you the opportunity to come to King Shalaman's Court, to negotiate."

"We see that you are civilized and responsible," said the man to the envoy's right, a gentleman who had been silent until now. "We noted the careful planning of White Gryphon, and it appears that you have endeavored to despoil the land as little as possible. We had expected brigands, and we find builders, architects." He smiled, revealing startlingly white teeth in his black face. "Such people would be valuable guards upon our northernmost border."

Amberdrake smiled back, and Skan bowed slightly. "I am of the same opinion," the gryphon said, with complete equanimity. "When would your monarch care to open negotiations?"

"Immediately, if possible," the envoy replied without a moment of hesitation. "We would be pleased to host a delegation of two with families and retainers, one human and one— other, such as yourself. There is room in our vessel to convey your initial delegation; others may follow you, if you so desire. We are authorized to wait here until you are ready to leave."

That made Amberdrake's eyebrows rise. Either these envoys had extraordinary power in making a decision here, or they had some way to communicate directly with their superiors.

Very possibly the latter. If their magic was working more reliably than magic used by the Kaled'a'in refugees, such communication would be simple enough.

Skandranon was equal to the challenge. "We would be pleased to host you in our city above for the night and show you a pale reflection of the hospitality we will be able to offer when our city is complete. In the morning Amberdrake and I and our families will be ready to leave with you. We are as anxious to conclude a treaty as you are."

"Excellent," the envoy said, as if he meant it. And for the first time, the three envoys stepped off their little strip of carpet and onto the dock.

Leaving their territory for ours! Whatever the gesture

meant, it seemed they were perfectly prepared to make the trip up the cliff.

Well, none of them are very old, nor do they look out-of-shape . . . and how better to show them that we're fortified for defense? Each of the envoys fell in beside one of the Councilors as they all began the walk to the path leading upward; the chief speaker beside Skan, the second man who spoke beside Amberdrake, and the one who had been silent the whole time beside Judeth.

The second man was thinner and a little taller than the other two, putting him at least a head taller than Amberdrake, who was not undersized by Kaled'a'in standards. His garments of red, black, and orange, while trimmed with heavy embroidery in gold threads, were made of very light material, perhaps silk. His walk and posture were relaxed now, and he strode beside Amberdrake with an easy gait that made the kestra'chern think that he was used to walking long distances. Perhaps they had no beasts of burden in his land.

"If you don't mind my asking," Amberdrake said hesitantly, "How is it that you speak our language so fluently? Our people have heard of the Haighlei Emperors, and how powerful they are, but nothing of any detail and certainly not your tongue."

"Oh," the man said, with a flashing smile and a wave of his hand, "That is simple. We have had many northern kestra'chern in the Courts of the Kings over the years—there is one with King Shalaman now."

"There is?" Amberdrake wondered—

"Oh, yes. A most remarkable and talented woman, and a great confidant of King Shalaman. Since he has no wife, she serves as Royal Companion. He even made her his Advisor for her wisdom. They call her *Ke Arigat Osorna*—that is, in your tongue and hers, The Silver Veil."

Somehow, Amberdrake managed not to choke.

Hadanelith

Three

Winterhart closed the pale-blue gauze curtains over the doorway to the balcony of the palace bedroom she shared with Amberdrake, and sighed contentedly. She left the doors open to the light breeze, a breeze that was already turning oppressively hot, and turned with all the grace of a courtier born, poised and elegant in the gown Lady Cinnabar had lent her. It was of a light cream silk, which complemented her skin. Her long hair, laced with cords of matching cream silk ornamented by bronze beads and cream-colored feathers, brushed her face as she smiled slowly at Amberdrake, and flicked her braids over her shoulder.

Then with all the abandon of a child, she flung herself between the pale-blue gauze bedcurtains into the heap of pale-blue silk pillows topping the bed. She grabbed one and hugged it to her chest, looking up at Amberdrake with a face full of mischief.

"A maid for the bath, another for the rooms—*two* nursemaids for Windsong—eating incredible delicacies at the royal table—and a suite of five rooms all to ourselves! And all Gesten has to do is oversee the Haighlei servants! I could get used to this very quickly," she said contentedly. "It certainly is a cut above spending my mornings weeding the vegetable garden, my afternoons tending to minor gryphonic ailments, and the rest of the time chasing a two-year-old with endless energy and a positive fascination for heights!"

Amberdrake smiled, and sat down on the bed beside her, reaching out to touch her cheek. "As far as I am concerned, the main benefit is the nursemaids, who give us the chance to be alone together! How is it that Windsong always knows the *moment* you and I—"

"Empathy, I suspect," Winterhart said impishly. "She certainly takes after you in every other respect, so I can't see any reason why she shouldn't have your gifts as well. And you know how little ones are, they want to be the center of attention, so when Mum and Da begin to shift that attention to each other. . . ."

Amberdrake sighed. "It is a perfectly rational explanation," he said ruefully. "But it doesn't suggest a solution to keep her from interrupting."

"But the nursemaids *will*," Winterhart said gleefully and waved her legs in the air, looking for all the world like a giddy adolescent. "Which means that we can spend as much time together as you can spare from being a diplomat."

"You are as much the diplomat as I, no matter how much you bounce on the beds," he reminded her with a slight grin. *Small wonder—she never had a chance to be giddy when she was an adolescent.* He ruffled her hair affectionately. *She is good at this business; she looked every bit as regal as the highest of the Haighlei at the court reception this afternoon.*

It had taken two weeks to sail down the coast to King Shalaman's capital city of Khimbata; a second vessel with more room for passengers would be arriving at White Gryphon shortly, to bring the rest of the delegation. The initial party consisted of Amberdrake and Winterhart, Skan and Zhaneel, the twin gryphlets and Windsong, and three hertasi, Gesten, Jewel, and a little female named Corvi. Jewel and Corvi were with Skan; Gesten mostly served (and lectured) Amberdrake these days, but he often stuck his bossy little snout into Skandranon's quarters to make certain that Jewel and Corvi were "doing things right by the old bird."

The first few days had been occupied with settling into their new quarters, a pair of side-by-side suites in the Royal Palace itself. The architecture of Khimbata was strange and fascinating, even to those who were used to the weirdly lovely buildings Urtho, the Mage of Silence, had raised over his lands. It had an oddly organic feeling to it, with pronounced woodgrains, and no exterior surface was ever left unornamented. The swirling curves were covered with mosaics and sculptured reliefs of plants, birds, and animals. There was seldom anything as simple as a straight line, either, even in the interiors of buildings. The corners and the joining of walls and ceilings were always gently rounded, forming arches; ceilings sloped slightly upward to the center of a room, where there was always a flower-shaped or globe-shaped lamp. There wasn't a right angle to be seen here, unlike the carved stone austerity of the buildings of long-lost Ka'venusho.

The private rooms all seemed to be decorated in pastels, and featured a number of ingenious ways to at least simulate coolness. There were gauze curtains to reflect away the worst of the sunlight, and huge windows and balcony doors to catch the least breeze. Fabrics were light and airy, smooth and soft to the touch. That was just as well because Khimbata lay in the heart of a jungle, and it was the most northerly of all the Haighlei Kingdoms. Amberdrake did not want to think about spending summer in one of the more southerly regions. One, at least, was a desert, with temperatures literally high enough to kill a man standing under the open sky for more than a few moments. So he had been told, at any rate, and he saw no reason to dispute the claim.

In the public chambers, however, the Haighlei love of color ran riot. The Haighlei felt as much at home in the jungle as within a building, and brought the jungle into their buildings as a pleasant reminder of the wealth of life lying outside the city. Huge, lush plants prospered inside, placed where sunlight would reach them and accompanied by cheerful fountains or pools with lazy fish of gold, white, and black. Tiny, huge-eyed furry creatures scampered tamely up the plants' trunks, and out onto their limbs, and loud, rainbow-bright birds sang, whistled, or spoke mockingly down at the humans passing beneath.

The birds made Amberdrake feel comfortable amid all the

alien architecture. They were like the tiny, rainbow-hued messenger-birds that the Kaled'a'in had brought with them, cherished, carefully nurtured, all the way from Urtho's Tower. These birds were larger, but like the messengers, spoke in human voices, with sense to their speech. He had already made friends with two, a salmon-pink one with a backward-curving crest of deep red, and one seemingly painted in blue, gold, and green.

The walls were covered with mosaics that were just as colorful as the birds, and cool, dim, deep-green passages between the vast public rooms brought to mind the cool, dim trails between huge forest giants.

The Haighlei themselves were as harlequin-bright in costume as their architecture; the clothing the three envoys had worn was fairly typical. Silk, raime, the finest linen imaginable, and a gauzy stuff made from fluffy plant fiber were dyed and fashioned into elaborate, fluttering robes, billowing trousers, and draped gowns, none of which incorporated less than three colors.

Amberdrake had pulled out all his most elaborately beaded and embroidered robes in anticipation of this; Winterhart would have been in some sartorial difficulty if it hadn't been for Lady Cinnabar. The Lady, it seemed, had used all of her old court gowns as padding on the floor of her floating-barge when planning for the evacuation of Urtho's Tower. That was clever of her, and reasonable given that fabric for padding was not a high priority and that her gowns were not made of stuffs that could be used as bandages or other useful articles. The clever aspect was that she had packed her gowns in a way that allowed her to retrieve the robes and dresses unharmed. "All" of her court gowns comprised a formidable number, and most of them were utterly unsuitable for the life of a Healer in a half-finished city.

Not all of the gowns were still pristine, and the lighter the fabric, the more it had suffered from wear and the intervening decade. Winterhart, however, was smaller than the aristocratic Cinnabar, and even those articles showing signs of wear or weakness at the seams could be cut down for her and look

new. Jewel and Corvi had spent most of the sea voyage frantically—but delightedly—retailoring those gowns to suit their
new owner. There was nothing a hertasi enjoyed more than
costume-making, and there had been little enough of that during the war with Ma'ar or the search for a new home. Even
Gesten had gotten into the act, much to the amusement of
Skandranon.

So now Winterhart could put on as fine a display as Amberdrake, wearing her elaborate gowns with all the aplomb of the
lady of nobility she had once been. The difference was, now
she was not suffering under the expectations of her high-
ranking family; now it was Amberdrake who was under the
careful scrutiny of countless critical eyes, and she who needed only smile and whisper a bit of advice unless she chose
otherwise.

She was enjoying it; Amberdrake was quite sure of that. He
thought about Winterhart with a wry smile as he looped string
on his fingers, preparatory to making a cat's cradle. She was
enjoying the luxury and pampering she had not had in decades.
For the past ten years she had done all of her own chores, her
own cleaning, her own cooking—or rather, she had done those
things with the help of Gesten and Amberdrake. For years before that, she had lived the rough life of a trondi'irn in Urtho's
army, a healer and tender of Urtho's gryphons, a post where
there were few luxuries and no pampering. Even Urtho himself had lived a life positively austere by the standards of the
Haighlei Courts.

"Is Silver Veil able to visit us this afternoon?" Winterhart
asked suddenly. Amberdrake covertly searched her face for
any hint of jealousy, but to his relief, there didn't seem to be
any signs of it. He would not have been at all surprised to discover that Winterhart was jealous of The Silver Veil. His mentor was one of those fine-boned, ageless women who, once
they achieve maturity, seem to hover at an indefinable perfec-
tion until they are very old indeed. Her hair had turned silver
in her teens, and she had capitalized on what might have been
a handicap for someone in her profession by growing and cul-
tivating it until it reached the floor, making it the trademark

that had become her name. She was as strikingly graceful and beautiful now as she had been when he knew her, and it would not have been unexpected for Winterhart to react with jealousy at the inevitable bond between astonishingly beautiful mentor and student.

"What do you think of her?" he asked cautiously, looping another strand. "Your own opinion, not what you think I want to hear."

"I like her," Winterhart said thoughtfully, her gaze turned inward for a moment. "If you can say you 'like' someone as self-contained as she is, that is. I want her to like me, and not just be polite to me, and that's not just because she is your old teacher and your friend. I like to listen to her talking; I think she is fascinating. I hope that I may age as gracefully."

Amberdrake nodded; it was a good observation. "To answer your question, she said she wanted to come to our suite this afternoon, if that is all right with you."

"When everyone else is taking a nap, which is a good time for northerners like us to get together and pretend we are accomplishing something even though we aren't," Winterhart chuckled. "I thought that was so absurd when we first arrived here, for everything to stop at the height of the day—but now, I can't imagine even trying to get anything done when it's so horribly hot. Even Windsong takes her nap without arguing now, and I thought that was nothing short of miraculous."

"But it's the perfect time of day to socialize," Amberdrake pointed out, verbally, since his fingers were weaving and unweaving intricate knots. "Especially if little 'why-mama' is chasing dream-butterflies. And if we northerners can't bear to sleep during the day when we should be getting work done, at least we can keep each other company."

Gesten appeared in the doorway, as if on cue. "Windsong is asleep, and Silver Veil is here, Drake," he said. "Would you prefer the sitting room or the garden?"

Amberdrake raised an eyebrow at Winterhart, signifying that it was her choice. After all, his hands were tied at the moment. "The garden, I think," she replied after a moment. "I hope the fountains in the pool will make it cooler than the sitting room."

By now, as always, even the cool stone of the floors was not helping cool the air much. It was always like this; shortly after noon, the heat began to collect, and it weighed down the very air until the sun neared the western horizon.

Gesten shrugged. "They're supposed to, so they tell me," the little hertasi said philosophically. "I'll have Jewel tell someone to send up the usual refreshments."

"I'd appreciate it if you'd serve us yourself, Gesten," Amberdrake said before Gesten could leave. "I don't think we're likely to say anything dubious, but it's hard to tell how the Haighlei would translate some of our conversations or mannerisms."

Gesten nodded and went off to attend to all of it; no need to elaborate with him. They all knew that the so-attentive servants were reporting whatever they saw and overheard to their superiors, and possibly to masters besides their superiors. That might have been the reason for Winterhart's choice of the garden as well; the sound of the fountains would cover any conversation from more than a few feet away.

Discretion, discretion. Still, this is better than facing the Haighlei warships. They were on sufferance here; how much, perhaps Silver Veil could tell them. That was what she had implied when she asked for this meeting; that she could tell him more about their position here, now that the delegation had settled in.

Winterhart smiled as Amberdrake showed off the finished cat's cradle, then she slipped off the side of the bed and smoothed down her skirt. Amberdrake unraveled the elaborate finger and string sculpture, rose to his feet and straightened wrinkles out of his robes. Together they made their way to the tiny garden in the center of every suite of rooms. The Palace sprawled out across the Royal Compound, rather than being built in the vertical as Urtho's Tower had been. It was a vast complex of suites connected by corridors, with tiny gardens everywhere, as if they had been scattered like seeds and the Palace had been built around them. Every garden had one

huge tree growing in the middle, shading everything, and most
had more of the same ubiquitous fountains and pools that
their own garden had. The theory was that this allowed more
air to flow through the rooms, and the falling water cooled the
breeze further. Since there was no need to worry about *heating*
this vast pile, there was no need to build so as to conserve
heat.

Their garden was mostly water, a complex of fountains and
connected pools with a fabulous collection of water-lilies,
water-irises, and flowering reeds to set off the fat fish in their
armor of red and black, gold and white. Their tree was a huge
giant, towering far above the roof three stories above, and shading the entire courtyard perfectly. Gesten had set a low wooden
table and three upholstered lounges out in the flagstoned midst
of the pools, and Silver Veil was already there, wearing a thin
gown of finger-pleated linen with gold ornaments on her arms
and bare ankles, trailing her fingers gracefully in the water.
Feeding the fish, perhaps? They were always greedy for
crumbs. She rose as they approached. Her thin, delicate face
was suffused with pleasure.

She kissed both of them on the cheek, impartially, and they
all took their seats as Gesten arrived with cool beverages and
slices of fruit arranged artfully on a plate. At the moment, the
earlier breeze had died away to nothing, leaving only the heat
and the babble of water; Winterhart picked up a fan made of
woven palm leaves and created a breeze of her own. The palm-
leaf fans woven into fanciful shapes were another Palace fix-
ture; servants left stacks of them everywhere.

"Does it ever get cold here?" she asked, a little desperately,
as Silver Veil followed her example with a fan shaped like a
spade blade.

Silver Veil shook her head, and her silver hair followed the
motion. "Never; in the deep of winter it is sometimes very
cool during the night, but only so that one wants a brazier of
coals in one's bedroom, and perhaps a light blanket. I never
thought that I would long for snow before I came here."

"Well, we of White Gryphon have snow enough in winter

for you," Amberdrake replied, "if you can get leave to come visit. You would be very welcome."

But Silver Veil only sighed. "I fear not," she said reluctantly. "I am one of Shalaman's Chief Advisors, you know; there is only Truthsayer Leyuet and Palisar, the Speaker to the Gods, besides me." She coughed delicately. "I fear that their advice is rather biased in some areas. I would rather be here to counter them, so to speak. In fact, that was why I wished to speak with you both, now that you have had time to settle in and view the situation."

"Oh? I am flattered that you would hold our welfare in such esteem, Lady," Winterhart said carefully.

Silver Veil laughed; it sounded like one of the fountains. "So discreet, Winterhart!" she exclaimed, with no hint of mockery. "From what northern court did *you* spring? It took me years to learn such discretion."

"Some are born with such grace," Amberdrake replied quickly, to save Winterhart from the question. Nevertheless he was enjoying the exchange, for this was like some of the conversations he had shared with her in the past, during the few moments of tranquillity during their flight from Kiamvir Ma'ar's forces. Now, however, the conversation was better, because it was between equals, not world-wise mentor and overstressed pupil. *I would not want to repeat that time for any amount of money, but I am glad to have experienced it, in a peculiar way. Certainly I am grateful for the privilege of learning from her.* When all was lost to him, she had taken him in. When he was adrift, she found him the avocation best suited to his talents. Who else would have done such a thing?

Silver Veil bowed her head in ironic acknowledgment of the truth of his answer. "Well, here and now comes the time to leave a certain amount of discretion outside the garden, and speak frankly, northerner to northerner, friend to friend." She leaned forward, her violet-gray eyes darkened momentarily. "I need to give you some small idea of the world you have blundered into."

"It baffles me," Amberdrake confessed. "I am not certain how to act, and I find myself doing nothing rather than chance an incident." He looked to Winterhart for confirmation, and she nodded.

Silver Veil fanned herself quietly. "Your instincts must be guiding you correctly," she told them both, "For that is the safest thing to do here; *nothing*. Had you noticed anything odd about the Court itself? Physical things, I mean; things that seem familiar, but antique."

Amberdrake frowned, for he had, although he could not name precisely what had set off those strange feelings of familiarity at one remove. But Winterhart was quite certain.

"There are strange echoes of *our* past here," she said. "I see it in the clothing, some of the customs, even some of the food. But none of it is like the North we left."

"Precisely," Silver Veil said, with a nod. "It is like the North of years, decades, even centuries ago. That was what gave me the key to understanding these people. *They both abhor, and adore, change.*"

Amberdrake shook his head. "I'm not sure I understand," he began.

Silver Veil interrupted him with a gesture of her fan. "The Haighlei are a people who avoid change at all cost. Their own customs go back in an unbroken line for hundreds of years. To them, our way of life with its constant changes and readjustments is one short step below blasphemy, for if the gods wanted men to change, would the gods not decree it?" She shrugged. "The point is, they not only hate change, it is mandated against by their holy writings. Change comes as the gods decree, when the gods decree."

Winterhart frowned. "But if that's the case, how is it that customs of ours have ended up in practice here?"

"A good point." Silver Veil looked pleased. "That is one reason why change, with all the attraction of the forbidden, is very appealing to many of them. And the answer to how change comes to them is this; someone, at some point, understood that without some changes taking place, this society would rot from within. So at some point in the past, the holy writings were modified. There is a celebration connected to an eclipse that takes place once every twenty years. The more of the sun that vanishes, the more change can be integrated into the society. Thereafter, however, it does not change, except for deep exploration of the details. That is why you see things here that have only been written about in our lands. And that is why the office and position of kestra'chern were established here in the first place."

"But it is the kestra'chern of a hundred years ago that they imitate?" Amberdrake hazarded.

"More like two hundred or more, the kestra'chern who were the pampered and cultured members of the households of the very elite, and never seen by the common folk at all." She pointed her fan at the two of them. "You are on sufferance here; you embody change. Only if Shalaman accepts you and adds you and your presence here to the Eclipse Ceremony will you be actually accepted by the Haighlei as a whole." She flicked her fan idly at a blue fly blundering past. "You don't have many friends here. The Speaker to the Gods is firmly against your presence. Others are curious, but fearful of all the changes you represent."

He nodded, slowly. "I understand. So the question becomes, how do we persuade others over to our side?"

She shook her head, and her jewelry sang softly. "Gentle persistence. It helps that you have Skandranon with you; he is such a novelty that he is keeping peoples' minds off what you folk truly represent. I was accepted because what I *am* fell within the bounds of what they had already accepted. You must tread a careful path, Amberdrake. You dare not give offense, or give reason for the Haighlei to dismiss you as mere barbarians."

"What else do we need to know?" Winterhart asked urgently.

"Mostly that the Heighlei are very literal people; they will tell you *exactly* what they mean to do, not a bit more, and not a bit less." She creased her brow in thought. "Of course, that is subject to modification, depending on how the person feels about you. If you asked one who felt indifferent toward you to guard your pet, he would guard your pet and ignore the thief taking your purse."

Amberdrake nodded, trying to absorb it all.

"What can you tell us about this Eclipse Ceremony?" he asked.

Silver Veil smiled.

"Well," she said, with another wave of her fan, "Obviously, it begins, ends, and centers around the Eclipse. . . ."

Zhaneel found the hot afternoons as soporific as any of the Haighlei, and usually followed their example in taking a long nap. Even the youngsters were inclined to sleep in the heat—her Tadrith and Keenath and Winterhart's energetic girl Windsong. Well, since the twins had been born, *she* had been short on sleep, so now she might have a chance to make it up at last. Let Skandranon poke his beak in and around the corners of this fascinating Palace; while it was this hot, *she* would luxuriate in a nest of silken cushions, or stretch her entire length along a slab of cool marble in the garden.

She was doing just that, when one of the servants entered, apparently unaware of her presence. The twins were asleep in the shade, curled up like a pair of fuzzy kittens beside one of the pools, for they liked to use the waterfall as a kind of lullaby. The servant spotted them and approached them curiously, then reached out a cautious hand to touch.

Not a good idea, since the little ones sometimes woke when startled in an instinctive defensive reaction. An unwary human could end up with a hand full of talons, which would be very painful, since each of the twins sported claws as formidable as an eagle's. She raised her head and cleared her throat discreetly.

The servant started, jerking upright, and stared at her for a single, shocked second, with the whites of his eyes showing all around the dark irises. Then he began to back up slowly, stammering something in his own language. She couldn't understand him, of course, but she had a good idea of the gist of it, since this wasn't the first time she'd startled a servant.

Nice kitty. Good kitty. Don't eat me, kitty—

She uttered one of the few phrases in his language she

knew, the equivalent of "Don't be afraid, I didn't know you were coming in; please don't wake the babies."

He stared at her in shock, and she added another of the phrases she'd learned. "I prefer not to eat anything that can speak back to me."

He uttered something very like a squeak, and bolted.

She sighed and put her head down on her foreclaws again. *Poor silly man. Doesn't anyone* tell *these people about us?* It wasn't that the Haighlei were prejudiced, exactly, it was just that they *were* used to seeing large, fierce, carnivorous creatures, but were *not* used to them being intelligent. Sooner or later she and Skan would convince them all that the gryphons were neither dangerous, nor unpredictable, but until they did, there would probably be a great many frightened servants setting new records for speed in exiting a room.

Those who accept us as intelligent are still having difficulty accepting us as full citizens, co-equal with the humans of White Gryphon, she reflected, wondering how they were going to overcome that much stickier problem. *At least I don't have to worry about that. Skan does, but I don't. All I have to do is be charming and attractive. And the old rogue says I have no trouble doing that! Still, he has to do that himself, plus he has to play "Skandranon, King of White Gryphon."*

The sound of someone *else* discreetly clearing her throat made Zhaneel raise her head again, wondering if she was ever going to get that nap.

But when she saw who it was, she was willing to do without the nap. "Makke!" she exclaimed, as the old, stooped human made her way carefully into the garden. "Can it be you actually have nothing to do? Can I tempt you to come sit in the garden?"

Makke was very old, and Zhaneel wondered why she still worked; her closely-cropped hair resembled a sheep's pelt, it was so white, and her back was bent with the weight of years and all the physical labor she had done in those years. Her black face was seamed with wrinkles and her hands bony with age, but she was still strong and incredibly alert. Zhaneel had first learned that Makke knew their language when the old woman asked her, in the politest of accented tones, if the young gryphlets would require any special toilet facilities or linens. Since then, although her assigned function was only to clean their rooms and do their laundry, Makke had been Gesten's invaluable resource. She adored the gryphlets, who adored her in return; she was often the only one who could make them sit still and listen for any length of time. Both Zhaneel and Gesten were of one accord that in Makke they had made a good friend in a strange place.

"I really should not," the old woman began reluctantly, although it was clear she could use a rest. "There is much work yet to be done. I came only to ask of you a question."

"But you should, Makke," Zhaneel coaxed. "I have more need of company than I have of having the floors swept for the third time this afternoon. I want to know more about the situation here, and how we can avoid trouble."

Makke made a little gesture of protest. "But the young ones," she said. "The feather-sheath fragments, everywhere—"

"And they will shed more as soon as you sweep up," Zhaneel told her firmly. "A little white dust can wait for now. Come sit, and be cool. It is too hot to work. Everyone else in the Palace is having a nap or a rest."

Makke allowed herself to be persuaded and joined Zhaneel, sitting on the cool marble rim of the pond. She sighed as she picked up a fan and used it to waft air toward her face. "I came to tell you, Gryphon Lady, that you have frightened another gardener. He swears that you leaped up at him out of the bushes, snarling fiercely. He ran off, and he says that he will not serve you unless you remain out of the garden while he works there."

"He is the one who entered while I was already here." Zhaneel snorted. "*You* were in the next room, Makke," she continued in a sharp retort. "Did you hear any snarling? Any leaping? Anything other than a fool fearing his shadow and running away?"

Makke laughed softly, her eyes disappearing into the wrinkles as she chuckled. "No, Gryphon Lady. I had thought there was something wrong with this tale. I shall say so when the Overseer asks."

Zhaneel and Makke sat quietly in easy silence, listening to the water trickle down the tiny waterfall. "*You* ought to be the Overseer," Zhaneel said, finally. "You know our language, and you know more about the other servants than the Overseer does. You know how to show people that we are not man-eating monsters. You are better at the Overseer's job than he is."

But Makke only shook her head at the very idea, and used her free hand to smooth down the saffron tunic and orange trews that were the uniform for all Palace servants, her expression one of resignation. "That is not possible, Gryphon Lady," she replied. "The Overseer was born to his place, and I to mine, as it was decreed at our births. So it is, and so it must remain. You must not say such things to others. It will make them suspect you of impiety. I know better because I have served the Northern Kestra'chern Silver Veil, but others are not so broad of thought."

Zhaneel looked at her with her head tilted to one side in puzzlement. This was new. "Why?" she asked. "And why would I be impious for saying such a thing?"

Makke fanned herself for a moment as she thought over her answer. She liked to take her time before answering, to give the question all the attention she felt it deserved. Zhaneel did not urge her to speak, for she knew old Makke by now and knew better than to try to force her to say anything before she was ready.

"All is decreed," she said finally, tapping the edge of her fan on her chin. "The Emperors, those you call the Black Kings, are above all mortals, and the gods are above them. The gods have their places, their duties, and their rankings, and as above, so it must be below. Mortals have their places, duties, and castes, with the Emperors at the highest and the collectors of offal and the like at the lowest. As the gods do not change in their rankings, so mortals must not. Only the soul may change castes, for each of the gods was once a mortal who rose to godhood by good works and piety. One is born into a caste and a position, one works in it, and one dies in it. One can make every effort to learn—become something of a scholar even, but one will never be permitted to *become* a Titled Scholar. Perhaps, if one is very diligent, one may rise from being the Palace cleaning woman for a minor noble to that of a cleaning woman to a Chief Advisor or to foreign dignitaries, but one will always be a cleaning woman."

"There is no change?" Zhaneel asked, her beak gaping open in surprise. This was entirely new to her, but it explained a great deal that had been inexplicable. "Never?"

Makke shook her round head. "Only if the Emperor declares it, and with him the Truthsayer and the Speaker to the Gods. You see, such change must be sanctioned by the gods before mortals may embrace it. When some skill or position, some craft or learning, is accepted from outside the Empire, it is brought in as a new caste and ranking, and remains as it was when it was adopted. Take—the kestra'chern. I am told that Amberdrake is a kestra'chern among your people?"

Zhaneel nodded proudly. "He is good! Very good. Perhaps as good or better than Silver Veil. He was friend to Urtho, the Mage of Silence." To her mind, there could be no higher praise.

"And yet he has no rank, he offers his services to whom he chooses, *and* he is one of your envoys." Makke shook her head. "Such a thing would not be possible here. Kestra'chern are strictly ranked and classed according to talent, knowledge, and ability. Each rank may only perform certain services, and may only serve the *nobles* and noble households of a particular rank. No kestra'chern may offer his services to anyone above *or* below that rank for which he is authorized. This, so Silver Veil told me once, is precisely as the kestra'chern first served in the north, five hundred years ago, when the Murasa Emperor Shelass declared that they were to be taken into our land. I believe her, for she is wise and learned."

Zhaneel blinked. Such a thing would never have occurred to her, and she stored all of this away in her capacious memory to tell Skan later. *No one can rise or fall? So where is the incentive to do a good job?*

"We are ruled by our scribes in many ways," Makke continued, a little ruefully. "All must be documented, and each of us, even the lowest of farmers and street sweepers, is followed through his life by a sheaf of paper in some Imperial Scribe's possession. The higher one's rank, the more paper is created. The Emperor has an entire archive devoted only to him. But he was born to be Emperor, and he cannot abdicate. He was trained from birth, and he will die in the Imperial robes. As I will be a cleaning woman for all this life, even though I have studied as much as many of higher birth to satisfy my curiosity, so he will be Emperor."

"But what about the accumulation of wealth?" Zhaneel asked. "If you cannot rise in rank, surely you can earn enough to make life more luxurious?" *That would be the only incentive that I can imagine for doing well in such a system.*

But Makke shook her head again. "One may acquire wealth to a certain point, depending upon one's rank, but after that, it is useless to accumulate more. What one *is* decrees what one may *own;* beyond a certain point, money is useless when one has all one is permitted by law to have. Once one has the home, the clothing, the possessions that one may own under law, what else is left? Luxurious food? The company of a skilled *mekasathay?* The hire of entertainers? Learning purely for the sake of learning? It is better to give the money to the temple, for this shows generosity, and the gods will permit one to be reborn into a higher rank if one shows virtues like generosity. I have given the temple many gifts of money, for besides dispensing books and teachers, the temple priests speak to the gods about one's virtue—all my gifts are recorded carefully, of course—and I will probably give the temple as many more gifts as I can while I am in this life."

Zhaneel could hardly keep her beak from gaping open. "This is astonishing to me," Zhaneel managed. "I can't imagine anyone I know living within such restrictions!"

Makke fanned herself and smiled slowly. "Perhaps they do not seem restrictive to us," she suggested.

"Makke?" Zhaneel added, suddenly concerned. "These things you tell me—is this forbidden, too?"

Makke sighed, but more with impatience than with weariness. "Technically, I could be punished for telling you these things in the *way* that I have told you, and some of the other things I have imparted to you are pieces of information that people here do not *talk* about, but I am old, and no one would punish an old woman for being blunt and speaking the truth." She laughed. "After all, that is one of the few advantages of age, is it not? Being able to speak one's mind? Likely, if anyone knowing your tongue overheard me, the observation would be that I am aged, infirm, and none too sound in my mind. And if I were taken to task for my words, that is precisely what I would say." Makke's smile was wry. "There are those who believe my interest in books and scholarly chat betokens an unsound mind anyway."

"But this is outside of my understanding and experience. It will take me a while to think in this way. In the meantime, what must we do to keep from making any dreadful mistakes?" Zhaneel asked, bewildered by the complexity of bureaucracy that all this implied.

"Trust Silver Veil," Makke replied, leaning forward to emphasize her advice and gesturing emphatically with her fan. "She knew something of the Courts before she arrived here, and she has been here long enough to know where all the pit traps and deadfalls are. She can keep you from disaster, but what is better, she can keep you from embarrassment. *I* cannot do that. I do not know enough of the higher stations."

"Because we can probably avoid disaster, but we might miss a potential for embarrassment?" Zhaneel hazarded, and Makke nodded.

And in a society like this one, surely embarrassment could be as deadly to our cause as a real incident. Oh, these people are so strange!

"There is something else that I believe you must know," Makke continued. "And since we are alone, this is a good time to give you my warning. Something of what Gesten said makes me think that the Gryphon Lord is also a worker of magic?"

Zhaneel nodded; something in Makke's expression warned

her not to do so too proudly. She looked troubled and now, for the first time, just a little fearful.

"Tell him—tell him he *must not* work any magics, without the explicit sanction of King Shalaman or Palisar, the Speaker to the Gods," Makke said urgently but in a very soft voice, as she glanced around as if to be certain that they were alone in the garden. "Magic is—is strictly controlled by the Speakers, the priests, that is. The ability to work magic is from the hands of the gods, the knowledge of how to use it is from the teachers, and the knowledge of *when* to use it must be decreed by priest or Emperor."

Zhaneel clicked her beak. "How can that be?" she objected. "Mages are the most willful people I know!"

Makke only raised her eyebrows. "Easily. When a child is born with that ability, he is taken from his parents by the priests before he reaches the age of seven, and they are given a dower-portion to compensate them for the loss of a child. The priests raise him and train him, then, from the age of seven to eighteen, when they return to their families, honored priests and Scholars. I say 'he,' though they take female children as well, though females are released at sixteen, for they tend to apply themselves to study better than boys in the early years, and so come to the end of training sooner."

"That still doesn't explain how the priests can keep them under such control," Zhaneel retorted.

"Training," Makke said succinctly. "They are trained in the idea of obedience, so deeply in the first year that they never depart from it. This, I know, for my only daughter is a priest, and all was explained to me. That, in part, is why I was given leave to study and learn, so that I might understand her better when she returned to me. The children are watched carefully, more carefully than they guess. If one is found flawed in character, if he habitually lies, is a thief, or uses his powers without leave and to the harm of others, he is—" she hesitated, then clearly chose her words with care. "He is removed from the school and from magic. Completely."

A horrible thought flashed through Zhaneel's mind at the ominous sound of that. "Makke!" she exclaimed, giving voice to her suspicions, "You don't mean that they—they *kill* him, do you?"

"In the old days, they did," Makke replied solemnly. "Magic is a terrible power, and not for hands that are unclean. How could anyone, much less a priest, allow someone who was insane in that way to continue to move in society? But that was in the old days—now, the priests remove the ability to touch magic, then send the child back to his family." She shrugged. "It would be better for him, in some ways, if they *did* kill him."

"Why?" Zhaneel blurted, uncomprehendingly.

"Why, think, Gryphon Lady. He can no longer touch magic. He returns to his family in disgrace. Everyone knows that he is fatally flawed, so no one will trust him with anything of any consequence. No woman would wed him, with such a disgrace upon him. He will, when grown, be granted no position of authority within his rank. If his rank and caste are low, he will be permitted only the most menial of tasks within that caste, and only under strict supervision. If he comes from high estate, he will be an idle ornament, also watched closely." Makke shook her head dolefully. "I have seen one of that sort, and he was a miserable creature. It was a terrible disgrace to his family, and worse for him, for although he is a man grown, he is given no more responsibility than a babe in napkins. He is seldom seen, but the lowest servant is happier than he. He is of very high caste, too, so let me assure you that no child is immune from this if a flaw is discovered in him."

Zhaneel shook her head. "Isn't there anything that someone like that can do?"

Makke shrugged. "The best he could do would be to try to accumulate wealth to grant to the temple so that the gods will give him an incarnation with no such flaws in the next lifetime. It would be better to die, I think, for what is a man or a woman but their work, and how can one *be* a person without work?"

Zhaneel was not convinced, but she said nothing. At least the Black Kings certainly seemed to have a system designed to prevent any more monsters like Kiamvir Ma'ar! There was something to be said for that.

Almost anything that prevented such a madman from getting the kind of power Ma'ar had would be worth bearing with, I think. Almost. And assuming that the system is not fatally flawed.

"Have the priests ever—made a mistake?" she asked, suddenly.

"Have they ever singled out a child who was *not* flawed for this punishment, you mean?" Makke asked. Then she shook her head. "Not to my knowledge, and I have seen many children go to the temples over the years. Truly, I have never seen one rejected that was not well-rejected. This is not done lightly or often, you know. The one I spoke of? He has no compassion; he uses whomever he meets, with no care for their good or ill. Whilst his mother lived, he used even her for his own gain, manipulating her against her worthier offspring. There are many of lesser caste who have learned of his flawed nature to their sorrow or loss."

Zhaneel chewed a talon thoughtfully.

"There is one other thing," Makke said, this time in a softer and much more reluctant voice. "I had not intended to speak of this, but I believe now perhaps I must, for I see by your face that you find much of what I have said disturbing."

"And that is—?" Zhaneel asked.

Makke lowered her voice still further. "That there is a magic which is more forbidden than any other. I would say nothing of it, except that I fear your people may treat it with great casualness, and if you revealed that, there would be no treaty, not now, and not in the future. Have your people the magic that—that looks into—into minds—and hears the thoughts of others?"

"It might be," Zhaneel said with delicate caution, suddenly now as alert as ever she had been on a scouting mission. All of her hackles prickled as they threatened to rise. There was something odd about that question. "I am not altogether certain what you mean, for I believe our definitions of magic and yours are not quite the same. Why do you ask?"

"Because *that* is the magic that is absolutely forbidden to all except the priests, and only then, the priests who are called to special duties by the gods," Makke said firmly. "I do not exaggerate. This is most important."

"Like Leyuet?" Zhaneel asked in surprise. She had not guessed that Truthsayer Leyuet was a priest of any kind. He did not have the look of one, nor did he wear the same kind of clothing as Palisar.

"Yes." Makke turned to look into her eyes and hold her gaze there for a long moment, with the same expression that a human mother would have in admonishing a child she suspects might try something stupid. "This magic is a horror. It is unclean," she said, with absolute conviction. "It allows mortals to look into a place where only the gods should look. Even a Truthsayer looks no farther than to determine the veracity of what is said—only into the soul, which has no words, and not the mind. If your people have it, say nothing. And do *not* use it here."

We had better not mention Kechara, ever, to one of these people! And Amberdrake had better be discreet about his own powers!

That was all she could think at just that moment. While Zhaneel tried to digest everything she'd been told, Makke stood, and carefully put the palm fan on the small pile left for the use of visitors. "I must go," she said apologetically. "A certain amount of rest is permitted to one my age, but the work remains to be done, and I would not trust it to the hands of those like that foolish gardener, who would probably think that Jewel and Corvi wish to rend him with their fearsome claws."

Since neither Jewel nor Corvi had anything more than a set of stubby, carefully filed down nails, Zhaneel laughed. Makke smiled and shuffled her way back into their suite.

The gryphlets looked ready to sleep for the rest of the afternoon; not even all that talking disturbed them in the least. Zhaneel settled herself on a new, cooler spot, and lay down again, letting the stone pull some of the dreadful heat out of her body.

She closed her eyes, but sleep had deserted her for the moment. *So Makke is an unTitled Scholar! No wonder she looks as if she were hiding secrets.* Now, more than ever, Zhaneel was glad that she and Gesten had made friends with the old woman. Next to the Silver Veil, it seemed they could not have picked a better informant. *That explains why she bothered to learn our language, anyway. She must have been very curious about Silver Veil and the north, and the best way to find out would have been to ask Silver Veil. It must have taken a lot of courage to dare that, though.*

But Makke was observant; perhaps she had noticed how kind Silver Veil was to her servants, and had decided that the kestra'chern would not take a few questions amiss.

An amateur scholar would also have been fascinated by the gryphons and the *hertasi*. Perhaps that was why Makke had responded to the overtures of friendship Zhaneel and Gesten had made toward her.

And when it became painfully evident how naive we were about the Haighlei— Zhaneel smiled to herself. There was a great deal of the maternal in Makke's demeanor toward Zhaneel, and there was no doubt that she thought the twins were utterly adorable, even if they looked nothing like a pair of human babies. Perhaps Makke had decided to adopt them, as a kind of honorary grandmother.

She said, only daughter. She could have meant only child as well. And if her child is now a priest—do the Haighlei allow their priests to marry and have children? I don't think so. Zhaneel sighed. *I wonder if her daughter is ashamed of Makke; she is only a cleaning woman, after all. For all that most priests preach humility, I never have seen one who particularly enjoyed being humble.* If that were the case, Makke could be looking on Zhaneel as a kind of quasi-daughter, too.

I shall have to make certain to ask her advice on the twins. I don't have to take it, after all! And that will make her feel wanted and needed. Zhaneel sighed, and turned so that her left flank was on the cool marble. *But the warning about magic—that is very disturbing. Except, of course, that we can't do much magic until the effect of the Cataclysm settles. That might not even be within our lifetimes.*

She would warn Skandranon, of course. And he would warn Amberdrake. Zhaneel was not certain how much of what Amberdrake did was magic of the mind, and how much was training and observation, but it would be a good thing for Drake to be very careful at this point. Winterhart, too, although her abilities could not possibly be as strong as Drake's. . . .

Healing. I shall have to ask Makke about Healing. Surely the Haighlei do not forbid that!

But the one thing they must not mention was the existence of Kechara. If the Haighlei were against the simpler versions of thought-reading, surely they would be horrified by poor little Kechara!

The fact that she is as simple-minded as she is would probably only revolt them further. And she is misborn; there is no getting around that. It's nothing short of a miracle that she has had as long and as healthy a life as she has. But she is not "normal" and we can't deny that.

So it was better not to say anything about her. It wasn't likely that anyone would *ask*, after all.

Let me think, though—they may ask how we are communicating so quickly with White Gryphon. So—this evening, Skan should ask permission from King Shalaman and Palisar to "communicate magically" with the rest of the Council back home. Since they do that, they shouldn't give Skan any problems about doing the same. He's clever; if they ask him how he can communicate when things are so magically unsettled, he can tell them about the messages we send with birds, or tell them something else that they'll believe, and not be lying. Then, when we get instant answers from home, they won't be surprised or upset because we didn't ask permission first.

So that much was settled. If the Haighlei sent resident envoys to White Gryphon, there was no reason to tell them what Kechara was—

And since she is there among all the other children of the

Silvers, her room just looks like a big nursery. Would they want to talk to her, though?

Would an envoy have any reason to talk to *any* child, except to pat it on the head because its parents were important? Probably not. And Cafri could keep her from bounding over and babbling everything to the envoys; he'd kept her from stepping on her own wings before this.

With all of that sorted out to Zhaneel's satisfaction, she finally felt sleep overcoming her. She made a little mental "tag" to remind her to tell Skan all about this conversation and the things she'd reasoned out, though. Gryphonic memory was excellent, but she wanted to make certain that nothing drove *this* out of her mind, even on a temporary basis.

Then, with her body finally cooled enough by the stone to relax, she stretched out just a little farther and drifted off into flower-scented dreams.

Silver Veil

Four

Winterhart moved easily among the Haighlei in their brilliant costumes of scarlet, vermilion, bittersweet and sunset-orange, wheat and burnt umber and the true gold of the metal; she seemed one of them despite her dress and light skin. She was distinctive, a single, long-stemmed lily among a riot of dahlias. Lady Cinnabar's refitted gown of white silk gauze and emerald silk damask was as startling in this crowd as one of the common robes of the Haighlei would be in a Northern Court.

A Northern Court. . . .

Assuming there *was* such a thing as a Northern Court anymore. The few bits of information trickling in seemed to indicate that the Cataclysm had a far more widespread effect than any of the Kaled'a'in had dreamed.

We were so concerned with our own survival, we never thought about what would become of the lands we left behind, she reflected, as she exchanged a polite greeting with a highborn maiden and her bored brother. *Oh, we knew that Urtho's Tower was gone, and the Palace with it, but we never thought about other lands.*

Without Ma'ar at the helm, the kingdoms he had conquered—the few that survived the Cataclysm—fell into chaos and intertribal warfare, the same kind of warfare that had devastated them before he came to rule.

And Winterhart could not help but feel a certain bitter satisfaction at that. If they had not been so eager to listen to his mad dreams of conquest, he would never have gotten as far as he had. Now, from being the acme of civilization, they were reduced to the copper knives and half-wild sheep herds of their ancestors, with the hand of every clan against members of any other clan. Their cities were in ruins, their veneer of civilization lost, all because they had followed a madman.

But beyond Ma'ar's lands, the Cataclysm utterly devastated other nations who relied heavily on magic. A few refugees had reached the Wtasi Empire to the east, on the Salten Sea, after all this time, and the word they brought of far-reaching consequences of the double explosion was terrible. Many lands had once relied on Gates to move supplies and food, especially into the cities. It wasn't possible to erect Gates anymore; there was no certainty that they would work. With no Gates, these cities starved; once people were starving and desperate, order collapsed. And worse was to come, for no sooner had the authorities—or what passed for them—sorted out some of the chaos, in poured hordes of leaderless troops who took what they needed by force of arms. Winterhart could only hope that those were Ma'ar's leaderless troops who were acting that way—but in her heart she knew better. It was likely that their own people, when faced with privation, would act just the same as their former enemies.

It is easy to assign the persona of a monster to the faceless enemy, but the fact is that most of them were just soldiers, following orders, no worse than our own soldiers. It had taken her a long time to work her way around to that conclusion, and it still wasn't a comfortable thought. But that was one unexpected result of living with Amberdrake: learning to seek or reason out truth, and accept it unflinchingly, no matter how uncomfortable it was.

The result of the Cataclysm was that there were no central governments worthy of the name up there now. For the most part, the largest body of organization was the small town, or the occasional place that those aforementioned soldiers had taken over and fortified. Old skills that did not require magic had to be relearned or rediscovered, and that took time. Civilization in the north was gone, as far as the Haighlei were concerned.

And where the Clan k'Leshya was concerned, as well, and all the adopted Kaled'a'in with them, Winterhart among them. There had been no communication from any of the other Kaled'a'in Clans, and no one really expected there to be any. K'Leshya had traveled far beyond the others, the distance of the maximum that two Gates could reach, rather than just one. That was too far for anyone except Kechara to reach with Mindspeech, and too far for the messenger-birds to go, assuming anyone was willing to risk them.

We are on our own, and we can only hope that the other Clans survived as well as we did. Our future is here, and we had better build a firm foundation for it.

So she walked among these strange people in their strange garb and accustomed herself to them, until they no longer seemed strange, until it was *her* dress and *her* pale skin that seemed odd. She moved through the gathering like one of the graceful slim silver fish that lived in the ponds with the fat, colorful ones. Unconsciously she imitated the slow, deliberate pace of their steps and the dancelike eddies and flows of the Court itself. She took all that into herself and made it a part of her.

That was, after all, precisely what she had been trained to do, so long ago. This was what she had been before she became the Trondi'irn Winterhart, serving the Sixth Wing gryphons in the army of Urtho, the Mage of Silence. Before, when she had borne another name, and a title, and the burden of rank, she had moved to the dancelike pattern of another Court.

Now rank was no longer a burden, but a cloak that trailed invisibly from the shoulders. The name she wore was hers, with no invisible baggage of long and distinguished lineage. The title? Hers as well, truly earned, like the name.

But the rest was familiar, as familiar as the feel of silk sliding along her body, as real as the exchange of banal courtesies and pleasantries. And since this was a Court like any other—with the folk of White Gryphon a strange and possibly hostile presence—there was caution and even malignity beneath the courtesies, and fear beneath the pleasantries. It was her task to discover where, who, and what hid under the posture and counterposture.

She often felt at a time like this as if she were a sword sliding into an old, well-worn sheath, or a white-hot blade sinking into a block of ice. She was Winterhart, the trondi'irn—but she was also much more than the Winterhart her fellow refugees knew. She had not used these old skills in a very, very long time, but they were a significant part of her, long disregarded. She stretched muscles long unused, and she relished the sensation.

Amberdrake, to her bemusement, simply smiled and bid her follow her instincts and her inclinations. "I have been *among* the well-born," he'd said this very evening, before they made their entrance. "I know how to act with them and comfort them. But I never was one of them. You were, and all that early training makes you something I cannot be, and can only imitate. It gives you an assurance that is part of you rather than assumed. Believe me, my love, it shows. So go and be your own gracious self, and show me how it is done. After all," he said with a grin and a wink, "I enjoy gazing at you anyway."

Like a hawk with the jesses cut, he sent her off, trusting she would return to his glove. And she would, of course, for like a *true* falconer and his bird, they were partners.

Or perhaps we are more like those Kaled'a'in scouts with their specially-bred birds, the bondbirds, who Mindspeak with the ones they are bonded to. She wondered what the Haighlei would make of those! They had relatively few domesticated animals, and most of them were herdbeasts. No horses, though—

They have sheep, goats, and cattle. They have those misshapen, hairy things that need so little water for riding and bearing burdens in the deserts, and donkeys for pulling carts. Dogs the size of small ponies! A few, a very few, of the Great Cats that have been partly domesticated. No house cats, no horses, no birds of prey. She smiled and nodded and exchanged small-talk with the envoy from the Kmbata Empire, and let part of her mind consider the possible impact that the introduction of each of these domesticated creatures could have on the Haighlei. The cats alone would cause a stir—those huge dogs had been bred to hunt equally large cats, and she could well imagine the delight that the elegant Haighlei would take in the graceful "little tigers" that the adopted Kaled'a'in had brought with them from their homes.

Trade and the possibilities of trade . . . it would be much easier on the citizens of White Gryphon if they could get their hands on *proper* plows, and not the trial-and-error instruments they had now, made by a weaponsmith who thought he recalled the one lesson he'd had in forging such things, twenty years ago. Proper boats, made for fishing, would save lives if the fishing fleet was ever caught by a big storm. Seeds bred to grow here—and the odd plants that the Haighlei themselves grew to eat—that would not fail in the heat, or sprout too late or too soon.

And in return—horses and cats, for a beginning. Lionwind, the k'Leshya Clan Chief, would be happy to learn of a "proper" market for his riding horses, which just at the moment were, to his injured pride, often trained to harness for pulling carts and plows. After that, there were surely skills they could exchange. Haighlei jewelry, for instance, was lovely and costly, but massive. Not crudely made, but with none of the detail that—for instance—the silversmith who made the Silver Gryphon badges could produce. Would the Haighlei like that sort of thing? They'd certainly admired the delicacy of Winterhart's ornaments, so they might—particularly if the northern jewelry became a fad item.

Odd. I feel so at home here, as if I were born for this place and this court, so rigidly structured, so refined in its subtleties. . . . The longer they were here, the more comfortable she felt.

The Haighlei ruled a territory more vast than anyone up north had ever dreamed; two Kingdoms—or Empires, for they had aspects of both—here, sharing the land between the Salten Sea and the Eastern Sea. Four more farther south, dividing yet another continent among them, a continent joined to this one by a relatively narrow bridge of land. The Haighlei called their rulers both "King" and "Emperor" indiscriminately, something that sounded strange to Winterhart's northern ears.

Another member of the Court greeted her, and Winterhart smiled warmly into Silver Veil's eyes, oddly relieved to see that she was no longer the only pale face with a northern gown here this evening. Silver Veil wore her hair loose, as always, and a pale gray silk gown that echoed the silver of her hair. "You are doing well, little sister," Silver Veil said softly. "I have been listening, watching. Amberdrake is respected for his office and his training, but *you* are acknowledge to be a Power."

She flushed, with embarrassment as well as pride. "Well, Skandranon has us all bested. He is doing more to impress the Haighlei simply by being himself than I could with all the clever words in the world."

But Silver Veil shook her head. "You underestimate yourself, my dear. That is your one fault, I think. But be aware that my people do not underestimate *you*. You are a Power among them, and they will all, from highest to lowest, accord you that respect."

Then she drifted away on another eddy of the crowd, as the dance of the Court carried them both off to other partners. Winterhart smiled and murmured greetings, and wondered about Silver Veil's words. *She* certainly didn't think of herself as particularly important beyond the fact that she was an envoy . . . but the kestra'chern was right, people were treating her with that sort of deference.

Not as if she were nobly born, but as if she were royal.

As royal as King Shalaman.

The King himself was here, sitting like a stiff statue on a platform about three steps above the rest of the room. He didn't have a throne, precisely; he sat on a gilded bench, shaped like a lion, with the head at his right and the tail at his left. He wore the pelt of the lion over one shoulder, but the rest of his costume consisted of a robe of a brilliant saffron color, belted with a sash made of thousands of links of pure gold, so finely made that at a distance it appeared woven. His pectoral collar was made to match, with the stylized mask of a lion on the front. He looked neither to left nor to right, and Winterhart found herself admiring him for the fine figure that he presented. It was difficult to believe that he was over sixty; if she had not been assured of that figure, she would have assumed he was a vigorous warrior in his early thirties at most, and that his white hair was due to premature graying—or to the fact that he was also an Adept-class mage, and working with node-magic had turned his hair white.

Evidently he was only supposed to grace these gatherings with his presence, he wasn't actually expected to mingle with his courtiers. She had the definite feeling, though, that he missed very little, and that what he himself did not notice, one of his advisors would tell him later.

Well, let them tell him that the Lady Winterhart is charming, well-spoken, and utterly opaque.

She smiled at that, and turned the smile on yet another Haighlei courtier. Even a smile could not be wasted. Not here, and not now.

Palisar watched the dance of the courtiers with only one eye, for the other was on his Emperor. The Emperor was watching one particular section of the dance, and Palisar did not care for the fact that the pale-skinned foreigner in her bizarre gown was at the center of that section.

"The Outland woman—" Shalaman murmured to the Speaker to the Gods. "She seems well at ease among us."

"She does, Serene One," Palisar replied, cautiously. *He* did not care for any of these new Outlanders, but it would not be a good idea to allow Shalaman to learn of this. Not while The Silver Veil, who favored them, was so great a favorite of the King, at any rate.

He was prepared to make many exceptions for The Silver Veil, who was a kestra'chern, and who had served Shalaman well and loyally for many years. That she so favored these Outlanders was understandable, since one of them was her own pupil. And their own audacity was forgivable, given that they *had* made their home in territory so far north that it was virtually uninhabitable. Still.

It does not make them our equals. Let them be made our clients, a liege-alliance, and then let them go home again.

That was what Palisar devoutly wished.

But Shalaman's next words to his Advisor nearly shocked Palisar into revealing his true feelings in the matter. "I would like you to bring her the Lion Lilies, impart to her my pleasure that she has blended so well into my court, and invite her to walk in the Royal Gardens tomorrow, if she so desires."

The Royal Countenance remained inscrutable, the Royal Voice was even and thoughtful. He might have been suggesting that Palisar order a new lionskin for him, rather than asking Palisar to upset every well-born princess in the court, and shock half of his courtiers numb and insensible. Granted, Shalaman was the son of the gods, but this—

—even the son of the gods could not reign for long by violating all the laws!

Only many years of serving Shalaman enabled Palisar to keep an outward seeming of composure. But he could not help but interject a note of caution—

Better a note of caution than to shout to the King that this could mean utter disaster!

"Is that entirely wise, Serenity?" he murmured, as if only faintly troubled. "So soon after they have arrived? This could betoken favoritism. You have other allies you have not invited to walk in the garden—and there are many other ladies, far more appropriate, to whom you have not sent the Lion Lilies."

All the while, he was choking on the words he wanted to say. *This is insanity! How can you even think of courting this barbarian Outlander when you have two, nay three dozen princesses from Haighlei Kingdoms here in your own court, waiting for such a gesture? You will offend your fellow Kings! You will offend the women themselves! And what has this woman done to deserve such attention, that The Silver Veil cannot do with more grace?*

But he knew the answer—for this woman was *like* Silver Veil, but differed from the kestra'chern in three important ways. She was not familiar. She was younger. And she was theoretically a good candidate to cement an alliance.

"My other allies do not need to be examined, for I know what they can and cannot do," Shalaman said, reasonably. "They are firmly my allies, and I need not strengthen those alliances any further than to see that the daughters are disposed of to high officials of my court. That *is* what they are here for, after all. And the 'appropriate' ladies do not interest me enough that I should send them the Lion Lilies. Impart to Lady Winterhart my words, give to her the Lilies, and bring me back word of what she said."

This was a direct order, which Palisar was helpless to disobey. With a sinking heart, he gathered up the Lilies from their brass vase, on an ebony stand beside the Lion Throne, while a stir of interest rippled through the court at his gesture. The Lilies, huge, tawny-gold, many-petaled bells on long, slender stems, spread their heavy fragrance as he moved them. There were three Lilies in the vase, as always, since Shalaman had not begun to court a consort in earnest. Three—for interest. Four betokened more than interest.

A dozen, along with the betrothal-necklace of ancient amber, gold, and bronze, became a proposition.

He bore the Lilies with a sinking heart, as the ladies he had to walk past looked hopeful, then excited, then downcast as he passed them by. He bore them toward Winterhart, that pallid, sickly-looking creature, like one of the Lilies herself, but a blighted one, colorless, stiff, and thin. All eyes followed his course across the highly polished floor of inlaid woods, and she, of course, must turn to see what everyone else was watching. When he stopped before her, he saw puzzlement in her eyes, quickly covered, as she bowed gracefully to him.

At least she can do that much. Pray to the gods she is feeble-minded, with no interests of her own. One conversation, and Shalaman will tire of her.

"Lady Winterhart," Palisar said, allowing no hint of his innermost thoughts to show in his voice. "The Emperor sends you the Lion Lilies, and has instructed me to convey his pleasure in the fact that you have fit yourself into our Court so gracefully and easily. He invites you to walk in the Royal Gardens in the afternoon."

He handed her the Lilies, praying that she might drop them, which would be a dreadful omen and would surely erode Shalaman's interest in her. But she smiled and took them from him without mishap. Clearly, she had no idea what an honor had just been bestowed upon her, nor what it might lead to. He was not inclined to tell her.

If she does not know, she may yet say or do something that Shalaman will not approve of.

"Please tell the Emperor that I am unworthy of his notice or his compliments, but that I am grateful that he deigns to allow his sun to shine upon this poor northern lily. I will accept his invitation for the morrow with great pleasure, though I by no means deserve such a privilege."

Palisar smiled, although he felt more like gritting his teeth. How had she learned precisely what the best sort of reply would be? It was exactly the right mixture of humility and graciousness. And that—that *dung* about "allowing his sun to shine upon this poor northern lily"—making a delicate play upon the Lion Lilies themselves, and making the comparison to herself that *he* had even noted—

Clever—no, not merely clever. Brilliant.

He bowed, and made his way back to the Emperor. Already a headache throbbed in his left temple. By the time court was over, it would be a torment. He always got these headaches when something went wrong, and he had the feeling that this was only the first of many such torturous headaches.

Shalaman waited for several long moments after Palisar took his place again before speaking to his Advisor. He watched Winterhart cradle the flowers carefully, watched her ignore the envious or avid glances from those other ladies who were too unschooled in the ways of the court to conceal their feelings beneath an urbane mask. Then, when at last the Emperor spoke, he spoke in that low voice that only Palisar was meant to hear, but casually. In fact, from the tone of his voice, he might have been asking what the weather in the gardens was like, and nothing of more import. But Palisar was not deceived by the casual tone. Shalaman knew the ways of dissembling better than anyone in his entire court.

"Well?" the Emperor said. "And what did she say?"

Palisar told him.

There was silence for a few more moments, then a sound which, again, only Palisar heard, but which was enough to make his headache worsen tenfold.

For quietly, deep within his chest, Shalaman was chuckling.

How do they light this garden so well? They are not using mage-lights, but the place is brighter than a night with a full moon! We need to learn how to do this, ourselves. White Gryphon would be made even brighter with such knowledge. Skandranon looked out into the Great Garden—which was more than a simple garden although it was shaded with more of the enormous trees that grew everywhere in the Palace. It was also a natural bowl-shaped amphitheater floored with grass, with carefully placed trees and beds of flowers beside carved benches on little terraces going up the sides for seating an audience. The only break in the bowl was the door from the Palace where he now stood. He gave his feathers a great shake to settle them, before stepping carefully into the bottom of the bowl.

As always, Evening Court was followed by some other kind of gathering, one which the King was not obligated to attend, although he often did. Perhaps the afternoon nap made people too restless to sleep until well after midnight, although Skan could think of things a lot more exciting to do than caper about at an official function, particularly with all those charming private and semiprivate gardens available.

And think, to one day have these in the White Gryphon settlement—grottoes and gardens for dalliances and courtship. Hertasi, tervardi, kyree, humans, and gryphons amid such beautiful landscaping. And perhaps even some Haighlei?

Tonight there was to be an enormous formal Dance, ostensibly in honor of the envoys from White Gryphon. This wasn't a dance as Skan was accustomed to thinking of a dance; more of a performance, really, rather than a gathering with music where everyone danced.

They didn't seem to have such things here. Instead, a Dance meant that most of the courtiers would be watching the trained dancers go through a long set-piece. All of the Royal Dancers and some of the courtiers would be participating, the courtiers as a kind of untrained, minimally-moving background to the Dancers, all two hundred of them, who were schooled from the time they were five and performed until they were deemed too old to be decorative.

That was interesting; there were a few people Skan had known—most of them kestra'chern or the odd perchi—who had gotten formal dance training. Virtually everyone else was self-taught.

But Drake said that before the wars there were dance troupes, so there must have been performances and people gathering to watch rather than participate.

These Dancers were different from that, though. They "belonged," in a sense, to the King—as the mages belonged to the Priests. They performed only for the King and his court. When they were too old to dance, they were turned into teachers for the next generation, if they had not already married. It was considered a great honor to be permitted to wed a Royal Dancer, and the marriage could not be consummated until the Dancer had a replacement.

The four envoys would be sitting on top of a little pyramid-shaped affair in the center of the performance area, a wooden structure erected for this purpose, surrounded by the dancers and the pivot point of the dance. Skan was rather disappointed that he wouldn't be able to perform this time; he had a notion that he could give these folk an eyeful!

Next time, he consoled himself. *Next time. The Dance-master has promised I may participate, and is planning aerial maneuvers to compliment the dancing on the ground.*

In fact, the Dancemaster already had a title for the next performance; *Phoenix Dancing with Dragon,* an old legend among these people. Skandranon would be the Phoenix, Air-Spirit and Fire-Spirit in one; the dancers would join together to form the earthbound serpentine Dragon, who embodied Water and Earth together.

The very notion had him chuckling with glee. He could hardly wait!

This performance would give him a good notion of how these people danced, and how to adapt his own skydancing techniques to their style.

Without that, I would look more alien to them than I really want to. Perhaps it's just as well that I'm not dancing tonight.

The others, including Zhaneel, had already preceded him, according to some sort of strict protocol that mandated that he, supposedly the highest in rank, be the last one seated. Now four of the Royal Dancers paced gravely up to him in their flowing robes of blue and green with short, cylindrical hats strapped to their heads; four young girls who could not be older than eleven, who looked up at him with solemn eyes and bowed to him until their foreheads touched the grass.

He bowed in return, just as low, and just as gracefully, bending over one extended foreleg until every muscle complained.

They took their places around him, forming a square with himself in the middle, and they all marched out into the garden together.

Murmurs of conversation rose on all sides, and he sensed the curious eyes of those ranked on the benches above him. What did he look like, the white gryphon parading on the green grass? Dangerous—or handsome?

Both! Oh, I hope so. I know I'm handsome, but I haven't felt dangerous all day.

The four girls split off as they all reached the pyramid, a smallish construction with a flat platform on top. He went on alone, climbing the wooden steps with ease, and discovered as he took his place beside Zhaneel why this was such a place of honor. From here, elevated above the dancers, you saw not only the dancers themselves, but the patterns they formed, abstract constructions created by the special colors of the costumes they wore.

Well, this should be fascinating. I can study their dance steps very well from here; the patterns ought to be incorporated into what I will do as well. As he settled in, a touch of a color he hadn't expected caught the corner of his eye—Zhaneel was buff and gray, Winterhart had worn green and white, and Amberdrake was all in green. So why the vivid, warm golden-yellow? He turned out of curiosity, and saw that Winterhart was cradling a bouquet of three large, tawny-gold lilies in her arms.

That's interesting. She didn't have those when we came down to Court, so she must have gotten them at Court itself. I wish I hadn't been so busy talking to Leyuet; I must have missed something. Wonder who gave them to her?

Chances were it was Amberdrake, that incurable romantic. But where had he found them? Skan had never seen anything like them before, and he *knew* there wasn't anything like them growing in the gardens. Gesten would have noticed; Gesten was always on the lookout for plants to take home to White Gryphon, and he would love these.

But before he could say anything to Winterhart, the musician struck up; Haighlei music wasn't anything like the Kaled'a'in stuff Skan remembered, nor like the music of the minstrels and Bards of the old northern courts. Like the Royal Dancers, these Royal Musicians were all trained to play together as a group, and their music lessons began in earliest childhood. They even wore a uniform that was unique among the Haighlei garments, in that there were no trailing sleeves or other encumbrances to interfere with the playing of instruments.

There were at least a dozen different kinds of drums alone in that group, plus gongs, bells, cymbals, zills—at least half of the musicians played percussion of one sort or another. The rest were equally divided between instruments with plucked or bowed strings, and various flutes.

As might be expected with that kind of balance, the music was heavily percussive in nature, and Skan was glad he wasn't sitting too near the ensemble.

You could go deaf quickly with that much pounding in

your ears—and I pity the poor creature with a headache! But when it all blends together, it is deep and driving. I like this a lot. It reminds me of—

Skandranon realized what it reminded him of. It was visceral. It reached deep into him; the vibrations carried through his chest, through his wings, through his bones. It felt like sex; it felt like skydancing and mating, when the blood thrummed in his ears and all the world shook.

Oh, I remember those times, when I weighed less. I was strong and virile. And fast! *And sleek and glossy black.*

Skandranon suppressed a delighted laugh. Those were the days!

Then the dancers struck their initial poses, right arms with their trailing sleeves raised high, left arm bent toward the earth, and bodies curved backward until it made *his* back ache to look at them. He forgot everything else from that moment on in his absorption in the dance, studying the details.

"Enjoy yourself?" Zhaneel asked with a saucy gape-grin on her delicate gryfalcon face, as they looked in on the twins before taking to their own bed. Skan was yawning; the performance had gone on for a very long time, and it was well after midnight when all the congratulations had been made to the Dancers, the Musicians, and the Dancemaster, and they could return to their rooms again.

Not that he hadn't savored every minutes of it!

The little ones were curled up in their nests of cushions, making a ball with two heads, four wings, and an indeterminate number of limbs—in other words, the usual nighttime position. In the heat of the day, they sprawled, belly-down on cool stone, looking rather squashed. But for now, they were puffballs.

"I liked it a great deal," he told her, as they left the twins to their dreams of mischief among the fishponds, and walked into their own room. The servants had already been and gone, leaving the suite prepared. The door to the balcony was wide open, the curtains pulled aside to allow entry to the cool breeze that always came up around midnight. The air that drifted in was scented with the heavy perfume of a flower that bloomed only at night, a tiny white blossom like a trumpet.

She is just as sweet. I wonder if she is in the mood?

Skan stretched luxuriously. "These Royal Dancers are quite amazing. I don't remember ever seeing anything like that be—"

Someone pounded on their door. Skan and Zhaneel exchanged startled glances as one of the Haighlei servants ran out of the servants' rooms to answer it.

Who can that be at this hour? Surely nothing can be so important that they need to summon us now! Unless— Skan suddenly felt a rush of chill. *Unless something's happened to Drake or Winterhart—*

The servant exchanged some half-dozen words with whoever was there, then quickly stood aside and flung the door open wide. Leyuet, the Truthsayer and Advisor to King Shalaman stood firmly in the doorway, looking both solemn and very upset, and with him were ten of Shalaman's guards, all armed to the teeth.

I don't like the look of this!

"You will please come with me," Leyuet said, trembling, his voice shaking a little as he looked into Skandranon's eyes, past the formidable beak. "Now."

Skan pulled himself up to his full height, and glared down at the thin Truthsayer standing in the doorway. *Better act important and upset. If this is some kind of a trap, I might be able to bluff my way out of it.* "Why?" he demanded. "It is midnight. It is time for sleep. And I am the envoy of my people and a ruler in my own right. What possible cause can you have to come bursting in here with armed guards at your back? What possible need can anyone have of my presence? What is so urgent that it cannot wait until morning?"

Is this some way to try and separate us? Have we come all this way only to find we've willingly become hostages? Was Drake wrong in trusting that Silver Veil would protect us?

But Leyuet only looked tired, and very, very frightened, but not by Skandranon. "You must come with me," he insisted as he clasped his hands together tightly in front of his chest.

"Please. You must not make me compel you. I tell you this for your benefit."

"Why?" Skan demanded again. *"Why?"*

"Because," Leyuet said at last, his face gray under the dark color of his complexion, "there has been a murder. And it was done by a creature with wings, with magic, or with both."

Zhaneel was not wanted along, so she stayed behind under guard. Skan was just as happy to have her elsewhere, although he doubted that she would get any rest until he returned. It looked as though it was going to be a long night for both of them.

And we were just getting our stamina back, too!

He was not under arrest. *Fortunately,* he and the others had been sitting in the middle of that Dance, under the scrutiny of the entire court, all the Dancers, and however many servants had managed to steal a moment and a place to watch from. Or rather, his "arrest" was a token only, and meant to last only so long as it took for half a dozen witnesses to be hauled from their beds and swear before the King that Skan had not once left his seat from the moment the Dance began. As he was counted as the highest authority among the newcomers, protocol dictated that he would be questioned first; presumably this was so that he would have the option of naming any of his underlings guilty of the crime, and thus save face.

Shalaman waited on his bench-throne, face stern and impassive, as six sleepy Haighlei—a Dancer, a servant, three courtiers, and an envoy from one of the other Kingdoms—all vouched for him at different times during the Dance. Evidently, they were leaving nothing to chance.

When the last of them left, Leyuet listened for a moment while the King spoke, then turned back to Skan. "The King would like your opinion on what transpired, and he requests that you accompany us to investigate the scene. As you pointed out, you have wings, and you know magic. The King believes that you will have insights into this tragedy that we may not."

As if I have any choice. If I refuse, it will look bad, perhaps suspicious, and these people are suspicious enough of me already.

Best to put a good face on it, then. He bowed as he had to the dancers. "Tell the King that I will be pleased to add whatever I can to help determine who is the author of this murder." He tried to look calm, dignified, and just as impassive as Shalaman himself.

His innocence ascertained, the King waited for Palisar, Silver Veil, and a gaggle of priests and official-looking fellows with spears that were both functional and decorative to arrive. Then all of them, Skan included, trooped off together to a far corner of the Palace, to one of the towers that housed some of the higher-ranking nobles.

The corridors were deserted, but not because people were sleeping. Skan sensed eyes behind the cracks of barely-opened doors behind them, and sensed fear rising like a fog all along their path. People knew that something terrible had happened although they didn't know what it was. Rumors were probably spreading already.

I only hope I look like an investigator and not a prisoner or a suspect in custody!

Up the wooden stairs of the tower they went, four stories' worth of climbing, with a landing and a closed door giving onto the staircase at each floor, until they came out onto the landing of the suite belonging to the victim. This was the uppermost floor of the flat-roofed tower, with only the staircase as an access route. Leyuet took pains to point that out, as they opened that final door into the victim's suite.

They didn't exactly have to search to find the body—or rather, most of the body. It was all still in the first room of the suite.

Skan didn't know the victim. When Leyuet had mentioned the name, it hadn't triggered a feeling of familiarity; there were a lot of high-ranking nobles, and he'd hardly had time to learn all of them by name. He might have recognized the face—if there had been anything left of the face to recognize.

The problem was that there wasn't anything left to recognize. The body had been shredded, flesh sprayed all over the

walls and furniture with such abandon that the hardened
guards looked sick, and the more susceptible Palisar and
Leyuet had to excuse themselves. The King, who presumably
had seen quite a bit of carnage over his lifetime, if only on one
of his fabled lion hunts, was visibly shaken. Silver Veil's face
was as white as her dressing gown, but her features remained
composed. Skan wondered how she managed it.

*Then again, she took her wagon and her apprentices through
Ma'ar's battle-lines, and before that, through the areas he'd
"pacified." Perhaps this isn't anything worse than she saw
back then.*

Well, that was a horrid thought. And, unfortunately, probably true.

Skan paced slowly around the room, avoiding the blood and
bits of flesh, noting how and where the blows had fallen.
There wasn't a great deal of furniture in this room, which
made his task easier. "I hope your Serenity will excuse what
might seem callousness on my part," he said absently, crouch-
ing to examine the path of a particular blood spurt. "But I am
a warrior. I have seen worse than this visited upon my own
people in my very presence. Silver Veil will have told you of
Ma'ar, of the wars. I assume that I am here in part because of
that experience, as well as the fact that I am a mage and I am
capable of flying."

Silver Veil translated, and Shalaman nodded. He said something, and Silver Veil turned toward Skan.

"His Serenity says that the woman who died was seen in
Court this evening, and left just as you entered the garden for
the Dance in your honor. She was known to oppose the
alliance, and chose to make her opposition public with her
withdrawal."

*Charming. My enemy, which makes me suspect all over
again.* "I was not aware that this particular woman felt that
strongly," Skan said mildly. "I do not feel it is my place or my
duty to interfere in the opinions of the Haighlei. Firstly, they
are *your* people, not mine, and your Serenity will deal with
them and their opinions as he sees fit. Secondly, actions tell
more than words; I behave with honor and candor, and that

will do more to reverse a poor opinion of me than all the arguing and attempts at persuasion of all the learned diplomats in the world."

Shalaman smiled faintly as Silver Veil translated this, and Skan went back to his examination. Since he had tacit permission to do so, he invoked mage-sight, although he frankly wasn't expecting it to work correctly. Sometimes it did, these days, and sometimes all it showed him was a wash of magical energy over everything like a fog, impossible to see through. Once in a while, very rarely, it showed him nothing. That might mean that it wasn't working—or it might mean there was nothing to see.

This time, he got that foggy wash of energy over everything, which was hardly useful.

He examined the windows, which were unlocked and open, and found nothing there, either. No bloodstains showing that the murderer had escaped that way, and no signs of clawmarks as there would be if the murderer had landed on the window ledge and grasped it as a gryphon would.

He reported both those nonfindings dutifully.

"Could a mage have done this?" Leyuet prompted.

"Certainly," Skan replied. "*If* any mage could gather enough power to overcome all the present difficulties in working magic—difficulties I am certain that Your Serenity's priests have already advised you of—this could be done at a distance, without the mage needing even to be near this room. It could also have been done physically. My opinion is that most of the damage was done while the victim was already unconscious or dead, probably the latter."

He pointed out with clinical precision why he had come to that conclusion—the lack of force in the blood sprays, the apparent lack of movement on the part of the victim. Leyuet looked sick but continued to translate.

I had better learn this language quickly if I am going to find myself fending off accusations of murder!

"I cannot tell if this was done by magic means or physical," he concluded. "There was time enough for someone to have done this by physical means before the body was discovered, since the victim dismissed her servants to brood alone during the Dance. I cannot tell if someone flew here or climbed up from below. The latter would be easy enough, for the north side of this tower is all in shadow, and does not overlook a guard post or a garden where someone might have been walking. If the murderer was very, very good, he could even have come up by the stairs and left the same way without anyone seeing him." He shrugged. "I am sorry to be of so little use."

Leyuet nodded, as Silver Veil translated, and then said something to Shalaman himself. The King spoke, and both of them listened gravely.

It was Silver Veil who translated the reply. "Skandranon," she said hesitantly, "I do not care to be the one who tells you this, but His Serenity decrees that while he is convinced for the moment that you had nothing to do with this, there are others who will not be convinced. You must therefore submit to his supervision."

Skan ground his beak, and Leyuet winced at the sound. "And what sort of supervision will that be?" he asked harshly. He could already tell from Silver Veil's expression that he wasn't going to like it, whatever it was.

"You must have one of the Spears of the Law with you at all times, or submit to being closed inside a locked and windowless room if you must have privacy," she told him apologetically. "That is the only way we can be certain of your whereabouts at all times. It is as much for your sake as ours, you know."

Oh, lovely. Either have one of these ebony spearcarriers watching my every move, or get closed up into a closet. Charming. This is not going to do a great deal for my love life! Somehow I doubt that Zhaneel will welcome a third party to our little trysts. . . .

And the idea of any kind of exertion in a locked and windowless room, especially in this climate, was not a pleasant one.

I shall certainly lose weight. It will be steamed off!

But what other choice did he have?

None, and that's the problem, isn't it!

"Very well," he growled, making no secret of his displeasure. "Tell everyone that I will suffer that they may feel more comfortable. Tell them I will voluntarily be their hostage in a closet. I can't see any other solution."

"Neither can I," Silver Veil replied with a sigh.

It was matched by Skan's. And there was one more problem to be faced.

I have to explain this one to Zhaneel!

There was a windowless room in their suite, as it turned out; normally used as a storage room, and hastily turned into a sleeping chamber. Fortunately for him, it might have been windowless, but it wasn't *airless*; he had forgotten the humidity that went along with the heat in this land. You didn't dare close things into an airless chamber, not and expect to extract them again in the same shape they went in. Mildew and mold were the twin enemies that housekeepers fought here, and mildew and mold would thrive in a completely closed chamber.

So there were air-slits cut just below the ceiling, no broader than the width of a woman's palm, but cut on all four walls, and providing a steady stream of fresh air into the room.

"At least it will be dark when we wish to sleep," Zhaneel said philosophically as she set a tiny lamp up on the wall, trying to make the best of the situation. It was a good thing that she *had* handlike foreclaws, and not Skan's fighting claws— with no mage-lights available, it was either a lamp or nothing, and *he* couldn't light a lamp. Except with magic, which he'd been warned not to use. "These slits cannot let in much light. And if the little ones wake at dawn and begin to play, the walls will muffle the noise."

Skan tried not to growl. It was not exactly compensation for being shut into a closet at night.

"I won't say I like this," he said, throwing himself down on their bed, and resisting the urge to claw it to bits in frustration. "I wish I had a better solution. *Sketi*, I wish I'd never come here in the first place! If I wasn't here, there'd be no one from White Gryphon to suspect!"

"I would not count on that," Zhaneel countered thoughtfully, stretching herself down beside him, and beginning to preen his ear-tufts to soothe his temper. "Consider; what if this were devised *precisely* to implicate you? Or rather, to implicate one of the White Gryphon envoys. If Judeth had been here in your stead, the murder might seem to have been performed by a fighter; if Lady Cinnabar, the victim might have been dissected with surgical precision. Or a weapon from the north might have been found in the room."

"Hmm." Skan pondered that; it had the right sound and feel to it. "But what does that mean for us at the moment?"

Zhaneel delicately spat out a tuft of down and answered him. "Whoever did this in the first place must not realize that you were under the eyes of hundreds of witnesses at the time of the murder. The best that we can do is be graceful and gracious beneath this burden, and wait for some other evidence to surface. What is needed is motive. Perhaps this courtier had some great enemy, or perhaps she owned something that will prove to be missing." She shrugged and went after the other ear-tuft. "In any case, it hardly matters at the moment. *I* think that there is magic involved."

"How, when mages are so watched and bound by laws and priests?" Skan asked skeptically.

She had no answer for that, but there was no reason why he couldn't pursue that particular quarry for a moment. "I suppose that accidents could happen," he mused aloud. "This is a large country. A child could be overlooked, or even run away from the school. Once he knew what he was, if he didn't turn himself in—"

"Then obviously he would already be a criminal," Zhaneel stated.

"A good point. Which would mean he would drift into the company of other criminals." He nodded, and leaned a little more into her preening; she knew where all the really itchy spots were.

"Which would mean that he would become a weapon in the hands of other criminals," she replied. "I think the most likely is that this woman had a great enemy, and that the enemy de-

cided to rid himself of the woman during a time when he was
unlikely to be caught."

"During the Dance, you mean? But everyone knew we were
going to be there, didn't they? After all, it was supposed to be
in our honor."

"That would be known to those in the Court itself. The fact
that the murder looked as if a gryphon did it might actually
only be a coincidence, if this was a crime of terrible and profound anger," she pointed out. "And the murderer could simply be incredibly lucky, to have gotten into his victim's suite,
killed her, and gotten out without being seen. People *do* have
that kind of luck, you know." She glanced at him slyly. "Certainly, you did."

"Huhrrr." He thought that over. It was possible. Not likely,
but barely possible. "He'd have to be lucky *and* good. And if
that's the case, we'll never catch him."

"But when nothing more happens, this will all evaporate in
a few days," Zhaneel pointed out. "After all, *you* could not
have done the deed, even Palisar admits that. As unreliable as
magic is, even if you had done this by magic, you would still
have needed privacy and a great deal of time, and there would
be traces. So, when nothing more is discovered, all the attention upon us will fade in importance in no more than a week,
and they will remove their guards and precautions." She
glanced at him, with a sideways tilt of her head. "They may
never find the murderer, but this will soon become only the
interest of what passes for a policing force here."

Skan sighed, and nuzzled her tiny ear-tufts. "You're right,
of course," he said as she craned her head upward to blow
out the lamp. "In a few days their suspicion of us will be
forgotten."

There. I have said what will comfort her. Why don't I be-
lieve it myself?

Shalaman

Five

There was a familiar knock at the door, a little after dinnertime and just before Court. The servant spoke a sentence or two in hushed tones.

"Don't tell me," Skandranon groaned, as the servant—once again—ushered in Leyuet and the Spears of the Law. This was the third time in six days. "Another murder."

Leyuet nodded grimly. His dark face was drawn and new worry-lines etched the corners of his mouth. And was there more gray in his hair? It seemed so. "Another murder. Another professed opponent of the treaty. This time, in a room locked and barred from within. It *must* be by magic. You were, of course, watched all afternoon during your sleep period?"

Skan gestured broadly to indicate the pair of heavily-muscled spear-bearers, standing stoically in what passed for the corners of the room. "They never left my side, and they never slept." After the second murder, a single watcher had not been deemed enough to insure Skandranon's innocence by some parties, so a second Spear of the Law had been added to make certain that the first was not duped or slumbering. "I've either been here or in the garden. Just ask them."

Leyuet sighed, a look of defeat creeping over him. "I do not need to, for I know that they will confirm your words. But I also know that no magician of the Haighlei could have done this. As you rightly pointed out, to overcome all the disturbances in the use of magic would require more power than any of our priests or mages has available to him. Thus the mage must be foreign, with foreign ways of working magic." He rubbed his eyes, a gesture that had become habitual over the past several days, as Leyuet clearly got less and less sleep. "No Haighlei would ever have committed murder so—so crudely, so impolitely, either."

Skan coughed to keep from choking with astonishment. Every time he thought he understood the Haighlei ways, someone said something that surprised him all over again. "You mean to tell me that there is a polite way to commit *murder?*" he blurted.

Leyuet did not rise to the bait; he just shook his head. "It is just the Haighlei way. Even murder has a certain protocol, a set ritualistic aspect to it. For one thing, a murderer must accomplish certain tasks to be certain that the spirit of his victim has been purged from the earth. How else could the perpetrator feel satisfaction? But this conforms to nothing Haighlei. It is not random, but there is no pattern to it, either."

Zhaneel coughed politely, drawing Leyuet's gaze toward her. "All the victims were women as well as being opposed to the alliance," Zhaneel suggested delicately. "Could it be a case of a jilted lover? Someone who approached all three of the women about an assignation and was rebuffed—or someone who once had affairs with them and was cast off for another?"

But Leyuet only shook his head again. "There would be even more of ritual in that case. No, this has no pattern, it was done by magic, and it is like nothing we have ever seen in the Empire."

As if some madman among the Haighlei could not act in a patternless fashion. "It is new, in other words," Skan said flatly. "And since it is new, and we are new, therefore—"

"Therefore I must summon you before the Emperor Shalaman once again," Leyuet finished for him, spreading his hands wide. "It is the pattern."

Skan simply bowed to the inevitable. *I have no choice, after all. I cannot even try to go back to White Gryphon now;*

they might decide that retreat was an admission of guilt and send an army. "Lead on," he replied, gesturing with his fore-claw. "I am at your disposal."

And I only hope that isn't a prophetic phrase! I would very much prefer not to be "disposed of!"

Kanshin worked the little wooden ball up and around his fingers, from the index to the littlest finger and back again, in an exercise often used by street-entertainers who prac-ticed sleight-of-hand and called it magic. He was no street-entertainer, however. He was a thief, and a master thief at that. More than any street-entertainer, he needed to keep his hands supple.

His father would be horrified, if he still lived, to know what "trade" Kanshin now plied. *Better to be a master thief than a master-ditchdigger.* That was what Kanshin's father had been, and his grandfather, and so on back for ten generations. That, so the priests and the gods decreed, was what Kanshin should have been.

Kanshin sneered at them all, at his father for being a fool, at the priests for the "decrees" that duped so many. *A pox upon priests and gods together. Assuming there even are any gods, which I doubt.*

He worked the ball around his left hand, across the palm, and up to the index finger again. *My father believed in the gods and the priests, and we starved. I like my way better.*

Kanshin had more intelligence than to believe the pious rhetoric spewed out in regular, measured doses by the priests—especially when the only way to "be certain" of a better posi-tion in one's next life was to bestow all of one's wealth on the priests in this one. Not that a ditchdigger was going to acquire much *wealth* over the course of a lifetime, but Kanshin's father had devoted every spare coin to the purchase of that new life, to the detriment and hardship of his own children.

Perhaps that was why Kanshin had seen through the scheme by the time he was five. Hunger undermined man-ners. Polite people didn't question.

He glanced at the door to the guest room, thinking he had heard a sound, but it was nothing.

Even our guest would certainly agree with me and not with my father. He might be insane, but he certainly isn't stupid.

He had hoped for a while that he might escape the endless cycle of backbreaking labor and poverty by being taken by the priests as a mage—but that never happened. *No mage-craft and easy life for me. What a joke! If the gods really existed, they'd have arranged for me to have the powers of magic, wouldn't they? If they had, I'd be one of their fat priests or fatter mages right now, and there would be many people still in the incarnations I cut short.* But there were no gods, of course, and no priest had come to spirit Kanshin away to a better life. So, one day, when his father and mother and bawling, brawling siblings were all sleeping the sleep of the stupefied, he ran away. Away to the city, to the wicked, worldly city of Khimbata, and a chance for something better than blisters on his hands, a permanently bent back, and an early grave.

Kanshin smiled with satisfaction at his own cleverness. So much for the gods, who sought to keep him in his place. For although he could not go higher in caste to win himself the fortune and luxury he craved—he *could* go lower.

He transferred the ball to his right hand, and began the exercise all over again.

He had started out as a begger, self-apprenticed to one of the old hands of the trade, aged Jacony. Jacony had taught him everything; how to wrap his body tightly with bandages to look thinner, how to make his face pale and wan or even leprous, how to create sores from flour, water, and henna, how to bind his leg or arm to make it look as if he were an amputee. That was all right for a while, as long as he was young and could look convincingly starved and pathetic—and as long as the sores and deformations his master put on him were strictly cosmetic. But when the old man let drop the fact that he was considering actually *removing* a hand or a foot to make Kanshin into a "wounded lion hunter," Kanshin decided that he'd better find another trade and another master.

I can't believe the old man thought I'd stand for that. I

*wasn't that desperate! But—maybe he was. And missing a
hand or a foot, I'd be a lot more conspicuous if I tried to run
off—a lot more dependent on him, too, I suppose.*

It didn't take him long to find a new master, now that he
knew his way around the city. By that time, he was quite con-
versant with the covert underground of beggars, whores, and
thieves that swarmed the soft underbelly of the lazy metropo-
lis, like fleas living in the belly-fur of a fat, pampered lapdog.
And he knew what he wanted, too.

*There were other masters ready to take me at that point.
Lakshe, for instance.* He hadn't ever given Lakshe's offer serious thought because he didn't intend to become a boy-whore,
although the trade paid well enough. He would have only one
chance in ten of earning enough before he became too old to be
called a "boy" anymore, and there wasn't a lot of call for aging
catamites.

*And the odds of becoming a procurer like Lakshe are even
lower than earning enough to keep you for the rest of your life.*

He'd tried being a beggar, and he just looked too healthy,
too strong; not all the paste-and-henna sores in the world
would convince people he was really suffering, not unless he
did undergo a self-amputation. *I didn't like begging, anyway.
No chance for a fortune. And scraping out a living that way
was hardly better than digging ditches.*

So—that left thief, an avocation he was already attracted to.
He smiled as he worked the ball across his fingers. *I'd even
picked a pocket or two by then, so I was ready, ready to learn
more.*

He was still young enough—just—to get a master. He chose
one of the oldest thieves in the city, an alcoholic sot who lived
on cadged drinks and a reputation many doubted. *No one
knew that Poldarn was more than a drunk and a liar.* Kanshin
had not doubted him after several of the stories had, on investigation, proven to be true. Nor had he doubted the man's ability to teach him, if only Kanshin could keep him sober and
alive long enough to do so.

He had managed both, and now, if he was not *the* master-
thief in the city, he was certainly among the masters. *Poldarn*

did know every trick of the trade, from picking locks to climbing up walls with no more gear than ten strong fingers and toes. He was good, I'll grant him that. Too bad drink addled his wits.

And his master? Dead, now; collapsed back into the gutter as soon as Kanshin left him on his own. *He couldn't stay sober a day without me. He was drunk the day I set up on my own, and I never saw him sober after that. I don't think he lived more than a fortnight after I left.*

Hardly a surprise; the man's liver must have been the size of a goose. *Either that—or he went back to drinking the same quantities of strong liquor that he had of weak, and the drink itself killed him. Small loss, to the world or to me. Where were the gods for him, when he was drinking himself into a stupor?*

The young thief had been good—and careful. He neither over- nor under-estimated his own abilities, and he always brought back the goods he'd been paid to take. Now Kanshin had all the things he had dreamed of; a house, slaves, fine foods to eat and wines to drink. The food was as good as that from the King's table, and the wines were often better.

The house was a grand affair, like the dream of a palace on the inside—granted, the house was in the heart of the Dakola District, but no one was stupid enough to try to rob Kanshin. The last fool who'd tried was still serving out his punishment, chained to a wall in Kanshin's basement, digging a new cesspit. That was a *far* more effective deterrent than simply killing or maiming interlopers. After all, most of them, like Kanshin himself, had become thieves to *avoid* hard labor. When they found themselves little better than slaves, forced to wield shovels and scrub dirty dishes, they never tried to rob him a second time.

He listened very carefully, and smiled when he heard the faint scrape of a shovel on dirt. Now *there* was one unhappy thief who would not be making a second visit to Kanshin.

The house itself looked like every other filthy, rundown heap in the district—outside. Inside, it was crammed with every luxury that Kanshin could buy or steal. Perhaps service was a little slower than in the homes of the nobles—the slaves were hobbled with chains to hinder their escape—but Kanshin didn't mind. In fact, he rather enjoyed seeing people who could probably boast higher birth than he, weighted down with iron and forced to obey his every whim. Slavery was not legal in this kingdom, but none of these people would dare to complain of their lot.

Not all of this was due entirely to his own work, but it *was* due to his own cleverness.

He set the ball aside, and began to run the same exercises using a coin. *It was clever to find this perfect partner. It was clever to see* his *cleverness.* Some eight or nine years ago, right after that strange winter when the priests all seemed to vanish for a time and there were rumors all over the city of magic gone horribly wrong, a young and comely stranger began walking the streets of the Dakola District. He claimed to be a mage, which all men knew to be impossible, since no mage—by definition a Law-Keeper—would ever frequent the haunts of the Law-Slayers. So all men laughed him to scorn when he told them this, and that he was looking for a thief to partner him in certain enterprises.

No one believed him. They should have known that a story so preposterous had to be true.

All men laughed at him but one—Kanshin, who bethought him that if a ditchdigger could slip through the Law to become a master-thief, could not a renegade mage slip through the Law as well to retain his magic? So he sought out this man, and discovered that what no one else would believe was nothing more nor less than the barest, leanest truth.

He—the man called himself "Noyoki," which meant "No one"—*was* a mage. And he had, by sheerest accident, slipped through the hands of the priests. At seventeen he had been discovered in some unsavory doing by the priests, his teachers—what, Kanshin never bothered to find out for true, although Noyoki said it had been because he used his powers to cheat at games of chance.

That seems unlikely . . . but then again, these priests find cheating to be a sin only second to murder. I suppose it never occurs to them that they *are the real cheats.* They had, of course, decreed that he should have his powers removed, as always. No child caught misusing his powers could be allowed to retain them. For that matter, it was rumored that adult mages had been stripped of their powers for misuse.

A useful rumor to circulate I suppose, if you are intent on preserving the illusion of the integrity of your adult mages.

It was the mad magic that had saved Noyoki, that first wave of mad magic ten years ago that had lit up the night skies, created abortive and mismade creatures, muddled everything and turned the world of the mages upside-down. The priest that should have burned the magic out of his head had been struck down unconscious and died the following week without ever waking again, but Noyoki had the wit to feign the sickness that came when such a deed had been done. And with magic gone quite unpredictable, no one of the priests could tell that it had *not* been done.

So he was sent back to his family in disgrace—powers intact, and lacking only a few months of training to be a full mage.

They were told he should never be trusted, never given power, a high office, or any responsibility. Kanshin smiled at that. Another challenge to the nonexistent gods; if they had never given this boy magic, he would never have turned against the world and cultivated Kanshin. If he had never met Kanshin, there were things stolen and deaths recorded that would never have happened.

So much for the gods.

It was a lofty house, for Noyoki had quarters of his own within the Palace itself. Noyoki had waited until they ceased to put eyes on him wherever he went, and left him in scorn to seek whatever excesses might soonest bring his cycle to the earliest end. That was what he was supposed to do. No one dreamed he had any ambitions at all; they should have been burned out with his magic.

Then, once no one bothered to watch him anymore, he went down into the quarter of the thieves, to seek a thief as a partner.

Kanshin and Noyoki were successful beyond Kanshin's original dreams of avarice—though Noyoki never seemed to want the gems and artifacts, the drugs and the rare essences that Kanshin stole with his help. No, Noyoki was most interested in paper, documents—

Well, that was fine with Kanshin. Let Noyoki have the documents; Kanshin knew better than to try to take them to use himself. That required subtlety which Kanshin had, but it also required knowledge of their owners and the enemies of their owners which he did not have. He was smart enough to know that he could and would never learn these things in time to make proper use of the stolen papers.

Noyoki also had another power—rarely used and hard on him—that allowed him to place Kanshin within a locked and barred room and extract him again. At first he had not been able to do this more than once a year or so, but lately, he had been able to accomplish it much oftener. For a thief, such a talent was beyond price, and Kanshin treasured his partnership, suffering insults and slights from Noyoki he would never have suffered from another living being.

Things have been going well. Kanshin frowned. *So why has Noyoki suddenly gotten greater ambitions?*

Everything had gone according to the plan Kanshin had worked out for his life—when the unexpected happened. Kanshin had wealth, power, a certain amount of fame, and needed only to work when he chose. But one day not long ago, Noyoki had brought the madman now in Kanshin's guest chamber to Kanshin's home and bade him care for the pale-skinned creature.

Hadanelith was the madman's name, a man with the white skin of a leper, the pale-blue eyes of a lemur, and hair like bleached straw. Kanshin would have thought that this "Hadanelith" was some kind of misbegotten sport, created from a normal man by the mad magic, if he had not once seen the Emperor's kestra'chern, The Silver Veil, with his own eyes. She had skin as pale, eyes as washed-out, and hair of an even stranger silver color. So the madman was not a misbegotten thing, but only a man from another land.

I do not understand this creature. Hadanelith found humor in things not even Kanshin found amusing; he made slaves of the slaves, manipulating their minds in such a way that Kanshin could remove their chains at any time and never fear their escaping. Of course, once Hadanelith had done with them, they were useless to anyone but him. Kanshin was just glad he had not given the man access to more than three, of which only two were female. Hadanelith had no use for males. Kanshin refused to allow himself to be intimidated by the man, but his strange behavior unnerved him.

On the other hand, he is frighteningly intelligent. He had learned their language so quickly that Kanshin wondered now and again if the man had plucked it from their minds. But no—he had only learned by listening, and when he finally spoke, it was with no real accent. He might giggle like an hysterical girl with pleasure in the work he had done for them, but it was competent work, and within the limits he and Noyoki set, Hadanelith worked well.

One of the slaves—one that Hadanelith had not spoiled—came to the door of Kanshin's work room, a chamber filled with the tools of his trade and the instruments he used to keep his body as supple as that of the *young* thief he had once been. "Master," said the man, his head lowered submissively, "Noyoki awaits your pleasure in the reception chamber."

"Good." Kanshin placed the coin back in the holder beside the ball, and rose from his chair. "Tell him I will be with him shortly."

With a faint clinking of chain, the slave bowed and shuffled out. Kanshin smiled at his back.

Then he surveyed himself in the full-length mirror to be certain there was nothing lacking in his appearance. He suspected Noyoki to be of extraordinarily high birth, and he had tried, since the beginning, to look as outwardly respectable as someone of high caste could. Noyoki himself cultivated a rapscallion appearance, wearing untidy robes of odd cut, his hair woven into braids like a working man, but that did not mean he was not influenced without his realizing it by the appearance of respectability. Every trick that came to hand was necessary when dealing with Noyoki.

There was nothing to mark Kanshin as a person of anything less than the caste of bankers and professionals. He smoothed his robes with a proprietary hand and went in search of his partner.

Noyoki sprawled casually on one of the couches in the reception chamber, his hair beaded as well as braided, his bright cotton robe made of patchwork material, like that of a mountebank or street-entertainer. He was examining a piece of carving that Hadanelith had left on one of the tables, looking it over with intense scrutiny, a frown of concentration on his handsome, chiseled features.

"What do you make of this?" he asked as Kanshin entered, followed by the slave with a tray of fruit ices for their refreshment. He held it up; there was no mistaking what it was meant for, but the shape was odd. It was carved to resemble a rabbit, with long ears pressed tightly together, and a misshapen, bulbous body. The expression on the rabbit's stupid face was that of sheer terror. Not the sort of expression one would expect to find on a toy of that nature. It was not unheard of for these toys to be shaped like animals, but the animals always looked as if they were cheerfully enjoying themselves.

"It is one of your friend's toys," Kanshin replied easily. "And I suspect it would give us a great deal of insight into his way of thinking if we knew why he had carved it that way. He presented me with it this afternoon. There was blood on it."

"Charming." Noyoki did not put it down immediately, as Kanshin had thought he might. Then again, given that he had turned to blood-magic, perhaps the thing held some arcane significance for him. "He performed well this afternoon."

"You would be the one to know, not I, by the results of your working." Kanshin raised his eyebrows in inquiry; Noyoki only smiled, and ran his fingers along the smooth wood of the carving, caressing the toy with his touch.

"If that is a question, yes, the blood-power came through strong and clear. It more than tripled the reserves I expended to put him in place and take him out again." Noyoki had told Kanshin that only the power that came through pain and spilled blood was strong enough to allow him to work magics in the old way, before magery had run wild. *What* he was doing, Kanshin did not ask. He really did not want to know. *The less I know of his doings, the safer I am.* He knew very well that Noyoki would not hesitate to be rid of him if the mage thought he knew too much.

Whatever magics the man worked now, it was something to put Noyoki back in a position of power, though whether overt or covert, Kanshin would not even guess. He knew that the victims Noyoki had chosen for his "pet" to slay were all rivals or former rivals; perhaps he was ridding himself of his male rivals by using the deaths of their females to undermine them.

"It is a pity that we cannot persuade the man to broaden his—ah—interests," he said carefully.

Noyoki frowned. "If I could find a way to coerce him to take men—well, perhaps coercion would be a bad idea. He *is* an artist in his way, and when one coerces an artist, the work is always flawed."

Kanshin nodded, although the turn of Noyoki's phrase surprised him. Had the mage spoken from past experience?

Their dual role in this was to use Hadanelith to simulate murder by magic. Kanshin would find a way to insert Hadanelith into the victim's chambers and get him out again; if there was no other way in, Noyoki would spirit him in and out by that odd talent of his when he was done, using the excess of the power released from the victim's suffering and death. In between, Hadanelith had free rein to work whatever atrocities on the victim that he chose, up until the moment he received the signal to kill.

A clever plan, which required a minimum of magic to carry out. At the moment, Kanshin's payment was coming through Noyoki, and both maintained the polite fiction that Noyoki was working for someone else, some great noble who wanted obstacles removed from his path, but in such a way that these dangerous new pale-skinned allies were also placed under suspicion.

It is easier to discredit foreigners anyway. It is just a good thing that their arrival coincided with the beginning of our plan. Kanshin had not told Hadanelith any more than was strictly necessary to carry out the work, but he wondered if the man had guessed who was taking the blame for the murders. If so, he did not seem at all displeased by the idea of what might be his own countrymen being falsely accused.

Perhaps he simply doesn't care. Or perhaps these people drove him out of their ranks. . . . That was an interesting thought. If Hadanelith had tortured and killed before, it would account for his peculiar competence in that area.

He was a good, if flawed, tool. He followed his instructions to the letter, as long as he knew why he was supposed to be doing something. When the signal to kill came, he never balked.

The trouble is, we cannot be certain how much longer he will remain tractable.

As Kanshin understood it, for Noyoki's blood-magic to work, the power he received had to be incredibly strong, which meant the murders must be committed with a diabolical, rabid brutality. Despite the fact that the Emperor was trying to keep the news suppressed, rumors of the murders were already in the lower districts of Khimbata, and hardened criminals spoke of the scenes and the victims with troubled awe, as if even they could not imagine doing such things.

"How much longer do you think we can keep a leash on our dog?" Noyoki asked, as if he was aware of Kanshin's doubts.

Kanshin shrugged. "How much longer do you need him? He seems stable enough for now. I think as long as he knows that we are the only route to what *he* wants, he will obey. But he is not sane, Noyoki. He could suddenly change, and we would have no warning of it."

Noyoki nodded, face solemn, the beads on the ends of his braids clicking with the movement of his head. "His carving might give us a clue."

"True." Hadanelith had a mania for carving; he always had a knife in his hands and a piece of wood, and there were more of his twisted little sculptures all over the house. Kanshin didn't mind the mess and the shavings at all; while Hadanelith carved, he was not getting into other mischief.

"I think he knows about the visitors taking the blame for the murders," Noyoki said, suddenly switching topics. "I think it pleases him. Perhaps these people were his enemies."

"Perhaps they were his jailers!" Kanshin retorted sharply. "Never forget what this man does, Noyoki! Never forget that Hadanelith is mad, and he could decide he wants to do it to you! We may turn the tiger upon the tracks of our foes, but the tiger can decide to turn back again and seek us instead!"

"Yes," Noyoki replied with an odd and disquieting smile. "And that is what makes the game all the more interesting, is it not?"

Madness must be contagious, for he surely is mad! Kanshin thought with astonishment.

"I am not mad, Kanshin," Noyoki said, in another uncanny answer to words left unspoken. "I am simply interested in a challenge, and Hadanelith presents such a challenge. If it is possible, I should like to tame him to my hand as I have tamed the lion and the pard."

Kanshin shrugged. "On your head be it," he replied. "I am interested only in getting rid of him once our tasks for him have been completed. If you choose to take him into your own household, I simply ask that you take him as far away from me as possible."

"Perhaps I will," Noyoki observed, stretching like a well-fed and very lazy cat. "And with that, I shall take my leave of you; I will bring you the information on the next of Hadanelith's playfellows tomorrow."

Kanshin bowed him out to the street and stood in the doorframe, watching his back as he disappeared into the swirling crowds. *He is not a fool, but he is foolhardy,* the thief thought as he closed the door and retreated into the perfumed safety of his own home and away from the noisome babble and stenches of the streets. *Too foolhardy for me. Once this set of jobs is over, I am retiring, far away from here.* He had just the place in mind too; a lake big enough to be considered an inland sea. *Such recklessness is like teasing a lion; you never get a second chance to learn how much is too much.*

He retreated deeply into the depths of his home, past rooms that only opened when he had picked a complicated lock, and which relocked themselves when the door closed. He took himself to the farthest of those rooms, a place where Hadanelith did not go and where, hopefully, he could not go.

The trouble was, the madman learned at a terrible speed. There was no reason why he could *not* learn to master all those locks, as he had already mastered the language and the thief's tricks that Kanshin had taught him.

Kanshin flung himself down on a couch, and laid his right arm across his eyes. How long would the madman remain "safe?" That was a good question.

He only wished he had an answer.

Skandranon was making some decisions as he marched toward the Audience Chamber under armed guard for the third time in a week. For one thing, he was getting *damned* tired of taking the blame for someone else's murders! Especially when the law-keepers didn't seem to him to be making much of an effort to find the real culprit!

His control over his temper had improved over the past several years, but he was just about to lose all that hard-won control. He felt the hackles on the back of his neck rising, despite a conscious effort to make them lie flat.

How can they even pretend that I'm still a suspect! he growled to himself. *I've been under guard for two of the three killings! After the second, they should have removed my guard, not doubled it!*

The situation was uncomfortable enough for him personally, but by now it was obvious that someone, probably someone in Shalaman's own court, was trying to discredit the Kaled'a'in. *We should be uniting to find the culprit,* he seethed. *They should have* asked *me to bring in the other mages from White Gryphon, mages who might know other techniques to get at the truth! Instead—here I am, being hauled up in front of the King again!*

These murders were jeopardizing everything he had worked for since Urtho's death, threatening to put the Kaled'a'in in the position having to make an untenable choice—abandon the city and rebuild elsewhere, where the arm of the Haighlei did not reach, or stand and fight for what they had built so far, against a vastly superior force.

By the time they reached the Audience Chamber, Skan was so angry he was just about ready to disembowel something.

So instead of parading meekly into the chamber as he had the past two times, *this* time he shouldered his guards aside and pushed his way up to King Shalaman. The courtiers quickly leaped aside when they saw the look on his face, the parted beak, the raised hackles, the anger in his eyes. The King's bodyguards instinctively stepped forward when the last of the courtiers jumped out of his way, leaving nothing between him and Shalaman but those two guards. But Skan waited for Leyuet and the escort to catch up—which didn't take long—and then he opened his beak and let the words pour out.

Leyuet was babbling, trying to keep up with his own flowing torrents of words. Skan ignored him, in part because he had a suspicion that Shalaman didn't need an interpreter.

". . . and what I don't understand is why no one has even *begun* to look for a suspect besides me!" he ranted, his voice coming close to a shriek on the last few words. People winced and tried to cover their ears. "What is wrong with you people? I mean, I know that magic's gone bad, but surely with enough power behind a simple spell your mages could make it work! If *your* mages don't know anything about using magic to find criminals, then *mine* do, and I'll bring them here from White Gryphon if that's what it takes!" He was in fine style now, pacing and lashing his tail, radiating enough anger to have sunburned anyone near him. "Are you deliberately obstructing the investigations? Have you even started them? I saw no signs of it!"

There was horrified scandal in the murmurs he heard, the faces he watched as he paced and ranted.

He was actually beginning to enjoy himself. Evidently this was something that was just Not Done in Haighlei society.

Well, murder is Not Done, and accusing someone falsely of murder is Not Done—and it's about time someone woke them up to that fact.

Since the polite approach had produced no obvious cooperation on their part, perhaps violating all their social rules would!

Leyuet watched in horror as the huge white gryphon broke away from his escort and began to force his way through the courtiers—although it didn't take long for the courtiers to notice what Skandranon was doing, and leap hastily out of the way. What did the creature think he was doing? Surely he wasn't going to—

But Skandranon stopped short of the throne and began to pace back and forth, his voice raised to a shout, accusing the Haighlei of trying to blame him for the murders for the sake of convenience. Accusing the *King* of originating the plan!

The gryphon was angry, showing more anger than Leyuet had ever seen demonstrated in his life. His rage was a palpable thing, radiating from him in waves of passion as he paced and turned, never once ceasing in his accusations.

He is innocent. Leyuet was sure of that on all counts; such rage could not be the product of guilt, and that was nothing more than simple fact. Leyuet himself had ascertained the gryphon's innocence a dozen times over, with far more than the simple facts to guide him.

So now what do we do? For the very first time since the strangers had arrived here, Skandranon was acting like a King, like the equal of any of the Haighlei Emperors, addressing Shalaman as an equal, demanding his rights, demanding action. This, along with their basic understanding of the gryphon's position as the Kaled'a'in leader, only confirmed his real position in Leyuet's eyes—and presumably in the eyes of every other Haighlei present.

And that only complicated the situation.

I will have to remove the guards, of course. A King simply

could *not* be imprisoned or under guard—or held for ransom—
or even *questioned* publicly!

"I swear to you, to you all, if *you* don't do something, I
will!" Skandranon shouted, his feathers standing on end with
rage, his beak snapping off the words as if he would like very
much to be closing it on someone's arm. "*I* will find the murderer! *I* will bring him to justice!"

Leyuet's dismay deepened, as he surreptitiously gestured to
Skandranon's guards to take themselves elsewhere. *Now* what
were they going to do? Kings didn't run about trying to solve a
murder! They left that up to the Truthsayers and the Spears Of
the Law!

Except that the Truthsayers and the Spears hadn't been doing very well. The gryphon was right enough about that.

Whatever were they going to do?

The Emperor caught Leyuet's eye and gave a slight nod in
Skandranon's direction. Leyuet cast his own eyes upward for a
moment, then nodded back. Some called it magic, some felt
that it bordered on the blasphemous powers of seeing into another's mind, but the Truthsayers were trained by the priests
to know, infallibly, whether or not someone was speaking the
truth. And Leyuet had just told Shalaman without words that
the white gryphon was doing just that. It was only a surface
touch of the soul; Leyuet dared not go deeper, as he would
with a human. He had no notion how his own soul would react to such an intimacy. But at the moment the surface touch
was all that was needed.

The skin around Shalaman's eyes twitched. That was all,
but it was an unusual display of emotion from the Emperor.

*We are in a tangle, and I see no way out of it. But I am not
the King. Perhaps Shalaman—*

The gryphon finally ran out of words—or his rage overcame
his ability to speak—and he stood quietly, sides heaving with
angry pants, glaring at Shalaman. The silence that fell over the
court was so profound that the calls of birds and monkeys pen-
etrated into the Audience Chamber from outside.

"I understand your anger," Shalaman said quietly in the

foreigners' own tongue—shocking Leyuet. The Emperor *never* demeaned himself by speaking the language of another!

Unless, of course, the other was a King in his own right. In one stroke, Shalaman had just confirmed the gryphon's status and changed the rules of the game.

"I understand it and sympathize with it," he continued. "Look about you—you are no longer under any sort of guard."

Skandranon nodded shortly without looking around. *Good. He is willing to take Shalaman's word for it.* Leyuet let out a tiny sigh of relief, for that was one small obstacle dealt with.

"I know that you have not seen any of *our* investigations; be assured that they are going on, even at this moment," Shalaman continued. "It is only that all such things must take place *within the grounds of the temples.* That is our way. That is probably also why you have noticed nothing of a magic nature taking place in the vicinity of the palace."

"Ah," the gryphon replied, a little more satisfied. "Now I understand. I had taken the lack of spell-energy for lack of effort."

"It is an effort," Shalaman admitted. "As you yourself are aware, that event you call the Cataclysm has changed everything for both our peoples. The mages and priests have, thus far, come up with no suspects—but they *have* eliminated you, which gives you yet one more voucher of innocence."

The gryphon muttered something under his breath. Both Leyuet and the Emperor pretended not to notice.

"*Please,* I earnestly ask you, do not bring your foreign mages here," Shalaman continued. "Such an act will only serve to drive a wedge between yourselves and our priests. That would be a bad thing for all concerned."

"Then what *can* I do?" Skandranon demanded.

"Be patient," Shalaman told him. "Please. You are once again free to come and go as you will in this Court and Palace. You will not be guarded nor watched."

Leyuet wondered if the gryphon realized that Shalaman was giving him tacit permission to go fly off and perform his own investigations.

Probably, he decided. *The gryphon is not stupid. If he can master the court dances the way he has, he will be able to read what is not said as well as what is said.*

But that would only give him one more personal headache; how to keep the gryphon safe while Skandranon was winging his way everywhere.

The gryphon's feathers slowly collapsed, bringing him down to a more normal appearance. He and Shalaman exchanged several more words, now in calmer tones, and with less vehemence behind them. That was when the gryphon surprised Leyuet yet again by replying to one of Shalaman's questions in the Haighlei tongue, neatly turning the diplomatic tables on the Emperor.

Although all of this was very good, a headache still throbbed in Leyuet's temple when it was all over and the gryphon had gone away, bowing gracefully.

Leyuet did not follow; the Emperor's eyes held him where he stood. For a moment, he feared that Shalaman would summon him to the side of the throne, but once the gryphon was well away, the Emperor only nodded, releasing Leyuet from any further need to dance attendance on him.

Shalaman's nod was accompanied by the faintest of sympathetic smiles, telling Leyuet that the Emperor had noticed the lines of pain about his eyes and mouth. Shalaman was good at noticing things, and was only unkind to his subordinates when need drove him to unkindness.

Leyuet took himself out, quickly.

Silver Veil had not been in *her* Advisor's position at the throne, and neither had Palisar. The latter was probably in the temple complex located on the Palace grounds, overseeing the magical investigations into the murders. The former must be in her quarters.

This was, for Leyuet's sake, a very good thing, the first good thing that had happened today.

A Truthsayer must always find the truth. A Truthsayer could not be bought for any coin. This was a weighty responsibility; and all those bearing weighty responsibilities went to Silver Veil for solace. That solace was generally *not* the kind of physical comfort that the lower classes assumed. Leyuet could have that at any time, from any number of skilled ladies. No, the solace that Silver Veil provided was of another order altogether.

His feet took him to Silver Veil's suite without a conscious decision on his part, purely in the hope that she might not be giving another the privilege of her skills. He had not gone to her in many days, respecting her need for privacy in the wake of the horrifying murders—but now, his own pain and need were too great. The physical pain of the headache warned him of worse to come if he did not have it tended to, *now*.

Silver Veil's servants answered his knock and ushered him into a room he knew well, a room where the harsh light of the sun was softened by gauze curtains drawn across many windows, where the scents of flowers blended gracefully with those of soothing herbs, where the only furnishings were low couches covered in soft, absorbent fabrics, couches that could also be used for massages.

The colors here were all cool; deep greens and blues, strong, clear colors that accentuated Silver Veil's pale beauty. She entered once the servants had settled him on one of the couches, and had clothed him in a light robe suitable for a massage.

She slipped among the gauze hangings like a slim silver fish through water-weeds, a silver-chased basket in her hands. She put it down beside him, and experimentally touched his shoulders with her fingers.

"My goodness," she said with an upraised eyebrow. "You should have come to me several days ago! Palisar certainly didn't hesitate."

"I am not Palisar," he reminded her.

"No, you aren't. You are Leyuet, who sacrifices his own comfort far too often. Here—" She flipped open the lid of the casket, revealing the contents.

It contained neither massage oils nor treasure, but Leyuet's own secret passion and guilty pleasure: sugar-powdered pastries and cookies.

"Oh—" he said ruefully, in mingled appreciation and concern. "Oh, my dear child, I shall eat these and put on so much weight that my robes will strain across my stomach!"

"You will eat those because a little bird told me you have eaten next to nothing these past three days," she said firmly. "You will eat these because you need them, for the soothing of your spirit, because you deserve them. Besides, they are good for you. I used special recipes. *I* do not ascribe to the belief that what is good for you must taste like so much old, dried-up hay."

Leyuet finally broke into a smile, selecting a plump pastry. He held it and devoured it first with his eyes, anticipating the sweet savor, the way that the first bite would melt away to nothing on his tongue, releasing the mingled flavors of almond, vanilla, and honey. He closed his eyes, brought the pastry to his mouth, and bit into the flaky crust, as sugar-glaze broke and scattered over his hand.

It tasted every bit as good as he had imagined, and before he realized it, he was licking the last crumbs from his fingers.

Leyuet opened his eyes to see that Silver Veil was watching him with a pleased smile on her lips, her hands folded in her lap. He laughed.

"Silver Veil," he asked, feeling a warm contentment begin to loosen those knotted muscles in his shoulders before she could even place a finger upon them, "how is it that you always know what someone needs before he himself knows? How is it that you can do the things that are *kind* as well as the things that are duties, in the face of all obstacles?"

She continued to smile serenely. "I could say it is a professional secret, dear heart—but the truth is that I simply think of another's hopes before my own, and the kindnesses follow, as naturally as flowers follow buds. It is really no more mysterious than that."

Leyuet shook his head. "If these strangers, these folk of the Gryphon King, could possibly be anything like you—"

"At least one is, for I taught him, and I think that I know him as well as any person can be said to know another," she interrupted, directing him to turn his back to her so that she could begin to work on the muscles of his neck and shoulders. He was tempted by the still-open casket beside him, but resisted the temptation.

"Amberdrake, you mean." He sighed. "He is so foreign—and their King, more alien still. I do not understand them, and I wonder how they could ever understand us. They *seem* to, but how could they, really? How could anyone who has a King like theirs ever hope to understand us?"

"Would that not make it easier?" she countered. "If someone can understand the ways of a creature like a gryphon, should it not be easier for them to understand the ways of fellow humans?"

He let out his breath in a hiss of pain as she struck a nerve, then shook his head again. "You and they are of a piece, my dear. Their lands gave birth to you and nurtured you. Yet somehow *you* fit in here as well as with them, and I find that even more mysterious than anything else about you. How can you move so well in two different worlds?"

Silver Veil worked on his muscles for a little longer before she answered.

"Perhaps—" she hesitated. "Perhaps because I have lived long enough that I no longer pay a great deal of attention to what is different, only to what is the same," she answered slowly. Then her tone grew lighter. "And one of the things that is universal is that no one can truly have his back worked on while he is sitting up like an old nursemaid displaying perfect posture!" She rapped him reprovingly on the shoulder. "Down, Truthsayer! Give me the space to work my will upon you!"

Chuckling, he obliged her, and for the space of an hour at least, he forgot the troubles that had brought him there.

Leyuet and Palisar

Six

Hadanelith carved another delicate sliver of dark wood from his current sculpture, and surveyed the result critically, lips pursed, humming a bit to himself.

Not quite perfect. Not yet. Soon, though. A little more here, and here. . . .

He had every reason to feel pleased. The last game he'd run for his "hosts" had been very satisfactory, particularly since they had consulted him before they told him what they wanted done. In fact, they had *asked* him for descriptions of some of the more interesting spells that dear old Ma'ar had used on his foes.

It's a pity I was never a mage. I'd know more about spells of destruction. Still, Hadanelith had a very good memory, and as a youngster he had always been very attentive when bodies were brought in from the front lines. No one ever paid any attention to him then; he'd been quite an unremarkable child, and since the concern of the Healers was for the living, he'd often been able to examine the dead quite closely. He remembered quite precisely what some of the most amusing effects Ma'ar had produced looked like. Well enough to counterfeit them, in fact, and that was what he had assured Noyoki and Kanshin.

His hosts had particularly liked the description of the flaying-spell, the one Ma'ar had preferred to use on gryphons.

"Copy that," they'd told him, leaving the ways and means up to him. That rather clever thief, Kanshin, had smuggled him into his target's rooms by way of a ventilation shaft, and had taken pains to assure him of a relatively satisfactory length of time alone with her.

Skandranon certainly recognized the result, although I doubt he guessed the method. What Ma'ar had accomplished with profligate use of magic and an exquisitely trained and honed talent, Hadanelith had duplicated with nothing more than determination and precise surgical skill. He'd taken care to leave nothing behind to betray that fact. *Poor Skandranon. By now he must be sure there's another Ma'ar around.*

Hadanelith giggled at the thought; he had thought that the role of a kestra'chern would give him ample scope for his fantasies, but what he had accomplished then was a pale shadow of the pleasures he had now. This situation had so much to recommend it! A free hand with his targets—even if they weren't of his choosing—was worth any amount of interference from his hosts, and, in fact, they actually gave him very little interference. The delicious moment when his targets realized that they were completely in his power and there was no help coming—that was better than all the tame slaves in the world!

Add to that the chance to terrify the so-powerful Skandranon and a way to undo everything that those presumptuous prigs from White Gryphon were trying to accomplish, and he had pleasure and revenge all in one tidy little packet.

All of these were equally delightful reasons to pursue his current course. But beyond those was the most delightful of all.

Personal revenge. Revenge on Amberdrake, who had dared to sit in judgment on *him.* Revenge on Skandranon, who had given Amberdrake the authority to throw Hadanelith to the wolves. Revenge on *all* of those fools of White Gryphon, who agreed with Amberdrake and Skandranon and who tamely went along with anything those two wanted.

Hadanelith would prove that he was cleverer, craftier, superior to all of them. Wasn't he proving it now? His hosts thought that they were the ones in control of the situation, that they held Hadanelith's leash. They didn't know he was the one using them.

Once the news of the Kaled'a'in settlement reached the Haighlei, Noyoki had scryed the area around White Gryphon during one of the few times that his magic worked properly. He was nobly educated; he knew several northern languages, and he had probably done his scrying in the vague hope of discovering a malcontent among the Kaled'a'in that he could make use of. He found Hadanelith, skulking around the guarded periphery, stealing from the gardens—and he'd scryed out people who knew something of Hadanelith's so-called "crimes."

He'd sent swift hunters and a small, fast vessel of his own to find Hadanelith and bring him back. That much, Noyoki had conveyed to him in his own language, obviously hoping to get some sort of gratitude in return.

Hadanelith kept his own counsel and simply looked agreeable. After he'd used his own rudimentary powers of mind-magic to pluck their own language out of their heads, he had made one small error out of sheer pique. He'd been so annoyed with Noyoki's callous remarks about how he planned to exploit Hadanelith's "madness" that he'd revealed his own knowledge of their tongue before he'd taken thought to what that slip might cost him.

Still, that sudden expertise in their tongue had impressed them no end. And he'd discovered with that slight mistake just how horrifying they found the bare concept of mind-magic. Forewarned, he'd managed to pass his sudden proficiency off as simple intelligence, and perhaps a side-effect of his "madness," rather than the use of anything forbidden.

So now he had a double advantage over them; he knew their language much better than they had any notion that he did, and he could occasionally read their thoughts. He knew that while they were aware he was of the same general race as Amberdrake, they did not know that he actually *knew* Amberdrake. They had no idea that he had his own little vendetta to pursue, and that they were helping him to do so.

So much the better. The less they realized that he *wanted* to do what he was doing for more reasons than just the obvious, the more power over them he held.

He shaved another sliver of wood from a curve of the sculpture and ran his finger over it to assure himself that there were no splinters or rough spots there. That would not do at all.

It was interesting that his "partners" were not at all horrified by the various acts he perpetrated on their chosen targets. In fact, so far as Noyoki was concerned, the more—artistic—the better. Noyoki apparently had more reasons than one himself for choosing these women; Hadanelith had sensed a deep and abiding resentment, even hatred, for each of them. That was interesting, too. Hadanelith intended to continue watching Noyoki's thoughts for more such information. Information was power, and one could never have too much power.

As for Kanshin, he was indifferent to the fate or plight of anyone except himself. Hadanelith found that attitude laudable as well as practical—and the exact opposite of those idiots from White Gryphon, who concerned themselves over the fate of every little social butterfly, slave, and useless leech.

Together the two of them fit very neatly into his plan. Noyoki obviously wanted the envoys from White Gryphon discredited and disgraced at the very least, and possibly destroyed at the most. Kanshin wouldn't care what Hadanelith did as long as *he* continued to get paid.

So now that some shadows had been cast over the reputations of the newcomers, Hadanelith would pour a little more fuel over the fire.

Before Amberdrake died—and he *would* die, in disgrace and despair—Hadanelith would see that he suffered all the agonies that only so sensitive a person was capable of suffering.

He had arranged via Kanshin to have some of Amberdrake's distinctive finery filched from the Palace laundry. Not enough of it to be missed, at least not immediately, but just enough to leave a few incriminating clues at the site of the next little exercise. Amberdrake's combination of Kaled'a'in styles and kestra'chern construction and luxury, with the specially woven fabrics and elaborate bead-fringes, were absolutely unique to him and him alone.

Hadanelith took up a fine wood rasp and began smoothing the surface of the carving, smiling with anticipation. This would be so sweet, so very sweet! The next victim would be left bound and gagged as well as whatever else Noyoki wanted him to simulate, and the Haighlei would find the tantalizing little bits of evidence nearby, as if torn from the murderer's clothing. There was no way that they could mistake these things for something Haighlei—oh, no. They would be identifiable immediately as distinctly foreign, and then as distinctly in the style of no one else but Amberdrake.

Suspicion would move from Skandranon—for the moment—to Amberdrake. Unlike Skandranon, however, it was not likely that Amberdrake would have any watchers to provide him with an alibi.

There *was* one small flaw in this plan. It was just barely possible that Amberdrake would recall Hadanelith and his predilection for bindings and gaggings . . . and might remember that Hadanelith knew more about him than anyone else outside the White Gryphon delegation. It might occur to him to wonder if somehow Hadanelith had found his way *here*, to Khimbata, Shalaman's capital.

But even if he did, there was still the large matter of convincing the Haighlei that Hadanelith could be the guilty party. His story of a mad kestra'chern banished into the wilderness, who had mysteriously transported himself to the capital to begin murdering high-ranked Haighlei, would be so ridiculous that no one would be foolish enough to give it credence. It would sound like something made up out of pure desperation—and not concocted very well, either.

In fact, if I told myself my own story, I wouldn't believe it. Hadanelith giggled and continued to smooth the dense, dark wood with his rasp. *No matter how logically he presents it, no one would* ever *believe a wild tale like that. He could bring all the witnesses he liked, and it would make no difference. No one here has seen me but my two partners, and my little playmates. My partners aren't likely to talk, and as for my*

*playmates—unless someone here has the ability to speak
with the spirits, they are otherwise occupied.*

He giggled hysterically at his own wit while he continued
to work on his latest sculpture. Perhaps, when he didn't need
it anymore, he would present this one to Noyoki.

I may never come to truly understand these people, Amberdrake thought with resignation. Winterhart told him that
he didn't need to understand them as long as he could follow
the logic of their customs, but he had been a kestra'chern for
too long to ever be content with anything that superficial. Life
at Court had gotten back to a semblance of normalcy—as normal as it could be, with three murders being gossiped about,
and foreigners under suspicion. Nevertheless, the Haighlei being what they were, custom, even in the face of murder, must
be observed.

Which meant that every night must contain Evening
Court, and every Evening Court must be followed by an Entertainment. Tonight the Entertainment was a play, a very
stylized play, accompanied by equally stylized music. Amberdrake had to admit that this one baffled him, even with his experience in all manner of entertainments. The actors wore
heavy masks and their dialogue was chanted to the sounds of
a drum and two particularly nasal-sounding instruments, one
a stringed thing and one a reed flute. Their multicolored, multilayered costumes were so complicated that the actors had to
move slowly when they could move at all. The scenery was
sketchy at best—a plant in a pot represented the jungle, a
screen invoked a bedroom, a spindly desk someone's office or
study. The tiniest gesture of a finger was supposed to convey
entire volumes of information, but the gestures were so arcane
that only an aficionado could ever decipher them. The result
was that Amberdrake had given up even pretending to watch
the play, and had moved away so that the music didn't give
him a headache.

He wasn't the only one ignoring the piece, however; it
seemed that most of the Haighlei were doing the same. One
wasn't required to sit and be a "proper" audience for this piece

the way one was for a performance of the Royal Dancers, and little knots of conversation had formed all over the room. Only a few folk still sat on the cushions provided in front of the tiny stage. Either the rest of them already knew this thing by heart, or it was as annoying to the natives as it was to a foreigner.

Very possibly the latter! he thought with amusement. It must be rather disheartening for the performers, however. Perhaps they were used to it. Perhaps they didn't care as long as they were paid. Or perhaps they were content to display their complicated art for the benefit of the few faithful. He managed to have a rather lively discussion with another envoy regarding the merits of several different massage-lotions for the treatment of aged joints, and he was looking for Winterhart when the musicians suddenly stopped in the middle of a phrase with a decidedly unmusical squawk, and the performance end of the room, where both Emperor Shalaman and "King" Skandranon were ensconced erupted into frenzied activity.

Naturally, Amberdrake and everyone else at his end of the room hurried over to find out what the fuss was about, expecting it to be something minor—someone who'd been slighted or insulted by another courtier, perhaps, or even word of a dangerous lion attacking a village. King Shalaman was famous for his lion hunts, but he never hunted anything but man-killers, and there hadn't been one of those in several years. Amberdrake found himself shuffled right up to the front of the crowd with absolutely no expectation of trouble in his mind—just as a grim-faced Leyuet and his brace of Spears of the Law laid bloody evidence of yet another murder down in front of Shalaman and Skan.

Amberdrake froze, as did everyone else within sight of the relics. There were bloodstained ropes and a ball-gag, torn clothing—

And then Amberdrake's heart stopped beating completely, for among the evidence was a bit of beaded fringe that could only have come from one of his own costumes.

No—no, it can't—

His face froze into an expression of absolute blankness, and his mind went numb, as he recognized more of the bits of torn clothing as his own.

This isn't possible!

Fear clutched a chilling hand around his throat, choking off his breath, and he went cold as all eyes turned toward him. He was not the only one to have recognized those telltale bits of finery.

How did that—where—how— His thoughts ran around like mice trapped in a barrel.

Skandranon rose from his seat, his hackles raised and his eyes dilated with rage, as a murmur passed through the crowd. At that point the courtiers began to back away from Amberdrake, leaving him the center of a very empty space, the evidence of terrible murder lying practically at his feet.

"These things—" Leyuet poked at the bead fringe, the torn cloth, with the end of his staff, "These things, clearly the property of the foreigner Amberdrake, were found with the body, oh King," he said stiffly, clearly continuing a statement he had begun before Amberdrake got there. "The bit of fringe was found in her hand. The death occurred at the afternoon recess, when Amberdrake dismissed his servants and there are thusly no witnesses to Amberdrake's whereabouts save only his own people—"

Skandranon let out his breath in a long, startlingly loud hiss, interrupting Leyuet in mid-sentence. "*I* can vouch for Amberdrake's whereabouts," he said fiercely, yet with surprising control. "But I will do more than vouch for it." He faced Shalaman, who sat his throne as impassively as a carving. "If you suspect Amberdrake of murder despite that, then I must stand prisoner alongside him. Pray recall, Serenity, that you suspected *me* of these murders less than a week ago!"

There was another murmur running through the crowd, these time of surprise mingled with shock, as Skandranon held up his head and challenged both the Emperor and Leyuet with his gaze. "I am as good as any of my fellows and companions from White Gryphon, and they are as trustworthy and law abiding as I. If their integrity is to be under question, then so must mine. I will offer my freedom in trust for their innocence."

Skan's voice carried to the farthest reaches of the room, and Amberdrake managed to shake himself out of shock enough to look around to see the effect of those words. *Oh, sun above, has Skandranon lost the last of his sanity? What is he doing . . . ?* The dumbfoundedness he saw on every face told him without any explanations how unheard of this kind of declaration was. Obviously, no Haighlei ruler would ever have stood personal surety for the honor of a subject; this went quite out of their understanding.

But Urtho would have done the same—

Skan raised himself to his full height, and Amberdrake realized that he was slimmer and more muscular than he had been a few weeks ago. He was changing somehow. Had the gryphon been exercising in secret? "Let it be known that the honor of those I trust is *my* honor!" he said, in the Haighlei tongue, clearly as the call of a trumpet. "This so-called evidence was concocted to cast suspicion upon one who is innocent, just as the other murders were accomplished in such a way as to cast suspicion on me! Amberdrake is innocent of any wrongdoing—and just as I urged the Spears of the Law to seek for the true perpetrator in the last murders, I urge them to do the same now! If you imprison him, you must imprison me as well, for I am as guilty or as innocent as he. I *demand* it! I stand by my companions, in honor and in suspicion!"

Amberdrake nearly choked. Did Skan realize what he was saying? By these peoples' customs, he was linking his *own* fate with that of Amberdrake!

Not that Urtho would not have done the same as well, but—but that was Urtho, Mage of Silence and Adept of more powers than Amberdrake could number!

"And if it is proved that Amberdrake *did* murder, will you die beside him?" That was Palisar, as cagy and crafty as ever, making certain that Skandranon knew what he was doing with his assertions, so that he could not claim later that he was not aware of all of the implications.

Skan snorted contemptuously. "No, of course not," the

gryphon replied immediately. "That would be ridiculous. My friends and I are honorable, but we are not stupid. But if you could *prove,* beyond a shadow of a doubt and to my personal satisfaction, that he had done such a thing, I would deliver the death sentence upon him myself, and I would carry it out myself."

The murmuring swelled to a low rumble, as Leyuet and Palisar stared at both Skan and Amberdrake, and the King blinked thoughtfully. Skandranon had now made it impossible to imprison Amberdrake and perhaps "question" him under torture to extract a spurious confession, yes, but—

But has he lost his mind? Amberdrake was practically ready to gibber and foam at the mouth, although the shrieking voice was only in his own thoughts. *Oh, he's been clever, all right—he's thinking on his feet—*

—and he moved like the old Skandranon, alive with a fire and an enthusiasm that could not be denied.

But had he lost his reasoning to recklessness?

And what about me? his thoughts wailed, as his knees turned weak with fear. *They think I've committed murder, and there's no way to prove them wrong! We can't use magic, we haven't any way to hunt a criminal out, we're strangers here, and the natives aren't likely to look for one of their own when they have a convenient suspect! What am I going to do?*

Never mind that Skan had already been a suspect—*he* at least had solid alibis. Amberdrake had nothing. And whoever was behind these deaths was smart enough to see to it that things remained that way. Except for the first murder, when Amberdrake had been watching the Dance with the others, *he* had no alibi at all for the times those other deaths had taken place. He could be charged, not only with this murder, but with all the rest as well!

What am I going to do? He wanted to run, but he knew he didn't dare even move. He felt horribly like a mouse looking up at the talons of an owl. Anything he did could look suspicious at this point!

As he stood there, frozen with fright and indecision, terror and shock, Skandranon continued to speak, taking the attention of everyone—even Leyuet—off of him. The removal of their multiplied regard freed him somewhat, and he felt the paralysis that had held his limbs weaken its hold over him, but he still didn't know what his very next action should be. How was he going to disprove all this? He was a kestra'chern, his skills didn't lie in investigation! And where was Winterhart? Had they already taken her into custody as an accomplice?

Oh, Star-Eyed, if they've taken her and they're torturing her right now— Paralysis was replaced by panic.

A gentle touch on his arm at that precise moment made him jump, and he began to shake as he turned. *Now* it came—despite anything Skan had said. Leyuet had sent Spears around to take him, arrest him, and carry him off under the cover of the crowd. They'd have a confession out of him in no time and—

But it was *not* a frowning, brawny man who had touched him to get his attention. He turned to gaze into the face of, not a dark and forbidding stranger, but an oh-so-welcome, calm visage he knew just as well as the face in his mirror.

"Silver Veil—what—is happening to—" he began, then forcibly shut his lips on what threatened to turn into hysterical babble as she laid a finger on her own lips.

"Come with me," she said, tucking her hand into the crook of his elbow and leading him to a side entrance of the Audience Chamber. "You and I must talk—and quickly."

Zhaneel did not want to attend Court or the Entertainment, and she had a perfect excuse not to: the gryphlets. Makke was better company than all the courtiers rolled into a bundle.

What was more, Makke was willing to help with them and more willing to learn about them than either of the "nursemaids."

"So, you see?" Zhaneel said, as Makke wiped down the feathers of both gryphlets with a very lightly oiled cloth. "First the bath, then the drying, then the oil. When they are older, they will oil themselves like any bird, but for now we must do so for them. Otherwise, if their feathers get too wet, if they decided to go fishing in the fountain after dark, for instance, they could take a chill."

Makke nodded and sent both of the little ones tumbling away with pats to their hindquarters. In the past few weeks, she had been spending more and more time in the gryphons' suite, time that had nothing to do with any cleaning that was needed. All Makke's children were gone, and the twins had obviously aroused in her all the old maternal urges. Zhaneel had been more confident with Makke in charge of the nursery than she had been in entrusting the safety of the little ones to the young and obviously childless "nursemaids" supplied by the chief of the serving staff.

Makke was clearly surprised, despite all her earlier talks with Zhaneel, that anyone of Zhaneel's rank would grant her such a privilege. She had even protested, once or twice, that this was not the sort of thing that she should be allowed to do.

"But you have been a mother, have you not?" Zhaneel had said, with patient logic.

Makke had nodded slowly.

"And you know and love children, you see my two imps as *children* and not as some sort of odd pet." That was the problem with the "nursemaids," who had probably been brought in from the ranks of those normally in attendance on the many animals that courtiers brought with them. The girls treated the gryphlets as beloved pet animals, not as children—expecting a degree of self-sufficiency from them that the youngsters simply didn't have yet. They might be as large as any of the biggest lion-hunting mastiffs, but you simply *couldn't* leave them alone for any length of time without them getting themselves into some kind of trouble. Tadrith, in particular, had a genius for getting himself into situations he couldn't get out of.

"That is so, great lady," Makke had admitted.

"Then you are the correct person to help me with them," Zhaneel had said firmly. "We of White Gryphon count what is in one's heart far more important than what caste one is born into. For those of us who shared the same trials, bore the same burdens, rank has come to mean very little."

Normally Makke came to the nursery with smiles wreathing her wrinkled old face, but tonight she had been unaccountably gloomy. Now she watched the two youngsters play with such a tragic hunger in her eyes that it might as well be the *last* time she ever expected to do so. Even as Zhaneel watched, the old woman blinked rapidly, as if she were attempting to hold back tears with an effort.

"Makke!" Zhaneel exclaimed, reaching out to her. "What is wrong?"

"Nothing, nothing, great lady—" Makke began, but then her resolve and her courage both crumpled, and she shook her head, tears spilling out of her soft dark eyes and pouring over her withered cheeks. "Oh, lady—" she whispered tightly, blotting at her eyes with her sash. "Oh, lady—I am old, my children are gone, I have nowhere to go—and I must leave the Court—I have disgraced myself and I will be dismissed, and once I have been dismissed, I will die. There is nowhere that will shelter me—"

"Dismissed?" Zhaneel interrupted sharply. "Why? What could you possible have done that they would dismiss you for? I *need* you, Makke, isn't that—"

"But you cannot trust me, lady!" Makke wailed softly, her face twisted with despair, the tears coming faster. "You must not trust me! I have failed in my duty and my trust, and you cannot ever dare to trust me with so precious a thing as your children, can you not see that? And I will be dismissed because I have failed in my trust! I *must* be dismissed! It is better that a worthless old rag as I should go after so failing in my duty!"

"But what have you *done?*" Zhaneel persisted, now seriously alarmed. "What on earth have you done?" A hundred dire possibilities ran through her mind. Makke was old, and sometimes the old made mistakes—oh, horrible thought! Could she have accidentally hurt or poisoned someone? Could she have let the fact that she suspected the Kaled'a'in of having mind-magic slip to one of the Priests? Could she have allowed someone of dubious reputation into the Palace?

Could she even, somehow, have been indirectly involved in the murders Skan had been accused of?

"Tell *me!*" Zhaneel demanded, insistently. "Tell me what you have done!"

"I—" Makke's face crumpled even further, and her voice shrank to a hoarse whisper, as she yielded to the long habit of instantly obeying those in a caste above hers. "I—oh, great lady! It is dreadful—dreadful! I have cast disgrace over myself for all time! I lost someone's—" Her voice fell to a tremulous whisper. "*laundry.*"

She—no— Zhaneel felt her beak gaping open. "You— what?" She shook her head violently. "You lost—laundry? And for *this* you would be dismissed and disgraced?" She shook her head again, and the words made no more sense than they had before. She blurted out the first thing that came into her mind. "Are you people *insane?*"

She did not doubt Makke, nor that events would follow precisely as Makke described. But—dismissal? For *that?*

"Great lady—" Makke dabbed at her eyes and straightened a little, trying to meet Zhaneel's gaze without breaking down again. "Great lady, it is a matter of honor, you see. If it were my own laundry, or that of the Chief of Servants—or even that of a ranking lady, it would be of—of less concern. But it is the *envoy's* laundry that I have lost. I *must* be dismissed, for there is no greater punishment for such carelessness, and it is our way that the punishment must equal the rank of the victim. This is—in our law, it is the same as if I had stolen his property. I am a thief, and I deserve no better, surely you must see this."

"I see nothing of the kind," Zhaneel said stoutly. "I see only that this is all nonsense, quickly put right with a word to Amberdrake. Unless—" She clenched her claws in vexation; if Makke had already told the Chief of the servants what had happened, there was no way that Zhaneel could save the situation. "You haven't told anyone but me yet, have you?"

Makke shook her head miserably. "I have not yet confessed my crime, great lady," she said, tears pouring down her cheeks afresh. "But I wanted to say farewell to you and to the little ones before my dismissal. Please forgive—"

"There is nothing to forgive, Makke, and I do *not* want you to report this until you and I have had a chance to speak with Skandranon and Amberdrake—" Zhaneel began, reaching out her left talon to surreptitiously hook the hem of Makke's robe so that the old woman could not run off without tearing herself free of Zhaneel's grip. "I—"

The door to the suite opened, thudding into the wall.

Makke and Zhaneel turned as one, as surprised by the fact that no one had knocked as the fact that the door had hit the wall.

Winterhart stood in the doorway, one hand clutching a wreath of tawny-gold lilies, the other at her throat, convulsed around an elaborate necklace of carved amber lilies and solid gold and bronze sun-disks. Her face was as pale as a cloud, and her expression that of a stunned deer.

She stumbled into the room as Makke and Zhaneel stared, and fumbled the door shut behind her.

"Winterhart?" Zhaneel said, into the leaden silence. "What is wrong?"

Winterhart looked at Zhaneel as if she had spoken in some strange tongue; she licked her lips, blinked several times, and made two or three efforts to reply before she finally got any words out.

"The—King," she said hoarsely, her eyes blank with disbelief. "Shalaman—"

"What *about* him?" Zhaneel persisted, when she fell silent.

But when Winterhart spoke again, it was Zhaneel's turn to stare with disbelief.

"He—" Winterhart's hands crushed the lilies, and her knuckles whitened under the strain. "He has asked me to marry him."

"You must confine us both to our suites," Skandranon was insisting, to an increasingly alarmed Leyuet. "You must place us under guard, if you will not imprison us."

Frantically, Leyuet looked around for a higher authority,

but the King and Palisar were both gone, Silver Veil had vanished earlier with Amberdrake, and only he and Skandranon were together in this little side-chamber. This, of course, was precisely the way Skan wanted things.

He's one of Shalaman's protocol administrators. These demands are going to send him into a spinning frenzy. He can't grant them, of course. I already made the bold, dramatic gesture, which forced the King to counter it with a bold, dramatic sign of trust.

"The Emperor has decreed that nothing of the kind is to occur," Leyuet said at last, forced to rely on his own judgment. "You must *not* be placed under arrest. Such a thing would be dishonorable. It is impossible to agree to this demand of yours."

I know, Skan thought smugly. *That's why I made it.*

"Are you saying that I am free to move about this Court as I will? That this is what the Emperor wants?" Skan retorted, allowing skepticism to creep into his voice. "That can't be right."

"I tell you, it is!" Leyuet insisted, his face now so contorted with concern that it resembled a withered fruit. "You must move freely about the Court—nay, the Court, the Palace, the entire city! This is the King's decree! This is how he shows his trust in you!"

There is a certain glint in his eyes . . . I think he has finally figured out that this might be a better move on their part than trying to keep us locked up. After all, that didn't work before. If we actually were guilty, this kind of freedom might make us careless, and give them a chance to trap us, and I'm sure those are precisely the thoughts that are going through Leyuet's mind at this very moment.

So, there would probably be watchers, covert and overt, keeping an eye on Skan and Amberdrake at all times. That was just fine with Skandranon. He *wanted* to be watched.

He continued to express doubt, though, and Leyuet continued to express the King's wishes, and all the while he was making plans, grateful that it was very difficult to read a gryphon's facial expressions.

*I will wait until Kechara contacts me tonight, and I will
tell Judeth to send only the Silvers and keep the rest of the
delegation at home. I'll tell her to fortify White Gryphon. We
might yet need to defend the settlement before this is over.*

And he had one more request of Judeth; one he knew that
she would understand. He had a list of things he wished her to
take out of the storage chests in his lair—and he would ask her
to prepare and send a cask of ebony feather-dye.

And last, but by no means least, he would bid her to tell the
settlement of White Gryphon that the Black Gryphon was
back.

The Black Gryphon is back.

Shalaman had long been in the habit of listening to his
court secretaries with half of his mind, while the other half
mused on subjects that had nothing to do with the minor is-
sues at hand. Whatever he left to the secretaries to read to him
was minor, after all; that was why he had them read these let-
ters to him after Evening Court and the Entertainment, and
just before he retired. He had a mind that was, perhaps, a trifle
too active; he needed to tire it or he would never be able to
sleep.

So the secretaries read the innumerable petitions, and he
grunted a "yes," "no," or "later—delay him," and he let his
thoughts circle around other quarry.

Tonight, they circled Winterhart, that strange, pale beauty
from the North. Engaging—nay, fascinating! She had many of
the attributes of the incomparable Silver Veil, but unlike a
kestra'chern, Winterhart was attainable. . . .

*Silver Veil could never give heart and soul to any single per-
son. No kestra'chern can. That is why they are kestra'chern;
their hearts are too wide for a single person to compass. But
Winterhart—ah, Winterhart—*

Like Silver Veil in elegance, in grace . . . not precisely a
shadow of the kestra'chern, but reachable. Shalaman had
learned, if he had learned anything at all, that there was no
point in yearning for the unattainable. Better to have the

moonflower that one could touch than to lose one's heart to the moon.

Logic gave him plenty of arrows to spend against the target of Palisar's inevitable objections. *This would be a valuable gesture; even in the light of the murders. Should Amberdrake prove to be the murderer, he will be repudiated, and wedding her would mollify the northerners. Marrying her would create the kind of alliance that would bring them into my Kingdom as vassals rather than allies. The gryphons alone are worth wedding her for!*

So he would tell Palisar and Leyuet—though he did not think that the Truthsayer would object, only the Speaker.

He would not tell them his other reasons.

This is the kind of woman, like Silver Veil, who could make me happy when I am not in the Court's gaze. Silver Veil was not always there when he needed—company, companionship, pure and simple. She had other duties, others who needed her skills as much as he. Winterhart could be only for him.

She said little enough about herself, but he sensed that she hid depths that she had not disclosed. She carried herself well, unconsciously projecting a nobility of spirit that spoke of noble birth, just like Silver Veil. But unlike Silver Veil, her surface was not entirely flawless; there were hints of vulnerability. One could reach her if one tried.

He had ten Year-Sons and two Year-Daughters, born of the Year-Brides of his first decade of rule. He need not wed her for heirs, for he needed none. He could wed her for himself alone.

The first secretary coughed and reached for water, his throat raw. Shalaman waved to the second to begin where the first had left off, as his thoughts drifted northward—not to Winterhart, but to the place where she had come from.

White Gryphon; no parrot in the world can crack that palm-fruit. His spies had drifted through the city in the guise of sailors and other harmless sorts, and the word that they sent back was of caution. The city was built for defense, and with very little work could be made impregnable. Technically, it was within his borders—but only technically. If he had to

make war upon them, his allies would rightly say that a settlement perched so precariously on the edge of his lands was
not worth disputing over. His allies would be correct. There
were troubles enough in his Empire without taking on a nasty
little border war. The sudden failure of magic and the strange
creatures emerging from the deserts and jungles in the wake of
magical catastrophe were quite enough to occupy the rest of
his tenure on the Lion Throne.

As for the newcomers themselves, unlike Palisar, he saw no
harm in them. They were a fact; they were not going to leave,
and their very existence meant a change in Haighlei ways,
whether or not anyone admitted it. Precedent was important, too, since there might yet be more Northerners to come.
If they came, they would mean change, too.

*We desire change even as we fear it. Like children looking
for demons in the dark, but hoping the demons will bring us
three wishes, or wealth, or magic carpets to ride. . . .*

And whether or not Palisar liked the presence of the newcomers and the changes they would bring, their discovery on
the eve of the twenty-year Eclipse Ceremony was too seren-
dipitous to be coincidental. *If I were a religious man, I would
call it an omen.*

Even Palisar would accept and embrace a change that was
mandated at the height of the Eclipse. *When the sun vanishes
at midday, then change comes to the Haighlei.* That was the
word in the holy books themselves, many of which had been
written following changes that came with the Ceremonies of
the past. *It was wise of our gods to give us this. We love things
to remain the same, but if they remain the same forever, we
will rot as a people. Pah, if they had remained the same forever, we would still be a collection of little villages of
thatched huts, hunting with copper-headed spears, growing
only yams, lying in fear of the lions in the dark! Or else—a na-
tion more flexible would have discovered us and carried us
away to be slaves in their fields.*

"Tell him it is impossible until after the Eclipse," he said,
in answer to one of the petitions. "If it is still an issue then, I
will reconsider."

Many of the current petitions could be put off until after the Eclipse. Many of them were not problems at all, only the perception of a problem, and simply delaying a decision would make it less of a perceived problem with every passing day. Others—well, they tied in with the decisions *he* would have to make about these people from White Gryphon, and none of them could be resolved until he decided what he was going to do about them *and* made his decrees . . .

. . . or did not.

At that point, it would become the problem of his successor, for he did not foresee himself living to see another Eclipse Ceremony. Nothing whatsoever could be done about the outlanders until the next Ceremony.

And there are a fair number of Emperors who resolved such tricky problems by just such a postponement, he thought wryly.

But again, Winterhart came into his thoughts. She could be the perfect, symbolic embodiment of that change; the focus for it, the way to present it to Shalaman's more doubting or hidebound subjects in an acceptable form.

If only Silver Veil—

But Silver Veil was a kestra'chern, and she, too, was bound by the edicts of the ages. She was not for any one man. Her office was too important, and not even the Emperor could take her for himself.

He had already proposed marriage to Winterhart anyway, this evening, before that dreadful interruption of the Entertainment.

She had been overwhelmed, of course, as any woman would. She had stammered something about being bound to Amberdrake, though, and there *was* a child, now that he came to think about it—

Shalaman was too well-schooled to frown, but his thoughts darkened for a moment.

Still, that may not be a problem for long, after this evening. In a way, the fourth murder had come as something of a blessing. It was rather difficult for even the most sensitive to be dreadfully upset about the death of that harridan, Lady Fanshane. She had moved into the life of Lady Sherisse years ago, turning the poor thing into a man-hating recluse, and she was cordially detested by most of the wiser folk in Shalaman's Court. And once Lady Sherisse had drunk herself into an early grave, Lady Fanshane had been circling the court like a vulture, looking for another victim to fatten on.

Still, she *had* been murdered, and murder was a crime most foul (and never mind that in the laws of return, Lady Fanshane could be considered guilty of the murder of her former paramour), and evidence was mounting that it was Amberdrake who was guilty of that crime, and perhaps the previous three murders as well. Once there was enough evidence, Amberdrake would be out of the way, and Winterhart would be free to accept the honor that the Emperor had offered her.

He might be innocent, muttered a third part of his mind, a part he seldom heard from. *This might be some strange conspiracy, and Amberdrake the victim of it as much as those who were slain.*

No. That was utter nonsense. If—*if*—Amberdrake were truly innocent, why had he not asked for the services of the Truthsayer immediately? If his conscience was clear, the Truthsayer would know; as the King's guest, he was entitled to the offices of the highest Truthsayer in the land, Leyuet, who was also the leader of the Spears of the Law. If Leyuet declared him innocent, not even Palisar would challenge that declaration.

So, obviously, he had something to fear from a Truthsayer's examination.

But what if these people know nothing of Truthsayers? niggled that annoying little voice. *What if he does not know he has the right to such an examination? It is magic, after all, and all the outlanders have been cautioned against the use of magic. Why, what if they do not even have such a thing as Truthsayers among them? How can he ask for something he is not aware exists?*

Oh, that was nonsense! Of course these people must have Truthsayers! How could any society exist without the means to tell truth from falsehood? That was insane! Besides, wouldn't

Silver Veil have said something if there were no such things as Truthsayers among the cultures of the north?

No, Amberdrake, if not directly guilty, knew something of the murders, enough to make him fear the touch of Leyuet's mind on his. That would make him guilty of conspiracy to murder, which was just as great a crime as murder itself.

It would be only a matter of time now. Either the evidence would become irrefutable, Amberdrake would slip up and be caught, or he would finally break down and confess.

And then Winterhart would be free—and once she was free, she would be his. Then he would be lonely no more.

Hadanelith flung open the windows of the darkened chamber, and the night breeze blew the gauzy curtains about, giving them the uncanny semblance of grasping, ectoplasmic hands.

This would be the first time he had dispatched two victims within a day of each other—but the Haighlei were expecting the same pattern as the last time, and they had all let their guards down in the wake of the last murder.

Fools; they patterned their lives like pieces on a gameboard, and expected everyone else to do the same!

Even this rather ineffectual old biddy; she had followed the same pattern every night for as long as he and Kanshin had watched her. It had been child's play to insinuate himself up the wall and into her chamber after she dismissed all of her servants for the night. She hated the sounds of other people breathing in their sleep (or worse, snoring), or so Kanshin said, and she would not abide another human being or animal in her chambers after she retired for the night. She would ring a bell to summon her servants once she awoke, but from the moment she took to her bed to the moment she left it, she was alone. And not even a murderer on the loose would induce her to change that pattern.

Fool.

Hadanelith had pinned Lady Linnay to her bed, stuffed the end of his latest special carving down her throat to prevent even the slightest sound out of her—

That was a bit unsatisfactory. I would have liked to have heard her beg.

Then he had dragged her over to the window, his skin pressed against her bedclothes, at precisely the spot she *might* have stood if she'd heard something large—say, the size of a gryphon—land on her balcony. Then he pretended to let her go.

Predictably—*Pah, these fools are so tediously predictable!*— she had turned to run, and he had struck her down from behind with his new sculpture, a club carved into the exact likeness of a gryphon's foreleg.

He opened the window now, so that the overwhelming body of evidence would be that it was open before she died. Then he stood over her unconscious body, and raised his club again.

As he brought it down in a punishing blow, regretting the necessity of doing this in the dark, he felt just a little bored. These Haighlei as a whole were just not interesting prey—the Kaled'a'in may have been sanctimonious, sickeningly sweet prigs, but at least they *did* something once in a while. The Haighlei just lined up like good little sheep for his knife. They didn't even alter their habits when it was obvious who and what kinds of folk his targets were!

Well, they aren't really important, he consoled himself with a grim smile, bringing the club down on the body with all of his strength. *They aren't my real prey, anyway. They're only tools. Their deaths are not the end, only the means. They're only the stepping stones to my real goal, the ladder to reach my revenge.*

Although—actually, this was turning out to be a little more interesting than he had thought it would. *I've never actually beaten anyone to death before. Hmm. Fascinating. I didn't realize how much punishment a body could take and still breathe!* He knew it could be done, of course; provided nothing like the spleen or the skull was injured, a great deal of injury could be inflicted in theory before the body was so broken that it literally bled to death from bruising. But he'd never actually witnessed such a thing.

In fact, he thought, beginning to feel some of that manic strength coming into his arm that only the best kills brought out in him, *this is rather fun!*

He wanted to giggle, but he kept his mirth well-contained as energy poured into him and the club felt as if it weighed no more than a straw. It rose and fell of its own accord, and he brought it down, over and over, harder and harder, the thudding of wood into flesh pounding in his ears like the thumping of his own heartbeat pounding with excitement and—

The club splintered. He heard the *crack* of the wood over the dull sound of the blow.

He stopped in mid-swing, immediately. *He* was too well-trained, and much too clever, to risk a final strike and leave behind even a single shred of evidence that it had *not* been the claw of a gryphon that had done the deed. Instead, he stood over the now-motionless body, breathing heavily, while he surveyed his handiwork as best he could by moonlight.

Quite impressive. He'd left the head intact except for the initial blow that had rendered her unconscious. For the rest—there was nothing to show that she had *not* been bludgeoned to death by the fisted claw of a gryphon. There were the cuts and tears in the skin that even a claw closed tightly could and *would* leave, and the telltale signs of the essentially bony nature of the "hand" that had beaten her. Virtually every bone in her torso had been smashed, however, and the stiff and structured Haighlei would assume that no human could do that.

Which will leave the obvious, of course. Skandranon.

Lady Linnay had been one of Lady Fanshane's few friends, and had been one of the loudest in her insistence that Amberdrake was guilty and must be made to pay then and there. And as such, she became an obvious target for Kaled'a'in elimination.

Hadanelith grinned as he moved carefully away from the body. Somewhere nearby, Noyoki was capturing all of the potent energy released by this death, and channeling it into whatever project *he* had in mind. Kanshin waited above, with a rope-ladder, ready to spirit him off the balcony and across two rooftops. Noyoki would meet them both there, and use a bit more of that channeled energy to lift them down to the ground, noiselessly, and efficiently, putting them all in a garden cul-de-sac where Kanshin had concealed the servants' livery they had worn earlier to move through the Palace grounds.

Of course, no one who was not a Palace servant would ever even *think* of wearing Palace livery—nor would the Spears of the Law consider that possibility. It was simply Not Done. Here, all crimes worked by ritual and custom!

Hadanelith backed up onto the balcony, glad for the first time of his pale skin, which blended into the stonework very nicely. Of course, Kanshin would have contrived to look like a shadow, but still—

Still, even he hasn't got the audacity to do work like this in the nude. Even if this murder was discovered before they got off the Palace grounds, watchers would search in vain for bloodstained clothing. There wouldn't be any. And one quick wash with the bucket of water that Kanshin had up there with the ladder would remove any trace of evidence from Hadanelith's person.

I will never forget their faces when I told them how I planned to avoid getting blood on my clothing. And of course, for all but one of these old hags, the sight of a naked man in their rooms was shocking enough to stun them all by itself. They didn't even think to scream until I'd made screaming impossible.

The only time he had worn *anything* had been this very afternoon, when he'd worn just a bit of Amberdrake's stolen finery. He'd let his target struggle just enough to tear the clothing from his back in an artistic fashion.

That time he'd brought his change of livery with him, of course. And he'd cleaned himself up in the pool in the prey's own little garden. Had anyone noticed a sign of blood there?

Probably not. But if they did, they'd assume it was Amberdrake cleaning up after himself.

That was the essence of making all of this work; attending to detail. With no bloody clothing to dispose of, that left one detail already taken care of. With no *blood* about, there was nothing for a mage to trace.

He would have to remind Noyoki to cleanse this club very thoroughly, though.

The rope-ladder dropped down from above, and Hadanelith grabbed it, clenching the end of the club between his teeth so that he could use both hands in climbing.

The night breeze felt very good, slipping along his skin like a caress. Was this how a gryphon felt when it flew? Was this how a gryphon felt when it made a good kill, and launched itself up into the vast dark vault of the night sky?

I should have been born a gryphon! he thought, laughing to himself, as he let his energy carry him up the ladder effortlessly. *But no, not a gryphon. Tonight—I was better than a gryphon! Tonight—I was the ultimate predator, the killer of gryphons! Yes. Oh, yes. Tonight, I was* makaar!

Winterhart

Seven

Leyuet was a sorely puzzled man, and his worries dogged his footsteps as he passed through the cool, dimly-lit hallways of the Palace. The rest of the Entertainment had been canceled, of course. That left most of the courtiers at loose ends, with nothing to do but gossip until their normal time to retire. And gossip they certainly would—but Leyuet felt certain that most of them would not come within a bowshot of the truth of tonight's drama.

Even though all the evidence pointed to the foreigner Amberdrake as the author of the latest murder, he himself would never have believed it to be so, *after* he witnessed the foreigner's reaction. Amberdrake had been as shocked as anyone in the room at the revelation of a fourth murder, and his reaction on being accused was to freeze, like a terrified bird. He had not been plotting means to escape the room, he had not come forth immediately with plausible alibis—he had frozen, struck dumb, as any innocent man would.

And seeing his bewilderment and terror, Leyuet would bet his professional reputation that, if he had been asked to perform a Truthsaying on the man, the results would mirror his intuition.

Furthermore, it occurred to him on reflection that the person who spirited himself into four rooms without detection, committed butchery without detection, and spirited himself out again without detection, would not have been stupid enough to leave so many clues behind as to his identity.

Still, though, the first three murders had been made without leaving a signature, as was customary among professional assassins. The foreigners' ways were not those of the Haighlei, though, so perhaps the murderer did not know what should be done. Even in assassinations, customs were to be observed— but only if the assassin knew the customs.

The foreigners don't know the customs of assassination any better than they know how to address a social convention in Court, if that is the case. That is circumstantial evidence, but evidence nonetheless, that a foreigner committed the murders.

He would have said as much to the Emperor in private, if the Gryphon King had not interrupted with his theatrical posturings and outrageous statements. By the time Skandranon was finished and Shalaman had been forced to order both of them free on their own recognizance, there was no point in saying anything, at least not until things calmed down a trifle.

Leyuet had intended to speak to the Emperor in private even before the murder was discovered, but he never got the chance. The Gryphon King had been spending a great deal of time today in the air, although Leyuet had not seen Skandranon anywhere near where the fourth murder had taken place—and anyway, there had been no way to get into the murder room from outside the building. But *why* was he flying about, spying? There was no reason for him to do so. This observation was of a piece with everything else about this series of murders—strange things were occurring all over the Palace, yet none of them fit with the murders or even with each other.

Strange things—such as the Emperor absenting himself from the Entertainment, and only reappearing after the Ho Play was well underway. I could not find him. Silver Veil and Palisar could not find him. Where was he? What was he doing? This play was about his own grandfather; what could have kept him from watching it?

There were others absent this evening, but the Emperor

was conspicuous in his absence. He only appeared after several people had been asking for him.

But there were other questions, more troubling than that, which plagued Leyuet this night—and they *were* about the murders.

I am the Chief Truthsayer of this Kingdom, and at the moment I would be willing to swear that Amberdrake is as innocent of murder as I. What is more, I would be willing to swear that Shalaman thinks so, too. So why *did he not call upon me to exercise my office and settle the accusation immediately?*

When it first appeared that the Gryphon King was a suspect, Leyuet had shrunk from the notion of touching such a strange creature's soul for a full and formal Truthsaying, and Shalaman had not asked it of him. There really had been no need, since the first murder had occurred when Skandranon—and his mate, which accounted for the only two gryphons besides their flightless children—was under the eyes of hundreds of spectators, and the next two when he was under guard. The suspicion was really only in the minds of those who hated and feared the foreigners in the first place, and was eventually dismissed without Leyuet's intervention, as the Truthsayer had hoped.

I could understand and appreciate the Emperor's reluctance to ask me to examine the mind of the Gryphon King— after all, I was reluctant myself and he surely saw that. Skandranon is not human, and I might not be able to read his soul, or trying to do so might cause me damage or distress. But Amberdrake is as human as I, and there should be no question of my being able to read him. Even if the foreigners are unaware that calling a Truthsayer is their right, the Emperor *certainly knows! So* why *did he not call upon me? I was waiting!*

Shalaman seldom forgot anything; with Leyuet standing there and Amberdrake accused of a terrible crime, surely he could not have "forgotten" to ask Leyuet to exercise his chief office! So *why* had Shalaman done nothing? Innocence *or* guilt could have been settled in a single evening!

And while under Shalaman's gaze—and command—it would have been improper of me to volunteer. Protocol must be observed.

Leyuet turned a corner and realized that he had quite missed the corridor he wanted; his feet had taken him in the direction of the Guest Quarters—and Silver Veil's suite—without him intending anything of the sort. He knew that Silver Veil was with Amberdrake now, possibly advising him, so there was no point in going on.

My heart knows what I need—but he has need of advice more than I. Surely I can unravel this by myself, if I can only see all the clues.

He turned, and was about to retrace his steps, when he saw that he was no longer alone in the corridor.

Stumbling blindly toward him, a look of stunned bewilderment on her face, was the foreign woman Winterhart. Leyuet would have attributed her expression to the terrible accusation laid against her mate, if not for two things. One, was that he knew that *she* had not been in the room when the accusation was laid.

And where was she if she was not there?

And two, an observation that left *him* stunned—she wore the Royal Betrothal Necklace of amber lilies and golden lion heads about her neck, and she carried in one hand the wreath of ten Lion Lilies, signifying the King's intention to wed her.

Her eyes saw nothing, and he pressed himself back up against the smooth wooden paneling of the wall, hoping the dim light would disguise his identity. With luck, she would take him for a servant.

She walked numbly past him, clearly lost in her own thoughts and paying no attention whatsoever to him, as he stared at her with his mouth slightly agape. His own thoughts swirled with confusion for a moment.

And suddenly, the reason for the King's inaction became blindingly, painfully clear.

Shalaman wanted Winterhart.

But Winterhart was bound to Amberdrake, by whatever simplistic rites these barbarians used as marriage. There was a child, in fact, a girl-child called Windsong, or so Silver Veil had told him.

Now, if Winterhart *chose* not to be bound by such things, then she would not be considered wedded, not by the laws of this land. Even among the Haighlei, most women would be so overwhelmed by the King's offer that even a legal marriage would be—dealt with.

Such things had happened before. If the woman were already wedded, she and her family, and possibly even her *husband* and his family, would do all that they could to hurry through a divorce so that she could be free to wed the King. Most marriages were arranged by parents, anyway, and a woman had only to declare her soul at complete opposite to that of her husband for a priest to make a marriage null and void. There was no particular disgrace in that, provided the husband also agreed. And in the case of the King's indicating his interest—well, there could be considerable status and profit in being the amiable and agreeable ex-husband of the new Royal Consort.

Fortunes had been made, and noble rank achieved, by men who had been willing to honor the King's interests before their own.

But that was only true where there were no bonds of the heart and soul. Now, admittedly, Winterhart was so poised and self-controlled that Shalaman might not be aware of any real attachment to Amberdrake—but it was Leyuet's experience in many long years as a Truthsayer that no woman packed up herself *and* a young and restless child to follow her mate into a strange land if she did not love him dearly, and could not bear to be parted from him.

Which meant that the King's interests would never be fulfilled.

Ordinarily.

He did not think that Winterhart was so dense as to be unaware of how singular an honor this was—but he also did not think that questions of status and opportunity would ever enter into Winterhart's considerations on this subject, either. In fact, he guessed that no threat or bribe would ever force her to break the bonds of the heart that she shared with Amberdrake.

But the death of Amberdrake, as a punishment for murder . . . *that* would break at least the earthly bonds of marriage, leaving the way clear for Shalaman. Even his imprisonment on suspicion alone might do that, if the imprisonment were made for life.

Or if something unfortunate happened to him in prison. Disease, a vengeful relative taking matters into his own hands—these things have happened before, too.

Leyuet stood frozen, his back still pressed up against the paneling of the corridor. It all made sense—horrible, dishonorable sense, but sense still.

He tried to find some other plausible reason for Shalaman's inaction. *The King might not know that they are unaware of the real meaning of my office. I only knew, because Silver Veil asked me about it when she first arrived, and she was astonished to hear that we had such a thing. He might not know that they do not know they can* demand *my services if he does not offer.*

He might not—but Leyuet had the horrible feeling that Shalaman would not raise even a whisper to find out. Not with Winterhart at stake.

Leyuet clenched his hands into fists at his sides, every muscle tight with anxiety. Oh, how was he to deal with this? What was he to do? It was a *dreadful* dilemma!

My duty as Chief Truthsayer is clear. If I even suspect there has been an attempt to circumvent my office, I must arrange for the barbarians to be informed of my function and my duties, and offer myself to them immediately. I must! That is fundamental to all of the oaths I swore! "Let no man be denied the Truth"—no man, be he Haighlei or foreign, and not even the King can deny that!

But his other oaths—the ones he swore when he took office as the King's Advisor, were now in direct conflict with his oaths as a Truthsayer.

I have a duty to honor the wishes of the King. All of this is supposition and suspicion on my part—except for the fact of the Lilies and the Necklace, which make the King's wishes clear to me.

His hands rose of their own accord to hold his temples. This was giving him a headache that surely rivaled any of Palisar's.

I shall never again be tempted to think lightly of his pain!

Which of his duties was the deeper? Shalaman *needed* a Consort; indeed, he and Palisar had been urging him for many, many years to select one. How could he continue in the next twenty-year cycle if there was no female principle beside him to balance his male? And he needed a Consort for his own sake as well; the Royal Consort was the equivalent of a personal kestra'chern in many ways, a kestra'chern Shalaman would never have to share with anyone.

Winterhart looked, to Leyuet's eyes at least, to be fully capable of serving that position admirably. In addition, wedding her would bring the foreigners neatly into the fold without having to concede anything. There would be no need for elaborate arrangements, or for special inclusion in the Eclipse Ceremony—they would become allies by virtue of marriage, the simplest way of all.

But my duty as a Truthsayer—

There had been nothing whatsoever in his training, arduous as it was, that dealt with a situation like *this!*

What do I do when the King, who is the embodiment of the honor of the Haighlei, is—is possibly—acting with less than honor?

Should he confront Shalaman? What good would that do? It was not his place or his right to confront Shalaman over anything—and anything less than an accusatory confrontation would serve no purpose. If Shalaman were innocent of these suspicions, he still would be shamed and lose face before Leyuet.

That would be unthinkable—and for suspecting such a thing, I should offer to take my own life.

If he were guilty—he would deny his guilt and probably still contrive to keep Amberdrake from exercising his rights.

And he might demand that I take my own life. How would

*I know without Truthsaying if he were innocent or guilty? I
cannot Truthsay the Emperor without his leave!*

There was really only one solution, and that was for Leyuet
to redeem Shalaman's honor himself. *The only way to save
this situation is to remove the temptation for Shalaman to act
wrongfully. If I circumvent the need to confront him, then
events will fall as they would have if he had not neglected to
call me forward in the first place.*

That meant that Leyuet, who abhorred taking direct action,
would have to do just that.

*You must make it impossible for Shalaman to make his
"convenient" oversight, Truthsayer,* said a stern, internal
voice, his own voice. *That is the deeper duty, both to your office and to your King. If he is acting without honor, he will be
forced to confront that for himself without having an outside
force confront him. If he was simply forgetful, he will be
saved from the results of that neglect, as is your duty to him
as an Advisor. You, yourself, must go to the barbarians and
make it clear to them what their options are.*

It might possibly be, still, that Shalaman knew something
that Leyuet did not. He might be aware of some reason why
the barbarians would not want Leyuet inside their hearts and
souls. But Leyuet would not *know* that unless he went to the
barbarians himself. Only then would his own conscience and
honor together be clean.

And I cannot sleep this night until I make them clean.

With a weary sigh, Leyuet turned again, and walked slowly
in the footsteps of Winterhart, making his way to her suite in
the Guest Quarters. He would tell her what he must. The next
steps would be up to her—

And to Amberdrake—for Amberdrake, after all, was the one
person around whom this tragedy was revolving, and the
one person who had the power to resolve at least part of it.

*And all of this so close to the Eclipse. Why do the gods tor-
ment and taunt us this way?*

Amberdrake's head and heart were already full of confusion
when he walked in through the door of his rooms, although he

had been relieved of a considerable burden of fear and tension by his graceful mentor.

Now the problems are not threatening my life—at least not immediately—but oh, the problems we've uncovered!

Thanks to Silver Veil, at least *now* he had the means to prove his innocence; the services of someone called a "Truthsayer" would put an end to any accusations. Unfortunately, now there were greater questions to be answered, for it was painfully obvious that someone in this land wanted the Kaled'a'in dead, discredited, or both. And it was absolutely imperative he find out who and why, and soon. . . .

And all this must be done before their Eclipse Ceremony, or we can bid farewell to any kind of arrangements with the Haighlei for another generation or more!

He was hoping to find Winterhart, sanity, and a tiny space of peace in which to muster his thoughts and come up with some plan of action.

Instead, he walked into chaos as soon as he opened the heavy wooden door.

The servant Makke was sitting on the floor and wailing, her face buried in her hands as she rocked back and forth. Zhaneel—and what was *she* doing there?—stood over her with wings mantled and hackles up, as if Makke were one of her gryphlets and under attack. Winterhart sat in the chair by the door that the servants used, staring blankly into space, her face white with shock and a crumpled wreath of flowers at her feet.

And the moment he entered, all three of them started, stared at him as if he was one of Ma'ar's worst creations, then began babbling like a trio of lunatics.

"Forgive me, great lord—I have betrayed you, I have stolen from you—"

"She didn't do anything, neither of them did anything, it is not their fault—"

"Oh, gods—I didn't mean to encourage him—please believe me—Drake, please, you must believe me—"

He clapped his hands over his aching temples and shook his head violently. What on *earth* were they all babbling about?

"Please—" he said faintly, over the din, "Please, one of you at a time—"

As if his plea, faint as it was, had been a thunderous roar, they all fell silent at once, staring at him. He knew he felt as if he had walked through the seven hells in his bare feet, but he didn't think he *looked* that way!

Unfortunately, the silence was just as uninformative as their babbling had been.

I must look worse than I thought. I must look like I've been dragged behind a horse through all the hells of all the religions of the world. They must not have heard . . . they expected me to be Amberdrake the Imperturbable, and I look as shaken as they are, and they don't know why.

This was clearly no time to fall apart and hope for them to pick *him* back up and put him together. It was also clear that what had happened to Winterhart, Zhaneel, and Makke was as serious as a murder accusation, at least in their own eyes.

My immediate problem is settled. Come on, Drake, get a hold on yourself, they need you! He took a deep breath, and pulled himself together. *I am a kestra'chern, dammit! I was a pillar of strength for others as a profession! If I cannot be a rock of sanity at this moment, I can at least pretend to be sane and calm!*

"Easy," he said, in a calm and soothing voice. "Let's sit down and get all this sorted out, shall we?" He smiled at Makke. "Now, what's all this about betrayal?"

In a few minutes, and at the expense of his own nerves, he had a sketchy idea of what had happened while *he* had been dealing with accusations of murder. He told them, with equal brevity, what had happened at the Entertainment. And there was a feeling of sickness in the pit of his stomach about the betrothal offer in light of what he had learned from Silver Veil, a nauseous unease that warned him that there was danger there he had not ever expected. There was also a rising sense of anger. King Shalaman wanted his *mate*. He had been struggling to be at peace with the King, and all the while, Shalaman had been coveting Winterhart! Had they all been fools, assuming that because the Haighlei were formal and civilized, they could not possibly be lustful or treacherous? What were Shalaman and his advisors orchestrating?

But he hadn't even begun to sort it all out, much less get the details from any of the three, when there was a knock at the door. Reflexively, because a kestra'chern was trained to *always* answer a knock, because it might be someone in grave need, he answered it.

He thought, when he opened the door, that he was either hallucinating or caught in a nightmare. It was Leyuet, the leader of those who administered Shalaman's justice—the very man who had just accused him of killing a woman in cold blood.

He's come to imprison me!

That was the first, panicked, thought. But there were no Spears of the Law with the Advisor, which meant he could not have come here for that, at least. But why? And in the name of the gods, why now?

"Ah, Leyuet—" he stammered, trying to think of what the Haighlei protocol would dictate in this situation, "I appreciate that you have come to my quarters, I presume to ask me some questions, but it is very late and this is not a good time—"

"I must speak with you, Lord Amberdrake," the rabbity little man said urgently, actually stepping forward so that Amberdrake had to move back, and thus managing to get himself inside the door. "I must. My honor, the King's, and your life may all depend upon this."

As Leyuet entered, he shut the door behind him, thus preventing Amberdrake from coaxing him out with similar trickery. And at the moment, he did not really look rabbity at all. Haggard, yes—but rather more like a determined and stubborn goat than a rabbit.

Determined, stubborn, and in extreme discomfort. The man was so ill at ease that he radiated it; even Winterhart stared at him with narrowed eyes as if she sensed it, and she was not as Gifted with Empathy as Amberdrake.

"You must listen to me—it is exceedingly important that you understand what I am and what my duties are," Leyuet blurted out, and then launched into a detailed explanation of what a Truthsayer was and did—and that his position as Advisor and Chief of the Spears of the Law was strictly secondary to his vocation as a Truthsayer.

"You are *entitled* to a Truthsayer to establish your innocence, Lord Amberdrake," Leyuet finished, his insides clearly knotted with anxiety, if the state of Amberdrake's own stomach was any indication. "Furthermore, as an envoy, you are entitled to the services of any Truthsayer you may wish to summon. It is serving no purpose to conceal from you that I am one of the best of my kind. If *I* declare you innocent, there can be no doubt of it."

Since Silver Veil had already gone through an even more detailed explanation of a Truthsayer's abilities and duties, Amberdrake saw no reason to doubt him. She had not recommended Leyuet by name—

But the hints she dropped were certainly specific enough that I should have made the connection already. Amberdrake nodded, aware that there was a lot more going on in Leyuet's mind and conscience than the Advisor wanted to admit—or be questioned about. The important thing was that he had offered his services, of his own accord. Silver Veil was of the opinion that the effectiveness of a Truthsayer was affected by whether or not he was bringing his gifts into play reluctantly, and she had warned him that he must find a Truthsayer who brought himself to his task with a whole heart. Leyuet, obviously, had made up his mind that he was not going to be reluctant.

Best not to question further. I do not want to know what he does not want to reveal.

"Leyuet—my Lord Leyuet—*thank* you for bringing this information to me, and so generously offering yourself as my Truthsayer," Amberdrake said, making sure that he projected sincerity and profound gratitude into every word. "Rest assured, your services will be called for shortly, perhaps even tonight—as it happens, the kestra'chern Silver Veil gave me identical advice, although she did not suggest you, specifically, and if anyone questions me I must in all honesty say that I ask for a Truthsayer on her word."

He had said precisely the right thing. Rather than taking offense, Leyuet visibly relaxed when Amberdrake said he would be giving Silver Veil the "credit" for advising him.

He doesn't want anyone to know he came to tell me the same things as Silver Veil. I think perhaps I'll ask her why later.

"I cannot begin to tell you how pleased I am that you have a true friend like The Silver Veil in this Court," Leyuet said, fervently, "And I will remain awake for a while yet, if you think you may wish to call upon me tonight—it is not that late—we would all still be watching the Entertainment under other circumstances—"

He broke off, embarrassed, as if he realized he was babbling.

There is a great deal of babbling going on tonight.

"I believe that will be the case," Amberdrake told him, gravely. "And I thank you in advance for going to such lengths for me."

"It is nothing more nor less than you deserve," Leyuet protested, opening the door and letting himself out quickly, as if he feared Amberdrake might want to question him further. "It is only my duty; it is only what is right. I bid you good night—for now."

And with that, he gratefully took himself out. Amberdrake had the feeling that if it had been within the bounds of propriety to *run* away, he would have.

There is something that he doesn't want me to ask about, and I would bet that it has to do with the King's proposal to Winterhart.

He turned back to the three anxious faces that were, at least, a little less anxious for hearing Leyuet's speech.

"Now," he told them, "let's get comfortable. The garden, I think—we're less likely to be overheard there. Makke, would you go fetch Gesten and have him bring us something to drink that will help keep our nerves steady? We have a great deal to sort out, and we must find a way to do it in a way that will keep anyone from being hurt."

When Makke rejoined them in the garden, with Gesten and a tray of strong tea and another of sugar-cakes, he ordered her to remain. "You have a part in this, little mother," he told her, patting a seat beside him and smiling at her as she took it, timidly. Gesten went around the garden lighting the insect-repelling lamps and candles. "Let us begin with the lost clothing, for that is what brought *me* to such a terrible accusation. I think you do not realize that you have been betrayed as badly as you believe you betrayed me."

She bowed her head to hide her face, her shoulders trembling. *Odd. I feel steadier now than I have all evening. I wonder why?* Was it because he was pretending to be the ever-serene kestra'chern? Or was it because they needed him to *be* the calm one?

Well, as a servant, she cannot demand the services of the Truthsayer, I suspect. But because the loss of my property is what led to my being accused of murder, I can demand she be examined myself. I think Leyuet will find she did not lose anything—that the missing clothing was stolen, and she cannot possibly be blamed for having clothing stolen by the crafty fiends who have successfully completed four murders!

He sensed Winterhart's anguish even as his mind raced through plans dealing with his quandary and Makke's, and he reached out for her hand even as he spoke soothing words to Makke. When the old woman finally raised her eyes to his, he smiled encouragingly at her and turned his attention to his own beloved.

"Amberdrake, I—" she began.

He managed a weak chuckle. "You are as blameless as poor Makke, if you think you somehow encouraged Shalaman to think you were interested in him," he said, taking a cup of tea from Gesten and pressing it into her trembling hand. "All you did was to be yourself. Dear gods—that was certainly enough to ensnare *me*, wasn't it?"

Her manners are flawless, in a Court which values manners and those things that have no flaws. Her mannerisms are all charming. She fits here as well as Silver Veil, and it is obvious even to a fool that she would never do anything that would disgrace her, in the purest sense of the word! Winterhart is surely as exotic as Silver Veil—though why Shalaman hasn't made this offer to her—well, it might be some stupid caste issue, I suppose. It irritated him to think that Silver Veil might somehow be considered unworthy of the King's matrimonial attentions, when he was obviously taking advantage of every one of that redoubtable lady's many talents.

Silver Veil would make such a Queen—and she loves him. Why can't he see that! Oh, damn. Let me get this settled first. A little matter of a murder accusation—I'll deal with hearts and minds later.

"All you did was to be yourself," he repeated. "And that was just a temptation that was too much for the Emperor to resist. I understand his desire, and I can hardly blame you if I can't blame him!"

She sensed his sincerity, even if she could not share his thoughts, and she managed a tremulous smile.

"The problem is—" he hesitated a moment, then said it out loud. "The problem is, it does appear that Shalaman was perfectly willing for me to stand accused of murder so that his way was clear to take you as his wife."

Makke's face turned gray, but both Zhaneel and Winterhart nodded. Zhaneel's hackles were up, and Winterhart's jaw clenched.

"The obvious answer is to demand Leyuet's services in Court," he continued, but Winterhart interrupted. And not, as he might have supposed, with angry words about the Emperor.

"You have to be careful not to imply in any way that Shalaman was using the accusation as a way to obtain me," she pointed out. "You can't even let other people make that implication. If *anyone* besides Leyuet suspects him of dishonorable intentions, he'll never forgive us."

Oh, that is the lady I love—thinking ahead, seeing all the implications, even while her own heart is in turmoil! He felt better with every passing moment, more alive than he had in years—the way he had right after the Catastrophe, when every day brought a new crisis, but she was there to help him solve it.

"Even if it all simply slipped his mind in the excitement, people could still suspect that if I act in public," he replied, thinking out loud. "If he *was* operating with those intentions—he'll become our enemy for exposing him. And if he wasn't, well, when people put facts together and come up with their own suspicions, however erroneous, wouldn't he lose face with his own Court?"

Winterhart nodded as Zhaneel looked from one to the other of them. She toyed with the necklace as she spoke. "It is almost as bad for the Haighlei to lose face as to *be* dishonorable, and while he might not become our enemy over his own mistake, he isn't going to be our friend, either." Winterhart frowned. "But we can't simply leave things the way they are!"

"If he is disgraced before his own people, might he not even declare war upon us in an attempt to show that he did not want Winterhart after all?" Zhaneel hazarded, her eyes narrowed with worry. "Oh, I wish that Skandranon were here!"

I'm just as glad he's not. He's more than a bit too direct for a situation like this one.

"In any event, if we do this in public, and everything came out *well*, we still must have Makke's part of the story—and that makes her a conspicuous target for anger," Amberdrake said, as Makke nodded and turned even grayer. "I can't have that. And we have to remember something else—there is *someone* out there who wants all of us dead or gotten rid of, and if we take care of this in public, he'll only try again to do just that. The next time he might be still more clever about it. As long as we don't know who our enemy is, we can't guard against him without just going home."

Winterhart clasped her hands together in her lap, around the cup of tea, and Amberdrake pretended not to notice that her knuckles were white.

"You are saying that we can't do anything, then?" she asked tightly. "But—"

"No, what I'm saying is that this can't be public. I spoke at length with Silver Veil, and she gave me another piece of advice—'That which is unthinkable in public is often conducted in private.' Is there a way, do you think, that we could get Shalaman alone, without any witnesses to what we say to him?"

"I don't see how," Winterhart began. "He always has bodyguards with him, even when he gave me the Necklace and the Lilies—"

Makke cleared her throat, interrupting Winterhart, and all eyes turned toward her.

"A bride-to-be accepts her betrothed's proposal in her own house," she said carefully. "She does so in private. This is an old custom, and one that dates back to the days when the Haighlei were barbarians, and occasionally kidnapped women they wished to wed. By making the groom come to her, alone, she prevents being coerced into acceptance."

"So—if I sent a message to Shalaman saying I wished to see him here, alone—" Winterhart began.

Makke nodded. "He would assume that you were going to accept the Necklace, and he would send away his guards, arriving at your door unaccompanied. He would, of course, expect that *you* would be alone as well." She coughed delicately. "It is often said that there are many children whose births come at intervals that are easily calculated back nine months to the date of the bride's acceptance. . . ."

"Would now be too soon?" Winterhart said, blushing furiously. "I—I wouldn't want to seem too forward."

"I suspect," Makke replied, with a hint of her old spirit, "that our King is pacing the floor, hoping that *you* will find it impossible to sleep until you have answered him."

Winterhart smiled, but it was a tight, thin smile. "So I shall," she said. "So I shall. . . ."

Skandranon, predictably, arrived just at the moment when they were about to send that carefully worded message to the King.

"I was on the roof," he said, looking at all of their tense faces with puzzlement. "I was waiting for Kechara to contact me. I was concerned that there might be an off chance that there was someone capable of sensing mind-magic at work within the Palace."

"Why go on the roof?" Amberdrake asked.

He shrugged. "If that was the case, I didn't want anyone to associate the messages passing between myself and our little gryphon with *me*. It wasn't our roof, you see."

They had to explain it all over again to him, which took a bit more time. Amberdrake was a little worried that Skan might come up with another one of his wild plans instead of falling in with theirs. To his relief, Skan was in complete agreement with all of them.

"I must admit I didn't expect you to go along with this without an argument," Amberdrake finally said, as Skan settled himself into a corner with Zhaneel tucked under a wing.

The gryphon looked up at him thoughtfully. "Not an argument, exactly," he replied. "More of an addition. It's unethical, of course—but you've had a game played on you that was worse than unethical, and I think this would just even the scales between you and Shalaman."

Amberdrake winced; whenever the gryphon suggested something "unethical," or something to "even the scales," there was no predicting what he was going to say. Gryphons were carnivores, and they showed it in their ideas of justice and fair play. "Well—what was your suggestion?"

"Two things, really," Skan said, preening a talon. "The first is the unethical one. You've got a rather formidable Gift in that Empathy of yours. Use it. You know very well you can make people feel things as well as feeling them yourself—so use that. Make Shalaman feel *very* guilty and in your debt for not exposing him. Shove your sincerity and good-will down his throat until he chokes on them. Make him eat kindness until he has to do us major favors or burst."

Amberdrake gritted his teeth over that one, but he had to admit that Skan had a good idea. He *hated* using his powers that way, but—

But if I'm going to ensure the success of this, I have to use every weapon I have. He's right.

"And the other?" he asked.

"Tell him you're lifebonded." Skan finished preening the talon, and regarded him with that direct gryphonic gaze. "From what I've learned, it's unusual here and it's important to these people. Leyuet can probably confirm that to him. I think telling him might just tip the scales in our favor."

Amberdrake considered that for a moment. "Well, I can't

see why it should, but I also can't see how it can hurt. All right, Gesten—are you ready to play messenger?"

The hertasi nodded tightly. "This is going to need a lot of fancy footwork, Drake, I hope you know that."

"Believe me," Amberdrake replied grimly. "No one knows it better than I do." He handed the hertasi the carefully worded messages, one to the Emperor and one to Leyuet. "We'll be waiting."

Gesten slipped off, and the five of them arranged themselves very carefully. Makke was off to one side, out of the way. Zhaneel and Skan placed themselves on either side of the door, ready to interpose their bodies if the King should decide to storm out. He would not get past them; they could simply block the door with their bodies, or an extended wing, using no force and no violence. Amberdrake stood beside Winterhart, who was seated on the floor, with the Necklace gleaming on a pillow, arranged in a pattern that Makke said signified "polite refusal." It seemed there were customs for the arrangement of the necklace, which included "angered refusal," "fearful refusal," "wistful refusal," "unexplainable refusal," and so on. There was a ritual for everything.

"What did Judeth have to say?" Amberdrake asked Skan, to fill in the time. "How much did you tell her?"

"Oh, as relayed through the little one, she was apoplectic about the murder accusations, of course," Skan said casually. "She wanted us to come home. I pointed out how stupid that would be, and how it might only get us in deeper trouble. Then she was going to cancel the next lot of diplomats; which wasn't a bad idea, but I had a better one. I told her to send us some of the human Silvers instead, ones that can at least go through diplomatic motions and leave the real work to us. She thought that was a pretty good notion, giving us our own little private guards. She wanted to send mages, but I told her that would be a very bad idea and why. She agreed, and started working out the details so things can move quickly and the Silvers can sail with the tide. That's pretty much where things stand."

Amberdrake had a shrewd notion that wasn't *all* Skan had

told Judeth to do, but it hardly mattered. At the moment, more strategy was required than diplomacy—the kind of leadership of a field commander rather than that of an administrator. Those were, and had always been, Skan's strengths. He was never better or more skillful than when he was alone, making decisions that only a single person could implement.

He hates being a leader. Now he's in his element. As dreadful as this situation is, it's good for him. And—is he losing weight?

At least this meant that there would be some skilled fighters showing up shortly, and if worse came to worst, as Skan said, they would have their own little guard contingent. If everything went wrong and they really did have to flee to save their lives—provided they could all escape the city—with the help of several skilled fighters, they *could* probably make their way across the jungle and back to White Gryphon.

It occurred to him that they ought to start making emergency escape plans, just in case. But before he could say anything, the sound of footsteps out in the hallway, coming through the slightly-open door, put all of them on alert.

Shalaman pushed the door open and took three eager steps into the room before he saw that there was a group waiting for him rather than Winterhart alone. His expression was so eager, and so *happy*, that Amberdrake's heart went out to him— despite the fact that Shalaman wanted him out of the way. Perhaps that was only a sign of how much a kestra'chern he was, that he could always see someone else's side.

Oh, gods, if only everyone could have everything they wanted out of this situation—But he knew very well that there were never such things as unadulterated happy endings, and that the very best that anyone could hope for here was that hearts would not be broken too badly. . . .

Shalaman was clearly taken aback when he saw Amberdrake; he stopped dead, and his face lost all expression. In the next heartbeat, his eyes dropped to Winterhart, then to the necklace on the pillow in front of her.

His eyes went back to Amberdrake, and turned cold. His face assumed an expression of anger. But his words surprised the kestra'chern. "Lady," he said softly, "if this man has threatened you—if—"

Winterhart raised her eyes to his, as Skan and Zhaneel closed the door very softly and put themselves between Shalaman and the exit. He did not appear to notice anything except Winterhart and Amberdrake.

"This is *my* answer, Serenity," she said steadily. No one who knew anything about her would ever have doubted the firm resolution in her voice. "If you think that anyone could threaten me to perform any action against my will, you are very much mistaken. Amberdrake is here because I wish him here, I asked him here, and because I wish to show you that we are of one heart in this and in all else."

Shalaman's face fell—but before he could react any further, Amberdrake spoke.

"You desired my lady," he said very gently, without even a hint of threat. "And you did not advise me that I had a right to a Truthsayer when accused of murder. I cannot think but that the two are connected."

He tried to keep the words neutral, tried to make his statement very casual, but the accusation was still there, and there was no real way to soften it.

Shalaman went absolutely rigid, as if struck with a sudden paralysis. His face froze except for a tic beside his right eye; he opened his mouth slightly, as if to speak, but nothing emerged.

Amberdrake sensed a turmoil of emotions—chief of which was panic. And overlaying that, real guilt. And beneath it all a terrible shame. All of his own doubts were resolved; consciously or not, Shalaman had tried to rid himself of his rival by underhanded means and had just been forced to acknowledge that.

Caught you. Now to soothe you.

"Serenity," he said swiftly, using his Gift just as Skan had advised, to emphasize his words and gently prod the Emperor's emotions in the direction *he* chose. "Winterhart is a beautiful woman, full of wit and wisdom and grace. She is a fit consort for any King, and I cannot fault you for desiring her.

We are private in our emotions, and you could not know that this was not a marriage of convenience between us."

"You are generous," Shalaman growled.

Amberdrake noted the dangerous anger behind that simple statement. *Time to turn that anger in the proper direction.*

"I also cannot fault you for falling into a trap that was laid for all of us," he continued with a little anger of his own. "A trap contrived by someone—or a conspiracy of someones— who must be the most clever and fiendish I have ever had the misfortune to encounter. The party behind it—whoever he or she is—saw your interest and did not scruple to use it against all of us."

Shalaman knitted his brows slightly in puzzlement. "I do not understand," he told the kestra'chern. "What are you trying to say? That these murders are serving another purpose?"

Amberdrake nodded. "There is *someone* in this land who wishes to be rid of the folk of White Gryphon. I dare say he or she would not be averse to seeing *you* come to grief as well, and this person contrived to put you in a situation where you might not see the threat to your honor." *There. No accusation, only point out the existence of the threat.* "That is why—or so we believe—these dreadful murders have occurred, all of them of people who objected to our presence but were completely loyal to you. That is why—so we conjecture—this person arranged a situation that *you* would also be entrapped by."

"So—I have a traitor in my own ranks?" the King asked, his expression darkening to anger, seizing gratefully on the suggestion that his actions had been manipulated by someone else—just as Amberdrake had known he would. It was an easier answer, one that was more palatable.

Better that, than be thought dishonorable, even by barbarians. Interesting. Amberdrake had the feeling that he was finally beginning to understand these people.

"We believe so. The problem is that we will never find this person unless we lull him into carelessness," Amberdrake told him earnestly as Skan and Zhaneel moved quietly away from the door. "So, before we go any further, that I may clear my name and honor before you, at least, I should like the services of Truthsayer Leyuet—but only in private."

Again, the King was taken aback. "Why in private? Do you not wish your name to be made clean?"

Amberdrake shrugged. "We are gambling with more than just my personal honor here," he said philosophically. "To ask for the Truthsayer before the Court would reveal that we are aware of some of what is going on, and I am willing for others to continue to suspect me if it will help us to catch the true villain. *That* is more important, and I can abide suspicious glares and the anger of your courtiers to achieve justice for the murders."

Sincerity, honesty, graciousness . . . do believe me, Shalaman. It all happens to be true.

Shalaman nodded cautiously; too much the diplomat himself to take even this at face value.

"I also request Leyuet's services on behalf of the servant Makke," he continued persuasively. "The reason will become clear when you hear what she has to say."

Shalaman frowned but nodded again. Gesten—who had left his message with Shalaman only to go fetch Leyuet—knocked in his familiar pattern at that precise moment, and Skan moved to open the door to let the hertasi and the Truthsayer in.

They almost lost their advantage at that moment as Shalaman realized how *they* had manipulated him. But his own good sense overcame his temper, and he managed to do no more than frown at his Advisor as Leyuet came in.

Leyuet made a formal obeisance to his leader which appeared to mollify the King somewhat. Shalaman gestured to the rest of them to take seats, then appropriated the best chair in the room and sat down in it with ill grace.

"I see you have all this planned," he growled, waving his hand at Leyuet. "Continue, then, before I lose my patience. Truthsayer, examine the man Amberdrake."

Good. He's angry. Now to turn that anger away from us and toward whoever is conspiring against us.

"There is only one thing more that I need to tell you,

Serenity," he said, very carefully. "But I needed the Truth-sayer here to confirm it so that you will believe it. If you would, please, Leyuet?"

The Truthsayer nodded and then knelt upon the floor at Amberdrake's feet, closing his eyes and assuming an expression of intense concentration. As Silver Veil had explained it, Leyuet would *not* actually read Amberdrake's thoughts as a Mindspeaker might, nor his emotions as an Empath would. She could only describe it as "soul-touching, perhaps, or heart-reading"—that Leyuet would take in what Amberdrake *was*, with no emotions or surface thoughts intruding, and relate that to the truth or falsehood of what he was saying. As she described it, the act would be far more intimate on Leyuet's part (for Amberdrake would sense nothing) than any Empathic sensing of emotion. It was impossible to lie to a Truthsayer, she claimed. If that was the case, Amberdrake did not envy Leyuet his Gift—

There are more than a few slimy souls I would never have wanted to touch in that way. Ma'ar, for instance, or Shaik-nam. The very idea makes me shudder.

"I wish to prove to you why my lady and I are more than we appear. Winterhart and I have a very unusual bond," he said, choosing his words with care. "In our tongue, it is called 'lifebonding.' I have not been able to find the equivalent in yours, but it is a binding of soul to soul—a partnership that completes both of us. What one feels, the other feels as well—"

He continued, trying to describe their relationship in terms that Shalaman might understand, groping through the unfamiliar Haighlei words, until suddenly Leyuet's eyes flew open and the Truthsayer exclaimed with dismay—

"Serenity! These two are *loriganalea!* Oh, dearest gods—what did you think you were doing?"

The look of horror on Leyuet's face was mirrored in Shalaman's.

What on earth! Why—

Amberdrake had no time for any other thoughts, for suddenly, the Emperor himself, the great Shalaman, was on *his* knees, clutching the hems of Amberdrake's garment and Winterhart's in turn, begging their forgiveness. Amberdrake had not seen anyone so terrified in ten years. What had Leyuet said?

Amberdrake was taken so aback he didn't know what to say or do next. Leyuet seemed to be completely paralyzed.

Finally it was Skan who broke the impasse.

"Well," he said, in a completely casual tone, as if he saw all-powerful Emperors groveling in front of his friends every day, "I always said you and Winterhart were something special."

Things were very confusing for several long moments. When a greatly-shaken Shalaman—who had by this time lost every aspect of Emperor and seemed to have decided that he would be, for now, only Shalaman the man—was calmed down and assured of both their forgiveness, they finally learned from him and from Leyuet why their reaction had been so violent. In fact, Leyuet was still looking a bit gray about the lips.

"This is a sacred bond," Leyuet said, carefully, so that there could be no mistake. "This is a marriage, made not for lust or for power or the sake of convenience, but made *by the gods.* The holy books are very plain; interfering in such a bond will bring the curses of the ages upon anyone who tries to break it, anyone who *helps* to break it and anyone who does not aid the bonded ones. If he who tried to interfere in the bonding is a ruler, the curses would fall even upon the people as a whole. You have done a good thing, Amberdrake, by recognizing this bond and telling us of it. You have not only saved the Emperor's honor, you have prevented the curses of all of our gods and yours as well from falling upon this land."

"You were well within your rights to withhold this knowledge from me," Shalaman said miserably, shaken to his bones. "If I had not the opportunity to obtain your forgiveness, it is possible that the curses would *still* have come, and you would have had your revenge upon me threefold. It would only have been justice—your withholding of information in exchange for my omission."

The Emperor shuddered, his lips pale with strain. "There is nothing I can give you in my entire Empire that can compensate you—"

This was too much. Amberdrake cast a glance of entreaty at the Truthsayer for help, since nothing he had said seemed to penetrate the Emperor's reaction. Leyuet placed a hand upon Shalaman's, keeping him from saying anything more. "It is enough. It did not happen. Amberdrake and Winterhart understand and forgive. They both know—well, enough."

"That is the truth," Amberdrake said hastily. "Remember, we were *all* caught in a web of deception. The blame should rightly fall on the spider who spun it; let the curses fall upon him."

That was evidently exactly the right thing to say; the Emperor closed his eyes and nodded, relaxing a little.

But Leyuet was not finished. "And *you* know, my Emperor, that even if Amberdrake were to perish in the next instant, Winterhart would *still* not be for you, nor for any other man. You may wish to consult Palisar on the matter, but I would say this proves that the gods regard those of White Gryphon as they would the Haighlei, in matters of the soul and love."

That last was said with a certain stern relish that made Amberdrake wonder if the pointed little reminder were not Leyuet's tiny act of revenge for his own mental and emotional strain over this situation. *Poor Leyuet. He walked a thread above a chasm, and he survived. I should not be surprised if he garnered more white hairs from this.*

Shalaman nodded weakly. "I know. And I swear that I will think of her from this moment as I would my own sister, my own mother, my own daughter—and with no other thoughts in my heart." He shook himself a little, then looked up at Amberdrake. "Now, you will assert your innocence in this matter, and Leyuet will verify it, and I will make this public if there is no other way to prove that you are blameless. Will that suit your plan to trap this plot-spinning spider?"

"It does. But do not reveal my innocence unless there is no other way to save my life," Amberdrake reminded him. "We must make our enemy think that he has us trapped, all of us. He will never make any mistakes unless he becomes over-confident."

We have to think of other things that will make it look as if I am still the chief suspect. . . .

Leyuet assumed his Truthsaying "trance" again, and Amberdrake carefully stated his innocence in *all* the murders. There was no point in doing this if Shalaman would still be wondering if Amberdrake had anything to do with the other three deaths. "Nor would I harm any other member of your court," he added, "except to bring this killer to justice."

There. I think that covers everything.

Shalaman hardly looked at Leyuet, who confirmed everything Amberdrake said in a dreamy, detached voice. *Odd; he looked so strained before, but now he actually seems to be experiencing something pleasant! I wonder why?*

"Now, for Makke—" Amberdrake brought the trembling woman to sit in front of Leyuet. She seemed to be on the verge of tears, but bravely held them back, looking only at Amberdrake. She seemed to take comfort and heart from his presence, and he put a steadying hand on hers as he knelt beside her chair, out of Leyuet's way.

"Makke, you are the servant and cleaning woman for myself, Winterhart, Zhaneel, and Skandranon, are you not?" he asked in a gentle voice.

She nodded mutely, and Leyuet echoed the gesture.

"One of your tasks is to see that our clothing is taken to the laundresses and returned, is that not so?" he continued; she nodded, and Leyuet confirmed the truth of the statement.

"Now—today, this morning, when you fetched the clean clothing, some of it was missing, correct? Whose was it?"

Makke's voice trembled with suppressed tears. "Yours, great lord."

"And that was before the afternoon recess, when all the Court takes a rest, was it not?"

"Yes, great lord," she replied, a single tear seeping out of the corner of her eye and escaping into the wrinkles of her cheeks.

"When you took it away yesterday, did it *ever* leave your hands from the moment you received it to the moment you delivered it to the laundresses?" he asked. She shook her head mutely.

"And when did you discover that there was a piece missing?" he asked her.

"When I opened the bundle as it came from the laundresses, in these rooms, great lord," she said and sobbed as she lost her tenuous control of herself. "I am—"

"No," he said quickly, putting a hand on her shoulder to stop her from saying anything more. "Describe the missing piece, if you can."

As he had hoped, she remembered it in minute detail, and it was obvious to anyone who had seen the bloody fragments that the robe she described and the pieces found with the last victim were the same.

"Good," he said. "Now, simply answer this. Did you leave the bundle anywhere, after you received it from their hands? Did you even leave it alone in our rooms?"

She shook her head.

"So during the entire time when the clothing was in *your* control, you did not leave it anywhere but in the hands of those who were to clean it?" It was a rhetorical question, but she nodded.

"The woman speaks the truth," Leyuet said tonelessly.

"So—*first*, the clothing that turned up with the last murder victim was missing from my possession this morning, so I could not have been wearing it," Amberdrake said triumphantly. "And *second*, it cannot possibly have been Makke's fault that it came into the possession of someone else. She was not careless, she didn't lose anything—it was stolen, and she can hardly be held responsible for the acts of someone who is a murderer, a traitor, and a thief."

Shalaman sighed wearily, and Makke suddenly looked up, her expression changing in an instant from one of despair to one of joy.

"That is so, Emperor," Leyuet said slowly as he shook himself out of his trance. "Though I fail to see why it was so important—"

He stopped himself, flushing with shame. "Forgive me, woman," he said to Makke, with stiff humility. "It was important to you, of course. Not all troubles involve the curses of gods and the fate of empires—but sometimes the fate of empires can devolve upon the small troubles."

Makke obviously didn't understand what Leyuet was trying to say, but she nodded timidly, shrinking back into the chair.

"The question is," Leyuet said, "what do we do with her? I do not know that she should continue as your cleaning woman. Perhaps a retirement?"

Makke shrank back further still.

"If I may make a request?" Zhaneel put in. "Makke is the only one who knows that the clothing was missing. This puts her in danger, if the murderer thinks of it. Could she not be protected if she were here, in our personal train? If she were to be made—oh—" Zhaneel's expression became crafty "—the nurse of my little ones? She would then be in our suite all the time, and under our guarding eyes and talons!"

Leyuet looked dubious. "Is this permitted?" he asked Shalaman. "She is of the caste of the Lower Servants, is not a nursemaid of the caste of Upper Servants?" He seemed far more concerned over the possible breach in caste than by the threat to Makke's life. Shalaman's brow creased with a similar concern.

Hang these people and their ranks and castes!

Skandranon snorted with derision before anyone else could say anything. "At the moment, the servants watching the little ones are from whatever caste takes care of pet dogs and parrots!" he said with thinly-veiled contempt. "This is, I believe, on the judgment of whoever it is that decides who should serve where. I hardly think that they can be of any higher caste than Makke. They are *certainly* of less intelligence!"

Leyuet looked a little happier. "It is true, Emperor, that there is no description or caste for one who would be a nursemaid to—to—" He groped for a tactful description, and Skan supplied him with an untactful one.

"Nursemaid to the offspring of intelligent animals," he said shortly. "And I don't see any reason why Shalaman can't declare it to be in Makke's caste and give her the job here and now."

"Nor do I," Shalaman said hastily, obviously wanting to get what seemed to him to be nonsense over with. "I declare it. Leyuet, have a secretary issue the orders."

Leyuet emerged from his trance feeling more like himself than he had since the foreigners arrived. His stomach was settled, his headache gone, his energy completely restored.

And it was—it was a pleasure to touch the soul of Amberdrake, he realized with wonder. *As noble a soul as Silver Veil—and how ever could I have doubted that? Was he not her pupil? Is he not still her friend? Why should I have forgotten these things?*

He did not even express impatience with the amount of time spent on the servant woman, where a few days ago he would have been offended at this waste of his gifts, and insisted that a lesser Truthsayer attend to her.

It would, of course, have been a great pity if anything happened to her, so the female gryphon's suggestion about how to keep her safe was a good one. But it was an insignificant detail in the greater work of this evening. He and Amberdrake between them had managed to engineer all of it without ever having Shalaman's honor publicly called into question.

And Amberdrake saved us all from the curses of the gods— and on the eve of the Eclipse, too! His relief at *that* was enough to make him weak in the knees. *The disaster that would be—the curses could have persisted for the next twenty years, or worse!*

But of course Amberdrake's forgiveness came quickly and readily; that was the kind of soul that Leyuet had touched.

He simply rested from his labor as Skandranon, Shalaman, and the rest worked out what the next moves would be.

"I think perhaps that we should do more than continue to

foster the illusion that I am the chief suspect," Amberdrake said gravely. "In fact—Winterhart, if you have no objections, perhaps we should also foster the illusion that you and I have quarreled over this, and that you have accepted the King's proposal."

Leyuet woke up at *that*. It was a bold move—and a frightening one. He would have been more concerned, except that he had violated custom and Read the King, and he knew that Shalaman had been truly frightened by his narrow escape, and that he would, indeed, regard Winterhart as purely and without lust as if she was his daughter from this moment on.

In the face of so great a threat, the violation of custom is a small matter. Shalaman could not have been permitted Winterhart's company if his heart had not changed.

"I don't object—as long as I can still—" Winterhart bit her lip and blushed redly, and Shalaman laughed for the first time that evening. These pale people showed their embarrassment in such an amusing fashion!

How far down does the red go, one wonders? It certainly crept down her neck and past her collar.

"I shall have Leyuet give you the key to the next suite," Shalaman said indulgently. "Just as the gryphons's suite connects to yours, there is one that connects to theirs. I shall put you there—it is a suitable arrangement for a Consort-To-Be, since the bride must remain with her relatives, and they are the closest you have to relatives here—and it will look as if I am placing the gryphons between you and Amberdrake as a kind of guard upon your honor and safety."

"Meanwhile, we are anything but. I like it," Skandranon said. "Just don't keep us awake at night, scampering through our quarters, all right, Amberdrake?"

Shalaman chuckled at this, as did Amberdrake. So did Leyuet. If the King had been having second thoughts, he would have put Winterhart in the Royal Apartments. All was well.

He relaxed back onto his cushion; his opinion was not needed in this, but he did need to know what they were planning, for Palisar and Silver Veil would have to be informed.

I shouldn't be relaxed, he tried to tell himself. *This is a per-*

ilous and horrible situation. There is a killer among us, a killer who is likely also a traitor, who kills in terrifying and obscene ways. It could be anyone! Well, almost anyone. Four ladies of the Court are dead—I did not know them, but still, I should not be sitting here thinking about being able to enjoy a meal for the first time in days. . . .

On the other hand, there was nothing more that he could do, and his Emperor was acting again like the Shalaman he knew, the warrior, the leader.

And he was seeing a side to the foreigners, especially Amberdrake, that he had never, ever guessed. They had seemed so different from the Haighlei before this moment—alien, tricky, crafty, possibly deceitful.

Amberdrake, in particular, had seemed too opaque to be trustworthy. How could he not have noticed that this very opacity was like Silver Veil's mannered detachment?

I thought that Silver Veil was unique. Is this how all northern kestra'chern are? Oh, perhaps not. Anyone can call himself a kestra'chern, after all. We have kestra'chern who are hardly worthy of the name. And there have been very few even of the good ones who have risen to the rank of Advisor.

But here were two who were worthy of the name and the highest of ranks—Silver Veil and Amberdrake—and an equally brilliant soul, if of a different order, in Winterhart. The strangers had turned out to be not so strange after all, despite their odd ways and their even odder friends, the gryphons.

Perhaps—one day I shall venture to read the gryphons. If they can be the friends of Amberdrake, then I think I should be in no danger of harm. . . .

With a start, he realized that the conference was coming to an end, at least as far as he was concerned.

"You may go, Leyuet," Shalaman said, dismissing him with a wave of his hand. "We have taken up enough of your rest as it is. In the morning, see that Palisar and Silver Veil learn of what we have discussed, but keep it all among yourselves."

Unspoken, but obvious to Leyuet—he should keep to *himself* the King's near-debacle in the matter of honor.

It was not the first time that he had kept such things to himself. That was something of the nature of a Truthsayer; he examined and watched the King more often than the King himself knew.

He rose, smiled his farewells, and bowed himself out.

But not to go to his rooms.

Silver Veil would probably learn of all of this from Amberdrake; he could make sure of that in the morning. But the rest of this was critical enough that Palisar should hear of it now.

Let Shalaman preserve his illusion that his Advisors wasted time on sleep when there was a delicate situation to be handled. Leyuet knew his duty, and so did Palisar. It would be a long night, but one well-spent.

Besides, he thought, humming a little to himself, *suddenly I seem to have much more energy than I did earlier.*

I wonder why that is?

Judeth, Aubri and
Snowstar

Eight

Skandranon woke early and went scouting on the wing, just after dawn, despite the late hours they had all kept the night before. He was restless and found it hard to sleep with so many problems burning away at him.

First and foremost, of course, was *who* the murderer was, and how he was accomplishing his crimes.

Skan was so angry that his muscles were all tight, but it was not the kind of hot, impulsive anger that had driven him in the past. This was a slow, smoldering rage, one that would send him wherever he had to go, to do whatever he had to do to catch the culprit. And when he caught the blackguard—well, he would probably wish that Leyuet and his Spears of the Law had gotten there first. *Whoever this smelly chunk of* sketi *is, he has to be getting into those rooms somehow. Maybe he left some sign on the roofs. Maybe I can find it. I doubt that Leyuet's people were really looking for it, not after they'd made up their minds that Drake or I had killed those people.*

He flung himself off the railing of his balcony and up into the air with a great lunge of his hind legs—a lunge no longer accompanied by the plaint of his muscles, although there was a tiny creak of his joints that was probably unavoidable. At least his campaign of reconditioning himself had worked. The creaking was because of the damp, and there wasn't much to be done about that. This place was always damp; cool and damp by night, hot and damp by day. The climate made for some spectacular foliage, thick with lushly beautiful flowers that were even now sending their fragrances up on warm thermals, but it was also rather bad for middle-aged joints.

It belatedly occurred to him as he took to the air and began a series of slow, lazy circles in the damp morning air that he made a dreadfully conspicuous target. *It isn't as if there are a lot of creatures the size of a horse or larger, pure white, flying about in the sky around here. If someone who happened to like one of those women happened to decide to take the law into his own hands, I could be in deep—*

Something sent a warning shrilling along his nerves.

Only years of dodging the inventive weaponry used by Ma'ar's soldiers—and the fact that his fighting instincts were coming back with a vengeance—saved him at that moment.

He thought later that he must have caught a hint of swift movement coming up from below, movement so subtle it didn't register consciously. His nerves just screamed a sudden alarm at him, and he sideslipped in the air, violently and unpredictably altering his path.

What in—oh, sketi!

And an arrow passed through the part of the sky where his chest had been a moment before, actually whiffling through his outermost three primaries on his left wing without touching the wing itself.

It was close enough that he reached out, still without thinking, to snatch it out of the sky.

A foolish move, of course—although it did give him the satisfaction that his reactions were quite good enough now that he caught it. He spiraled violently away before a second arrow could follow it, scanning the ground below him for signs of the archer.

There was nothing, of course. Whoever had sent off the shot wasn't willing to risk a second. And he wasn't about to show himself with a bow in his hand, either.

The arrow was plain, quite ordinary, without owners' marks or fancy fletching. It was probably nothing more than a plain target arrow, one of a hundred thousand like it in this

city alone. It might not even have been shot at him; someone
might have been stupid, overly exuberant, or a very bad hand
with a bow.

*Oh, yes. Surely. And pigs are flying in parade formation
around the sun at this moment.*

There was no point in pretending that this arrow had come
zinging at him with any innocence involved in its flight. Someone down there on the ground did not like him. Someone in the
Palace wanted him perforated. Suddenly he could hardly wait
for a particular barrel to arrive with the augmented "diplomatic" corps. For some reason, even by day, it was harder to hit
a black target in the air than a white one. Human perception,
perhaps.

But this arrow carried far more implications than that. For
someone among the Haighlei to bypass law, custom, and protocol and go shooting at Skandranon personally meant that
the situation had eroded to a very dangerous point indeed.
These people simply did not *do* that. They were so law-abiding
that it was ridiculous.

And neither he, nor anyone else, had taken that possibility
into their considerations last night. It might be a lot more dangerous to be the chief suspect of all these killings now than
they had thought. That put Amberdrake in a very precarious
position.

*I think I'd better talk to Drake. Quickly. Besides, the sky
is not a healthy place to be at the moment.*

Mere heartbeats later, he was backwinging to a landing on
Amberdrake's balcony—and Amberdrake, much to *his* surprise, was pushing his way through the curtains to meet his
early-morning visitor.

The kestra'chern looked as if he hadn't gotten a lot of sleep,
either. His eyes were red and a little swollen with a hint of
dark circles beneath them, his long hair was tangled, and the
loose robe of rich, multicolored silk was something he had
clearly just pulled on when he heard Skan's wings outside his
bedroom.

It's a good thing that Winterhart sleeps as deeply as she

does, or I'd be in trouble. She hates being wakened too early. At least Drake will put up with it.

He made one of the better landings of the last several months, at least, touching down gracefully and sending Amberdrake's hair whipping around his face with the wind from his wings.

"Drake, we have more trouble," he said shortly, as Amberdrake looked up at him, with one hand absently rubbing his temple, a sure sign the kestra'chern had a headache. Well, there were a lot of headaches in the Palace this morning. "Look." He held out the arrow, and Amberdrake took it. "Someone thinks foreigners make great targets, especially flying foreigners. That could change, though. Walking targets in silk robes might be next on the target range."

Amberdrake chewed his lip thoughtfully, his brows knitted with worry. "Meant to warn, or to strike?" he asked, coming straight to the point.

"To strike, unless they were counting on my being able to dodge it," Skan told him bluntly. "The thing is, you don't get out of the way as well as I do, especially if you're on a balcony or in a corridor. We might want to rethink this plan of ours; Winterhart isn't going to be very happy with me if you end up full of holes."

You're not a warrior-hero, Drake, he thought silently, willing the kestra'chern to be sensible. *You were never meant to be on the front lines. You don't have to do this if you don't want to. Don't pretend to be something you aren't.*

"If I become the chief suspect, I can keep to my rooms," Amberdrake pointed out reasonably. "In fact, if I become the chief suspect, I'll have a good reason to keep to my rooms. The others will be here in a few days; I'll have guards enough then to keep me safe, don't you think?"

"You can never have enough guards," Skan muttered, but he nodded reluctantly. "I want to go on the record as thinking this is a very bad idea, though," he continued. "You aren't and never were a fighter, no matter what most of the Kaled'a'in are. You never got any closer to the front lines than the Healers' tents. You haven't got a fighter's instincts. I—"

"Skan, you forget what I was before I was a kestra'chern," Amberdrake interrupted softly. "I haven't been sheltered from violence my entire life. I weathered the flight from Ma'ar's troops as a boy, I weathered the war with his army, and I managed to do all right on the journey into the West. And I may not be a fighter, but I've kept myself in shape the whole time."

If that remark was supposed to annoy the gryphon, it fell wide of the mark. "I've gotten myself back in shape, too, Drake," Skan said, just as pointedly. "I make a better target than you. I'm not human, and I *am* a fighter, with plenty of practice at dodging whatever is thrown or shot at me."

"You make a much more conspicuous target than I do, and I'd say that disqualifies you," Amberdrake snapped, then looked contrite. "I'm sorry; I'm short on sleep and on tolerance, and this hasn't helped. I promise, I will be *very* careful, but this thing is too important not to take some risks in order to get it solved. Is that enough?"

Skan closed his eyes for a moment, trying to quell the sick feeling he had in the pit of his stomach when he thought of pulling that same arrow in his talon out of Amberdrake. *Odd. I was always the one who went charging off into danger, and it never bothered me like this. But put Drake on the line of fire—* The sick feeling rose to his crop, and he fought the nausea down. *Is this how my friends felt about me? I can't stand the idea of him being in danger! I not only want to protect him, I want to keep him out of it!*

Yet wasn't it Amberdrake's right to decide what he did, what he volunteered for? *I certainly didn't need anyone telling me what to do with my life, and I'd have resented anything Drake did to "protect" me. And he is right, damn him. These murders are going to wreck everything with the Haighlei and may send us into a war neither side can win if we can't solve them.*

"If you *aren't* careful," Skan said savagely, through a clenched beak, "what this enemy of ours does to you will be *nothing* compared to what *I'll* do to you if you get hurt!"

"Fair enough." Amberdrake ran a hand through his long, tangled hair, and smiled wanly up at Skan, who glowered down at him. "As long as I'm awake, why don't you tell me everything you said to the people back home, and what they said to you. The less Winterhart knows, the better, and I don't want to worry Zhaneel, but *I* need to know what you've ordered. If I'm going make a target out of myself, the least you can do is keep me completely informed."

Of all the nerve! Skan folded his wings tightly, and gave Amberdrake a nasty look. "That's not fair, Drake," he growled. "That's blackmail."

"So it is." Amberdrake nodded agreeably, then pulled his robe more tightly around himself, folded his arms, and leaned against the wall. It constantly amazed Skan how the man could look so attractive even when he was disheveled. "You might as well talk because I'll continue to make you feel guilty until you tell me what I want to know. I'm very good at it—as you very well know."

Damn him. He is good at it. All he has to do is put on a certain expression—or drop the right word or two. He could have been my mother.

Skan growled wordlessly and gave in. "Mostly, I told *them* what was going to happen. If they're going to insist that I'm their leader, then in a situation like this one, damn if I'm not going to get arbitrary."

Amberdrake nodded as if he had expected something of the sort. "And who were 'they'? You mentioned Judeth; who else was in on the conversation?"

"Judeth, Snowstar, Vikteren, Aubri. That was the most Kechara could handle over the distance, and she simply repeated to me what Judeth and Vikteren were saying rather than relaying their mind-voices." He tilted his head to one side. "I put Snowstar in charge of White Gryphon, taking my place indefinitely. He didn't like it, but he agreed. Vikteren is staying, too. Judeth and Aubri are coming here themselves."

I think Snowstar guesses I plan to put him in charge permanently. I'm no leader—and I think once people get used to deferring to Snowstar in this emergency, they won't have any more trouble deferring to him ever again. I suspect he'd have been made the Kaled'a'in k'Leshya Clan Leader if Lionwind hadn't been so charismatic and capable.

"Your idea or theirs?" Amberdrake asked, raising an eyebrow in inquiry.

"Theirs mostly, but—hell, Drake, we've worked together before, and I'd rather have them than some green gryphlet who thinks I'm only a legend." He turned away from Amberdrake for a moment and gazed back north, in the direction of the settlement. All that was visible past the buildings of the city and Palace were trees, but his heart knew where home was, and he wished he could be back there now.

And yet—no, he wouldn't have missed this for the world. He felt his blood stirring again, felt *effective* for the first time in years. "I told them to bring black feather-dye with them. I'm going to be the Black Gryphon again."

He expected Amberdrake to protest, but there was only silence from the kestra'chern. He turned back to see his friend nodding.

"Oddly enough, this is not a surprise," Amberdrake said, startling him a little. The kestra'chern smiled at Skan's reaction. "You are remembering who you are, after being made into someone else by the needs of others. Others may not see it, but a close friend or a kestra'chern can. I *am* a kestra'chern. Accurate perception is part of the job."

"So it is." Skan bowed slightly in his direction. "Well, I told them what the situation was here—that we had an enemy who was more interested in taking us out than confronting us. I told them that there was no point in arguing about whether or not we were going to do something about him, because we couldn't afford not to."

"True enough. We discussed that to death last night." Amberdrake sighed, and leaned his head back against the stone of the wall. "Who's coming, then?"

"No mages," Skan said quickly. "Judeth wanted Vikteren there; he didn't want to go because we're still getting mage-storms and you never know what they're going to kick up. I thought about it, and agreed with him—more because these people don't want mages around than because I think he's right about being indispensable."

"There *is* Snowstar, after all," Amberdrake pointed out with a smile. "Vikteren would be very useful, if we could just keep the fact that he's a mage a secret."

"Oh, yes, we all know Snowstar is more powerful than he is, and there are half a dozen others as good as he is. Still." Skan clicked his beak a little. "On more reflection, I would still want him in place in White Gryphon. He *does* have a knack for handling situations no one else has ever seen or heard of before. So he stays. The main thing I told them, though, was that I had to get to the heart of this mess, or I might not have a settlement to come back to—" he snapped his beak, "—or else, the Black Gryphon Skandranon might come back to a blackened city. That would be bad. So all I wanted on this job were experienced Silvers with good sense and good judgment—which ought to let out Aubri, but I'm sentimental," he added with a gape-grin.

"I hope you haven't emptied White Gryphon of every competent Silver there," Amberdrake protested. "We can't bring an army in here, either!"

Skan shook his head. "Only asked for a couple of them who are as long in talon or tooth as we are—even if I haven't *got* any teeth—and a couple of youngsters who never saw fighting against Ma'ar but proved themselves since. Judeth's entire contingent won't number more than ten. Enough to be useful, not so many as to be a burden or get in the way. If we *have* to cut our way out and run, we'd better not have too many people to keep track of."

Amberdrake nodded agreement. "I suppose that's all I needed to hear, then, if that's *all* you said and did." He squinted tiredly against the sunlight.

Skan chuckled. No point in telling Amberdrake about the "no questioning allowed, this is orders," attitude he'd taken with the folks back home. What would the point be, after all? Amberdrake would only worry about his "image," and he frankly didn't care about his "image" at the moment.

And no point in telling him about Kechara, either, he thought with a pang.

The little misborn had been unhappy that her "Papa Skan" had been away so long, and even more unhappy when she sensed the worry in the others as Skan issued his orders. He had spent quite a bit of time Mindspeaking only to her before he went to sleep.

I tried to tell her that everything was fine. I tried to reassure her. He thought he'd been very convincing, but then again, it wasn't too hard to convince Kechara of much of anything. She believed him because she was Kechara, and she believed in everyone and everything.

He'd told her how proud he was of her, praised her for her hard work in watching all of them from such a great distance. Judeth had told him about that—how Kechara had decided all on her own to keep a watchful eye on all of them, touching their surface thoughts several times a day without them ever being aware of it. He was only grateful that purest chance had caused her to pick times when none of them had been worried about their situation.

Then she had to ask me when Father Urtho was coming back, and if he was with me here. That had given him a serious wrench, although he'd managed to cover it without her noticing.

So far as Kechara knew, her "Father" was still alive, somewhere, doing something vague but important. No one had ever tried to tell her anything to the contrary. The deception made her happy, after all—and in a sense, that was probably just what Urtho, or Urtho's spirit, *was* doing.

Besides, no one was entirely sure she understood what death meant—and if she didn't know, no one wanted to be the one to tell her.

I had to tell her he wasn't with me, and that I didn't know when he'd be back. Sketi, I'm not altogether certain that I'm going to be back. How could I tell her that?

He had tried to prepare her—if anyone could prepare simple little Kechara for such a terrible revelation—that sometimes people went away and didn't come back again. He'd meant Urtho, but—well—he could only hope and pray that it *wasn't* going to apply to him. . . .

Damn it, it's not going to apply to any of us!

Amberdrake yawned hugely, then apologized, covering his mouth with his hand. "Skan, I'm tired, and I'm going back inside; frankly, the less I show of myself, the more people are going to talk, and that's good for us right now. So I'm going to get some sleep. The Morning Court can proceed without me. I wouldn't be popular there today anyway. But tell Leyuet about this as soon as you can."

Skan ruefully regarded the arrow in his talons. "Given that the skies seem to be more than a bit dangerous today, I probably ought to do the same, at least as far as going back inside and not doing any more flying today goes," he admitted. "I wish I could have spotted the archer. I think I'm strong enough now to lift a struggling body—or a dead one. Just—watch your back for me. Tell Gesten about this."

"Gesten already knows," said a rasping, humorless voice from inside the room, in tones of disgust. "You didn't think you'd get away with me not finding out, did you?"

"Hardly," Skan snorted. "You are the Emperor of all busy-bodies, the King of eavesdroppers. I would never even dream of having a conversation you didn't manage to overhear. I hold all my conversations assuming you will be lurking behind a curtain or beneath a piece of furniture." Then, since he seldom got the last word in any such exchange with the hertasi, he took advantage of the situation and vaulted lightly over to the next balcony, his own, before Gesten could manage to form a reply.

Behind him, he heard Gesten giving Amberdrake a healthy piece of his mind, and chuckled with relief. *Now there is one danger I am* glad *to avoid! Gesten's tongue is worse than all the arrows in the Haighlei arsenal!*

Amberdrake woke for the second time that morning, this time when Winterhart came back in from attending Morning Court in her new role as Consort-To-Be. He stretched with care, and sat up, feeling much the better for the few extra hours of sleep.

She had dressed very carefully for Morning Court, and the transformation she had undergone while he was asleep was amazing. She looked spectacular.

The amber silk gown she wore had been altered slightly; enough to make it into something of a compromise between a northern costume and Haighlei robes. Bands of geometric applique in white and gold had been applied to the wide sleeves and the hem, although there was no matching band at the collar the way a Haighlei costume would have been adorned. Instead, the gold and amber Betrothal Necklace took the place of such a decoration. Her hair had been put up in an intricate arrangement of braids with one of the Lion Lilies nestled in the front, and she wore bracelets matching the Betrothal Necklace around her wrists and a belt of amber plaques carved in lions' heads at her waist. She looked like a statue of marble and golden amber, and not human at all.

Some of the strain she was under showed in the serene expression she wore; the worse she felt, the more like a statue she looked.

"So it's official?" he asked, as she sat down on the side of the bed beside him. "Is that where the bracelets and belt came from?"

She nodded and sighed, fingering the heavy gold of the bracelets. "The rumor is that I have abandoned you for your terrible crimes, even though nothing has been proved against you yet. I, of course, have said nothing. We've already taken enough of my belongings over to the other suite that it will look credible—and I took Windsong with me, too. Or, to be precise, I moved her into the nursery with Tadrith and Keenath." She eyed him apprehensively as if she expected him to object. "She'll be safer there, in case this person gets the bright idea to go after the children."

His stomach turned over at the merest suggestion that harm could come to their daughter. *Gods. That was a possibility I didn't want to think of. I'd better warn Skan.*

He smiled wanly, though, and tried to make light of the situation. "Well, at least I'll be able to sleep late in the morning, now, and she'll have her two playmates from the moment she opens her eyes. Frankly, I pity anyone trying to get in at her—especially if they're trying to get past Makke."

He meant it as a joke, but she only raised an eyebrow, and said quite seriously, "So do I. There's more to Makke than you think."

He raised his own eyebrow. *One mother recognizes and trusts another, I suspect. I must remember never to underestimate maternal protectiveness. Or Makke, for that matter.* "So, from now on, officially you are no longer associating with me." He couldn't help the feeling of depression and abandonment that gave him, though he tried not to show it. That was the one part he really hated about all this. He'd been alone for so very long, and then found Winterhart—he'd never thought he'd have to face an empty bed again.

Now she dropped her mask of serenity. From the bereft expression in her face, she felt the same as he did about any kind of separation—

That gave him a perverse kind of comfort. It made him feel better, knowing that she would be as lonely as he, it made him feel needed and valuable. Did she know that? She might.

It was a good thing, though, that she was a consummate actress. He knew her, and knew without a shadow of a doubt that she would never betray how she felt in public. She had managed a much more difficult task in her past—of completely hiding who and what she was from people who might have recognized her.

And it is just as well that I am as certain of her as she is of me, or when we met in public I would have terrible doubts. He laid his hand on hers as her eyes darkened with unspoken unhappiness. He sensed her heart growing as heavy as his own.

She squared her shoulders and tried to shake her mood off with brave words, as he had known she would. "It won't be forever. And at least if I have to avoid you in public, things can be the same in private." She bit her lip, and he tightened his hand on hers. "In case you are curious, Shalaman has been very sweet, attentive, and entirely brotherly. I doubt anyone else has noticed the difference, but he treats me as if I were a sacred object, and not for such profane hands as his."

"And you are conducting yourself as if you were not only his affianced, but had lost all faith in me." He smiled as she nodded, comforted no end, as much by the fact that she knew to give him that comfort as by the words themselves. "That has to be feeding right into our nonfriend's plans. The more he can sow dissension in our own ranks and make us avoid each other, the more chance he has of implicating all of us in one or another of these murders."

Well, the worst was over; the actual acknowledgment of the separation, the physical fact of it. He found his mind was working again, thinking of possible parameters, now that the emotion was out of the way. In a curious way, he realized that he was enjoying this, despite all the danger, implicit and real, despite the artificial rift between him and his beloved. Skan might be the strategist, but *he* was turning out to be a more than adequate coordinator.

And speaking of that—he should change the subject. Thinking of strategy and tactics would keep both of them from becoming too depressed by their personal thoughts. "Skan Mindspoke with Judeth and some of the others last night. Judeth is coming, along with nine of the Silvers, instead of the diplomatic experts that were originally supposed to join us."

She pondered that for a moment, tracing a pattern on the bed with her fingers. "That's not a bad idea, but I wish we dared have some mages among them. Well, it's not possible, since we don't dare offend Palisar; he's just marginally on our side at the moment, and if we had a mage—"

"He'd probably make up his mind that we'd had somehow had the mage working the killings, and never mind what the Truthsayer said." At her nod, he felt a great deal of satisfaction in his reading of the third Advisor. "How does he feel about the Consort-To-Be?"

She laughed, but without real humor. "He'll put up with me, but only because this isn't real. He really doesn't like us very much. I think we disturb him."

"And I think I need a bath." Amberdrake rose, and headed for the bathroom, gesturing for her to follow. That was one place where they were sure to be left undisturbed even by servants. "I believe you are right," he said, as he slid out of his robe and lowered himself into the bath that had been prepared for him with a little shock at the feel of the cool water against his skin. The tub was sunk into the floor, and Winterhart sat next to the head of the tub to talk to him. These people preferred cool baths over hot; not surprising, given the climate. "Silver Veil told us that the Haighlei both crave and fear changes. I think Palisar is probably the representative of the Haighlei who are most afraid of change—and Leyuet represents those who are somewhere in the middle. The Emperor himself probably represents the Haighlei—the *few* Haighlei— who would welcome changes."

"And Silver Veil?" she asked. "How does she fit into this pattern of change and denying change?"

"Silver Veil is change itself, but hiding within a changeless package." He was rather proud of himself for such a poetic simile, but she made a face and splashed water at him.

He shook the drops out of his eyes, ducked under the surface to rinse his hair, then came up with a new thought.

"I'd like to keep the real identities and purpose of our new 'diplomats' secret even to the Emperor," he continued, combing his clean hair with his fingers. "The only outsider I want to tell is Leyuet—since he's in charge of the Spears, we'll need him to cooperate with Judeth, and he'll have no reason to do that unless we tell him what she is."

Winterhart just shook her head and shrugged helplessly. "Whatever you and Skan decide is fine with me," she told him. "I'm out of my depth with all this skulking-about talk. The best I can do is keep up my part of the deception. You just tell me what you want me to say and do, and I will."

Good gods, am I becoming a leader!

Surely not.

"Exactly as you have been doing." He tilted his head back in open invitation, and she leaned down and planted a warm and lingering kiss, sweet and bitter at the same time, on his lips. "I wonder if you know how remarkable you are," he breathed to her, as her lips left his.

"Oh, I know," she said, with a smile. "But only if you keep telling me."

"In that case," he said, as she reached down to him, ignoring the danger to her robe, and despite the fact that he was soaking wet, "I shall never stop."

They were all together in the gryphons' garden when Leyuet walked in on them with the stiff expression and gray cast around the lips that they had all come to associate with very bad news. This time, at least, he did not bring the Spears with him, but his face betrayed his thoughts, and they were as dark as his skin.

They stared at him in shocked silence for a moment. The sound of falling water seemed unnaturally loud.

Only one thing can have put that particular expression on his face.

"Oh, gods—" Amberdrake exclaimed. "Not *another*—"

He did not have to say anything more. Leyuet nodded grimly, and sat down in a carved wooden seat as if he were exhausted.

He probably is. This is very, very hard on him.

"We discovered it not long ago, but it happened last night, and I'm certain there will be more folk than I who will recall that Skandranon was flying at the time," the Truthsayer said through clenched teeth. "This is the insidious part; whoever is behind this must know where the two of you are at all times now, and makes the murder appear to be the work of the one without an alibi at that time. He must be learning from his mistake the first time."

"I would be surprised if he were not," Amberdrake said, and ran a hand through his hair. "Can I assume that our killer left evidence pointing to Skan?"

"Are marks of a gryphon's claw enough?" Leyuet countered, but now with an odd and ironic air of triumph. "This victim appeared to have been clawed to death by something that came in by way of the open door of the balcony."

He's holding back something, Amberdrake realized—but also realized that he should allow the man to reveal whatever it was in his own good time. *One does not force the conjurer's hand. It isn't polite, and it spoils the trick for everyone, especially the conjurer.*

"And Palisar isn't beating down our door?" Skan said in surprise—obviously the gryphon hadn't seen what Amberdrake had. "I am astonished! How have you kept him muzzled?"

"He kept himself muzzled," Leyuet told them, and fished in the capacious sleeve of his robe for something, the sleeves that every Haighlei seemed to use instead of pockets or pouches.

Ah. Now we have the moment of revelation.

He found whatever it was he was looking for, and held out a silk-wrapped trifle in triumph. Whatever it was, it was about the size of a human finger under the wrapping of black silk.

No one touched it, and Leyuet carefully undid the folds of silk from around it. The last fold fell away, revealing a bit of wood.

Very hard, dark wood from the look of it—and very skillfully carved, into the shape of a gryphon's talon. By the rough bit ending the third "knuckle," there had been a weakness in the wood the carver hadn't noticed, and it had broken off.

"Well!" Amberdrake said, picking the thing up with a bit of silk between it and his fingers, and holding it up to the light. If there were any traces of the carver's identity still on it after contact with so much blood and pain, he didn't want to muddle them by leaving his own traces. "So Palisar is finally convinced?"

Odd. Something about the carving seemed familiar, but he just couldn't place it.

"He couldn't explain *that* away," Leyuet countered, with a grim smile. "He's had temple mages on it, and so far they've found nothing, but he thinks the problem is with them and not the claw; you know how magic is these days. By evening their spells could suddenly go right again."

"Hmm." Amberdrake put the claw back in Leyuet's hand, wrapped again in the insulating silk. "Does anyone else know?"

Leyuet shook his head, and tucked the betraying bit of evidence away again. "Not even the temple mages; Palisar told them nothing. Only the King, the Advisors, and now you know where it was found."

This is important. This might be just what we've been hoping for. "Suppress it," Amberdrake decided instantly. "Let it leak that the victim was clawed to death by something like a huge lion. It isn't going to hurt anything at this stage if Skan goes back on the list of suspects, and if he doesn't—then a rumor just might spread that I'm a mighty mage and can call up demonic creatures to murder my enemies at a distance." He smiled grimly himself. "The latter rumor might help keep me in one piece. If people think I can call up demons, they may think twice about attacking me on their own."

Leyuet nodded; Skan must have told him about the arrow at Morning Court. "The King is coming here to discuss this in a moment, as soon as he can free himself from his guards. Technically, he is coming to have a private moment with Winterhart—"

"Which is an excellent excuse for conferring with all of you," said the King from the door into the gryphons' garden. "No one will dare intrude on the Emperor and his affianced."

Shalaman's baritone voice and steps were full of the vigor and energy of a man many years his junior, and he had donned robes this morning that were a complement, in their color scheme of deep brown, amber, and gold, to Winterhart's. He took a seat beside Amberdrake with the ease of a long-time friend.

"We'd counted on that, Serenity," Amberdrake replied, pleased by the King's casual manner, especially around *him*. It said a great deal—

It tells me also that Shalaman was not exactly in love with Winterhart; he was in love—or at least desired—what she represented. That's rather different from being in love with the person, and easier to get over. Evidently Shalaman had gotten over both his desire for Winterhart and his disappointment in a remarkably short time. *That is an old lesson of the kestra'chern; often, one can be in love with who they think someone is, while being blinded by their own desires. And just as often, instead of being in love with a lover, one is in love with love.*

"Another murder—" Shalaman shook his head, grimacing, but as if he were discussing the death of a complete stranger. Perhaps he was—his Court was enormous, and there was no reason to assume he knew everyone in it personally. "It is interesting that all of the victims have been rather outspoken people with both powerful and disagreeable personalities. They all had—or had at one time—considerable influence, they all had great wealth and personal power, and they all collected many enemies. And—this is not the sort of thing that one wishes an ally to know, but I fear that assassination has been something of a way of life in the Haighlei Courts of the past. Not in *my* Court, or not until this moment, but it still happens in the Courts of some of the other Emperors. If all the signs did not point so forcefully to you foreigners, it might have been accepted as the result of acquiring too many enemies."

"In the case of at least two, there is very little mourning in the gardens of the women," Leyuet said dryly, regaining some of his composure. "They were hardly popular. If the rumors were that one of their enemies had rid the world of their presence, I think this might have been little more than a matter for quiet investigation. One simply cannot have this sort of thing go on in a civilized Court."

Amberdrake suppressed the urge to laugh at the prim look to Leyuet's mouth as he made that last statement. Shalaman caught his eye at that moment, and the two of them exchanged a look of private amusement that flashed between them like a signal between two mischievous small boys.

"Nevertheless, because the evidence points to the foreigners, it now becomes a case of Haighlei against the wicked outsiders," Shalaman said, as his expression sobered. "How did the last die?"

"Clawed to death, it would seem—but look here!" Once again Leyuet displayed his bit of carved wood. The King bent over his outstretched hand with interest, but did not offer to

touch the thing. "This was found in one of the wounds. Now
we have proof that someone is trying to force us to take action
against the folk of White Gryphon."

"But I want this kept secret," Amberdrake interjected. "For
now, at least."

Shalaman straightened, and his mouth twitched with distaste. "I do not like this idea, my friend," he said. "It greatly
troubles me. How can I keep you safe when the hand of every
person in my court is against you?"

Amberdrake licked his lips and chose his words with care.
"We have an enemy, Serenity," he said. "This enemy is very
clever, very cunning. He is intelligent enough to learn from
his mistakes—so we must not let him know that he has made
any. At the moment, the evidence is only that the victim was
clawed to death, and any number of supernatural horrors
could have been called up or created, or even imported, to have
done this thing."

Shalaman pondered Amberdrake's statement, as the sounds
of the garden provided an ironically soothing background.

"But magic is no longer functioning—" Leyuet protested.
"All men know this."

"Someone could have found a live makaar somewhere,"
Skandranon pointed out suddenly. "It doesn't take much
magic to coerce them. They fly, they're intelligent enough to
obey orders, they have claws and fight with them, and they're
absolutely vicious. If I hadn't seen that bit of wood, that's the
first thing I'd have thought of. In fact, when you bring an accusation against me, that's what I'm going to claim—that
Ma'ar must have had an agent with a flock of makaar lurking
down here, and now he's using them to make me look like a
murderer."

"That will sound contrived," the King replied doubtfully,
shaking his head. "Surely you see that."

Skan shrugged, his feathers rustling. "Can't be helped, and
it's a good enough suggestion that some people might think
about it a little before they jump to any conclusions."

"What I am trying to say, is that it is absolutely vital that
we make this enemy of ours think that everything is going

well, so he has no reason to alter his methods," Amberdrake said, bringing the discussion back to his original point. "If our enemies are convinced that there are no flaws in their scheme, that we are all falling into their trap, they will have no reason to alter the way they have been working. If we make them overconfident, they may become careless, and make an even bigger mistake than the one that left behind that claw—and a large enough mistake will be fatal for them."

Shalaman leaned forward to concentrate on Amberdrake's words, and he nodded, though reluctantly. "My concern is this; as I pointed out, although there have been no wars-of-assassination within my Court in my reign, the Haighlei are inclined to such things. I do not want your blood on my hands, because relatives wanted vengeance and were not willing to wait for the Spears to bring it to them."

"I understand," Amberdrake said, feeling Shalaman's very real concern and anxiety for him. He was touched by it; Shalaman had made one of those abrupt internal decisions of many men of great passion and high power—he had decided that Amberdrake was his friend in the moment that Amberdrake forgave him. It was not the first time that Amberdrake had seen such a change of heart in a man of this type, but it was always a little startling when it happened to him personally. "I suggested to Skan in jest that perhaps we should encourage the rumors to spread that one of us is doing this by magic—at least people would think twice about trying to attack one of us, then."

"There is another problem," Leyuet interjected, "One that we had not needed to consider until this latest killing, which points so clearly to Skandranon. We are nearing the Eclipse Ceremony, and we simply cannot make a public decision then on your status as allies while there is such a specter of guilt hovering over you!"

The King nodded. "Now that is true. We cannot make a decision without either declaring your innocence as determined by the Truthsayer, or finding the real killer."

Amberdrake shrugged. "Surely it can wait a little longer than the ceremony—"

"Oh, no," Shalaman said forcefully. "And if we do not make the decision then, we *cannot* do so until the next ceremony. Everything *must* be resolved by the Eclipse itself, or— well, at the very best, you will all have to remain here as virtual prisoners until we catch the real murderer, and then return to your city, and *we* will have to make at least a token effort at evicting you."

Skan sat up straight at that. "What? No one ever said anything about that! How token?" he asked.

Shalaman's expression was not encouraging. "Blood spilled on both sides, to satisfy honor," he said. "Deaths, perhaps. Obviously, I cannot now wed Winterhart to make you my allies without the declaration; that was the only way the question could have been resolved. As you would not be allies, and would be occupying our land without permission, you would have to pay for your presumption in personal currency. I am sorry, but unless we have instituted a change, we must uphold the old ways. If I do not do this, I have no doubt that some of my courtiers will take their own private armies and do it themselves. We are not a peaceful people by nature; it is only our law that makes us so. Every chance to make war within the law is eagerly seized upon."

Amberdrake groaned and buried his head in his hands, his heart sinking. In all of his worst nightmares, he had not thought that the Haighlei would react this way! It wasn't logical!

Then again, our logic and these people seem to have very little in common. Now I understand why Leyuet and Silver Veil kept emphasizing the Ceremony. I hadn't realized that it was quite such an imperative. . . .

Oh, well. I work better under pressure, or at least I can look that way. Calmness in a crisis fosters trust, even if only by contrast.

He raised his head from his hands, and saw that everyone in the garden looked as discouraged as he felt.

He took a deep breath and rearranged his own expression. If Winterhart could pretend convincingly to be estranged from him, he could pretend convincingly to be optimistic.

"We'll worry about that after the Ceremony," he said, firmly. "Unless we concentrate on one thing at a time, we're bound to feel overwhelmed. Right now, the thing to concentrate on is catching this fiend!"

Leyuet's gloomy face brightened as he projected a cheer he did not feel. The King slapped his shoulders heartily, and Skan cocked his head to one side, as if he was holding back a question he'd decided not to ask.

Like whether or not I'm still sane. Or whether I know something I'm not telling all of them.

Perhaps he wasn't sane—but he knew he was right in this. They had to keep their minds focused on catching the murderer, and worrying about the approaching Ceremony would only distract them from that purpose.

"Like any good commander, you see to the heart of the matter and work from there, Amberdrake," Shalaman said, his cheer restored. "So—let us plan our next actions, so as to bring this villain to his knees the sooner!"

Hadanelith leaned forward, threw the wooden claw on the kitchen fire, and chuckled as it burned. Noyoki had mentioned this morning when they all met at breakfast that his magics were coming to him with greater ease now—and perhaps that had been in an effort to compliment Hadanelith for his work in creating as much blood-born power as he had. But the explanation might also be that enough time had passed since the last mage-storm that magic power was resuming some of its old pathways, and if *that* was the case, the Haighlei mages would soon be discovering that fact. While Hadanelith was no mage himself, he had made it his job to find out as much as he could about the spells that "lawkeepers" used to hunt down criminals. No amount of scrubbing would get blood-contamination off a murder weapon; only burning would break the link between it and the last victim.

So that lovely carving must go, consigned to the flames along with every other souvenir that Hadanelith still had in his personal possession. There was that other carving, of course, but that was not his problem. If Kanshin didn't take the proper precautions, that was Kanshin's lookout.

The cheerful bonfire fit in with his feeling of celebration, though, and did not invoke any kind of sense of loss. Everything was going so *well!*

He sat back in the cook's favorite chair and watched the flames crackle merrily. The cook and all of her underlings pointedly ignored him, but he didn't mind. They weren't worth bothering about, and they were all Kanshin's slaves, so they wouldn't go running off to tell someone what he'd done. Even if they told Kanshin, the thief wouldn't care.

But oh, the pure pleasure he got from hearing the latest news from the court, straight from Noyoki's own lips!

Elation made him hungry; he barked an order for fruit into the air, and a slave brought sliced fruit to him directly from the shaking hands of the cook. They might pretend to ignore him, but they didn't dare ignore a direct order. And they feared him; he knew that, and he reveled in it.

He stayed in the kitchen, making the slaves nervous, and eating fruit, until the last of the contaminated objects had been reduced to nothing but ashes in the heat of the bake-oven. Then he stood up and left, overturning the cook's chair with his foot and scattering rinds and cores carelessly before he walked off.

That would teach them not to ignore him!

But the morning's news was too good for a little insubordination to ruin his mood. He strolled back to his rooms, whistling a little, as he contemplated the results of his own genius.

Amberdrake was in the deepest disgrace, of course, and rumor held he was under house arrest. Now most people believed that Amberdrake and Skandranon between them had contrived the murders of their most outspoken foes in the Court, even though the evidence linking them to the deaths was tenuous at best.

So Amberdrake is suffering because he is a murder suspect, and suffering twice because his dear gryphon friend is as much a suspect as he is. He may even be suffering three times over, thinking that the stupid beast might *have decided to do away with some of their opponents in a more direct fashion than simply arguing them down!*

He giggled, for that in itself was a sheer delight. But there was more, much more.

Winterhart had broken off publicly with the kestra'chern, declaring that she could not remain bound to one who was tainted with the suspicion of murder. According to Noyoki, her speech before the Court had been short, but passionate, and had taken everyone by surprise.

It didn't take *him* by surprise; Winterhart was a rigid bitch, and proud to boot. She would never stand for even a hint of impropriety, and her own pride would not tolerate a fall in status. He could have predicted this, although he would have thought it would not happen quite this soon.

But once he learned she had made her break, he knew what Noyoki's next revelation would be. She would either find someone of higher rank than Amberdrake to attach herself to, like any other parasitic, leeching female, or she would turn around and go back to the city.

So he wasn't particularly shocked when Noyoki revealed that the King had declared she had accepted his offer of marriage. It had simply fit in with Winterhart's personality.

It had delighted him, though. Amberdrake must have been shattered; Noyoki didn't know his reaction because he hadn't emerged from his suite. *She* had moved out, though, into private apartments, which put the stamp of finality on the rift between them.

He giggled again, as he flung open the door to his room and glided inside, with a grace even Amberdrake couldn't replicate. Oh, Amberdrake must be reduced to emotional shards, now—for there was nothing he could do to get Winterhart back! Not even if against all odds he proved himself innocent could he get her back! She would never, ever choose to return to someone like *him*, when she was to be the wife of a King!

The greedy little status hunter was probably rolling on her solitary bed right now in an ecstasy of pleasure over her coup and her good fortune.

He would have to find a way to bring her down, too, but without bringing her back to Amberdrake. That would make him suffer even more.

Now—how to go about that? And what to do to her, I wonder?

He sat himself down in *his* favorite chair, the one built into a replica of the little throne he had in his special room back in the settlement. The one with all the delightful surprises built into it. . . .

But before he could settle himself into a good planning session, there was a knock at the door. Frowning, he started to rise, but the door opened before he could get to it, and Noyoki and Kanshin strolled in as though they belonged there.

He glared at them in outrage, and they ignored the glare to appropriate two of the best chairs in the room for themselves. They sat down without even asking if he minded!

Anger held him breathless, which in turn made him speechless.

"You've done exactly as we wanted so far, Hadanelith," Noyoki said, in that supercilious, ever-so-superior tone he always adopted when he spoke to Hadanelith. "The results have been excellent, and Kanshin and I are agreed that you have passed all the tests we set for you."

Tests? Tests? These weren't tests! What is he talking about? The overfed, obnoxious base-born bastard! What does he think he's doing? Who does he think he's dealing with?

"We've selected your next target, Hadanelith," Kanshin said—nervously though. Very nervously. Hadanelith quieted his rage and set it aside. This was odd; he'd never seen the scrawny little thief nervous about any assignment ever before. What could be so difficult about this one?

"Your next victim will be Shalaman," Noyoki said with such careless casualness that it had to be an act.

"Shalaman? The Emperor?" Hadanelith was incredulous, and even angrier than before. He jumped to his feet and faced them both with his fists clenched at his side. "What have you been drinking? You *know* I won't handle a man, I have no interest in them!"

He felt his face flush with fury and outrage. Just who did these two think they were? He'd told them he wouldn't target males—not for *that*, anyway! There was only one man he'd ever be willing to kill, and only after he'd made Amberdrake suffer a great deal more than he had so far! It would take years, decades, to inflict all the misery he'd planned on Amberdrake's soul!

"Now, Hadanelith, we know it's going to be dangerous," Kanshin said in a wheedling voice, as if he were a recalcitrant child. "We're prepared to take care of that. Haven't we always?"

Hadanelith shook his head violently in disgust, his vision turning red around the edges, he was so angry with them. What was the matter with them? Danger didn't worry him, and they knew it—danger was only a spice!

"I am *not* targeting a male!" he spat. "I told you that before, and I'm not changing my mind just because you think you have a way to kill the Emperor and get away with it!"

"Well, if you're afraid—" Noyoki began.

Hadanelith spat on the floor at his feet in a deliberate insult. "Hardly! Why should I fear one fat old man? I *won't* take him as a target, that's all! That was our bargain—I get targets I like!" He narrowed his eyes, and the red of thwarted rage suffused his entire field of vision. "You're trying to cheat me!"

"Not cheat you—offering you a challenge to your talents!" Noyoki replied, in a coaxing tone of voice. "We know you're brilliant, we planned to give you something with more spice to it than that last target." He gave Hadanelith a sly, sideways look. "How can you resist a chance to assassinate Shalaman at the height of the Eclipse Ceremony?"

Anger vanished, collapsing into itself like a deflated bladder. He gaped at the two of them, certain now that they *had* gone mad—or else that they had been drinking or otherwise ingesting something that had turned their brains to mush in the past few hours.

Assassinate the King! In public!

"You're both mad," he repeated flatly, a chill creeping up

his spine. "Completely mad. You only think *I'm* mad; you two ought to be locked away for your own good."

Neither of them changed their expressions, or even said anything. They just watched him.

"What could you possibly tell me that would make me think you weren't mad?" he challenged, beginning to wonder himself. "Killing Shalaman—that's nothing more than suicidal! I'm not stupid, you know! And you're going to have a fine time dragging me up to the Emperor, strapping a knife into my hand, and throwing me at him, because that's the only way it's going to happen!"

In spite of himself, he felt a tiny bit of intrigue as they continued to watch him narrowly but did not reply. They must have *something* up their capacious sleeves to make this idea possible!

Something besides making the sacrificial lamb out of me, anyway.

It was enough to pique even his curiosity. He wanted to know—but he still had no intention of doing anything about it.

Let them *do it, if it's such a good scheme.* And besides, they still hadn't overcome his basic objection. Shalaman was male. They had given him no reason whatsoever for him to target a male. Males were males, they were not inherently tainted like females were. There would be no thrill in it, and without the thrill, why bother?

"We have an absolutely foolproof scheme," Noyoki said with confidence. "We can get you right next to the King, you can kill him, and we can get you away before he drops to the ground."

Fine. There's still no thrill. His mood turned again, back to anger, this time a sullen anger. What did they think he was, some sort of automaton, a killing machine like a makaar, something that could be sent out on a whim and didn't care what it killed?

"No," he said flatly, folding his arms across his chest. "I don't care how well you planned this, or how foolproof it is. Shalaman's male. Our bargains never included males."

"They didn't include Winterhart, either," Noyoki said, off-handedly.

Hadanelith went cold, then hot, then cold again. His groin flared with excitement, and he fought to get himself back under control before there were any visible signs of his interest. "Winterhart?" he said, lightly, and laughed. "And just how does she enter into this?"

If I could take Winterhart—better if I could have her, mold her—but I'll never get her away from Shalaman. Death would be better; I could hold her in death forever. To be the last thing she saw as she died—to fill her mind and soul with my power to bring her down—

That would make her his forever. He would mark her, brand her as his, and take her away from Amberdrake at the same time.

"She'll be at the ceremony at Shalaman's side," Noyoki told him. "And it fits our plans very well for you to get both of them at once. Unless, of course, you don't think you have the strength and skill to kill the King." He frowned. "I wouldn't have thought that of you. Or is it that you haven't the stomach or the courage?"

"I have all of those," Hadanelith snapped. "It's that I'm not—there's no—I'm not interested in men!"

Noyoki's eyes flashed for a moment, as if something had just come clear to him. Hadanelith ignored his expression; this was a quandary, and no mistake about it. Was it worth wasting time on the King to get Winterhart?

I've done it before; gone through men to get to their women. Back in the camp, it was . . . and here, too. There is a thrill to that—actually—

When the women saw their protectors going down under Hadanelith's skilled blade, when they realized that there was no one left to defend them—there was a real thrill in that. Could he possibly manage that in this case?

"We can get you all the time of the full Eclipse to do what you want," Kanshin said persuasively. "Think of it—coming in out of the dark like a demon, striking and bringing fear as well as death! Besides, we haven't told you the best part yet!"

The best part? There's something more?

He felt his interest rising, and gave up trying to pretend otherwise. They had him, at least for the moment. He might just as well hear them out.

But he was going to do so in comfort.

He sat down again, assumed an expression of total boredom, and yawned. "All right," he drawled, picking a tone of voice sure to infuriate both of them. "I can't get rid of you until you get done trying to persuade me that you both aren't fit only to be locked away, so you might just as well speak your piece."

But they were neither infuriated nor offended, at least not openly, and Noyoki leaned forward in his chair with an eagerness that made Hadanelith think of a night-heron about to spear a fish.

"It's very simple—" he began.

And before Noyoki was finished with the explanation, Hadanelith was giggling. This could be more fun than ever.

Kechara and Zhaneel

Nine

Skandranon spread his newly-dyed wings to dry in the hot sun, knowing he looked entirely too much like an oversized cormorant hanging its wings out to dry, and waiting for the inevitable sarcastic comments. Aubri would never be able to resist this opportunity.

"You look like a short-necked, crook-beaked, fisher-bird, old crow," Aubri chuckled from his position atop a pile of pillows in the cool of the shaded garden. "Maybe one that ran into a rock because he wasn't watching where he was going. I can't wait to see the size of the trout *you'll* pull up."

"I am the one with the taste for fresh fish, lazy Aubri," Zhaneel chided. "You are as forgetful as you are slothful." She poked Aubri with a wingtip, then got up and circled Skan, eying him dubiously. "You will be lucky if those feathers dry at all by nightfall, as humid as it is."

"They'll dry," Skan said, with as much dignity as he could muster, given the undignified circumstances. "Drake is good at this feather-painting business. He used every trick there was to make sure I dry out properly. Don't you remember how humid it used to get in the summer, when Ma'ar pounded the camp with thunderstorms?"

Aubri shook his head. "I think you're going about this all wrong. Damned if I know why you want to play the Black Gryphon again. These people already think that you're a murderer—now you're dyeing yourself black and flying around at night? Are you trying to give them *more* reasons to point fingers at you?"

Skan growled under his breath, while he continued to fluff his body-feathers. Were they sticky? He didn't think so, but until they were dry and he'd had the excess dye rinsed off, he couldn't preen them to find out. "They'll be pointing a lot worse than fingers at me if I'm flying around at night as a *white* gryphon," he pointed out. "I've been shot at once already. If we're going to help catch the real culprits, I've got to find out how they're getting at their victims. Drake thinks they're using magic, but I don't think so, or at least, they're not using magic all the time. I may not be the greatest mage in the world, but I can tell when someone has used magic and there's no trace of it."

"You can tell, when magic is working right, you mean," Aubri countered. "Not even Snowstar is relying on what used to work anymore."

Skan just leveled a look of extreme skepticism at him. "*I* think they're somehow sneaking onto the Palace grounds, maybe in disguise, lingering for a while to watch several potential victims, then taking the first opportunity they see. Or else they already live in the Palace, and they're either servants or nobles. *I* think they're outsiders, Drake thinks they're insiders."

He and Amberdrake had hashed out every possible combination of ideas, and they both had their pet theories. Amberdrake thought the murderers were in the Court and using magic to transport themselves from their own rooms to those of the murder victims and back again. It would be a very nice theory, if anyone could find a trace of magic as powerful as a Gate or Pass-through, and if magic was working at all reliably. Skandranon thought they were disguising themselves as servants and sneaking into the Palace complex, then using perfectly ordinary tricks of thieves to climb into the rooms from the outside.

Which is a nice theory if every guard and every servant is conveniently blind and deaf at the time, is what he says. And

*I must admit there's something rather odd about the idea, be-
cause why would a thief who's that good waste his time on
something like this? He'd be robbing the Palace bare, then
taking the loot off to live in luxury somewhere. Granted, a lot
of what he'd take is identifiable, but it's not that hard to melt
down gold.*

"I don't know, old bird," Aubri said dubiously. "I think
you've picked prey too heavy to carry."

Skan only shrugged. "You can think whatever you want,"
he replied tartly, "but I've made my decisions, and until evidence comes along to make me change my plans, I'm sticking
to them."

"You'd stick to anything with feathers that wet," Aubri
retorted.

"Except you, you filthy buzzard," Skan snapped back. "You
people put me in charge, and that is the way I am going to approach this."

Judeth chuckled sardonically from the deeper shadows under a low-hanging cascade of flowering vines. "I hate to be the
one to tell you this, Skan, but you aren't the one in charge.
Amberdrake is."

The words hit him like a pailful of cold water in the face.
He almost dislocated his neck, whipping his head around to
stare at her.

"Amberdrake is better at coordinating things than you are.
You're better at anything that requires action. Anyone who
knows you both knows that." Judeth shrugged. "Besides, Amberdrake can keep secrets. When have you ever been able to
keep a secret?"

Skan just stared at her, unable to formulate a reply.

"And further, when the evidence comes along that shows
you're being a foolhardy old feather-brain, risking your life
like this, you'll ignore it. We know you, Skan. We know what
you're like. That's the other reason Amberdrake's in charge."
She examined the leather trim on her black tunic with care,
avoiding his eyes. "On the other hand, right now, stupid as it
seems to me, he says you know what you're doing and we
might as well let you go ahead with it."

Skandranon thought about pretending he hadn't heard her, but that would only prove her point rather than refute it. *She's taking Drake as the leader here? Does Drake know this? How could he not? But he didn't say anything to me.*

He felt as if he'd been caught in an invisible whirlwind, in the middle of a cloudless sky. Why would Amberdrake do this? And why not even mention it to Skan?

Maybe he didn't think he needed to. Skan had made no secret of the fact that he was tired of being the leader, of making all the decisions. But—it would have been nice if someone had asked him before they arbitrarily decided to give the job to Amberdrake.

"Drake is risking his life as much as I am mine," he said stoutly, as he tried to rearrange his thoughts to cope with the new situation. No point in making an issue of it here and now, but later—

No, first deal with convincing them that I know what I'm doing. At least Drake is with me on this.

He waved his wings to emphasize his point. "Drake's the one these people think is the real mastermind, if not the author of most of the murders. He's in danger from anyone who decides to go back to the old ways of court assassinations. Shalaman told us that much."

"But he's staying mewed up in his quarters like a sensible person, not lurking in the gardens at night, trying to catch someone climbing in a window," Aubri countered.

"That's because he can't," Skan interrupted. "He never *was* a spy or a fighter, and I was both. And I can beat you, broadwinger, at any game you care to mention."

Aubri shook his massive head, and clacked his beak at Skandranon. "You won't catch me in that trap. I'm *not* in shape, and I'll admit you are. That still doesn't make the game you're playing any saner."

Skan sighed. He'd done his best to convey the urgency of their situation to the Silvers who'd arrived in the guise of diplomats. He thought he'd convinced Judeth, and she was really the only one he needed to convince, since the others were all her underlings. But Aubri was stubborn—

Aubri is old, said a small voice inside him, noting the weight at the keelbone, the slightly shabby plumage, the care with which the broadwinger moved. *He's older than you are, and he took a lot of damage in the war. Well, you did, too, but you were young when you took it, and the young heal fast and thoroughly. He's old, and he's as cautious as any old creature would be. He's forgotten how intoxicating danger can be, and all he remembers is the pain of failure.*

Not that Skan had forgotten the pain of failure—but he wasn't willing to let his actions be dictated by it. Not when the safety of all the people in White Gryphon depended on it.

To his way of thinking, "token" warfare all too often became real warfare. If Shalaman's casual description of the restless nature of his young fighters was at all accurate, Skan didn't think that a "token" effort to displace the settlement would remain that way for long. The first time a Haighlei was hurt or killed in their "token" siege, all the rules would change. Shalaman would be far away, and commanders with a grudge to repay would be on the site.

"Just remember the old soldier's rule, Skan," Judeth said, from her couch among the shadows. "Battle plans seldom survive past the first engagement with the enemy. Be flexible, and be prepared to change your mind and your plans."

She was right, and Skan knew it, and she knew that he knew. He didn't have to like it.

"Who knows?" he said instead. "It may turn out that it's so important that I fly night patrols that you dye Aubri and send him out too!"

"Not if I can help it," Aubri growled. "One crook-beaked fisher-bird is enough."

Skan flexed his wings, testing the feathers for lack of anything better to do.

Who decided that Drake was in charge? Judeth? Drake himself? Both of them together?

Amberdrake had been one of the most expert feather-painters in the whole of Urtho's contingent, and he had learned a lot about feather-dyes in that much-different time. He had sworn to Skan that he could take the barrel of black dye the others had brought, thin it with certain chemicals, and produce something that would dry quickly and without stickiness in the oppressive humidity of this place. It would also have the possibly beneficial side effect of coming out glossy.

Well, no use trying to deny to yourself that you're hurt, Skan. Now be reasonable. Does it matter who's in charge? Objectively, it probably didn't; Skan would do whatever he thought was best, and both Amberdrake and Judeth probably knew that. Objectively, it was actually better for everyone if Skan didn't have to worry about coordinating plans and keeping everyone informed while he was flying clandestine missions.

But it was hard to be objective when you thought you were the Gryphon King and you walked in to find someone else sitting on your throne.

Still, he was going to have to think this one through, calmly and rationally. There was no point in getting upset.

I don't want to be calm and rational! I want to be upset about this! But—no, I guess I'm not really upset. I guess I just have hurt feelings because nobody consulted me.

"Where's Drake, anyway?" he growled. "I think Evening Court is about to start; shouldn't he be here?"

"He said he was going to give everyone something to think about besides the murders," Judeth replied, her lips thinned with disapproval. "He wouldn't tell me what it was; he said he wanted Winterhart to react naturally."

Once again, Skan whipped his head around to stare at her fully, but this time it was with dismay.

He wouldn't tell Judeth, and he must not have told Winterhart—oh, no! Oh Drake, what are you getting yourself into this time?

Shalaman sighed and patted Amberdrake on the shoulder in a surprisingly fraternal gesture. "I hope you know what you're doing, my friend," he said heavily. "This all seems very dangerous to me—not to mention unkind to the lady."

Amberdrake half shrugged, then shook his head. "I hope so

too, Serenity," he replied with honesty. "I hope Winterhart forgives me for doing this to her—but you know my reasons."

Shalaman nodded and knotted the sash on his tunic a little tighter. As always, he looked magnificent, an imposing figure of a man dressed immaculately (if by Amberdrake's standards rather flamboyantly) in a long tunic and loose, flowing trousers of shimmering saffron silk decorated with heavy red, black, and gold embroidery, with a heavy gold pectoral and armbands in a motif of lions. By contrast, Amberdrake looked dreadful.

This, of course, was precisely the image he wanted to have. He was an innocent man, wrongly accused of hideous crimes, whose lady had abandoned him. Anyone in that situation should look dreadful.

His long hair was unbound and artfully disheveled, his robe looked as if it had been slept in and not changed for days (thanks to an extended romp with his daughter and the two gryphlets), he was unshaven, and he had altered his posture to a defeated slump. Shalaman had been gratifyingly shocked to see him.

Unfortunately, he hadn't needed to resort to cosmetics to create the dark circles under his eyes. He'd earned those naturally.

"I can see why you would want to give my Court something to think and gossip about besides the murders," Shalaman said thoughtfully as he got up to pace the confines of the tiny Private Audience Chamber. "But will this accomplish what you hope?"

"If I'm dramatic enough, and if Winterhart responds the way I think she will, they won't be able to talk about anything else," Amberdrake told him grimly. "I'm very good at creating unpleasant scenes. It comes from needing to know how to prevent them."

Shalaman accepted that without comment. "I'm sure, given time, that Leyuet and Palisar could arrive at something that would accomplish the same thing." His eyes, as he turned to look into Amberdrake's face, were troubled. "I do not like to see Winterhart hurt."

"Neither do I—but I must be honest with you. I don't believe that Palisar is particularly motivated to help us, and Leyuet is not very good at gauging what ordinary people are fascinated by," Amberdrake replied, with complete candor. "Most of all, we don't have time. The Eclipse Ceremony is less than a fortnight away. Idle people want scandal and drama, which I'm about to provide in abundance. This will give the courtiers something to take their minds off the deaths of some rather unpleasant people who were fairly minor fixtures of your court. It will also give me a good reason to appear to be locked away in my suite without being under house arrest. And I think doing both these things will force our enemies to show their hands again."

Shalaman sighed, then motioned to his servant to open the door for him. This servant, like the two bodyguards who were also in on the plot, had been with the Emperor for years, and Shalaman swore they were as trustworthy as himself. Amberdrake had to accept that. After all, one of the possibilities he and the others had discussed was that Shalaman himself was at the heart of this mess, creating a situation in which he could declare a full war on White Gryphon with the heartfelt blessings of everyone with any power in his kingdom. It was an outside possibility, very low on their list, but it *could* be the case.

We have to trust someone, somewhere, or nothing is going to happen.

"Very well," the Emperor said. "I bow to your better judgment, my friend. Thank you for warning me."

Amberdrake smiled wanly as Shalaman left, taking the servant with him. He paced the floor himself, measuring out the proper length of time as dripped out by a waterclock, waiting for Court to get underway and all the participants to be in place. Skan wouldn't be there—he'd insured that fact by choosing the afternoon rest period to dye the gryphon's feathers black again. Judeth and her Silvers wouldn't be there, either; he'd simply told her not to attend.

Her reactions had been odd, though, since the time she'd arrived. She'd held herself back from saluting him more than once; he'd seen the little twitch as she restrained the automatic impulse. Judeth hadn't saluted anyone since Urtho died, not even Skan. . . .

Does this mean she thinks I'm the real leader around here? He wasn't certain he was comfortable with that idea—but he also wasn't comfortable with the notion of Skandranon leading this group in the current circumstances. The old Skan was impulsive, quick to think but also quick to act, and likely to run off and do things without consulting anyone. Skandranon's old ways were coming back with a vengeance. This wasn't the best time or place for someone like that to be the leader.

And you aren't acting impulsively? his conscience chided.

I thought this through completely, he told it sternly. *And I consulted Shalaman. If I'd let anyone else in on the plan, Winterhart would have gotten word of it, and I have to have a real reaction out of her, not something feigned. Leyuet's not the only Truthsayer in the place and besides, she's good at hiding emotions. She isn't very good at creating them.*

His conscience grumbled that he was underestimating her. Well, he might be, but it was too late now.

He took a deep breath and slumped his shoulders, opened the door of the small room Shalaman used for private appointments, and headed toward the Audience Chamber. If he did his work right, this would be something that the courtiers here would talk about for decades.

If he did it wrong, they would still talk about it for decades, but Winterhart would rightfully never speak to him again.

He waited at the edge of the crowd for the best possible moment to act. At this instant, Winterhart had no idea that she was in the same room with him—but he knew very well that both his appearance and his reputation as a killer would soon clear a path between them. That, and the expectation induced by his appearance that something dramatic was going to happen.

Whispered word spread through the crowd as if by magic, and as if by magic the courtiers parted along the line his eyes followed toward his lady. The gathered Haighlei parted neatly, as if invisible guards were clearing a path for him, and as they moved back they turned to stare avidly at him.

He waited; she suddenly realized by the stares and stir he created that he was standing near the door to the Audience Chamber, at the end of a cleared corridor that divided the courtiers into near-equal groups. She turned, met his eyes, and started. Silence descended, the heavy silence that falls whenever a mob senses drama.

"Oh, *gods!*" he shouted into the silence, clutching his robe melodramatically at his throat. "Oh, gods, it is *true!* I thought they were lying, I thought—"

He advanced toward her, where she stood at the foot of the platform holding the Emperor's bench. Shalaman might have been a statue; he neither stirred nor spoke. "You bitch!" he snarled. "You faithless dog, running to lick the hand of the first man who offers you a better bone and wallow at his feet! You mongrel cur! You—you—*perchi!*"

She stood staring at him, her eyes round and shocked, her mouth open in disbelief.

"It is not enough that I am accused of vile crimes I know nothing about!" he cried, his voice already hoarse with shouting. "It is not enough that I am a prisoner without a trial! It is not enough that *you* lose faith in me! But to run to fawn at the feet of *him*, to use this as an excuse to make yourself a queen—you are lower than a *perchi!* At least a *perchi* gives satisfaction for the money! You give nothing but hollow lies and false smiles, you feign what you cannot feel, and you don't even do it well!"

He went on with an extensive account of her faults, ranting graphically and at length about her failures as a lover. Finally she reddened, lost the look of utter shock, and he knew he was about to get as good as he had just given.

She was a lady—but she had worked in an army. She had worked among soldiers who saw no reason to temper their language around her, and she had tended gryphons, who were the earthiest creatures he knew. She was absolutely outraged and not thinking at all, and all she wanted to do was to strike back.

By the time she was well wound up and in full voice, if he'd *had* a reputation left, it would have been in shreds.

He got caught up in her hysteria, which fed back to her, and only made the performance better. They railed at each other like a pair of gutter-whores, and for several agonizing moments he was afraid that he *had* done his work too well. She wasn't holding back—and she sounded as if she meant it all.

Then, just as his voice began to hold the intimation of *real* heartache, he caught a familiar sparkle in her eyes.

Relief nearly made him faint—which certainly would have been a dramatic ending to the fight, but not the one he'd intended!

End it now, before she starts laughing!

"I cannot bear this!" he cried, pulling out the knife he'd concealed in the breast of his robe. He raised it over his head—making the motion vague enough that it was open to interpretation whether he was going to kill himself or her.

It didn't matter; the King's bodyguards, specifically warned by the King to watch for this particular gesture, rushed at him, seized him and the knife, and bundled him out. He heard the King issuing orders over his screams to lock him in his rooms.

Now he had every reason in the world never to appear in public—*as himself.*

He was a kestra'chern, adept with costume and drama; he was confident that he could look like a dozen people, all very different from each other—and there were an unspecified number of new "diplomats" from White Gryphon who had just arrived. "Poor, mad Amberdrake" could stay locked in his suite. Someone else would join Judeth's people. Someone taller than Amberdrake, with austere tastes, funereal leather clothing, and a forbidding demeanor, whose slicked-back, dark hair (there were more uses for feather-dye than dyeing feathers) never escaped the mathematically-precise tail at the back of his neck. A personal bodyguard appointed for Skandranon—

And he is going to love that!

The King's two guards only manhandled him as long as they were all in sight of the courtiers. The moment that the doors closed on his private rooms, they released him with apologies.

He thanked them—and handed over the knife with a wink. "I'd rather you gentlemen had this—just in case someone asks what you did with it! I'm a dangerous fellow, you know, and you shouldn't leave me in possession of a weapon!"

They both grinned—showing very white, even teeth in extremely black faces; unlike most of the folk of Shalaman's land, their skin tone was a true black, with a bluish cast to it. "Thank you," said the taller of the two. "It *would* be like that idiot of a Chamberlain to ask that, in front of the Court!"

Amberdrake looked from one friendly face to the other, as something occurred to him. "You seem very—accommodating—to someone who's been accused of murder."

The tall one shrugged. "Here is our logic. The Emperor must believe that you are innocent, or why go through all this? If he believes that you are innocent, he must have brought in his Truthsayer, and for some reason, doubtless a reason that seems good to him, he has not made that public. That is enough for me."

The shorter fellow tossed the "confiscated" knife from hand to hand for a moment, before sheathing it in his belt. "Also—we have seen what was done to those women," the man pointed out. "And we have seen the rooms. Now, this *might* have been done by a mage—but you are not a mage, or you would have gotten rid of them in much subtler ways. It would have been much easier to have them drop over dead with no sign upon them. It might have been done by someone who was both a skilled thief and a skilled torturer, and while as a kestra'chern you have the knowledge to *be* a torturer, it takes a lifetime to learn the craft of the kestra'chern. Therefore, unless you are much, much older than you look, you could not also have become a skilled thief. It might have been done by several people working together—but there has never, during these murders, been a time when three out of the four of you have not had witnesses to prove where you were. I believe in my Emperor, and I believe in the power of the Truthsayer, but I also believe in logic."

Amberdrake had listened to this well-reasoned discourse with astonishment. *This* was a bodyguard?

"You have thought of all that, and you are *only* a bodyguard?" he blurted. "The gods forbid I should encounter a scholar!"

The man laughed aloud.

"Not only a bodyguard, good kestra'chern Amberdrake," he said, with a little bow. "Also the son of King Sulemeth, the Emperor of Ghandai. This is my brother." He indicated the other guard, who bowed also. "This is how Shalaman and every other Haighlei Emperor preserves the peace among us and our lands—they all have sons who are their neighbors' personal bodyguards, as well as daughters who are Healers, Household Priestesses, Wives, or Consorts."

"But I thought—" Amberdrake began, confused, "I thought Shalaman had no wife, no children."

"Shalaman does not yet have sons and daughters by a Chief Wife and Consort," the man corrected with a smile, "But he does have them by the ten Priestess Year-Wives of the first decade of his reign, and that is sufficient to the purpose. Year-Sons and Year-Daughters can inherit if there is no heir by a Chief Wife."

"It is not wise to contemplate violence when your potential foe's sons are the men guarding your back, but this is neither the best time or place for a discussion of our customs. Now, let us leave you to your rest."

"Indeed." Amberdrake came back to his mission with a start. "Thank you for being so civilized."

The taller guard smiled again. "At first, you were thought to be barbarians. We who are at Shalaman's side are also his voices in matters that would be improper for him to speak of. All I can say is that you are not barbaric—you are civilized, only different. The time of Change is upon us all—even the Emperor."

Winterhart stormed into the bathing room just as he was putting the finishing touches on his disguise.

"You! You beast! You miserable dog!" she said, picking up

the first thing that came to hand—which fortunately was a dish of soap and not the feather-dye. "You *bastard!*" She flung it at him; he ducked, and it smashed against the wall.

The single act of destruction seemed to run all of her rage out of her. "How could you?" she wailed, turning from anger to tears in a heartbeat. He froze in dismay; he'd thought she understood back there! "How could you *say* those things? How could—"

"I could say them because I didn't mean them!" he cried, as her distress spilled over into him. "Oh *ke'chara*, how could you think I meant any of that?"

"But the things about—you *know* I'm sensitive about—" she dissolved into sobs, and he dropped everything he was holding to take her in his arms—leaving behind more shards of glass and pottery in his wake.

The moment he touched her, *he* was overcome by the same terrible grief, and for one moment, he could not shut it out. He was so used to leaving himself completely open to her it struck him like a great wave.

Close up, close up now or you never will—

It was a struggle, but he managed to close up his shields before he was overwhelmed and lost.

Think of her as a client, Drake—get her out of this. It's just hysteria and strain, she was close to laughing in the Audience Chamber, and that was as much hysteria as this is. Besides, she's had all this time to brood on it all, and you know how she makes things worse by brooding! Maybe you knew it was just a sham—but she didn't, not for certain, not at the time of the shock. No matter how much she trusts you, it was a shock and she couldn't be positive in her own mind that there wasn't some truth in what you said to her.

He calmed and soothed her with all the resources at his command, now very grateful that their daughter was nowhere nearby. This was the last way he'd want Windsong to see her parents, and as sensitive as she was, she might very well be affected by it all. Such small things as a child built one reaction upon another.

Gentle deflection while appearing to stay on the subject. . . .

"You handled yourself well, lover. You stood in the midst of the Court and spoke your mind without fear. Now, no one will ever think you are hiding your true feelings. I don't see how anyone *could!* The breeze we feel tonight should be from their lips flapping!"

Finally he had her laughing again, mostly at the absurdity of the situation, at the shocked and avid expression he'd seen on the courtiers' faces, at the effect the outburst had invoked in the staid and mannered life of the Haighlei Court.

"They looked as if we'd dropped a muck pile in the middle of the floor," he chuckled. "If this shocked them, I wonder what they would have thought of the tantrums some of Urtho's people used to pull in public?"

"Oh, you've quite driven every thought of the murders out of their minds, beloved," she said as he wiped her face with a damp cloth to remove all traces of tears, then led her back into the bedroom. "You've driven all thoughts of *anything* else out of their minds, at least for the next day or so. It was all they could talk about, and now I know who favors what faction, just by whether or not they came up to sympathize with me or politely gloat at my situation."

"Gloat?" he said. "The ones who don't want you as Consort, do you suppose?"

She nodded as they both sat down on the bed. Sunset had come and gone, and the usual evening breeze had sprung up, driving the stale humidity from the room. "And those very few, mostly women, who really don't believe that you're guilty and who think I'm everything you said about me for deserting you and taking the Necklace." She quirked an eyebrow at him, with just the faintest hint of jealousy. "You have *quite* a devoted following in some quarters. I wouldn't be the least bit surprised if they start showing up at your door, wanting to console you in your deep distress."

"Console me?" he said in dismay. "There are women who feel sorry for me and want to console me?" That was a possibility that hadn't occurred to him and it presented any number of unpleasant and inconvenient possibilities!

"Hadn't counted on that, hmm?" She was smiling smugly

now, and didn't bother to hide it—probably in just retribution for what he had just put her through. "Oh, yes, I'm sure they'll be eager to console you, personally and intimately. However, the King's physicians have said you're mad and not to be trusted without a keeper. Theoretically, he has sent one to take charge of you, so no one is going to get in here unless you let him—or her—in."

He heaved a sigh of relief. Trust Shalaman to think of that! He knew his courtiers better than Amberdrake had suspected.

She blinked then and touched his hair as if she had only just that moment noticed it. "What's this?" she asked, startled. "You won't be able to show up in public like that—"

"Not as Amberdrake, but as Hawkwind, Skandranon's bodyguard, there shouldn't be a problem," he told her, and laughed. "Besides, this is a carrier version of the feather-dye. It washes right out again. I won't be able to swim or take a bath in public, but not everyone swims, and these people don't have public baths. I'll just hope it doesn't rain much. Come to think of it, I'd better have a hood with me."

"Why do this at all?" she asked. "We have enough people now. You don't need to go out in public."

"Three reasons." He sat back and stretched his shoulder muscles as he spoke, easing the tension out of them. "Skan should have a bodyguard, and he won't listen to anyone but me. Granted, he doesn't often listen to me either, but at least I have a better chance of getting through to him. Two, if I'm *not* here and an assassin comes calling, I won't be killed, and only the assassin would know I wasn't here. So anyone who would accuse me of sneaking out would be the assassin, or have hired one. Three, no one ever pays any attention to a bodyguard, as I just had brought home to me. I might hear or see something you and Skan don't, since you are Personages and I won't be."

She nodded, and added another reason. "Four, you're going crazy here, cooped up in these rooms."

"I hadn't wanted to mention that," he admitted, "But yes. You're right. It's very lonely here."

He hadn't intended to admit that, but somehow it came out. She blinked thoughtfully, and nodded.

"I can see that," she began, when there was a tapping on the door to the balcony.

Before either of them could answer it, the door opened, and the Black Gryphon stepped in, leaving the door ajar to let in more of the fresh breeze that followed him inside.

"I," he said to both of them, "am one frustrated gryphon."

Skandranon finished the third night of his patrols the way he had finished the first two; with empty talons.

Well, not quite empty—he had already caught three thieves this evening alone. One was not exactly a petty thief, either; he'd managed to scale one of the lesser treasure-towers, and was about to break in through a window hardly big enough to admit a child. Of course, since this man was either a dwarf or of some race that was naturally stunted, the window made a fine entrance. Since the thief was so small, he was able to comfortably snatch the small man from the wall. The Black Gryphon carried the man's tiny, terrified body to the proper authorities, whereupon the thief blurted out a full confession, as they all had. Leyuet's Spears had them all in custody, a neat arrangement so far as Skan was concerned.

He'd assumed that since magic wasn't working properly, their enemies couldn't be using it even to disguise their movement or hide themselves—and that his old night-combat and night-spying skills would be better suited to spotting the culprits from above than even the most experienced Haighlei guard from below. Whoever this was might not think about hiding himself from a watcher above him. Even Ma'ar's people, as accustomed as they were to dealing with gryphons, still occasionally forgot.

All it had netted him, though, was the common and not-so-common thief. No killers. Most of the little rats had not been any kind of threat physically.

Put a bedridden old woman with a cane against any of these clowns, and I would bet on the old woman to beat them senseless.

But he was not going to give up. For one thing, Drake was watching.

The fact that Amberdrake was still considered to be the person in charge of this whole operation still rankled, even though he agreed logically with it. It rankled even though he agreed emotionally—at least in part.

He just hated to think he'd been superseded, and worst of all, no one had *asked* him about it. They'd all just assumed it would be all right with him.

That was what left the really sour taste in his mouth.

As he glided on still-rising thermals, circling with a minimum of wingbeats, it continued to rankle.

Drake is a terrific planner. Drake is a fine organizer. Drake knows what he's doing, and yes, I am a bit too reckless, as long as it's only my own neck I'm baring to the makaar's talon. But still—if they'd just asked me. . . .

He probably would have said yes. He probably would have cheered. Now, it itched like an ingrown feather, and he couldn't stop obsessing on it.

Only a few days to the Eclipse Ceremony, and we still don't have our killer. That was his second ingrown feather. *Shalaman can't marry Winterhart, so he can't ally with us that way. He can't declare us allies while we're still under suspicion. He can't declare us innocent, not without forcing the hand of our enemy in some way we probably won't like. Probably what would happen would be that he would just quit, leaving us with several corpses and no answers, but there are other things he could do—and Drake's histrionics should make him go after another victim before the Ceremony. He'll probably make it look as if I did it, since I'm making myself so conveniently obvious as a potential killer.*

Wait a moment. What's this?

He turned a slow, lazy circle in the sky and peered down at the hint of movement below. There was something or someone climbing up the side of that tower—

Now, it *could* have been a simie, one of those furry little creatures that looked so very human; normally they lived in some of the gardens and made the paintbox-birds miserable

with their antics. But the simies often got out of their desig-
nated "areas" and went looking for something to do, some
new mischief to get into, when they ran out of ways to torment the birds.

*I thought the shadow looked too big to be a simie,
though—heyla!*

There he was. . . .

Skan spiraled down, taking care not to betray himself with
the flapping of wings, and drew nearer.

Silence. . . .

The man was scaling the side of the tower, which was odd,
because there were a dozen better ways to get into it, all of
them involving a whole let less work.

If he was *just* a thief, why bypass all those easier ways in?
He moved with a skill that told Skan he knew exactly what he
was doing. . . .

In fact, he moved in a way that put Skan's hackles up. Move
a little—then freeze in a distorted pose that looked more like
an odd shadow than the outline of a human. Move a little
more, freezing again, this time in a different, but equally distorted pose. He wasn't going straight to his goal, either, but
working his way back and forth along the face of the building
to take advantage of all the real shadows.

This has to be the one!

Just as Skan thought that, the man suddenly vanished, and
only by accident did Skan see the darker shape of a window inside the irregular shadow-shape he had entered.

Skan folded his wings and dove headfirst for the spot,
backwinging at the last moment and thrusting out with all
four claws to catch the sides of the window, and hold him
there.

He clung there for just a heartbeat, long enough to see that
the window was open and that it was big enough for him to enter. Then he plunged forward with a powerful thrust of his
hindlegs, wings folded tightly against his body, head down and
foreclaws out.

Where i— was his last thought.

*   *   *

He woke all at once, which argued that a spell had knocked him unconscious rather than a blow to the head or an inhaled drug. He was, however, still quite unable to move; he was bound in a dozen ways. No matter how he strained against the bindings, he could not move even a talon-length.

He lay on his side staring at a wall, with a rigid bar or board stretched all along his spine. His neck was bound to this bar, and his tail; his head was tethered to the end of it as well, and he thought he had been bound to it in several places along his chest and stomach. His wings were certainly bound. He counted three straps at least, and there might be more.

He was muzzled, but not blindfolded or hooded. There were more bars, this time of metal, fastened to his ankles, holding all of his legs apart in a rigid pose, and rendering his talons useless. He could flex them, and his legs a little, but it wasn't going to do him any good; the ends of the metal bars were against the wall and floor and weren't going anywhere. A collar around his neck was tied to the muzzle and to the bar between his foreclaws.

A soft footfall behind his back warned him that he was not alone. "Quite an artistic arrangement, don't you think?" said a voice that sounded vaguely familiar. "I thought it up myself."

Skan discovered the muzzle was just large enough to permit him to speak. "Fascinating," he said flatly. "And now that you know you've got a successful arrangement for gryphon trussing, would you like to let me go?"

"No," said the speaker. "I like you this way. It reminds me of home."

Why does he sound familiar? Who is this idiot? He's speaking our language, not Haighlei—could he be one of Judeth's people? No, or how would he have killed all those Haighlei women before Judeth got here?

Something about that combination was teasing at the back of his mind, but he couldn't seem to put the clues together into a whole.

"Haven't you recognized me yet?" The voice sounded disappointed. "Oh, this is really too bad! Either *you* are becoming a senile old fool, Black Gryphon, or I am simply not notorious enough. I am inclined to believe the former."

"Which means you have outwitted a senile old fool," Skan replied instantly, with a growl. "Hardly impressive."

He hoped to annoy this person enough to get some useful reaction out of him, but he was again disappointed when the man giggled.

"But *you* aren't the important one, gryphon," the man said smugly. "You're only an annoyance that we had to get out of the way so you couldn't interfere in our real work. We have bigger prey in mind than you."

"We?" Skan asked.

The man giggled again. "Oh, no. You won't catch me in *that* little trap. You have the most remarkable knack for escaping at the last minute—unlike those old bitches I practiced on." The voice took on a sullen quality, rather like an aural pout. "They were hardly good material. All flaws, and nothing really to work on. Very disappointing. Unartistic. Not worth my time, when it came down to that. You have some potential, at least, and I am truly going to enjoy showing him—ah— what you're made of." Another giggle, and this one was definitely not sane. "Now mind you," the man went on, in a belligerent tone, "I don't usually practice my arts on males, but I'm going to make an exception in your case, just to impress Amberdrake."

Skandranon lunged without thinking, succeeding only in throttling himself against the collar. As he choked, he realized how diabolically efficient his captor's bindings truly were, although they gave a little bit more than their creator had intended. *Amberdrake? What's he got to do with this?*

The man wasn't done yet. "I do owe him more than a few favors for what he did to me."

And with that, the last piece clicked into place in Skandranon's mind. *Amberdrake—punishment?—women—tying up— cutting up—*

Hadanelith!

"Hadanelith, you're out of your mind," he said flatly.

"Whatever sanity you had when you lived in White Gryphon coughed once and died when they threw you out on your nose."

"Oh, good—you guessed!" The mocking tone sounded more pleased than anything else. "How nice to be given the recognition one deserves at last! How nice to know one's hard work hasn't been in vain!"

"And just what did you intend to accomplish with all of this nonsense?" Skan asked, making his own voice sound as bored as possible. *Eventually Kechara is going to test my thoughts—she'll find out I'm in trouble and tell the others.*

The only problem is, I haven't the foggiest notion where I am. Hard to rescue me when they have an entire city or more to cover.

"Well, disposing of those old bats was meant to make you lot look like bad little boys and girls," Hadanelith said. "It worked, too—no one likes you anymore. Even the charming and lovely Winterhart deserted you."

There was *no* doubt about the tone of his voice now; gloating. And he lingered over Winterhart's name in a way that was just enough to make every feather on Skan's body stand straight on end. He practically breathed the name. *Winterhart.*

Oh, Kechara, I hope you're listening for me now!

On the other hand, Winterhart's apparent defection from the Kaled'a'in had fooled even Hadenelith. Would that be enough to keep her safe?

"My colleagues have continuing plans, however, which I do not particularly feel like discussing with you," Hadanelith continued lightly. "I trust you'll forgive me. And I hope you won't mind waiting until I acquire Amberdrake before I introduce you to the delights of my skill. I want him to watch. He might learn something. I might even let him live afterward; being left alive would be a better revenge than disposing of him."

Hadanelith's voice took on a grating tone. "Before we all went on this mad flight to 'safety' and you morons built White Gryphon, I practiced my hobbies in Urtho's camp, on all the little human hens huddled around his Tower. I used to watch you and all your oh-so-glorious feathered brethren go off to fight Ma'ar, and inside I cheered when fewer of you came back. Urtho the 'artist' created the gryphons, but he quit too early. He made you to be pretty but shallow. The Black Gryphon will die the shallowest of them all."

With another half-hearted struggle and a gasp, Skan replied softly, almost pleadingly, "Don't mock Urtho."

"Mock Urtho?" Hadanelith laughed very near Skan's head, probably hoping for Skan to lash out fruitlessly again. "Uttering Urtho's name is mockery enough. Still, it would be below my honor to mock a lesser artist. If I had any."

Another of his maniacal giggles, this time farther away.

"Ma'ar, at least, came closer to worthy creation than that so-sweet 'Mage of Boredom.' Ma'ar took what Urtho limply tried with the gryphons and created the *makaar*. Now there was something closer to art. Makaar weren't flatulent, preening extravagances made by a pretend leader, they were hunters. They hunted and enslaved with style. And while on the subject of style, let me tell you of how my next carving will go. I believe an amusing end for the failed legend, the 'Black Gryphon,' would be to carve and rebuild him, into a female makaar."

Oh. My. Word. I can't say I like the way this is headed at all.

"Think of it as being remade into a tribute to the departed lesser artist Ma'ar, Skandranon! Like Ma'ar himself, though, the lifespan of the work will be only temporary. A pity, but then again, transforming the 'Black Gryphon' into the 'Bleeding Makaar' is art enough. The knifestrokes begin *here. . . .*"

He went on at some length and in great detail, describing all of the things he had in mind to do to Skandranon, starting with that most private of parts. He tried to push the mental images of what was going to be done to him away from the fore of his thoughts, although it was difficult. The descriptions of the mutilations were bad enough, but Hadanelith gloated over how the agony could be made to linger. Skandranon had never liked pain at all.

Skan could only stare at the wall, listen, and hope that

there were no mind-shields around this place, that none of Hadanelith's "colleagues" were aware of the gryphonic ability to Mindspeak, and that Kechara would find him quickly enough for the others to search for him.

Because, in three days' time, it was all going to be too late for Skandranon's life to make a difference in the relationship between White Gryphon and the Haighlei. Hadanelith, without a shadow of a doubt, had timed his plans to come to fruition before then.

Zhaneel was doing an admirable job of not panicking, but she wasn't far from it. Her ear-tufts were flat to her head, and her entire posture suggested she was restraining herself by pure will alone.

"Where was he supposed to be flying last night?" Amberdrake asked her. It was hard to think; he was very tired, and last night had been a late one for him. He rubbed his temple, trying to will his fatigue headache away.

She shook her head. "Mostly over the Palace, but he also intended to fly some patterns over the city nearest the Palace walls," she told him. Her feathers already showed signs of overgrooming, ragged around the edges and a bit frayed. "Leyuet says that he last heard from Skan at three on the waterclock, when he brought in another trespasser. This one was let go—he was only trying to sneak in to see his lover among the servants."

"Did Leyuet check that out this morning?" Amberdrake asked sharply.

"I don't know—" She shook her head, sadly. "They did not let the boy go until dawn, to frighten him."

"He couldn't have anything to do with it, then." Amberdrake bit his thumbnail and tried to think. "Skan *must* have discovered the murderers, maybe even stopped them before they could strike again—but then what? Why would he disappear?"

"What could they want with him? Where could they have taken him?" Zhaneel echoed, her voice shrill with worry.

"Kechara has not yet found him!" She dropped her head with distress.

"Remember, she has to know *where* to look, what minds to find him among," Amberdrake told her, patting her shoulder to comfort her. "Right now, she's going to have to search through the whole city to find him."

And we have to hope they don't have shields up to cover him. Kechara is good, but I don't know that she's ever broken a shield. Would she know what to look for?

"Does Kechara know anything about mind-shields?" he asked, wanting to give her something she could act on. "All I know is that they exist, and that some kinds of magic shielding acts like a mind-shield. Could she break one if she found it to see if Skan's under it?"

Zhaneel brought her head up, quickly. "I do not know, but I think I can explain it to her!" the gryfalcon exclaimed. "It would be much faster to search for a shield than to search for Skan! As for breaking one—Amberdrake, there is nothing she has tried with Mindspeech that she cannot do, and she might well be able to break one."

"Talk to her, then, the next time she calls you, and ask her." This was the maddening part; the only time the people here, where Skan was presumably captive, could speak to Kechara was when the little gryphon stopped searching long enough to talk to one of the strong Mindspeakers here. There were only two, with Skan gone—Zhaneel and a Kaled'a'in trondi'irn named Summerhawk. Aubri was a Mindspeaker, but not very strong; Winterhart was on a par with Aubri, and Amberdrake's Gifts were in the sensing of emotions and the healing of the spirit, not in Mindspeaking. It was incredibly frustrating—

But at least Snowstar was in charge of Kechara and her search, and he was interrupting her at regular intervals to get her to talk to one or more of them and to rest and eat. Otherwise, the poor little thing was so frantic to find her "Papa Skan" that she was likely to drive herself until she dropped.

If ever we find her limits, it will probably be now.

He racked his brain, trying to think of any other way they

could look for the gryphon. No new murders this morning, and all courtiers accounted for at Morning Court, so if Skan had intercepted the killers, he'd done so before they even got at their potential victim.

And at least he won't be blamed for another killing.

So what else could they do? Ask for a room-by-room search of the Palace? What would that accomplish, besides getting people more annoyed with the Kaled'a'in than they already were?

And besides, if they know there is a search going on, they could and would move him.

"You stay here, just in case he comes flying in with his tail singed," he ordered Zhaneel. "I'm going to go talk to Silver Veil. Maybe she can help."

He left Zhaneel consoling herself with her twins, who played on, oblivious to their mother's worries, and left the suite in his "guard" guise. Like most kestra'chern, by the very nature of her work, Silver Veil was usually alone in the mornings and early afternoon, and he found her enjoying a solitary lunch beside the pool in her own garden. She knew immediately that something was very wrong, of course, even though she did not have the level of Empathy he did.

"What is it?" she asked, leaving her lunch forgotten and hurrying across the garden as soon as she spotted him. "What has happened? I heard nothing of another death!"

"No death that we know of, but Skan is missing," he told her, taking the hands she held out to him with gratitude. "We have a Mindspeaker searching for him, but that takes time."

Her eyes went wide when he said that Skandranon was missing, and her hands tightened on his. "Is there anything I can do to help?" she asked quickly.

"I was going to ask you that; can you think of anything?" He tried not to show his disappointment when she shook her head, but his heart fell a little anyway. He hadn't exactly counted on her coming up with a brilliant plan on the spur of the moment, but he'd hoped, just a bit. She was so resourceful, it was hard to realize that she couldn't do everything, solve every problem.

"I cannot solve every problem," she said softly, as if she had read his thoughts. "I cannot even solve my own."

Only then did he see that her eyes were red, as if she had been weeping, and that there were shadows beneath them that told him she had been spending some sleepless nights.

"I can't do anything more to look for Skan," he told her quietly, drawing her back over to her seat under the trees. "Why don't you tell me about your troubles? I may not be able to help, but at least I can provide a sympathetic ear."

She let him lead her there passively, and sat down again with a sigh. "It is nothing I had not known about when I came here," she said wearily. "It is just that I had not known how it would affect me until I saw Winterhart with the Necklace."

"Winterhart?" he said, puzzled. "What—" But the question was answered by her woeful expression before she could even say a word. "Oh, my very dear! You have gone and fallen in love with Shalaman, haven't you!"

She nodded, a tinge of color creeping over her cheeks. "A dreadful confession for a kestra'chern, to say she has fallen in love with her chief client."

"I did with mine—" he objected, but she waved the objection away.

"Winterhart was not the King," she pointed out. "And you were not in Haighlei lands. It is assumed here, among the Haighlei, that a true kestra'chern is a precious thing, too precious for any one person to have to himself. Yet the King's Consort obviously could not—well. I am caught in a double bind, you see."

"And it would be bad enough that you love him, but he is also in love with you, I suspect," Amberdrake hazarded. "Ah, now a great deal makes sense. That was why he thought he was in love with Winterhart! It was really a reflection of his true feelings for you!"

She nodded. "Your lady is very like me in many ways, and he had every reason to believe that she was accessible to him. I have not let him know of my feelings, and I suspect that custom has made him deny his. As flexible as my King is, he is surprisingly custom-bound."

He let go of her hands and reached out to hold her instead. She did not resist at all but rested her head on his chest with a sigh that conveyed more heartbreak than all the tears in the world.

"I was able to manage when there was no serious contender for his affection," she said softly into his collar. "But when he offered Winterhart the Necklace—oh, it hurt, it hurt! It stabbed me to the heart, and I could scarcely bear to stand there and smile, and pretend to be glad! And even now, although I know it is all a sham, I cannot bear to stay in the Court for very long and watch her in the place of Consort-To-Be at his side!"

"One way or another, in two days it will all be over," he reminded her, with a stab of pain and fear in his own heart, as he wondered just how it would all end. With laughter and triumph—or in bloody war?

"But the situation will still remain," she replied, every word an unshed tear, a whispered fragment of pain. "One day soon, he must take a real Consort, and I know this now, as does he. I will bear it because I must—but, oh, my friend, I shall walk from that moment on upon knifeblades, with spears in my heart until the day I die!"

He stroked her hair, unable to arrive at a satisfactory answer for her. "I wish that I had a magic means of helping you," he said at last. "If there were a kestra'chern of your skill available to take your place, do you think—"

"I do not know," she said, but sadly. "It has never happened before that an Emperor took as his Consort a kestra'chern. I suspect he could order it to be so only at the Eclipse Ceremony."

So much hinges on that damned Ceremony! he thought bitterly. *Even the barest hope of happiness for Silver Veil!*

"I cannot promise anything," he said at last, "but I will do what I can to help you, as you have so often helped me. Perhaps—perhaps, if everything works out properly at the Ceremony, there may be a solution for you as well."

"But you must not tell him of my feelings for him!" she insisted. "You must not! It is bad enough now, but it would be worse for both of us if you do! Loving in silence is misery, but loving, knowing the other loves, and remaining parted is twice the misery! I have seen it happen all too often that way."

Sadly, so had he. "I swear it," he pledged her. "Yet I also swear that I will do what I can to remedy the situation, if a remedy can be found." He cupped her face in his hands, kissed her forehead, and smiled into her eyes. "'I might even offer my own services to the Emperor," he said, only half in jest. "Then, at least, there would be a substitute for you. You often said that I am the one pupil who is your equal."

"You surpass me, and beware lest I hold you to that," she murmured, but she managed a wan smile. "And meanwhile— I shall consult with Leyuet. There may be something that the Spears can do quietly to help search for Skandranon."

"Thank you." He took her hands again, squeezed them gently, and stood up. "I must go back to Zhaneel before she begins plucking her feathers. I will let you know if we learn anything."

"And I, you." She smiled up into his face, this time with more feeling. "Odd, how we can forget our troubles in the troubles of others."

"Isn't it?" he responded.

She escorted him to the door of her suite herself, and let him out with another embrace.

But the moment he left her presence, all the fears for Skan and for their entire precarious situation came back a hundred-fold. He hurried back to the gryphons' quarters, half in hope, and half in fear.

Zhaneel was where he had left her, but her muscles were the tiniest bit less tense. "I have spoken to Kechara," she announced before he could ask anything. "I think she understands the concept of shields, and she is going to look for them. Snowstar is to show her one, and he will teach her to break in if she can. He thinks that she should be able to, especially since these people do not know as much about mind-shields as we."

He heaved a sigh of relief. At least that was one bit of good news in all the bad.

"So now we wait," she finished, with tired and worried resignation.

"Now we wait," he confirmed. "But—we also hope. After all, isn't he the Black Gryphon again? And hasn't the Black Gryphon *always* been able to return, no matter how harsh the odds?"

She nodded. And that seemed to be all the answer she needed, at least for the moment.

Makke, Gesten and the
Gryphon Twins

Ten

Amberdrake paced the floor of the gryphons' suite, surrounded by the rest of the White Gryphon contingent, who were fretting and worrying each in his own fashion. While he knotted and untied a length of satin rope, Zhaneel preened her feathers with exquisite care for each one—preening to the point where she was doing them damage around the edges. Judeth sharpened a knife; by now, it must be the sharpest knife on the continent. The rest of her Silvers were following their leader's example, including Aubri, who sharpened his claws. And Winterhart braided, unraveled, and rebraided the fringes of her sash.

It had been two days since Skan's disappearance, and in all that time Kechara had not been able to contact him.

What she *had* been able to do was to learn what long-distance mind-shields "tasted" like, and how to break or bypass them. That had taken her a day, and Amberdrake was astonished that she had learned in so little time. He had not thought she had the mental capacity to learn *anything* in so short a time period, much less something fraught with so many sophisticated concepts.

She had been searching for mind-shields since dawn, and systematically getting past them. Most of them, predictably enough, were crude things, masking only the minds of those who were Gifted and had shielded themselves against the outside world. Some had been put in place over temples or the minds of Haighlei priests, which again was not surprising, given how these people felt about Mindspeaking in the first place.

Faithfully, she reported every shield found, and every shield broken, although Snowstar was reportedly growing worried that she was nearing the end of her strength.

But time was growing short as well. The Eclipse Ceremony would take place beginning at dawn and ending later tomorrow. Everyone intending to take part in the Ceremony— which was everyone except Zhaneel and Amberdrake—was supposed to meet with the Haighlei priests for a special cleansing that would take until sunrise. Amberdrake was excused by dint of his insanity, and "Hawkwind" because "he" was supposed to be guarding Amberdrake. The servants were due at any moment to come and fetch them all.

There was a knock at the door in the next room. Gesten went to answer it, coming back with the expected result.

"They're here," he said in a toneless voice. "We'd better get going."

Judeth rose from her seat, and the rest stood up with her. "If we're going to have any hope of pulling our tails out of this fire, we have to play along with this," she said, for at least the twentieth time.

Amberdrake nodded, deciding not to answer because as short as his temper was, he was likely to snap at her. She waited for a few moments, then taking the nod and the silence as her orders, ushered everyone else out, including Gesten. Only Makke remained behind to watch the children. Winterhart was the last to go, casting an anxious glance back at him.

He sensed that she wanted to say something—like "don't do anything stupid while we're gone"—but she wisely kept her own thoughts behind her lips. He smiled at her, and mimed a kiss. She did the same.

Then they were all gone. The silence in the suite was enough to make him shake his head with the feeling that he must somehow have gone deaf.

"Well?" he asked finally, just to hear something, even if it was his own voice.

Zhaneel raised her weary head from her foreclaws; she hadn't slept in all this time, and she looked it. "She has found another shield, and she is working on it. This one tastes magical in nature."

He frowned, rubbing his weary, aching eyes. That was odd. That was *distinctly* odd. The chief effect of every mage-storm so far had been to destabilize or knock down shields, so this one would have to have been put up since the last storm.

And to put up a magical shield right now would take an enormous amount of power. Why bother, especially here?

Unless whoever was beneath that shield had something to hide from the priests. . . .

Like more magic! Like—blood-magic!

He had hoped so many times, and had his hopes dashed, that he was afraid to hope this time. And yet—and yet this time all the parameters fit, all of them, and not just some of them.

He waited, and Zhaneel waited, as the water-clock dripped toward three.

Zhaneel suddenly jumped to her feet, uttering a cry that made his ears ring and every hair on his head stand straight up.

"Drake!" she shouted as his heart lurched into a gallop. "Drake, she found him! He is alive!"

Alive, but not necessarily well . . . according to Zhaneel, Skan was trussed up like a bird for the spit, had been cut on a bit, and had not eaten or drunk since his capture. With his high energy needs, he was not in very good shape at the moment, and he was light-headed with exhaustion. Getting details from a tipsy gryphon through a gryphon with the mind of a child to a gryphon who was giddy with lack of sleep was a lesson in patience.

"Little Kechara is worried about her Papa Skan. I can feel it. She hasn't yet admitted to herself that Skandranon's in trouble, but she can tell something isn't quite right. Skan's been trying to soothe her, but he isn't in very good shape, Drake."

"All right, I want every single detail that she can get from him," Amberdrake said wearily. "I want her to describe everything he's hearing, smelling, and seeing. If he's anywhere in the Palace complex, I might be able to identify the place. The gods know I've walked over every inch of it, looking for clues."

Zhaneel nodded, her eyes closed. "There is the smell of peppers, and of night-trumpet," she said, slowly. "The stone of the wall is a pale yellow, and—it is marble." She lapsed back into silence for a moment. "She looks in his memory, and there are fine furnishings, like the ones in our rooms."

"Could be anywhere," he muttered, mostly to himself. "Could even be out in the city. Damn!"

"Sounds, though. There is no sound of people or traffic, and there are always those sounds in the city," she said, and his heart rose a little. If Skan was somewhere, *anywhere,* within the complex, it would make things much easier.

"The sound of falling water," Zhaneel continued. "And windchimes, wooden ones. Oh, there are night-singers, nearby, perhaps in a garden!"

That narrowed it down a little, to one of the less-desirable, older sections of the complex. Night-singers, which were a type of singing insect, had fallen out of favor a century or so ago, but no one had bothered to eradicate them from the gardens of those who themselves were not particularly in favor. The fashion now was for birds that sang at night, or no singers at all—or, more accurately, the fashion three generations ago was thus, and nothing had changed.

"Anything else?" he asked, in desperation, as his back and neck clenched with tension. She spasmed her talons in her pillows, her eyes squeezed tightly shut.

"No—yes!" she said, and her eyes flew open. "There is a sentry, calling the hour, within hearing distance of the room!"

He leaped to his feet, every nerve alive with excitement, his heart racing again. There was only one place where one could hear the hours called as sentries made their rounds, and that was near the outer walls of the huge complex. And because most people did not care to have their sleep disturbed, there was only one building near enough to the walls to hear that—

"He's in the Hall of Fragrant Joy!" Amberdrake said, fiercely. "He has to be!" He thought quickly. "Zhaneel, try to get the priests to let you in to the others. I'll go after him now, while we still have a chance of getting to him before they really hurt him."

"You?" she said incredulously. "You? You are not a fighter! How could you—"

I will not think about this, or I will not have the courage.

"Zhaneel, it is a moonless night and you *know* you don't fly well at night! Skan has enhanced night-vision, but you don't, and if you can't see to fly, you'd have to walk. That puts you on the ground, where you are terribly vulnerable, and that's in the open. Inside—well, I may not be a fighter, but the hallways in that old section of the Palace are narrow, and you would hardly be able to move, much less fight!" He took her head between his hands and looked deeply into her eyes. "And I do *not* intend to fight! I intend to slip in, find him, turn him loose, and get *out* of there! If I go now, I can probably manage so that no one notices me. You couldn't be inconspicuous no matter how hard you try."

She made a growling sound but nodded in agreement.

"Go get the others; badger the priests until they let you in," he urged. "Send them after me. Now, I've got to go!"

He was already wearing the best possible clothing for night prowling; his guise of Hawkwind, black-on-black. She clicked her beak in anxiety for a moment, then appeared to make up her mind, and rushed out the door.

He didn't bother with the door; perhaps he wasn't a fighter, but he hadn't been spending all these years helping to build White Gryphon without learning some rather odd skills for a kestra'chern.

I will not think about this, only do it.

He had a balcony, and it was a lot faster to get to the ground by sliding down the spiral support poles.

And what was more—if their enemies were watching the door, they'd never see him leave.

He went over the balcony railing and hung by his fingertips
for a moment, as he felt for the support pole with his feet. In a
moment, he had it; he wrapped his legs around it and let go of
the railing, sliding down the pole like a naughty boy fleeing
confinement to his room.

Except that, unlike the boy, he had no sense of exhilaration.
His muscles all shivered, and his heart beat double-time with
fear and tension. He was only too aware that he was one man,
alone, and that this course was madness.

A moment later, he was crouched in the shadow of the
bushes at the foot of the pole, listening for the sounds of anyone else out in the garden. *I suppose I could have dropped
straight down; one story isn't too far to fall. Yes, but if I'd broken an ankle, I wouldn't be able to do Skan much good now,
would I?*

He felt the stir of the night breeze against his skin with un-
natural clarity. As far as he could tell, there wasn't anyone
nearby on the grounds. That was the way it should be; everyone of any consequence was in the various cleansing ceremonies, and the only people who were excused from the
ceremonies were the sick, the injured, the mad (like Amberdrake), and those whose duties forced them to work, like the
guards and some of the servants, and probably less than a third
of those. This was the quietest the Palace had ever been.
Lights were going out in every direction he looked, as servants
went from room to deserted room, extinguishing them, in
preparation for the Ceremony.

In this case, the best way to be inconspicuous—if a man
with a face as pale as his ever *would* be inconspicuous here—
would be to act as if he was going somewhere on orders. So
once he made certain there was no one in the immediate area
watching him, he stood up, straightened his tunic, and set off
for the Hall of Fragrant Joy at a fast walk.

He felt as if there were hundreds of eyes on him, and the
skin of his back prickled, as if anticipating an arrow.

He wanted to run, but that was hardly the way to remain
inconspicuous. No one ran, here. It simply wasn't done.

He couldn't have run in any case; the path was visible only

because it was white gravel in the midst of dark green grass. If he tried to run, he'd probably fall and break his neck.

Oh, this is bright, Drake. You're going off by yourself, without any reinforcements. You've assumed that Skan will be alone and relatively unguarded, but you can't be sure of that, now, can you? So you're going off to play the hero, and you aren't exactly suited to the role, you know! And what are you going to do when you get there and find out that Skan isn't alone, hmm? Try and talk your way out of it! I don't think anyone is going to believe you just went out for a stroll and happened to show up where he's being held! And with a pale face like yours, you aren't going to pass for Haighlei!

The internal voice did nothing to still the fear; not even clenching his hands into fists kept them from shaking.

Buildings loomed all around him, poking up above the carefully sculptured foliage of the grounds, dark and lifeless. There wasn't a hint of the sounds that usually filled the night here; no music, no conversation, nothing. Just lightless buildings, with the star-filled sky up ahead, and the white of the path barely discernible in the heavy, flower-scented dark. He couldn't even make out much beyond the bare shape of the bushes and trees beside the path.

Thank you so much, Skan, for running off and not taking anyone to back you up. Even leaving Aubri up on a rooftop while you played mighty warrior would have been enough! Now you're in trouble and I'm running to your rescue like the fool I am. In the dark. Alone. Oh, brilliant, Amberdrake.

This was as close to being blind as he cared to go, and it took all of his concentration to keep from stumbling over uneven places in the dark.

Which was precisely why, when a shadow separated itself from the trunk of a tree overhanging the path and flung itself at him, he didn't have any time to react.

And he didn't even feel the blow to his head that sent him into unconsciousness; there was only a sense of timelessness where awareness should have been.

*   *   *

His head hurt—

It throbbed, horribly, with every beat of his heart. His stomach turned over and there was a taste of blood and something bitter in his mouth. His lower lip stung; he tested it with his tongue, finding more blood, finding it swollen and cut.

His arms were twisted under him and behind his back in an awfully odd pose. He groaned, and tried to roll over. What had he done last night that—

A tugging at his neck stopped him. He couldn't roll over. In fact, he couldn't move at all.

Amberdrake's eyes opened, but slowly, slowly, for they were sticky and felt swollen, and hurt too, though not as much as his head. He didn't learn much of anything, however, for there was nothing more enlightening than a yellow marble wall in front of him. He was lying on his side, but someone had "considerately" propped him up and padded him with cushions placed beneath him in a primitive mattress.

Why does this not comfort me? Possibly because I have obviously been bludgeoned and am now tied hand and foot?

Moving even a little woke pain in his arms and neck, but also told him that much. His arms were pinned together by a restraint at the elbows, behind his back, although they had not been tied so tightly as to be uncomfortable.

Yet. Of course, I'm a kestra'chern, and I can force my muscles to relax, which might help.

His wrists were also strapped together, and there was a collar around his neck that was fastened to something behind him; that was what had kept him from rolling over.

So much for rescuing Skan. Whoever has him must have been watching our rooms. Gods, I hope they didn't get Zhaneel!

Blinding pain washed a red haze over everything for a moment; when it subsided, he continued to take inventory of his situation. Curiously, though, he began to realize that he wasn't afraid any longer. *Maybe because the worst has already happened, so why be afraid?*

His ankles were tied together, and his knees, although he could bend both. He craned his neck a little and bent at the waist as much as the collar would allow, to get a peek at the bindings on his legs. His head throbbed, but there was enough slack in his bindings for him to think about getting himself loose.

If I didn't know better—

"Awake?" Skan rumbled.

"Yes," he said shortly. "What time is it?"

"Mid-morning I think. Well after dawn. Which means the Ceremony is already underway." Skan sighed gustily. "Which completes this disaster, as far as we're concerned."

Mid-morning? Oh, sketi. *That means Zhaneel couldn't get the priests to let her in—or else that they let her in, but wouldn't let her see the others and started her on her own purification rites. Oh, hell. Oh, bloody hell. She's the only one who knows where we are! Or where I thought we'd be—but we may not even be there.*

Not just fear rose up in him—but a hint of panic. This was not just a disaster, this was catastrophe!

He rolled, this time in the direction of the pull on his collar, and managed to get himself faced away from the wall. There was a leash fastened to a ring in the floor to which he'd been tethered, which answered that question, at least.

Skandranon was indeed trussed up like a bird waiting for the spit. He looked very much the worse for wear, but not really visibly damaged—certainly not as damaged as Amberdrake himself was. Another moment of blinding pain held him breathless for a few heartbeats. Then Amberdrake sat up, but slowly, for he had to inch his way over to the tether point of his leash before he could get the slack to sit.

His head protested every move with throbs of pain, reminding him sharply of why it had been a very stupid idea to go rushing off to Skan's rescue without additional help. As if he needed reminding.

"I suppose you rushed off to my rescue without any additional help, right?" Skan said with resignation. "Of course—everyone was being prepared for the Ceremony, but you're supposed to be mad *and* guarding yourself in the persona of

Hawkwind, so you were excused as Amberdrake and Hawk-wind both."

"So that's where the extra Kaled'a'in came from!" said a delighted voice. "I wondered. There were ten new bodies from White Gryphon, but *eleven* new bodies parading about!"

Amberdrake looked up at the grinning madman in the doorway, and his stomach turned over again, sending sour bile into the back of his throat. "Hadanelith," he said tonelessly, his head echoing painfully. "I won't say it's a pleasure to see you again. I suppose you've come to gloat? That's trite enough to be in your style."

Hadanelith strolled over to Amberdrake in a leisurely fashion, and stood just out of range of a kick, frowning down at him. "You know, Amberdrake, you should never have dyed your hair. It's just not a good look for you."

Amberdrake raised an eyebrow at Hadanelith, and his battered mind finally took in the lunatic's costume. He blinked, certain he was seeing things. Why would Hadanelith be wearing a copy of one of Amberdrake's formal outfits?

"At least you've gotten some sense of fashion," he replied, his mind searching frantically for some guess at what the madman was about to do. His stomach lurched again, and his skin crawled. He'd *seen* Hadanelith's handiwork. . . .

"Oh, this little thing?" Hadanelith smoothed down the beaded placket at the neck of his tunic. "It's part of the plan, you see."

"Which you are going to tell us in excruciating detail," Skan moaned, as if he at least was not the slightest bit afraid of Hadanelith's plans, as if being bored was the worst of all possible tortures. "Oh *spare* us, will you? Good gods, does every half-baked villain have to boast about what he's going to do before he does it? Can't you just kill us so we don't have to endure your boring speech?"

Hadanelith turned to glare at the gryphon, and crossed his arms angrily over his chest. "Yes I *do* 'have to boast about it.' I want you to know how and why and the means. I want you to know everything, because there isn't anything you can do to stop it all, and I want you to lie there in agony because you're both helpless."

Skan groaned, but it was the groan of someone who was in dread of having to endure an after-dinner speech, not someone in fear of death. "You haven't come up with anything new, you know," he complained. "Whatever you think you've invented, some other idiot has tried before you. And Ma'ar was better and more imaginative at gloating than you. Trust me, I know."

Amberdrake clenched his muscles to keep from trembling; he knew exactly what the gryphon was up to, and he feigned an equal boredom as Hadanelith turned his back to the gryphon, his spine straight with indignation.

Listen to what he says, pretend to be interested, and he'll shut up. Tell him to get lost and take his little speech elsewhere, and he'll babble like a brook.

"You and all your friends are finished, kestra'chern," Hadanelith spat, turning back to Amberdrake.

Amberdrake yawned stiffly. His lip split and bled a little more. "Yes?" he replied indifferently. "And?"

Hadanelith's face grew red with rage. "You think you're all so clever," he snarled, flecks of spittle forming at the corners of his mouth. "You think you have everything taken care of. But you hadn't planned on magic, had you? *We* have magic, magic that works, *blood*-magic from those foolish women, and a few slaves and scum we took off the streets. We have magic enough to overcome anything; even if a mage-storm came right this moment, we have power enough to push through whatever we want."

Oh, gods. That explains everything. Amberdrake went very, very cold, and struggled not to show it. That was indeed one of the things no one had counted on—that someone was using the power of blood-born magic to push through spells that no longer worked in ordinary circumstances. He began to shake.

"We have a little surprise planned for the Eclipse Ceremony," Hadanelith continued, smiling now. "My friends here have a job they want me to do. Now normally, I wouldn't handle a job like this, but we're such good friends I thought I'd do them the favor." He raised an eyebrow archly. "Don't you want to know what it is?"

"Find the mind you lost?" Skan suggested. "Or could it be the virility you misplaced?"

Hadanelith flushed again, and ground his teeth together with rage. Amberdrake was fascinated, despite his screaming nerves. He'd never actually seen anyone grind his teeth with rage before. It was something you could actually *hear*—and all this time he'd thought it was just a cliché. "We are going to kill the King," Hadanelith got out from between his clenched jaws. "Publicly. At the height of the Ceremony."

He got himself back under control again, with a speed that would have been impressive if he hadn't been insane. He smiled sweetly at Amberdrake, a smile that struck the kestra'chern like a blow and stopped even his shivering. "And as a little present to you, dear Amberdrake," he said in a caressing tone, "we are going to kill Winterhart as well."

Amberdrake felt his face and body freezing into stone, along with his mind. His vision misted, and there was a roaring in his ears.

Hadanelith saw his reaction, and his smile widened. "My friends have more than enough power to whisk me away as soon as I finish the job," he continued with satisfaction. "Everyone will blame you Kaled'a'in, of course. The Black Gryphon will be proclaimed a coward and traitor to his own people, since he disappeared before the King's disposal. One of my friends has positioned himself to take advantage of all this, since the King hasn't yet declared an heir. He'll see to it that the rest of your contingent is rounded up and executed, and that war is declared on White Gryphon. At the end of it all, he'll be the great hero, and they'll probably demand that he take the Lion Throne before he can even claim it himself."

Amberdrake closed his eyes, fighting off a faint. *Winterhart—oh, gods—* He had to think, had to keep Hadanelith talking so he could get the *time* to think.

"Why should the Kaled'a'in take the blame?" he asked thickly, opening his eyes again. "The Haighlei aren't fools, you know—they don't think all Outlanders look alike! You aren't going to fool them by dressing up in one of my outfits."

"Oh, my very dear Amberdrake," Hadanelith said with a laugh that sent chills down his spine. "My dear, dear kestra'chern! They won't see *me* when they see the murderer!"

His features blurred, and for a moment Amberdrake wondered frantically if the blow to his head had done something to his eyes as well. But nothing else was blurring, and in a moment, Hadanelith's face sharpened into focus again.

Except that now it wasn't *Hadanelith's* face.

It was a face Amberdrake knew only too well, for he looked at it in mirrors several times every day. It was the face that Winterhart knew as her own beloved's.

"You see?" said Hadanelith. "These people so abhor magic that they'll never dream someone might be wearing an illusion! That is the gift I have given these people—my originality. They would never have thought of this. They won't see me when they see a Kaled'a'in murdering their King and his Consort-To-Be. They'll see you."

He laughed—or rather, giggled—a high-pitched whining sound that set Amberdrake even further on edge. *I'd have banished him for that laugh alone,* he thought irrelevantly.

"And the last thing, the very last thing that your dear, faithless lady will see," Hadanelith continued gleefully, "is her former lover gutting her with a smile on his face. *No one* will doubt that you are completely capable of killing her and her betrothed; you made that perfectly clear with your dramatic scene in front of the entire Court."

With a sickening wrench, Amberdrake realized that he himself had set the pattern for all of this. And it wasn't the King that Hadanelith wanted—it was Winterhart. He was murdering the King because that was the only way he could get at Winterhart.

"She should have been mine," Hadanelith said softly, as if he didn't realize that he was speaking aloud. Amberdrake sensed the depth of obsession there, and shuddered. How long had Hadanelith been like this? How long had he wanted Winterhart? He must have known he could never have her!

All those women back at White Gryphon—they were in Winterhart's pattern. Lean, elegant, strong-willed until he broke their will—why didn't I see that before?

"If I cannot have her for my own, then I shall make sure no one else has a chance to carve her into another image," Hadanelith whispered, confirming what Amberdrake had been thinking. Then he shook himself, and looked down at Amberdrake again with that odd, foam-flecked smile.

"A gut-stroke, I think," he said meditatively. "In at the navel, to the left, and up. She will linger quite agonizingly, but not long enough for a Healer to get to her in time to save her. Treasure that image in your mind, Amberdrake. Hold it until I come back. Then Skandranon and I will play some charming little games, until I decide whether I'm going to teach you some of my arts, or let you go."

"Let me go?" Amberdrake said, blinking stupidly, struggling against the multiple blows to his soul.

"Of course!" Hadanelith giggled again. "Why not? No one would ever believe you, and it would be such a major help to my friends if they were the ones to 'capture' you and bring you to justice! I understand that Haighlei executions are terribly entertaining."

As Amberdrake stared at him, Hadanelith raised his right hand and wiggled the fingers at him in a childish gesture of leavetaking. "Fare, but not well, dear Amberdrake."

Amberdrake expected him to walk out of the room in a normal fashion, but evidently that was not dramatic enough for him. He pirouetted in place—stepped to one side—and vanished.

"Kechara has all of this," Skan said hoarsely as soon as he disappeared. "That's why I wasn't talking much. She's relaying it to the others now."

Which was, of course, one thing that *Hadanelith* hadn't counted on.

"The problem is that everyone except Winterhart is too far back in the crowd to do any good," Skan continued desperately. "And Winterhart isn't a Mindspeaker, so they can't warn her. They've decked Aubri out with a ceremonial drape that's strapped down over his wings—he can't fly—"

"Never mind," Amberdrake said fiercely, as he willed his muscles to relax *here* and contract down hard *there,* and wriggled carefully in place. *Got to get the strap around my elbows down first—* His muscles protested sharply as he tried to squeeze his elbows together even tighter. *Got to get some slack in the ropes—* "There's something else Hadanelith forgot—"

They were silk ropes, very impressive to look at and very strong, but also very slick. If you knew what you were doing, silk was the worst of all possible bindings, though the most ostentatious.

The elbow ties dropped past the joints. Now he could ease them further down.

By squirming and shaking, he managed to inch the bindings around his elbows down to his wrists.

Thank the gods he didn't tether the elbow bindings to the back of the collar. Inexperienced binders work along the spine only, without thinking diagonally. The way he bound me, it looks nice, but isn't very hard to get out of—something a real *kestra'chern would know.*

He curled over backward until he got his wrists passed under his buttocks, then curled over forward and passed his legs through the arch of his arms. A moment later, he had his wrists in front of him and was untying the bindings on them with his teeth.

"I'm—a kestra'chern—Skan," he said, around the mouthful of slick cord. "A *real*—kestra'chern. I've probably—forgotten—more about knots—and restraints—than that impostor—ever learned. There!"

The cords fell away from his wrists, and the ones that had held his elbows followed them. He unfastened the collar—which was looped through but not even locked!—and crawled over to Skandranon. He could get his legs free later. *Now* it was important to get Skandranon out of here and into the air!

Skan's restraints were artistic, but not particularly clever or difficult to undo, either. "Dilettante!" he muttered, as he untied more silk cords and undid buckles. He had to mutter, to keep the fear at bay a little longer, or else it would paralyze him. "Rank amateur!"

Damn knots! Damn Hadanelith! Damn all these people to the coldest hells! I swear, if I had a knife—if Winterhart—oh, gods, if Winterhart—

Knife—Winterhart—

He blinked, and shook his head as the light took on a thin quality. "Is it me, or is the light fading—"

"It's not you," Skan said, his own voice rasping and frantic. "It's the Eclipse! That idiot Hadanelith *has* to be dramatic, he would never strike at any time but the height of the Eclipse! Hurry!"

"I'm *hurrying*," Amberdrake snarled, doubtful if the red haze he saw was due to the Eclipse. "I'm *hurrying!*"

Shalaman stood tall and proud beneath his heavy weight of fine ceremonial robes, and surveyed his people.

They were gathered below him in a vast sea of faces, as many as could fit into the largest open section of Palace grounds. The Palace gates had been opened today to the public, as they were only opened on the most important of ceremonial occasions, and citizens of the city had been lined up for days to enter, squeezed in together on the other side of a barrier of guards, to view the Eclipse Ceremony with the Court. They were jammed together so tightly that none of them could move. The sheer numbers were overwhelming. Colors warred with each other, and the glare of sunlight on jewelry threw rainbow-hued flashes up into his eyes at unpredictable moments.

The heat down there must have been unbearable, but no one complained or showed any sign of it. This was the Eclipse Ceremony, and time for changes, and no one here wanted to miss a single word.

They were all silent, as his people seldom were. It was entirely possible to hear birds singing evening songs above the faint murmur of breathing and whispers. The light had been thinning for some time now—triggering the birds to go into their sunset melodies—and although it could not be said that the air was getting colder, the sunlight on his skin burned less with every passing moment.

To his right stood Winterhart, and to his left his three Advisors; otherwise, he was alone on the platform of three steps raising up above the level of the crowd. In his mind, he *was* alone, for he and he alone could make the decision about the people of White Gryphon. He was the King; they would listen. They loved him; they knew his loyalty to their interests.

He turned his troubled attention, though not his eyes, on the pale-skinned people from the north. They stood in a group, held away from the platform by an intervening phalanx of his personal bodyguards. He had not wanted to show them any particular favor until he had made up his mind.

He had to recalculate everything he had planned last night. All along, although he had permitted them to remain in doubt, he had planned to bring them into the "changes to come" portion of the ceremony, whether or not the actual murderers were found in time. It would have been better if they had been, of course, but that wasn't strictly necessary. Any words spoken by a Truthsayer during the latter half of the Ceremony had special import, and only today Shalaman had decided to call upon Leyuet to impart publicly all he had learned from the minds of Amberdrake and Winterhart. Having a Bound Couple in the Court would bring special blessings from the gods, and having Leyuet declare Amberdrake's innocence at that point in the Ceremony would give his words all the force of the Gods' Voices.

But he would need the Gryphon King to do that, to speak for his friend—and the Gryphon King was not in evidence. Amberdrake could not be there to speak for himself—officially, he was supposedly mad, and the mad were specifically excluded from the Ceremony.

Without either of the two principals, there was nothing he *could* do about the settlement and the people in it, not with murder charges hanging over them and no one to receive Leyuet's blessing and declaration of innocence.

He'd sent his men for the kestra'chern a few moments ago

anyway, out of pure desperation. The priests wouldn't like the fact that Amberdrake hadn't been cleansed, but that was too bad. If Leyuet declared him sane, his presence wouldn't taint the Ceremony, and once that innocence was made public, the White Gryphon folk could be made allies. But his men weren't back yet, either, and he had taken up as much time with prayer and chanting as he could.

The one thing he could not delay was the Eclipse itself, and it was about to move into its final phase.

He looked down at the image of the sun's face, cleverly duplicated in the middle of a square of shadow at his feet. The shadow itself was cast by a thin plate of stone with a round hole in it, which allowed a single round beam of light to shine directly in front of the King. What happened to that round dot of sunlight was replicated in the heavens above, and there was a substantial bite in the circle, a bite of darkness that was visibly increasing. Out there in the gardens, the beams of light that filtered through the tree branches to fall on the ground also had bites of shadow taken out of them, forming dapples of crescents, and those who were wise were watching them instead of squinting up impotently at the sun-disk itself.

Still no sign of the Gryphon King or of Amberdrake.

This must be as the gods have willed it; we have certainly tried for another solution. With a heavy heart, he raised the staff of his office high over his head and began to intone the Words of Change.

And at that precise moment, as if the gesture had called him there, Amberdrake appeared on the second step of the platform out of thin air.

Shalaman stared at him, mouth agape. *What—the men must have found him—the priests must have built him a magical Portal and sent him directly here so that he would be in time!* He felt giddy with relief. Things were going to be fine after all.

But in the next instant, his relief turned to confusion. There was shouting and pushing down among the Kaled'a'in, and instead of rushing to greet her beloved, Winterhart gasped and recoiled from him.

And there was something very odd, and very *wrong*, with the hungry expression on Amberdrake's face. No sane human wore an expression like that!

Shalaman backed up a pace himself, a cold chill falling over his heart as he looked into Amberdrake's eyes. There was *no* sign of sanity there, and he wondered wildly if this were the real Amberdrake after all—if the man was demon-ridden, and this demonic side of him had been the one responsible for the murders! Certainly this man looked capable of any kind of evil!

The guards were not responding. *Of course they aren't! I told them myself to let him through when he arrived, and they can't see his face, so they don't know anything is wrong!*

Shalaman opened his mouth to call for help—

And could not get any sound to come out.

Nor could he move. He was held in place as securely as if someone had bound him in chains and stood him there. He struggled against his invisible bonds to no avail; they held him fast in the position he had last taken, staff held above his head and free arm outstretched to the sun.

And the last of the sun slipped behind the moon, throwing them all into darkness.

Amberdrake laughed, a horrible, high-pitched giggling; he pulled a knife out of the breast of his tunic, and lunged up the stairs toward Shalaman while the folk of White Gryphon struggled against the guards, shouting incoherently.

Amberdrake screamed and lunged forward with the knife in a vicious series of slashes, cutting the darkness with the glitter of his blade, displaying a knife-fighter's threat show, weaving a pattern of death in the air.

The space of a single breath passed, and a slim figure in silver interposed itself between Shalaman and his assassin.

It was *not* Winterhart—who was dressed in gold, and who was backing away from the assailant with her face frozen in a silent scream.

It was Silver Veil.

Every kestra'chern is taught self-defense, for every kestra'chern may one day require it, she had said once, when he'd expressed worry over her safety. *Every kestra'chern knows the body of man and woman, and knows where to strike if need be.* He had smiled indulgently, then, and with a hint of disbelief. Those were the sort of things a warrior-trainer said to impress his Captain, and were usually of dubious worth. *Now he believed!*

The lovely kestra'chern whirled in a flurry of skirts, and kicked at the assassin's legs, connecting with them expertly and bringing him down on his knees.

But the man was faster than Shalaman could have believed possible; he scrambled to his feet again, and as she tried a second kick, he caught her foot in one hand, then twisted in place and whirled, sending her crashing, gasping, to the ground in a tangle of silver fabric.

And once again, the assassin lunged toward Shalaman, this time unopposed.

Shalaman closed his eyes, the only parts of him that he could still move, and commended his soul to the gods.

At least I shall perish bravely, though I shall not perish as a warrior. Silver Veil, I shall never forget you—

The gods, however, decided that they did not want his soul—at least not right then.

A battle-screech rang out from overhead, and all heads searched the dim sky for its source. Even the assassin jumped, turned, and stared.

Out of the black sun-disk, out of the midnight-at-noon, the Gryphon King plunged with a scream of defiance that shattered the confusion and pierced the spell holding Shalaman captive.

Shalaman flung himself away from the assassin—and toward Silver Veil. The assassin frantically found the right direction—just in time to fling his paltry knife up in puny defense against ten razor-talons and the unstoppable force of stooping predator.

Skandranon, the Black Gryphon, drove the assassin into the stone with a great crunch of breaking bone, sending the blade skittering away—

Just as the sun appeared again from behind the moon, frosting the great gryphon's wings and glinting off his eyes.

The guards at last realized what was happening and started to rush up to the platform, but the Black Gryphon was not yet finished with his wonder-working. He gripped the assassin's face with one clawed hand, made a savage gesture in the air with one talon of the other hand—

And the face of Amberdrake melted away, leaving an entirely unfamiliar—and rapidly bruising—stranger beneath the claws of the gryphon.

Shalaman straightened, still keeping himself between the assassin and Silver Veil. The stranger squealed and struggled, then shrieked with pain as his many freshly broken bones announced themselves to him.

Winterhart took a single look at the man and gasped in recognition.

She started to babble something at Shalaman, but in her distress she was speaking in her own tongue and he couldn't make out a single hysterical word, so he waved at her to be silent. Skandranon mantled at the stranger, all but killing him with his glare. The crushed man soiled himself, unable to stop moving in his sobs of terror.

"Here is your murderer, King Shalaman," Skandranon rumbled angrily. "Here is the man who slew your courtiers in ways not even a mad beast would contemplate, for the sake of collecting the magic power of death and blood, and who held both myself and Amberdrake captive so that his plan to murder you could be completed. He is an exile from among our own people, and I regret that we cast him out instead of finishing him then. We left it to the forest to dispose of a mad beast that we should have dealt with ourselves. He is the one who used his skill in killing to counterfeit the effects of magic, mimicking death-spells with death-skill. *That* was why it looked as if a mage had done the deeds."

"If he is yours—" Shalaman began doubtfully.

Skandranon shook his head. "He is no more 'ours' than the garbage that we bury in the clean earth," the gryphon replied. "We repudiated him and cast him out before we ever met your people. He is not ours, if you are offering him up to our judgment. He is as much yours as any mankilling beast who murders the innocent. He has committed crimes against you and yours, and you may do with him what you will."

Shalaman took a long, steadying breath. "Then you turn him over to us, to be dealt with by our laws?"

Skandranon narrowed his eyes at the whimpering Hadanelith. "He should live so long."

"Lies!" shrieked the captive suddenly. "It is all lies! They cast me out because I would not use my skills for their plans! They—"

"Silence!" Skandranon boomed, tightening his claws on the man's throat until only a faint wheeze could be heard. Sweat stood out on the assassin's pale forehead, and Shalaman might have been tempted to feel sorry for him, if the accusations against him had not been so terrible, and his guilt so sure.

But just to be certain, Shalaman looked to Leyuet, who shook his head. "I need not even trance, Serenity," he said clearly, but with immense dignity. "It is this man who lies. His soul—I dare not touch it." The Truthsayer was gray, and he shivered as if with a fever. "It is vile, filthy—as fully unclean as yours is pure."

There were murmurs of fear and anger from those in the crowd who were near enough to hear, but no doubt—and those in the first ranks turned to spread the word back to the ones behind. The word passed rapidly as Shalaman waved to his guards to come forward.

The man began screaming again, but his words made no sense. "Noyoki, you bastard!" he howled. "Get me away! You promised! Get me away! Help me! *Help me!*"

Was there some rescue that was supposed to have taken place? If so, it appeared that this assassin had colleagues. But "Noyoki?" No one? What kind of a name was that?

"Your conspirators have deserted you, fool," Shalaman said sternly to the struggling, screaming man. "Think of this, as you wait my justice."

Where is Amberdrake? Could he be the reason that no one had rescued the assassin?

No time to think of that now. The guards dragged the assassin away, followed by two priests, hastily waved there by Palisar, who presumably would prevent any escapes by magic means. The assassin was screaming at the top of his lungs, but his words were no longer coherent.

Shalaman could and would deal with him later. What was important was the completion of the Ceremony.

Silver Veil had gathered herself back up again, although evidencing a limp, and was back in her place. The Gryphon King remained beside Winterhart on the platform. Shalaman turned again to face his people, resolutely putting Amberdrake and his fate out of his mind.

"By the grace of the gods and the strength of my friends, I have been spared to serve you!" he called out in a voice that would carry to the edges of the courtyard. "Here is the omen for changes—that Skandranon, the Gryphon King, once as White as his city, has come to my aid in the shape of a Black Gryphon King, and has struck down the murderer of our nobles with his own hands! What say you, my people? Shall we ally ourselves with these honorable folk of the north? Shall we add another Black King to the ranks of the Haighlei?"

The roar of assent was more than enough to drown out any few dissenters. Shalaman bowed slightly in acknowledgment, and turned to Winterhart. He pitched his voice deeply, so as to be heard over the crowd noise.

"Would you give me back the Necklace, my dear?" he asked, looking into her strange, foreign eyes.

She smiled and pulled it off over her head, handing it to him with relief that she did not even try to conceal.

She is soul-bonded to Amberdrake. Surely if something had happened to him, she would know. Wouldn't she?

He took the Necklace, and walked to Silver Veil's side of the platform, where she stood flanked by Palisar and Leyuet. One thing at a time, and the first thing *must* be Silver Veil. She looked shaken, but otherwise unhurt.

Unhurt—except for the fear she had felt for *his* sake, the

shadows of which still lingered in her eyes. That was enough; it gave him all the insight that he needed to see into his own heart.

I never wanted Winterhart. I will find a solution for the problems this will make, later. I will not let this opportunity escape.

"You would have died for me," he said, as the crowd quieted, sensing more drama to come. He felt their presence at his back, heavy, uncomprehending—but in the joy of the moment, willing to accept anything he decreed. He was the King, and this was the time of changes.

She nodded; Leyuet held his breath. But Palisar, grim, dour Palisar, was—was he smiling? And would he remain smiling when he saw what Shalaman meant to do?

"You would have died for me. Would you live for me as well?" he asked. "Would you live for me only?"

He held out the Necklace to her, keeping his eyes on her face and nothing else.

She did not feign surprise, nor did she affect a coy shyness. She was too complex for the former and too honest for the latter. But her eyes lit up with a joy that told *him* everything he needed to know.

His heart's desire had matched hers, and she had kept hers hidden all this time to avoid putting pressure on him. He knew that as if he had been a Truthsayer, to read her soul.

Her joy was doubled by the fact that she had never truly expected to have that heart's desire fulfilled.

"I would, my King," she said simply, "If you will have me."

He raised the Necklace high overhead, then lowered it to place it around her neck as she bent her head to receive it.

Shalaman spared a glance to his other two Advisors. Leyuet's hands were clasped in front of him and *his* face was alive with pleasure—but oddly enough, so was Palisar's!

"You have Year-Sons enough to choose an heir, Serenity," Palisar said, very softly. "Marry now for joy."

That had been the final real obstacle; Palisar's supposed disapproval had fallen like a card balanced upon one edge, and with as little fuss.

He took Silver Veil's hand and led her to the edge of the platform. Once again, a complete silence fell over the crowd.

"To help flush out the murderer, Lady Winterhart posed as my bride-to-be, and honorable Amberdrake feigned madness in a plan to lure the true madman. Let it be known that the honorable leaders of White Gryphon risked their lives and reputations to save Haighlei from murder. Let it be known that the gods themselves have blessed this Palace with a Soul-bonded pair—Lady Winterhart and Kestra'chern Amberdrake."

The people were clearly stunned, even after mentally preparing themselves for the Eclipse Ceremony and all that it entailed. "This is the season of changes," he said into that silence. "And let it begin with the King wedding his beloved Silver Veil!"

The crowd went insane, cheering and bouncing in place, waving scarves in the air where there was room to move. Even the guards were smiling!

He had not realized that Silver Veil was so popular with the people—all the more reason to wed her! A King could not do better with his people, if his Consort proved to be a popular Advisor, popular with the people as well as the nobles.

She moved to the position that Winterhart had held during the first half of the ceremony. Winterhart had already fallen modestly back to a new place beside the weary Gryphon King.

Shalaman surveyed his cheering, joyous people, as the sun brightened with every passing moment, and his heart filled with a content he had never expected to experience.

He held up the staff, and they fell silent again, this time in pleasurable expectation.

"Hear, all ye people, the changes that are to come!" he boomed into the stillness. "We shall ally with the people of White Gryphon, who bring us new arts and new beasts, a touch of the new to every part of our land and life. We add another King to the Haighlei, Skandranon, the Black Gryphon. I take as my bride, my Consort, and my Advisor, the Silver Veil. From this day, it will be allowable that a King may choose to wed his kestra'chern."

He continued, enumerating all the changes, great and

small, that he and his Advisors had determined would be reasonable and acceptable for the next years. The litany went on, but his real thoughts were elsewhere.

I have been given my life by these strangers, he thought, *And—I have been given awareness of my true love. What more could they have given me? I will be in debt to them for the rest of my life, but it is a debt I will joyfully strive to repay.*

Shalaman felt the supporting presence of his beloved and his friends at his back, and smiled at the crowd. He even smiled at Skandranon's grumbling.

"I hope this is over soon. I'm scheduled to fall down and twitch," the gryphon murmured. "Then I'm due to eat everything in sight and sleep for two days, and then—"

Shalaman stifled a laugh at the explicit description of what the Gryphon King would be doing with his mate Zhaneel. These people of White Gryphon would shock and delight his Court for a long time.

Only one shadow still darkened his joy.

Where was Amberdrake?

The Black Gryphon

Eleven

Amberdrake worked the last of his bonds loose, and stood up, hands and feet still tingling. He wished he could ignore the sensation; the best he could do was to keep from making too much noise about it.

Now—find those others Hadanelith mentioned. There are probably two; maybe more, but he talked as if there were only two.

If anyone had ever described Amberdrake to his face as a courageous man, he would have laughed. He had never considered bravery to be one of his chief attributes; that was for others, not for him. He was able to recognize bravery when he saw it, but it was never a quality he would have granted to himself. He was often afraid, and knew it, and did not scruple to show it. Not that brave people weren't afraid, but they were able to get beyond their fear to act. Amberdrake knew, in his heart, that fear often paralyzed him.

Thinking on it, he would not have granted himself *physical* bravery, the kind of bravery that made Skan and Zhaneel fly off and risk their lives, over and over, as if such risk was no worse than a cold bath on a winter morning.

And right now, he felt as if he were the biggest coward in this whole shattered world. As Skan vanished out of sight, all Amberdrake wanted to do was find somewhere to hide until the whole mess was over. He wished he could find a nice, secure room and lock the door so that no one could get at him. That *would* be the sensible course, really—what could he expect to accomplish?

There's no way I can just hide when the most powerful and dangerous of our enemies are both here, somewhere, wherever that is. Something has to be done about them. They may be engrossed with whatever magic they're controlling, or they may be confident they've already won, or—

With no real Mindspeaking ability of his own, he would not know whether Skan arrived in time to save the King and Winterhart until long after the fact. The light grew dimmer with every passing heartbeat—and Hadanelith was due to strike at the darkest part of the Eclipse. No one knew he was here except Skandranon and Kechara. Assuming that Kechara wasn't watching Skan, *she* would know what was happening on his side of this little battle, but otherwise he was on his own.

And somehow I doubt she'll be able to tear her mind away from her "Papa Skan."

Was this how Skan felt when he went off on one of those famous solitary missions? Lonely—and deserted—and completely terrified?

Not terrified, not Skan. He's been scared, but always confident in himself.

Kechara might be able to call for help if things went wrong and she *was* watching him, but that also assumed that she had enough understanding of what she saw to tell the others if Amberdrake was in trouble. She had shown a surprising grasp of abstracts lately, but—well, she was tired, and stressed, and under a great deal of pressure, more than she ever should have had to bear. Little Kechara was more toddler than warrior.

No. I'm on my own here. His insides knotted up as he acknowledged that. *I have to find those so-called "friends" of Hadanelith's, and I have to neutralize them before they can rescue him. If all that means is that I occupy their attention until he's secured against magic, then that's what I'll do.*

That certainly sounded brave enough. He only wished that it was going to be as easy as it sounded.

But they were all running out of time; he'd better find Hadanelith's co-conspirators before the full Eclipse fell!

He gathered up what "weapons" he could find—the ropes he'd been bound with, and a length of metal bar. He picked them all up so quietly that there wasn't even a scrape of metal against the floor, even though he knew objectively that the noise was negligible. At least while he was concentrating on keeping quiet, he could convince his body to move, and not freeze like a frightened tree-hare. He crept toward the door, listening with all his concentration after he made each step. His hands shook so hard he nearly dropped the bar. He closed his eyes and swallowed, willing his hands to stop shaking, but they wouldn't. Finally he reached the doorway; he plastered himself flat against the wall next to the door, and listened again, this time holding his breath.

Nothing. Not even a distant murmur of voices. No matter how thick the walls were, this close to the door he'd surely hear something if there was anyone out there! Wouldn't he?

Carefully, he reached out to the door handle, and eased the door open a crack, his teeth clenched as he waited for the hinges to groan. *That would be just my luck.* But the hinges were silent, and he heard nothing, and there was no sign of a guard on the other side.

Meanwhile, the logical part of his mind was still worrying away at the problem of who Hadanelith's co-conspirators were. *This is—probably—a suite in the Palace, which means that one of Hadanelith's friends* must *belong to the Court. But who could it be!* Unfortunately, Amberdrake had no idea who was quartered where; probably only the Chamberlain would know that. He'd been under the impression that this section of the Palace was about empty. The rooms were not very desirable; they were all too near the outer walls, and the sentries and far-off noise of the city disturbed the nights. There were only a few gardens shared among the suites here, and the entire section was a little too damp during the winter. The only people who lived here, so *he'd* thought, were those too lowly in status to complain about the rooms they were granted. That seemed to fit with someone of low rank, perhaps exacting revenge for being overlooked and slighted, and finding a shortcut to exalted status as well.

But that didn't mean that someone who was quite *high* in status couldn't commandeer a suite or two, especially if they were empty. The conspirators' knowledge of the movements of the courtiers seemed to be that of someone familiar with the ebb and flow of the court.

Then there was Hadanelith's assertion that one of his "friends" could take the Lion Throne, which also argued for a high status. Yet, all the King's Year–Sons were in the guard of his fellow rulers, which would make it rather difficult for one of them to be there and here at the same time.

Unless a Year-Son is using magic to transport himself! Oh, surely that would have been noticed! Or—could he have found someone to impersonate him, and crept back here! That's even more far-fetched a notion than the use of magic to transport him. Impersonators are less reliable than magic—

Or were they? He clenched his eyes closed as he thought about Hadanelith impersonating him, closing in on Winterhart, cutting once to the side, again, up—

Pull yourself together, Amberdrake. Think. Think about what you have learned. Lifebonded pairs can feel each other. If she was hurt, you'd feel—

He'd feel sick, he realized with a lurch of his stomach. What if it wasn't fear for himself that was making his hands shake so? What if this was the side effect of feeling his beloved Winterhart die, somewhere far away?

And what if it isn't! Think, Amberdrake—alive or dead or dying, would Winterhart admire you for shaking and hiding! You have to act. No matter what happens to Winterhart or you, you have to act for the good of White Gryphon.

Amberdrake eased the door open a little more; there was still no reaction indicating someone out in the hallway. He turned his intellect back to narrowing down or eliminate possible suspects; he had a particular suspicion of his own, and he devoutly hoped it was wrong.

But the doubt kept recurring—*could it be Palisar!*

It was a horrible suspicion, no matter how you looked at it.

It was an unworthy suspicion, because he knew very well he would never have entertained it if Palisar hadn't been so openly hostile to the foreigners. But if the Haighlei had customs and rituals for everything, perhaps the Speaker was prohibited from hiding his true feelings, even if it would mean giving himself away to those he plotted against.

But he kept wondering . . . for certainly there was no one better placed than Palisar to know everything about the movements of every courtier in the Palace. Who better to know exactly what was going on, and who better to know which courtier was vulnerable and which was not?

Add to that the fact that Palisar was a priest, a trusted priest. Who better to *ensure* that the chosen victim was alone? If Palisar sent messages to each of the women who'd been murdered, telling them he needed to talk to them alone, wouldn't they have made sure to send every servant off on errands to obey him? He was the King's Advisor, and it might be presumed that the King had a message he wished to send discreetly. He was a priest, and it might be thought that as a priest he had something of a spiritual nature to discuss. Both of those would require absolute privacy.

And he's a mage—there's another thing. If he's anything like our mages, he's been frantic with frustration at the way magic has been rendered unreliable. Our people have tried every way short of blood-magic to bring things back under control, and even Snowstar admitted to me that the temptation to resort to that is a great one after you've had your spells abort one too many times. What if Palisar has gotten his hands burnt too many times by the storms? What if he didn't resist that temptation to resort to blood-bought power?

Granted, every single one of those arguments could be applied to every single priest-mage among the Haighlei, but still—Palisar disapproved of the foreigners, of change in general, and possessed everything required to be the one holding Hadanelith's leash.

I don't know how the succession goes around here, but as a powerful Advisor, he could have some blood-ties to the

King. If he has royal blood, he could see a chance at the throne he wouldn't otherwise get.

Amberdrake touched the door again, easing it open still more. Now it was held ajar enough he could squeeze through it if he wanted to.

I don't want to, but I don't have a choice. He shivered, and clenched his trembling fingers tightly around the iron bar he carried. Even if Skan made it to the Ceremony in time to stop Hadanelith, if Hadanelith got away somehow, things would be worse than they had been before the Ceremony. It would still *look* as if Amberdrake had been the one trying to kill the King.

They're going to want to kill me on sight! The King is going to have orders out to strike first and bring back the body, and I doubt he's going to listen to anything Skan has to say!

Not that Amberdrake could blame him, in the abstract.

What am I doing, just standing here? I have to do something to keep the conspirators from rescuing Hadanelith. Good answer, Drake—and as soon as you magically transform into a squad of mercenaries, it will be no worry at all.

The room began to darken visibly. The last part of the Eclipse must be starting. His time was running out; Hadanelith would strike any moment now! And what if the mages—or mage—wasn't *here*, but was somewhere else entirely?

For a moment, he panicked, then logic asserted itself. *Hadanelith's not predictable enough to be left unsupervised. He was gloating, so he wouldn't see a need to lie. He is insane, but he was never known to lie. He implied they were here, so they have to be here, probably scrying the Ceremony to see when to snatch their assassin back again.*

That made good sense. It also meant that he'd better do something *now.*

Something physical? Against two or more people? Not a good idea. *I'm not a fighter. I do know self-defense, but that isn't going to help me attack someone. What do I have left?*

Bluff?

Well, why not? It couldn't hurt. It could buy time, and as soon as everything is over, Skan can send me help. While I'm bluffing them, they aren't going to be doing anything but watching me. If Skan can catch Hadanelith, the time I buy could give the King's people a chance to shield him against rescue.

Assuming one of them isn't Palisar—

He shook his head angrily, with cold fear a great lump of ice lodged just below his heart. If he kept on arguing with himself, he wouldn't *get* a chance to do anything! Time was slipping away, and the Eclipse wasn't going to delay for anyone or anything.

He pushed the door open, to find himself, not in a hallway, but on the top of a set of stairs. This must be one of the corner towers of Fragrant Joy, where the "suite" was a series of rooms on a private staircase. Very handy, if one was expecting to send an accomplice out over the rooftops at night. And very convenient, if you wanted to isolate a madman in a place he'd find it hard to escape from.

He stalked noiselessly down the staircase as the light grew dimmer and dimmer, listening for the sound of voices. The hand holding the iron bar was beginning to go numb, he was squeezing it so hard. He passed one room without hearing anything, but halfway down to the ground floor he picked up a distant, uneven hum that might have been conversation. A few steps downward, around the turn, and he knew it was voices. A few more, and he distinctly caught the word, "Hadanelith."

He clenched his free hand on the stair-rail, grimly, as his knees went to jelly. It was the other conspirators, all right. Two of them, just as he'd thought, from the sound of the voices. Unless there were others there who weren't speaking.

He pushed the thought that he might be struck down the moment he crossed the threshold resolutely out of his mind. If he thought about it, he'd faint or bolt right back up the stairs again. His throat was tight, and his breath came short; every muscle in his back and neck was knotted up. Every sound was terribly loud, and his eyes felt hot. He forced himself onward. One step. Another. He reached the bottom; there were no more stairs now. He faced a hallway, with several doors along it. He knew which one he wanted, though. It was the first one;

the one that was open just a crack, enough to let light from inside shine out into the hall.

The staircase was lit by a skylight with frosted glass at the top; it grew darker and darker in the stairwell, until by the time he reached the door he wanted, it was as dark as early dusk. The voices on the other side of the door were very clear, and it was with a feeling of relief that left him light-headed that he realized neither of the two speakers was Palisar.

It didn't sound as if there was anyone else there; he took a chance, braced himself, and kicked the door open.

It crashed into the wall on the other side; hit so hard that the entire wall shook, and the two men sitting at a small, round table looked up at him with wide and startled eyes.

Bluff, Drake!

The room was well-lit by three lanterns; a smallish chamber without windows, it held the round table in the middle, some bookcases against the walls, and not much else. There were more things on the shelves than books, though he didn't have the time to identify anything. The men had something between them on the tabletop—a ceramic scrying-bowl, he thought. So his guess had been right!

"Put your hands flat on the table, both of you!" he boomed, using his voice as he'd been taught, so long ago, to control a crowd. He hadn't used command-voice much until the journey west; now it came easily, second nature. "I am a special agent for Leyuet and the Spears of the Law! You are to surrender!"

The two men obeyed, warily and not instantly. That was a bad sign. . . .

"We know everything," he continued, stepping boldly into the room. "We have Hadanelith in custody, and he is being *quite* cooperative. You might as well save all of us time and trouble, and do the same. We know he was working for you; we also know that he was the only one who committed those murders. Since you didn't actually commit the crimes themselves, His Serenity the Emperor might be lenient enough to grant you your lives if you show remorse and confess."

Was that a good enough bluff? Do they believe me? They

still looked shocked and a bit surprised, but the signs of both reactions were vanishing rapidly. Too rapidly.

At that moment, the last of the light faded behind him. Hadanelith was about to strike! He had to keep their attention off that bowl and on him! Or, eliminate the bowl itself—

Oh, gods. What do I do if they try something? He repeated himself, nearly word for word, taking another step forward every few seconds. And meanwhile, he kept straining his senses, hoping for some warning if either of them moved, hoping to have an instant or two in which to act.

And do what?

Skandranon felt a deep-in-the-flesh pain he hadn't felt in a decade, and it radiated out from him badly enough to make Winterhart, Silver Veil, and anyone else sensitive wince. He had been starved and dehydrated, trapped in an unforgiving position for many hours—days!—regardless of his bodily needs, and then forced to fly and fight at a moment's notice. His wingtips shivered with the strain of burning off his body's last reserves.

I am useless now, physically—I'll be lucky to reach our quarters without collapsing. So all I have left is my mind and words.

So he muttered about this and that while the last of the Eclipse Ceremony went on, purposely keeping his voice omnipresent. When at last it felt right, and Palisar was speaking to the assembled sea of people, the Black Gryphon caught Shalaman's attention.

"Amberdrake freed me to save you, before freeing himself," he rumbled. "He may still be in great danger from Hadanelith's accomplices."

Shalaman's countenance took on a new expression, one that the gryphon instinctively knew as that of the King on one of his famous Hunts. To Skandranon's amazement, he unclasped his ceremonial robes and let them fall, leaving only his loose Court robe, then snatched a spear from one of Leyuet's men. "You tell me where," Shalaman said, steely-eyed and commanding, while his personal bodyguards fell in behind him.

The Black Gryphon nodded, then closed his eyes, reaching out with hope. :*Kechara! Kechara, love—please hear me.*:

:*Papa Skan!*:

The voice was there as clear as always, with only a little more than usual of the odd echo that usually accompanied fatigued Mindspeaking. :*Papa! Are you having fun?*:

Skandranon couldn't resist a huge mental smile. Kechara wouldn't understand what was going on if he spent two lifetimes trying to explain it to her. What was important to her was "fun" or "not-as-much-fun."

:*Papa! Are you hurt? You feel like you have an "ow."*:

:*Yes, dear heart, I got hurt a little. I'm very tired. Kechara, love, I need you to look for Amberdrake. Find Amberdrake and help him. Can you do that for me?*:

There was a pause, and then, :*All right! I miss you!*:

Then Kechara was gone from his mind.

King Shalaman straightened up and repeated himself. "You tell me where."

Skandranon met the King's eyes and understood. It was The Haighlei Way. He opened his beak to say, "Follow me," then stopped himself. No. That was not what a King would say to another on his own ground.

Skandranon took a deep breath, refolded his wings, and summoned his last bit of endurance. "Run beside me, King Shalaman, as you run in your great lion hunts, and I will guide you. But we must make haste."

Amberdrake knew, as he flexed his grip on the silk rope and the bar, that his words and acting had failed him. The novelty of his speech was gone. Bluff or not, his status as just one man would catch up with him. Despite what history would show, for better or worse, now was the time for him to throw himself on fate's mercy.

He flung the coil of rope at the table, then pulled, twisting his body sideways with all the strength he could muster.

There was a splash and a scrape, and a moment later, a re-

sounding *thunk* as the scrying-bowl struck the floor. Amberdrake continued his twist and brought the iron bar down on
the bowl to shatter it into a dozen pieces.

That was it, Drake—your one move.

He came to rest on one knee, looking up at the two.

But at that moment, he heard—well, it wasn't precisely a
voice in his mind, and he didn't quite *hear* it—

It was a sense of presence; not words, just feelings, and the
aura of boundless cheer and playfulness overlaid with weariness, but bolstered by endless curiosity.

Kechara! he thought, hard, trying to project the image of
herself back to her.

Feeling of assent. Before he could respond, she sent him a
new sensation; intensified curiosity. It didn't take a genius to
figure out what she was asking, either. "What are you doing?"
was as clear in feelings as in words.

He was breathless with relief—dizzy with the feeling that
he was, at last, no longer alone.

But how had she figured out how to reach him? She was using his *strongest* Gift, that of Empathy, to speak with him
without Mindspeech! Where had she gotten *that* idea?

Fear rose screaming inside him. He didn't have any way to
explain what he was doing—not without words!

*Do what Skandranon would do, Drake—do without words—
without focused intellect—let her feel it—let her in!*

He had never, ever, lowered his barriers completely with
anyone but Winterhart, for an Empath always has to fear being
lost in another's emotions—but how could he ever fear little
Kechara? There wasn't an unkind bone in her body! He
dropped every barrier he had to her, and let her come directly
into his mind, just as the light began to creep back and the
Eclipse to pass off.

He felt his body slip away from him—felt his back and arms
go limp—

One of the two men at the table slid noiselessly out of his
chair and seized something from a bookcase against the wall.
As the man turned, he came fully into the lamplight, making
what was in his hand gruesomely plain.

Amberdrake's stomach lurched, and he sensed Kechara recoiling as well, mimicking his reaction, though she couldn't have any idea what they were both looking at.

It was a wand, crudely fashioned from bone. It *could* have been made of animal bone, but somehow Amberdrake knew that it wasn't. No, this was not just *any* bone, but a human bone, the large bone from the thigh. From one of the earlier victims? *Probably. Probably the first. We'll never know who, I suspect.* Somehow that just made it worse.

This grisly relic must be the mage's primary power-focus, the place where he was storing all the power stolen from those Hadanelith had murdered for him, and all the people he had murdered on his own.

Amberdrake stared at it, his gorge rising and bile collecting at the back of his throat. He couldn't move; he couldn't even think. He could only stare at the nauseating thing, as the mage took in his shock and paralysis, and smiled, slightly. The light strengthened, and the mage moved the wand in front of him, holding it between his palms, and his smile deepened. The other man leaned back in his chair and chuckled. That was when Amberdrake realized that neither of these two had been fooled for an instant. His heart and courage plummeted. They knew he was alone.

This mage was about to level a magical blow at him—and he didn't even have the defenses of a mouse.

He tried to move, and discovered that he couldn't; the bar dropped from his numb fingers and clattered on the floor. This was no spell. It was nothing but pure, overwhelming fear.

I am going to die.

It wasn't even a guess. It was a fact.

:BAD MANS!: Kechara screamed into his mind.

He reeled and dropped to both knees beside his iron bar, momentarily "blinded" and "deafened" by her mental shout, so strong it was clear even to someone who was not a Mindspeaker. Both of the men facing him went stiff with surprise, as if they "heard" it too. Instinctively, he threw up his shields again—which was what she had been waiting for.

:*Bad, bad mans!*: she screeched again, this time accompanying her angry scream with a building mental shriek, aimed at the two facing him. It came like a windstorm that would not stop building, filling his ears.

The two conspirators were *not* expecting anything of the sort. Neither was Amberdrake, for that matter. He was so used to thinking of Kechara as a child, as a complete and total innocent, that he had underestimated her entirely. He had forgotten that she had more than enough experience to recognize a "bad man" when she saw one.

Both of Amberdrake's opponents collapsed on the spot.

:*Ow*,: said Kechara, with a mental wince—and her presence vanished from his mind.

Ow, indeed. For one moment, he took the time to shiver in awe at her power—and to be very glad that she had the guidance of all of her friends who loved and cared for her. *Now* he understood why Urtho had kept her locked up in his Tower for so very long. Her range in Mindspeaking was impressive enough to have made her valuable, but this demonstration of her full potential had been considerably more than impressive. With that kind of mental power, she could have been so dangerous—

Danger. He hadn't been mindblasted by Kechara, but he couldn't move either. He had just experienced, with certainty, imminent death, and he could only sit among the pieces of broken pottery and stare at the still bodies of the two conspirators.

"*Drake!*" a voice called from above, after an indeterminate amount of time. All he could tell, when such matters came to mind through the shock, was that it was fully light again outside. "*Drake! Are you all right! Where are you!*"

"Down here, at the bottom of the stairs!" he croaked back. A few moments later, Skan, Aubri, *and* Zhaneel came tumbling breathlessly down the staircase, following the sounds of a great many hard-shod feet from the presumed direction of the outer door.

"*Drake!*" Skan bellowed, as soon as he caught sight of Amberdrake, making him wince and shake his head as his ears rang. The gryphon grabbed him with both foreclaws, seizing him and staring at him as if he was afraid that Amberdrake would vanish or crumble into dust in the next instant. "Drake—Kechara said you were in trouble, then she just—just blanked out on us. We thought something had happened to both of you! We thought you were—"

"Kechara was right, I was in trouble," Amberdrake interrupted, before Skan could work himself up into hysterics.

Not that he hasn't earned a few hysterics. For that matter, so have I!

With a dazed look he was certain made him look very silly—as if vanity could matter at a moment like this—he peered around at the people filling the area. That was when he recognized King Shalaman.

"This one—" he pointed at the larger man "—is your blood-mage. He was just about to level me with a magical attack, when—I broke their scrying-bowl and they fell down." Amberdrake shrugged. He and the gryphons exchanged hasty warning glances; they all knew Kechara was somehow involved, and they also knew about the prohibition on Mind-speaking. It would be a great deal better for all concerned if the Haighlei never learned about Kechara.

Shalaman said nothing, staring unflinchingly through slit-ted eyes at one of the motionless—but still living—bodies.

"Gods save us!" one of Shalaman's bodyguards stammered. "That is the Disgraced One. The Nameless One."

"Who?" Skan said, "What? What are you talking about?"

"This is the One With No Honor," Shalaman said levelly. "My brother."

The "Nameless One" was bundled up like so much trash, put under as many magical bindings and coercions as the priests could get to work, and then hustled off to some unknown destination. His compatriot was not even treated with the respect one gives sewage. Somehow, Amberdrake had the feeling that this was going to be the most pleasant portion of their experiences with the priests. . . .

Neither Amberdrake nor Skandranon were permitted to leave, although Aubri and Zhaneel were told politely to return to the main part of the Palace with Shalaman and his bodyguard, and wait for them. Amberdrake wasn't particularly worried; actually, he was *wearied,* not worried. In many ways, he and Skan were the heroes of the moment; you don't mistreat your heroes, not even when they've learned something politically delicate, so he didn't have any fear that the "escort" was a thinly veiled guard. In the meantime, he leaned against Skandranon, resting in the glossy black feathers.

Eventually, Leyuet himself arrived, and with him, Palisar.

Skan pulled himself up to his full height as they came through the door, and leveled a stern eye on both of them. "All right," he said. "I assume that we are still here because we now know something that is delicate. So you wanted to speak to us in relative privacy, with no other ears about but those of the Spears. So—speak. You can start with this so-called Nameless One, and what he did to get that way. The sooner we know, the sooner we can eat and bathe and sleep and climb our mates, in whatever order feels right at the time."

"I understand. I would rather not speak of this one," Palisar said with distaste as he took a seat. "Hadanelith has already revealed to us that this piece of trash called himself Noyoki, which means No One, and we would all wish he had *been* no one." Palisar's brows knitted together as he frowned. "He is a blot upon the honor of his family. Still, you have earned the right to know all, and Shalaman has ordered us to reveal it to you. I will not swear you to an oath, but I would ask that what we tell you goes no farther than your respective mates. The fewer who know the whole of this, the better."

He looked pointedly at the two Spears still in the room. They took the hint, and left, closing the door behind him firmly. Amberdrake leaned forward, expectantly.

"The 'Nameless One' is Shalaman's brother," Leyuet began, but Palisar interrupted him with a wave of his hand.

"Half-brother," the priest corrected. "Shalaman's mother was King Ibram's First Consort, and—let us continue to call him Noyoki—this man Noyoki was the last son of the Third Consort, who would be ashamed to have given birth to him were she still alive."

"She was a good woman," Leyuet agreed. He rubbed his

temples wearily; by now he must have a headache that matched Amberdrake's. "There is no blame to her for giving birth to a creature without honor. Perhaps if others had the rearing of him—well, it may be that we shall never know. Perhaps he was without honor from the beginning. Perhaps he was born with some lack of understanding of honor."

Palisar raised a skeptical eyebrow but did not comment upon that observation. "Noyoki was selected as a child as one who had many powers," Palisar continued. "He was sent to the priest-school, just as others of his kind have been and will be. He then misused his magical powers and supposedly was rendered magically impotent. Somehow this did not take place, and you may be certain we will find out what it was that prevented the removal of his powers, and why it was not discovered that he had been left potent."

"I should warn you, out of my experience with northern-style magic," Skan rumbled, "Even if your priests had done their job, it is still possible that with enough will and focus, Noyoki *might* have been able to use the power released by blood-magic to work some kinds of spells."

Palisar sat up in alarm. "Tell me that this is not true!" he exclaimed.

Amberdrake shook his head. "I wish I could, but that is something that is well known in the north. Even with minimal talent or none, *some* people can focus their will enough to make use of powers that they cannot now or could never sense, or could sense only dimly. With more refugees coming down from the north, eventually this knowledge will come to the Haighlei. This is one of the many things we would have told you, if circumstances had not gotten so tangled. Sooner or later, an unTalented blood-mage *will* enter your Empires, and he *will* teach others."

"We cannot stop it." Palisar nodded grimly. "Very well. Then we must work to deal with it when it comes. Together. That will be one of the first items on our agenda."

"Noyoki," Skan prompted. "I want to hear all of this."

"What made this man all the more dangerous was that he had not only possessed the ability to work magic, he also had one other, even rarer ability," Leyuet said gravely. "One we had not seen in decades, even centuries, in this city."

"Which the priests were *supposed* to have blocked before they took away his magic," Palisar continued. "I recall the day that I saw him demonstrate this very clearly. He was able to move things from one end of the city to the other with the power of his will alone."

Amberdrake nodded; now he had the whole picture. "I heard something about Noyoki's story, although my informant would not tell me anything about him, when we were warned that the Haighlei do not permit the use of magic by anyone but the priests. But I would never have guessed this other ability of his. Was that what he had been using to cheat with?"

Palisar nodded grimly. "That was why we priests were so terrified of the idea of a dishonorable man loose with that kind of power. That was why we were to have burnt out that ability first, before we ever blocked away his magic."

"And of course, that was how he got Hadanelith in and out of at least one locked room without a trace, not even a trace of magic," Skan put in, with a decisive nod of his own. "And of course, how he was to put Hadanelith in place to kill Shalaman, and get him away again. It begins to make sense, now."

"We didn't know at the time that he could move anything larger than—say—a water jug, not for any real distance," Palisar replied, grimacing with chagrin, as Leyuet toyed with the carving on the arm of his chair. "He didn't openly use it often, of course. We didn't know such an ability could be strengthened with practice."

Amberdrake looked at Skan. "You and Urtho talked about such things, do you remember talking about anything like this ability?"

Skan flexed his talons and flared his nostrils as he thought. "Such things can be strengthened up to a point. I suspect he couldn't move an object the size of a human very often or for a great distance. That would be why he needed to bring his confederates here, and why he only used it when there was no other way to get at a chosen victim. If it's any comfort to you, it's as rare among our people as it is among yours."

Palisar shrugged. "We'll find it all out for certain in short order," he replied, his eyes focused on some point beyond Amberdrake. "We do not lightly use those whose abilities grant them the means to see the thoughts of others, but when we do call upon them, they are dealing with those whose guilt is known, and they employ their skills without mercy or regard for the consequences."

Amberdrake blinked. Was the priest saying what he *thought? Are they prepared to use coercive force to strip their minds away?*

"Their minds will be broken like eggs before we meet with Shalaman again," Leyuet confirmed grimly. "And like eggs, the contents will be extracted, and the empty shells left behind. We will not slay them. We will not need to. They will, all three, live out their lives in a public place as examples of what the ultimate penalties may be. And in sifting through their minds, we may, perhaps, learn what made them what they are and prevent such a monster from appearing among us again."

Amberdrake shuddered at the ruthlessness in the slender Advisor's words. He knew what a powerful Mindspeaker could do to someone just by accident, having been on the receiving end of Kechara's first "shout," and the edge of the second. He could only imagine the sensation of having one's mind scraped away, layer by layer, until there was nothing left. On the whole—death might have been more merciful.

Did they warrant mercy? Especially after the way they tortured and murdered people? I—I don't know, and I'm glad I'm not the one making the decision. The sounds of birds singing in the gardens outside seemed unnaturally loud and cheerful.

"That, I think is all that needs be said for now." Palisar stood up, then, and gestured to them, a wordless invitation to leave this room and return to the main section of the Palace. Amberdrake was not loath to leave.

I think the strength of fear is wearing off. His joints hurt, his muscles ached with the need to lie down. His mind was in a fog. Later, he would have the strength to think about all of this, but right now—

Right now, he just wanted to fall into Winterhart's arms and rest.

It's over. It's finally over.

The walk back was a long one, and it was accomplished mainly in silence. Both Palisar and Leyuet brooded over their own thoughts, Amberdrake was too tired at the moment to really think of anything to say, and Skan moved haltingly, in no mood to talk. It was only when they reached the door of the Emperor's portion of the Palace that Palisar stopped them all with a lifted hand.

Hot, brilliant white sunlight beat down on them all, but Palisar seemed immune to its effects. "I have some things I must say. I do not favor change," he said, still frowning, "And I did not want you foreigners here among us. I was certain when the murders began that you had brought the contamination of your people here, and that you were the cause, witting or unwitting, of all our current troubles. But I am not a fool, or blind; the *cause* was already here, and your people merely gave birth to the tool. Sooner or later, Noyoki would have found another way to reach for his brother—a man does not recruit a notorious thief to his cause if he is planning to build temples. You tried to be rid of Hadanelith without making the punishment greater than the crimes he committed called for. It was not your fault that he fell into the hands of one who readily used him."

Amberdrake nodded, and waited for Palisar to continue. *He's about to make a concession. I wonder just how large a concession it will be!*

"I said that I do not favor change," Palisar went on. "That is my role, my purpose as the Emperor's Advisor. I do not intend to alter that. But I do not oppose change when it is obvious that it is inevitable. And I do not place blame where there is none." He held out his hand to Amberdrake; not grudgingly, but not with warmth, either. It was very obvious that he was not ready to be the friend of the Kaled'a'in, but at least he was no longer their enemy.

Amberdrake clasped his hand with the same reserve. Palisar nodded, with brusque satisfaction, and they all resumed the walk to the Audience Chamber, the one place where all their answers—or at least, the answers they would get for now—would be waiting."

Two weeks later, Skandranon and Amberdrake watched as Makke packed up the last of the myriad of gifts that the Haighlei had presented to Skan and Zhaneel. The Black Gryphon would never again lack for personal ornaments; he had enough jewelry especially crafted for gryphons to allow him to deck himself like a veritable kestra'chern!

"They're going to make me vain," Skin remarked, as yet another casket of jeweled collars and ear-tuft cuffs went into the packing crate. The curtains at the window and the doors of the balcony billowed in a soft, soporific breeze.

Amberdrake laughed, as he reclined on the only couch in this room. "No they won't. You already are."

Skandranon stared at him with mock effrontery. "I am *not* vain," he protested. "I am merely aware of my considerable attributes and talents. There is such a thing as false modesty, you know."

Amberdrake snorted with derision, and took another sip from the cool drink he held. Skan was pleased to see that the dark circles under his eyes, and the gray cast to his skin, were both gone. The first week after the Ceremony had been rather bad for his friend; all the horrors of what might have been came home to him as soon as he got a little rest. According to Winterhart, he'd had four solid nights of nightmares from which he would wake up screaming.

"I'll be glad to see you back at White Gryphon," Skan continued wistfully. "It's going to be very quiet there without you around."

Amberdrake gazed thoughtfully out the balcony door for a moment before replying. "I don't want to go home for a while," he said, very quietly. "There are things I need to think about before I get back, and this is a good place to be working while I do that." He returned his gaze to meet Skandranon's eyes. "Snowstar sent word that he doesn't want to run White Gryphon."

"Then what I told you a few days ago still applies," Skan told him, wondering tensely if he was going to *have* to return only to shoulder responsibilities that he now knew he was ill-suited to handle. "I had to give him the first chance, since he's been handling everything for me since we arrived here, but—"

"But that's one of the things I need to think about." Amberdrake turned the cup in his hands. "Being the leader of White Gryphon is not something I'd take on without thinking about it."

"I wouldn't want you to," Skan said hastily. "But you'd be good at it, Drake! Listen, I'm already a symbol, and I can't get away from that. I'm an example, and I can't avoid that, either. But if I've learned one thing, it's that I'm not a leader—or at least, I'm not the kind of leader that Urtho was."

"You're a different kind of leader," Amberdrake said, nodding. "When people need a focus and someone to make a quick decision, you're good at that. I've seen you act in that capacity far too often for you to deny it, Skan. You have a knack for making people want to follow you, and the instinct for making the right choices."

"That's all very well, but a *real* leader needs to be more than that." Skan sighed as he watched Makke pack away more gifts, this time of priceless fabrics. "I admire those leaders, but I can't emulate them." His nares flushed hot with embarrassment. "I get bored, Drake, handling the day-to-day snarls and messes that people get into. I get bored and I lose track of things. I get bored and I go stale and I get fat. I make up crisis after crisis to solve, when there aren't any. I turn ordinary problems into a crisis, just so I feel as if I'm doing something. You, though—you're *good* at that kind of thing. I think it's just an extension of what you were trained for."

"What, as a kestra'chern?" Amberdrake raised an eyebrow. "Well, you may be right. There's a certain amount of organizational skill we have to learn—how to handle people, of course—how to delegate authority and when to take it back. Huh. I hadn't thought of it that way."

"And you *won't* get bored and fat." Skan nodded his head decisively. "Judeth says I can have my old job back, so to speak. She'll put me in charge of the gryphon wing of the Silvers. Provided I can find someone to take over my administrative jobs."

"Oh, really?" Amberdrake looked as if he might be suppressing a smile. "Fascinating. I wonder how you talked her into that."

Privately, Skandranon wondered, too. Judeth had been entirely too accommodating.

Then again—leading a gryphon wing took some special talents, and they were talents a mere human wasn't likely to have.

Sometimes getting them to work together feels like herding grasshoppers. It's hard to get them to understand that teamwork is necessary off the battlefield.

"We aren't the only people emigrating out of the battle zone, just the first. She thinks that we're going to need to help the Haighlei deal with more refugees, and they're as likely to be from Ma'ar's army as ours," he said by way of reply. "She wants to have the wing set up and ready to move the first time there's trouble. We're a lot more mobile than you two-leggers; we'll make a good strike and run force."

I just hope that all of those damned makaar died with their master.

"And the more cooperative we show ourselves, the easier it will be to get the diehards like Palisar to fully accept us," Amberdrake acknowledged. "Well, she's right, and you're right, and I have the feeling that we aren't out of the woods yet." His expression turned thoughtful. "You know, the mage-storms are settling down to squalls and dying out altogether, and one of these days magic will go back to being what it used to be. Ma'ar and Urtho weren't the only powerful Adepts up there, just the two *most* powerful. And right now, there probably aren't too many places that are pleasant to live in the North."

Skandranon thought about that for a moment, and he didn't

much like the taste of it. Amberdrake was right; there had been plenty of mages up there, and not all of them died or were burned out in that last conflagration. Most mages had either joined forces with Urtho or with Ma'ar; there was no point in worrying too much about those who had been with Urtho, but those who had been with Ma'ar couldn't *all* have been eliminated.

And there had been a few mages, Adepts all, who had opted to sit out the conflict between Urtho and Ma'ar—to wait and watch from within hiding, and see precisely who won before making moves of their own. And where were they?

No one knew. No one would know, unless they came out of hiding. *When a wizard chooses to go into hiding, there isn't much that can pry him out until he's good and ready to come out.*

But no other mage had ever had anything like the gryphons. They had proved to be Ma'ar's downfall.

We could surprise someone else, too.

Well, that didn't matter at this very moment. What *did* matter was that there were two tasks facing the people of White Gryphon that needed to be finished. They needed to complete their city and learn how to run it—and they needed to learn how to live in this new situation and society.

I can take care of contingency battle plans for dealing with possible enemies, if Drake can take over the city. Skan chuckled to himself. *The old team. Just like before. With Gesten putting us both in our place.*

"Well, right now, what if we agree to wait until I have the permanent delegation here set up and running smoothly?" Amberdrake asked. "If I manage that—well, perhaps my skills might be up to administering a city."

"I'll agree to that!" Skan said readily.

People are already deferring to him. Judeth does, and so do the rest of the Silvers. The Haighlei are—I think they're rather in awe of the way he could play so many roles, too.

"Besides, I need to be here to help Silver Veil interview her replacement," Amberdrake continued, but this time with an amused sparkle in his eye. "We both agreed that, on the whole,

I am not particularly suited to the position since Leyuet would never be able to unburden himself to someone he thinks of as being god-touched, but she's willing to talk to anyone from White Gryphon that I send for. I have a candidate or two. Jessamine, for one. She's competent, and she would be a complete change of pace from Silver Veil—which would make it impossible for anyone to ever compare the two."

Skan sighed with relief when he realized that Amberdrake was not even thinking about taking the job himself. That *had* been a private worry of his; that Amberdrake would decide to stay here as Silver Veil's successor, with Winterhart in charge of the actual ambassadorial delegation. In many ways, it would be a good positioning of resources. Winterhart was admirably suited to such a task—and if Amberdrake was in the position of Imperial Kestra'chern, his people would be very well appraised of whatever situation currently prevailed in Shalaman's land.

But I want him home, Skan thought stubbornly. *We're a good team, and I need him back home where he belongs.*

Besides, he needs to take over from Lionwind, as well as taking over the city. The Kaled'a'in are more than they were before, and Lionwind is still acting as if they were just one of the Clans, with no outsiders among them to change things. I think he realizes that, too.

In fact—*Hmm. There were some stirrings in that direction, before we left. It seemed to me that Lionwind was spending an awful lot of time with the shaman. Maybe he's thinking that he ought to move on to something else, too.*

Change or stagnate. Keep moving or die. That always seemed to be the choices facing Urtho's folk.

But if we change, we grow. If Drake takes all this leader business on, it will make him grow. He's been stagnating, too.

This was going to wake him up, and that would be good, not only for him, but for Winterhart. *She'll be his partner, just like always— Now that's interesting. She really wasn't suited—or trained—to be his partner when all he was doing was speaking for the kestra'chern. But as the full administra-*

tor! *Oh, they'll handle that job together like two trained horses in harness!*

"Winterhart would probably enjoy sharing the administrative things out with me," Amberdrake mused aloud, in an unconscious echo of Skandranon's thoughts. "She'd been wasting her talents, really, until we got here. She *was* trained to rule, not only a household, but a full estate with a substantial number of retainers. It would be a shame to let that kind of training and skill go to waste."

"You're going to do it, then." Skan could hardly conceal his glee.

Amberdrake gave him a wry smile. "Sounds as though I've talked myself into it, haven't I? Well—yes. *We* will do it. Provided we don't make total fools of ourselves, setting things up here."

"Good!" Skan settled back to watch Makke pack with a much lighter heart. Everything was settled—and exactly as he wanted!

And now *he* would be able to get back to doing what he did best—being the Black Gryphon, and all that entailed!

I won't be stagnating, either. We'll have to figure out how to work with the Haighlei forces; we have no idea what may be coming down out of the north. We gryphons really should put some thought into organizing ourselves in some way—

He gryphon-grinned at Amberdrake, and the kestra'chern's wry smile softened into a real one.

And Skandranon Rashkae sat back on his haunches and pulled himself straight up in a deliberately statuesque pose against the sunlit sky, content with himself and the world. Life was good.

And his heart had never been quite so full of light.